The
WARM SOUTH

The

WARM SOUTH

A NOVEL

by

PAUL KERSCHEN

ROUNDABOUT PRESS
WEST HARTFORD, CT
MMXIX

Roundabout Press
P.O. Box 370310
West Hartford, CT 06137
www.roundaboutpress.com

ISBN 978-1-948072-03-8
Library of Congress Control Number: 2018943857

Printed in the United States of America

First Edition
10 9 8 7 6 5 4 3 2 1

This one is for J.C. and R.D., who extended it credit

CONTENTS

Ther God thi maker yet, er that he dye,
So sende myght to mak in som comedye!

Troilus and Criseyde

FIRST PART

Prologue in Hell

HE DIED; BUT THEY TURNED the lock on his bones and shut the ghost inside. Everything had to go on as before. He discovered the persistence of walls, the dominion of furniture. Look long enough into the ceiling and the ceiling ends up inside you.

I have not begun the last work, that of losing things.

They fed him on milk and toast. They bled him from the neck, and they took away the cork-stoppered bottle of laudanum that he had been saving in his travel chest, under the *Paradise Lost*. Think of your soul! they said. He wept. That bottle, which he had never uncorked, had been his last comfort. The pain cannot get worse. The pain did get worse, every time, and the consolations of his soul went up in bonfires, except for the knowledge that he might kill it. He would swallow from the bottle only once and endure five seconds more. The five seconds stretched forward their fibers, became an hour, and his senses were cut away.

I will tell you what is the life you have saved… the cough and hemorrhage you know. The night sweats are to come. The palpitations. The wasting diarrhea, that empties the structure. You are tending a corpse….

He couldn't draw breath. His throat scorched. An ocean hung at his lips and he could not drink for weakness. He started awake at night with his sheets drenched and his heart skipping in him like something tumbling over ice. Instead of the old scarlet spittle he now brought up a black vomit into the chamberpot, threaded with clots. Yet he always had enough blood to fill the leeches in the morning. How, then, could anyone believe in his death?

The pain prowled him from side to side and scratched for its exit. He knew it as he had known faces. His skin had begun to sag at the joints, with a waxy cast as if ready to peel away.

He could not play this game forever, always extending the same five seconds.

Say farewell.

His ambitions were forgotten. Friendship and love were fond, faraway dreams. Lay them into bed, let them drowse. His secrets were harder to let go, being his alone. That evening field of wheat, dipping its stalks in the wind—will it not survive me? No. Nor the very near things. The wall, the slant of yellow sun. Unwind them from your heart. This sheet and blanket are the span of your being. You lie still as a saint. Do not cling to breath, neither shrink from pain. The world spins outside your door, and from now on will have to answer its own questions. For you there is drowsing and letting go.

He dreamed his death. A physician's scalpel slit him from sternum to navel. A violet track, the mark of poison, touched his innards.

Was I betrayed?

Someone laughed. You may go to law.

Kindling was heaped under his pallet and set alight. Everything he had touched in life must be burned.

Deep in the earth, where the dead had their courtroom, up and down were turned about. Benches hung in rows above his head and he clambered down an arched ceiling into the well of a dome. A crowd was gathered around a magistrate, and he shoved between their shoulders, calling, who is not dead, let him live! In fact he was saying, I alone am living, let me die, since in the courtroom of the dead every word had its meaning turned about. The pages in his hand were out of order. He could not read a single line from beginning to end, and everything was mixed in with his poems and plays, not his finished work but the abandoned things he had never brought to print. He tried to hide them against his breast, but a bailiff in riding clothes leaned from behind and said, ah, Cockney poetry, the rare wild weed.

On the far side of the crowd there showed a woman's white hand, a color cool as water. To touch it would end him. He tried to reach around the bailiff, but the man's shoulders kept moving to block his way.

Thou, spoke the magistrate. Unsay thy farewells.

Sir?

Thou shalt take up each thread at the place it was dropped. Ravel them back into the whole.

The key turned in the lock. The bone cage cracked open. He was flung upward, tumbling fast as if rising from the bottom of the ocean. The blue arm of night flowed up his limbs, kissed his temples, and a trickle of snow touched his throat. He lifted his chest to suck and a torrent of ice poured into him. He was penetrated to the fingertips and could not be filled. What was this power?

He was drowned; he was alive. With all his heart he had expected to be finished.

Piazza di Spagna 26

A ROMAN MORNING IS A glass bead on the horizon, pearl-gray to start, then stained by lower lights. Blue rises from the roofs, flat white follows and in a flash of gold the sun mounts the sky and divides the world into light and shade. Knife-sharp shadows cut the piazzas, a lesson in perspective: things stand as they stand. There shall be no doubting of place, nor time, nor substance. All dreams are locked in their cabinets for the day. The light's edge touched bricks and deep-carved porticos, the bright Bourbon flag over the Spanish embassy, church steps and apartments across the way and the upper-story window that dropped a bar of sun onto the lids of John Keats. He winced and moved his head. The shutters traced a golden diamond on the hearth.

A tread on the steps, a soft rap at the outer door would be the doctor. Severn would receive him in the outer chamber, which was Severn's to sleep in but outfitted during the day as a sitting room, with a couple of French chairs and a hired pianoforte. Severn set up his easels to block the bed and shuttled around between wooden panels with bright oil sketches, watercolors of Roman scenes and the half-length canvas where he'd chalked out the start of his Royal Academy painting. The doctor, a sober Scotsman who knew his landscapes and classical themes, always stopped to admire the works in progress before continuing into the sickroom. Severn laughed nervously at his compliments.

"Doctor Clark, you very much flatter me. I am always afraid my daubing shall disturb you...."

"But, Mr. Severn, I should say you *prefer* to daub before a public. Did you not sketch these upon the Pincio?"

Severn gave another high laugh. "One works from life. I

can't very well get the Pincio to come to me." But he really did take pleasure in being watched. Every so often he would set down his brush and strike poses, running his hand through his curls. He had twenty-seven years to Keats's twenty-five but had always seemed the younger man.

"Good morning, Mr. Keats."

The doctor was large, the doorway small, and his shoulders and elbows had a way of filling it. His frock coat blocked the light. As he stepped in, one saw his thin ginger hair and the hooked nose that gave him the look of an eagle, though a kindly eagle, perhaps from a storybook. He opened the shutters and threw southern sun over Keats in bed.

"How did we pass the night?"

Keats muttered in answer. So early in the morning, he felt the breath uneasy in him.

"I think no leech today. If you would oblige me by lifting the nightshirt."

His large hands undid the clasp of the medical bag, took out the wooden auscultation tube and held it to the patient's breast. Keats inspired and expired, and the doctor nestled his balding head below, just as Keats had nestled his head against Severn those nights that Severn had carried him choking from room to room.

"Good." The doctor raised his head. "Clearer by the day. Sit upright, please, and turn your back."

Keats pushed himself up, arms slightly quaking, and hung his head out the window three stories over the piazza. The steps of Trinità dei Monti had sprouted their carpet of hats and parasols over the young women for hire as artists' models. At the bottom of the steps carriages stood in line and fountain water shipped over the bow of the elder Bernini's sinking boat. At times Keats would start in his room, realizing that for hours he had been hearing phantom patterns in the splash, a triple-time dance measure or the iambs from *Philaster*:

As you are living, all your better deeds
Shall be in water writ—

"What do you feel if I press here?" asked the doctor.

"Pressure," Keats gasped, "but no inflammation. I should say the liver and pancreas are very well."

The doctor chuckled, glad to hear the patient making a sally. In Keats's own ears his voice sounded high, almost childish, since the illness. No one else had remarked on any change. The doctor returned his instruments to their bag, exactly reversing the order in which he'd taken them out, and Severn showed his face at the door.

"The liver is sound," said Doctor Clark. "The pancreas is sound. I suspect the lungs were well from the start. The greater part may have been an affliction of the mind."

"The mind," said Keats.

"A nervous complaint."

Doctor Clark could talk at length of nervous complaints, their various forms, their connection to bodily ailments—inasmuch as the brain, we now understand, is a fibrous organ like any other. He was kind. More than a doctor he'd been their factotum. He'd secured their rooms across the piazza from his own, gone out to find books in English, arranged for the hire of carriages and the pianoforte, brought sheet music of Haydn for Severn to play. What he said about the nerves was surely correct, and it struck Keats as an attack. He spoke from inside his profession as if it were a coat he had pulled around him, knowing that Keats, who had never taken the surgeon's examination, must face him naked.

Keats sank back into bed. In his new, weak voice he asked, "Then I may soon return to England?"

The doctor shut his bag. "I recommend against haste. You haven't the look of a man who has much encountered the Roman sun. Have you been about the city?"

Keats was coming back to walking as a child. His feet had become hilarious foreign implements, to be trusted only while he kept them in sight.

"Mr. Severn? You haven't taken Mr. Keats onto the Pincio?"

Severn smiled narrowly. "Mr. Keats yesterday said that he found the stairs, er, of a difficulty to rank with German philosophy."

"My life is in England," said Keats.

"It shall wait for you there," said the doctor. "I fear to send you on a sea voyage if the onset of winter should precipitate another attack and require you to be shipped back here in six months. Let the Roman spring do its work. Given the Roman summer, in a month or two I might suggest a removal to the hill country."

"Consumption killed my younger brother," Keats said.

The doctor lifted his brows and, getting no further information, turned his look to Severn.

"They prescribed him bloodletting," he continued, "and a vegetable diet. Tom would not quarrel with physicians. Only when he was near his end did he whisper that more than anything in the world he wanted a beefsteak. We didn't give him it. At times my heart is pierced to think we kept it from him."

The piazza's sounds receded, becoming remembered sounds. From far above the doctor replied, "It is a truly sad necessity."

"Nor to dispute your diagnosis," said Keats, "but you are aware, are you not, that my hemorrhages in England were of arterial blood, not from the stomach. They came up in a froth—"

"Bless me!" cried Severn, shuddering, "must you say 'froth?'"

"It is a fact."

"I understand," said the doctor. "You are not quarreling with me, Mr. Keats, but with the gods."

Keats crossed his arms and made a wry face.

"I cannot encourage you to travel. The risk that we would gladly run ourselves, we shrink from imposing on another. If it does not sound too parsonical from a man in middle life, I would counsel patience, to think of the years you have left, and to recall that as recently as Christmas, it was doubtful you should get to live any of them."

Under his folded arms Keats felt his own slightness. "Believe me to be grateful for all you have done, Doctor Clark."

"Believe me to be sorry I can do no more." The doctor bowed. "Until tomorrow. I always look forward to the effects of another day upon Alcibiades"—he gestured to Severn's canvas— "and I have your volume, Mr. Keats, on order from Taylor and Hessey."

"My volume?" The frontispiece came faintly to mind. "They will have a happy surprise that anyone wants it."

The doctor made a strange face and reached as if to touch Keats's shoulder, but withdrew. "Mr. Severn," he said, "if I might trouble you apart for a moment."

They stepped out. Keats heard the door unlatch and swing open, and murmurs from the entryway, in the embarrassed tones of people with nowhere private to talk. They lived very close here. A muslin drape screened the landlady and her daughter from sight, but their footsteps were as clear as one's own. One heard their food on the gridiron, their water jars and chamberpots being emptied. They were always boiling egg noodles and filling the place with steam. The mother never stopped exclaiming in her Roman dialect; the daughter was silent. During his fever Keats had forgotten she was there. Now that he sat in the front room, he would see her step past the drape in bright, coarse calico, hair pulled up from her long neck and a basket in her hand. Her shy glance as she walked to the door struck him dumb. He felt himself viewed: slight, ill, poor, from a foreign land. A quarter hour later she came back with bread or a wrap from the butcher and was hurried by her mother behind the drape.

Footsteps went down the stairs and Severn stepped in with a dejected look.

"What was that?" asked Keats.

"Nothing," said Severn. "The bill. As courteous as a duke, of course."

"The purse is a fibrous organ like any other."

Severn blinked and forced a smile, but his eyes darted about the room. He muttered, not quite to himself, "The lodging—full-crown dinners—seven for the pianoforte."

"Are we very poor now, Severn?"

"Poor!" Severn raised both hands and brushed back his curls. "On my honor, Keats, I spared you every trouble so long as I could. I cooked for economy's sake; I washed up; I made you coffee," he cried, waving at the hearth, "and you threw it away, and I made it again, and you threw it out the window again, and I made it a third time—and then you would have me read to you. And I was supposed to begin a painting! With my son yet in London, nearly two years old and not baptized—"

"It was good of you."

Severn colored and looked down. "It is a fortnight since I drew the last on your publishers' letter of credit. Doctor Clark was not inquiring after professional fees. He has been providing for us out of his own pocket."

A pot clanged in the outer room and the landlady shouted. Past these walls were other walls in morning light, and others again, then farther roads, country hills and mountains, all the lands of Europe that Keats knew only from guidebooks and poetry, each stood up as a barrier between him and the life he had loved.

"I had made peace with this country being my grave," he said. "It can't be my home."

"You are advised to stay," said Severn.

"I am *desired* to stay. And how? With the good doctor dispensing scudi from the one hand and asking them back with the other—only around the corner, so as to spare my condition? It is not tolerable."

"He has been kind," Severn said haltingly. "There was that

certain fish."

"Fish?"

"Last month. He went all over Rome to find it, and had in his wife to cook, though you couldn't eat—"

"Then mightn't I as well have choked?"

Severn winced. The blood began to ebb from Keats's face and very slowly, as if guided by an older hand, he sat up in his blankets. The stream of the world had found its way back to him. The moment he set foot out of bed, it would take him up again.

"Forgive me, Joe," he said. "It is the melancholy. It came first of my illnesses, and it will be the last to take leave."

"So says Doctor Clark. The nervous fibers."

"I do not speak of fibers," said Keats. "It is the trouble I have put you to. I've so depended on you, and on everyone, I don't know how I am to make good."

"It is nothing," said Severn.

"I shall settle my debts to the penny."

He had said it to give confidence. But Severn turned aside with a twist to his mouth, and Keats realized he was embarrassed to have such a promise made him by a sickly man in a nightshirt, sitting up in the cot that ought to have been his deathbed.

Morning Post

IN SLEEP HE RETURNED TO ENGLAND. He saw clouds, green hills and dog-rose bushes; he walked through fogs. Sometimes he was ill in the dream and a cloth was pressed to his mouth or forehead, but he was always able to find his feet again. The landscape might be sunny or snowy; all the seasons came at once, and Fanny was always with him. Her long face moved like a bird's. She declared her love and drew him close and warm, but her blue eyes wouldn't stay fixed on his. She was dressed in silks and lace, on her way somewhere he wasn't invited. Even in his arms she couldn't be stilled, she laughed at hidden things, he couldn't find her hand to clasp it, his eyes snapped open and the room's embossment jumped down at him. The pattern assumed one shape after another till he remembered—he was in Rome, this was the ceiling—at which it leaped back to its full height. He was not dying and Fanny was far away.

Dante was thirty-five, it is said, when he imagined himself straying into a forest so dark that his master poet and lost love had to return from the dead to save him. Keats was ten years younger and lost in the same wood. At twenty-one he had published his first volume, at twenty-two a second. They had won him the admiration of a few, ridicule in the magazines and no money. He borrowed from Charles Brown while they wrote a tragedy; he borrowed from his publisher against his next volume; and the tragedy was rejected by Drury Lane and Covent Garden, and his mythological epic collapsed after two books. His parents were long dead, his youngest brother expiring from consumption. The other, who had gone to America with most of Keats's money on loan, sent word that he'd been bankrupted in a scheme involving a cotton mill.

In the depth of this wood he fell in love. It was poisoned from the start. He was five feet high with a mouth like a bullfrog's, didn't know how to dance, didn't know how to court, and lived in fear of losing Fanny to another. Severn and Brown were easy with women; they found mistresses for a season, took pleasure and moved elsewhere without catching their hearts in birdlime. Keats was caught. Fanny was everything to him, but he hadn't possessed her, nor would he till he got money to marry. Surely it was a ludicrous passion. A year ago he would have laughed to hear of someone in his predicament. He wrote Fanny wild letters swearing that his two sweetest thoughts were her beauty and the hour of his death, that he longed to possess both in the same moment. She had sense enough not to answer that kind of thing. Her mother spoke of him as a very odd young man.

Ought he to send his publishers a volume of fragments, the odes and sonnets that his failed epic had dropped by the wayside? Ought he to go to Edinburgh and study surgery? Ought he to take up the apothecary trade in London, become a ship's surgeon on the India line, take rooms in Westminster and write for magazines? When his hemorrhages began, they merely occluded these questions behind a briefer one—shall I live?—which was only now fading out like a dark sun. A third, patchwork volume had been published while he was ill and had done better than the others. But his quandaries were as before, except that he faced them poorer than ever and far from home.

Out of bed, he moved slowly in pulling on shirt and trousers. Asleep he had been all spirit, and it took time to knit the body around him. Touching real things he became more real. Yellow light fell through the window, in the next room Severn was boiling water. Thinking of coffee, he sucked his teeth; but he must be careful, he didn't know how his mood would turn. Joy and melancholy always brimmed in him like two colored vials, one bright silver, the other dank brown, and either ready at the least touch to upset itself on the world. He must train his senses on their proper objects. There was his bright window, the desk, his books. At the bottom of his illness he'd passed a confused night when he couldn't read two words together but longed to have them near, so Severn had carried them all to his bedside, where they now stacked like dolmens: Shakespeare in seven green volumes, his Milton, his Burton and black-letter Chaucer, Dante and Tasso and Ariosto in Italian and English both, Spenser, Wordsworth, Bailey's and Lemprière's dictionaries, Ovid and Terence in Latin, guidebooks and grammars and atlases, everything he'd packed in London to make a millstone of his travel chest.

The dank brown things, the frightening things, he would ignore. He kept Fanny's parting gifts shut in his desk. She had hemmed the collar and sleeves of his blue coat, cut him a lock of hair and given him paper to write her letters. He hadn't written one.

"Hullo!" called Severn, "are you up? The courier's come."

His stocking feet pressed the tiles. They were solid, he was solid. He walked out and found Severn whirling around in an open collar, rattling the dishes as he dragged a side table to meet the chairs.

"Hi," said Keats, "you'll ignite your trousers," and pulled Severn back from the hearth. He grabbed the rattling kettle from the trivet and poured it into the cups, coffee bags bobbing up with the smell of morning.

"White bread," said Severn, "butter and jam, good Roman milk—and I've a letter from Brown to read you."

"A letter to the Romans! Is it decent for breakfast?"

"It is the work of Charles Brown. *Scripsit*—" and Severn cleared his throat and sat. "My dear Severn—'tis your name that graces the envelope, for I am maiden-shy of Keats's condition, yet if he be so far recovered as I hope, you won't make me cold to him, but will take this as a letter to you both."

"Maiden was never shy," said Keats, "once Brown was in the

room five minutes," and helped himself to the bread. As Severn read on, Brown took shape before him: a heavy figure with thirty-four years on his good-humored cheeks, beard and balding crown over a dinner suit, with the dinner to match, say a roast chop and claret, for when one imagined Brown it was always over a good meal. For Severn's benefit, he began with gossip about London painting. Haydon had exhibited his *Agony in the Garden* at the Great Room and had not created much enthusiasm. The picture was melodramatic, people said, and represented Judas as too palpable a villain—surely, wrote Brown, Judas ought to possess a good talking face, one an honest man might trust. But the profits were in and Brown promised to recover the money Keats had loaned the painter.

"I shall have to turn bank-clerk to Keats," Severn read, "since there is no getting him to do it himself. I am yet waiting to hear of a remittance from George in America. Should a sum arrive, Keats will want me to appropriate some part of it, but let there be no question of that so long as he continues disabled from writing— O, I saw Taylor the other day, but had not time to press him on the sale of the new poems."

"They want quite a sale to recover the advance," said Keats. "I hope the letter is not altogether about money?"

"No, no. He writes: I hope still to come to Rome, though my affairs are in a muddle. I can't let the house at present. Abby is living with me again, though not, thank God, in the same capacity as before—she keeps to her own bed and I keep myself continent. One child is quite enough. Between you and me, I think an infant is disagreeable, it is all gut and squall, yet if she holds the little scrap apart it gives me pain. The baptism was Catholic and I hope well enough for the child's soul, but to speak in a lawyer's phrase, with the Church of England not a party I may get clear of these entanglements the sooner. Keats is—ah, well, never mind that." Severn broke off and slid his finger down the page.

"Why," asked Keats, "what does he write?"

"Nothing of consequence," said Severn. "He must have forgotten he was writing us both."

"Certainly Brown forgets things. May I ask what he writes?"

Severn dropped the page and set Brown's looped writing before Keats's eyes, as if to disavow it. "You may see. He writes: Keats is fortunate that he and Miss Brawne never risked any such predicament."

Keats frowned and brushed away the sheet. "Well, that is boorish of him. He knows perfectly well how things stand between me and Miss Brawne."

"Oh, it was idly meant—"

"Idly! And does he think *I* mean so idly toward Miss Brawne, that I might treat her as he treated his kitchen-maid? Really, it is only the lawyer in Brown that is not idle."

"Keats!" cried Severn, with pain in his face. "If you rebuke him you rebuke me as well." He stirred the jam pot uneasily. "You can't know what it is to have a child. You may say it was laxity that brought my Henry into the world. But he is in the world now, and I swear to you, it is nothing but care."

"I don't mean to deny it. You are not Brown."

"Brown understands me better than you do on this point." Severn picked up the letter again. "He writes that the family who are keeping Henry have been round to my sister for money, and that they've embarrassed my parents. But it is only his safety I care for, Keats. I'll be a father to him one day, when I have the means. But a child is a fragile vessel. If an accident should take his soul, before he is baptized? I have terrors in the night. I dream of him drowned, or in a fever."

"You mustn't." Keats took Severn's arm. "I'm sorry, Joe, this is no stuff for breakfast."

"Indeed no," said Severn, and tried to smile, but his own emotion had startled him.

"You will get your Academy scholarship, and that will reconcile you to your family. And you'll get the means to claim your child, I'm sure of it. In the meantime," he said, letting Severn go, "you know I can't hold to a faith that refuses heaven to a dry forehead. But as you trust in Providence, you can't believe such an end is meant for your boy."

Severn blinked a little, mastering his emotion. "Well, on the matter of faith—" He dropped Brown's letter and reached for a packet on the mantel. "You have another to try those questions."

The letter was addressed to Naples, where they hadn't been since November, and from its worn corners and thick collection of postmarks seemed to have enjoyed a long adventure through the Italian post. Keats's name appeared in large, elegant letters; but, he said, he didn't recognize the hand.

Severn grinned. "See the top postmark. Pisa."

Their only knife was smeared with butter. Keats sucked the jam spoon clean and slit its handle through the seal. Unfolding the sheet, he found a page in the same neat script.

Casa Galletti, Pisa, 20 January

My dear Keats,

I need not say what anxiety I have had these past months for news of you. Knowing that you were bound for this Peninsula, & in grave physical danger, but unable to get further intelligence on either point, I have been in a suspense which is only slightly relieved now that I hear you are at Naples; for this news comes with no clear assurance as to your condition. No doubt you are better already, & will write soon to satisfy my mind that the Italian climate is doing what it ought, & that your Life is to be preserved in the service of many verses to come. On your "Hyperion," which I have much reread lately, I have more to say than a letter will contain, & would rather have it held in the ampler bounds of conversation. Mrs. Shelley joins me in hoping that you will come to Pisa, where I aim to be-

stow every necessary attention on your body & spirit—to
keep the one warm, & to teach the other Greek & Spanish.
Meanwhile be assured that I remain ever,

Your sincere well-wisher,
P.B. Shelley.

"Well?" Severn asked through his bread.

"It is brief," said Keats, "and gentlemanly. He invites me to
Pisa again."

"I expected he would do it. But can you imagine staying with
him? To dine on broccoli and cauliflower, and be told there is no
God, and that government should be chosen in sweepstakes?"

"There is none of that in his letter. He wants to teach me
Spanish."

"Spanish? What use has a poet for Spanish?"

Keats sipped his coffee and gently set down the letter. "If I
were the son of a baronet," he said, "and had Shelley's income,
I don't know *what* I mightn't have use for. If he wants to take a
villa and arrange Spanish lessons for all the poets of the kingdom,
who's to tell him he may not?"

"Oh, he may do as he likes. But you aren't obliged to go and
amuse him, surely?" Severn widened his eyes. Keats did not return
the look; he was lifting and dropping his spent coffee bag on the
saucer, watching the folds in the wet silk.

"The whole world has come to breakfast this morning," he
said.

"Well, it can't stay to luncheon," said Severn, and pulled the
saucer away. "Come, are you dressed to go out? We're waited for
on the Pincio."

SPQR

In the winter Dr. Clark had recommended, on unspecified authority, that Keats take up riding; so an expensive horse had been hired to jog at a snail's pace down the streets and public walks, grimly bouncing him over its chestnut withers, until his condition had put a stop to the excursions. Now that he was able to go out again, he was glad to do it on his own feet. Past the Piazza di Spagna, with its steps and sunny fountain, the cobbled ground sloped into a narrow lane between three-story buildings that were strange as a first sight of Rome, since their walls were freshly whitewashed as in England, their doors and shutters bright with verdigris as in England, and the people leaning out the windows all pale foreigners who seemed perplexed to find the street full of copies of themselves. One came to Rome expecting to meet gallant and noble Italians, and perhaps wicked and cruel Italians as well; but among the hotels one saw only serving boys, carrying up baskets of chicken and macaroni from the trattorie on the ground floors. England floated on top of Italy; turned brilliant under the Roman sky, it stared itself in the face; and Keats walked through it as if through a mirror until England came to a sudden end. He stood alone before the dim windows of a small piazza, where dark-faced people in dingy clothes watched from doorways. Here was the mystery. It was strange to think that this was an ordinary scene, that Rome was a city like any other, of whose natural life he knew nothing.

He and Severn had seen washing hung from windows and smelled laundry soap masking the cabbage in the gutters, come across charcoaled graffiti they couldn't read, met soldiers in Papal uniform leaning on their bayonets and been followed by stray dogs with full paps. On the wider avenues were open-air stalls with men carving stone miniatures of monuments that, when you actually came across them, seemed to be miniature themselves, hemmed among higher, newer walls. The Pantheon, worn and soot-blackened on its outside, was inside transformed to a palace of gilt and rose-colored marble, full of kneeling pilgrims and plaster saints with heaped offerings: candles, dried flowers, paper scraps and—was it to symbolize afflictions?—a tin nose, a wooden leg. The height of St. Peter's made Keats dizzy. Its outer square was gray and empty and gave no hint of the work within, only flagstones and palm trees, blue sky and the Pope's prisoners in particolored garments, hoeing up weeds and rattling their ankle chains as they went.

They had gone outside the modern city too, out to the stretches of open campagna where the ruins were. Keats had expected the Forum to look like an enormous Bank of England, but in fact it was a park grown wild, with grass smothering its crumbled walls and brilliant red poppies shaking their early blooms in the breeze. The field was governed by a scattering of marble facades and arches whose carved boasts, where they hadn't been broken up, were just within reach of Keats's grammar-school Latin. Severn knew which emperors had left which memorials, and which had stolen and defaced the works of their predecessors; he also wondered aloud, as every traveler did, whether the banks of the Thames were one day to look like this. Keats couldn't keep track of the history and spent a long time watching a gray cat slink among the stones and grass. It twisted now and then to lick the fur on its back. At the Colosseum they spent most of a day sitting on an overgrown upper ridge, Severn laying boards on his lap to sketch pastels of the changing light and Keats looking on with an empty head. Myrtles and olives had taken root below. There were dirt paths that seemed worn by human feet, but very few others were in the ruins, only some pilgrims clambering at bottom between the stations of the Cross.

Today they were not going so far, only up the Pincio from the

English hotels. Severn was afraid of arriving late and kept darting up the street past the foreigners and their porters, then looking back and frowning as he waited for Keats to catch up. They were supposed to meet a genuine Roman, a young sculptor that Severn had gotten to know in one of the academies. Since their arrival they had seen no Italians socially, nor indeed anyone else, and Keats was suddenly shy. Suppose he was taken for the obnoxious sort of touring Englishman who took his guidebook everywhere; suppose he looked like a pauper? He kept pushing his hair back from his brow, and took a careful pace behind Severn lest he lose his breath. The high gate of the Villa Medici cast a terrible judgment on him. But Severn was already calling and waving, and a figure in nankeen jacket and trousers strode up with arms spread wide. He was tall and quite dark; he greeted Severn in loud, fast, strongly accented English; then he turned and clasped Keats's hand in both his own. His hair was thick and slightly curled, flattened with a great deal of bear's grease. Over his beaked nose were set deep, wide, feminine eyes with long lashes. Keats felt an immediate warmth for him, as he'd felt in the past for very tall people who seemed benign in their height. It seemed he could take them as protectors.

The sculptor seemed happy with any conversation they might offer, and Severn began to talk about art. He had just made a visit to Canova's studio, where the great man had received him with the warmest hospitality and promised to write the Pope so that Severn might get permission to study in the palazzi.

"I wouldn't say it to a painter," said Severn, "but I may say it to you—I think to go far beyond any of the modern Italian painters I have seen so far. Does it not seem to you that they have no original or native idea of painting left? That everyone is in thrall to his dead masters?"

"Ah," said the sculptor, delicately moving his hands, "it may be so, I can't judge. I have never seen England. To know the galleries of London!"

They took a path of smooth earth between wild hedges that

had burst the bounds of English style and splayed in all directions, hungry for light. Women with parasols and wide hats walked in the other direction and glanced with half smiles at the passing men. They halted at a stone fountain under pines and Severn leaned confidentially close. "Now let me tell you of Keats," he said. "I've said as much privately, but let me say it in his hearing—you see in him the greatest English poet of our time. He is a rival to Wordsworth already. Soon enough he'll rival Milton."

Keats shook his head. "For pity's sake, Severn."

"No," said the sculptor, touching Keats's shoulder, "I believe your friend. I am honored to meet you." He lowered his gaze and said, "I love English books. But it is not easy, you know, to find them in Italy. To import foreign books is restricted here." His eyes flickered regretfully up, and Keats realized the man was trying to apologize for not having read his work. His face grew hot. He had been put in a false position, and the last thing he wanted to talk of was his own poetry.

"You wouldn't see my books anyhow," he blurted. "It's the women."

"I beg pardon?" said the sculptor.

"I am not the poet Severn claims." Keats shook his head quickly. "What I say about women is a matter of commerce. I don't know how things stand in Italy, but in England it is women who buy all literature. The reviewers cater to their sensibilities. This is all to the detriment of my sales, for Severn would not have told you that my poems are prurient, and vulgar—"

"Why no," said Severn.

"But they are, Severn, and you know it. You read *Blackwood's*, the same as anyone." To the sculptor he said, "I published a mythological poem in England, which represented the goddess Diana taking a mortal lover. I was young when I wrote it, and I am sensible of its defects. But the choice of subject was its particular ruin."

The sculptor's quick eyes darted between the Englishmen. "A goddess, you say? A goddess can never be vulgar."

"Thank you," said Keats. "As I say, it is the ladies who take offense."

"The Italian woman would not find her vulgar," declared the sculptor. "She understands the passions, she has not the fear of them. If the book is not moral to the Church, she must perhaps tell her confessor—but this is not what you said, *offense*."

He spoke insistently, with wide gestures, and as they turned to walk on they found the hill's obelisk raised on a pedestal before them. It thrust upward for several dozen stone yards, with glyphs along its shaft and the sun glinting on its tip. Severn giggled and glanced between the others with his hand at his mouth.

"I look forward to meeting the Italian woman," said Keats. "Now, if Severn has pity on me, he'll talk of something other than my poems."

But they had run out of talk. The sculptor folded his hands into the sleeves of his jacket and seemed very foreign to Keats, full of secrets. They circled the obelisk and came to a low stone wall overlooking a gap in the pines. There was the piazza they had climbed from, the narrow streets tumbling toward the river and farther off the campagna's yellow fields hazing into blue.

"Castel Sant'Angelo," said the sculptor, and pointed. "See, they have filled the moat."

The city's bridges ran slight over the water, skewing with the river's bend like the spokes of a wheel. At their hub was the castle; a silver thread lapped the fortress within its outer wall.

"Why?" asked Keats. "Is that usually done in the spring?"

The sculptor turned in shock. "It is war," he said. "You know that, don't you? The cannons are getting ready." Black blots were stationed at the fortress's rim and tiny figures went between them.

Keats looked to Severn, with the sense of failing an examination. "I was ill. I've been shut in."

"Excuse me," the sculptor said. "Then it is natural." But he seemed uneasy at Keats's ignorance. "You know, surely, that we have Austria to the north and Naples to the south, and that they will have their fight here, in the Pope's territories? The Austrians have already crossed the Po. But the cardinals fear more a march from Naples. There will be smoke from the south," he said, pointing into the campagna, "if an army is seen."

"They fear the carbonari, you mean?" Severn asked.

"The carbonari, the revolution, the new constitution in Naples. You know a revolution does not stop at a border. Suppose they march on Rome; why should they not seize the Holy See— even the, ah, person of the Pope? That is the prize."

His eyes were fierce, but there was a faint smile around his mouth, and Keats said cautiously, "But you yourself don't fear that chance?"

The sculptor glanced at the women strolling some distance away. "You will find many in Italy," he said quietly, "to tell you that Austria is our jailor and that Count von Metternich has locked us up under a guard of kings, and dukes, and popes. They would tell you the people of Naples are the first to break free."

"We saw King Ferdinand in Naples," said Severn, "parading with his troops. I thought he looked like a goat. Keats said—what did you say, Keats?"

"I said—and understand, please," he told the sculptor, in the same low tone, "I know nothing of affairs here. But I thought history had started to run backward. Bonaparte was a plague, but why, after his defeat, should we restore the old princes to their plots? Imagine the fallen Titans seizing back their thrones, and Saturn swallowing his children a second time! I am ashamed of the part the English had in it."

The sculptor threw back his head laughing—he seemed to have forgotten about secrecy—and clapped Keats's shoulder. "Bravo! Bravo, signor poeta! Only," he said, now serious, "I cannot agree with you on Napoleon. Read even the grafitti here, and always you will see his name with the cause of liberty. *Costituzione* on the one side, *Evviva Napoleone* on the other."

"But the two can't agree. Where is the liberty in changing a king for an emperor?"

The sculptor looked into the treetops. "I think the English can never understand Napoleon. You have an old constitution, and ancient ideas of your rights. We in the South had no such things, not until Napoleon brought the beginnings of civilization. And if that is not the end, if he returns—"

"Returns!" cried Severn. "How, from his island?"

The fierce smile showed again on the sculptor's lips. "The ocean is wide," he said, "but not empty. Some would tell you to watch for American ships in our harbors." He opened his arms to his companions. "It is lucky, signori, to come to Italy in this time. Great spirits are at work."

They reflected on this. Keats looked again into the countryside, and the sculptor coughed and doubled over. His hand went to his lips; Keats caught him in both hands and pressed his heaving breast and back.

"There, lift your head," said Keats. "Try not to bend—sit if you must—" But already the sculptor was shaking his head and gasping that it had passed, thank you, he was well. His face was a dark ash color and his forehead glistened. Severn stood aside in hesitation, hands half raised.

"Your lip!" said Keats.

Along the sculptor's mouth and fingers were red droplets, spread thin and flecked with foam. He made a quick nod, unfolded a white handkerchief from his jacket and wiped his lips slowly, with conscious dignity, as if recovering from an embarrassment. Keats wanted to press his ear to the man's chest, to test the lungs, but he would hear nothing through the jacket. A proper examination was needed. "How long have you had the symptoms?"

The sculptor's thin fingers tucked away the handkerchief and he made an effort to smile. "Long enough that I don't worry. It is never severe."

"But are you under a doctor's care?"

"A doctor costs money."

"We must find you someone. Severn, do you think Doctor Clark—?"

"Thank you," said the sculptor. "What can a doctor do? In England he would tell me to go to Rome. In Rome he will tell me to pray."

His eyes were wide, but there was no appeal in them. Something else was in his face, a quietude and refusal of sympathy that stopped Keats cold. He was not to feel the sculptor's sufferings as his own, and he was not to offer aid. The sculptor watched him as if from behind a window, with a touch of pity that Keats did not understand their separation.

Pine boughs cooled the yellow light above them, and the passing gowns and umbrellas had vanished into the farther gardens. Distant laughter struck the air, like pebbles dropped in water, and faint bells began to sound from St. Peter's. The miles of intervening air washed out their harshness, as if they were not being struck at all but coaxed into song by fine brushes.

"I think it a richer sound than St. Paul's," Keats murmured.

Severn had been looking on and biting his lip. Now he tentatively said, "But for richness of sound, you know, nothing bests the Roman chamber pot."

"Chamber pot!" said the sculptor, with a weak smile.

"Why yes," said Severn, with more energy, "owing to how thick you Romans make them. Do you not know what a fine tone is produced by kicking one? Thus—" His boot mimed a blow and he called, "Barummm!"

His face was earnest, and Keats felt very glad to know him. "Not at all," he said. "It is rather, prawwng!"

"What! Shall you instruct me in the chamber-organ?" His foot skated through the dappled light, striking again and again until the sculptor started to laugh.

"Baroooom!"

"Praaayng!"

The Death of Alcibiades

It was evening. Severn worked by lamplight at his canvas. The painting looked its best at this dim hour; the burning house on the left caught the glow of the Argand lamp and really seemed to be dissolving in fire. Flames pulsed and black smoke belched with palpable thickness to smother the palm trees and Greek portico that Severn had copied from the Roman streets. Still, one might wonder—Keats had wondered—if it was really to the painting's advantage that it looked so much better under a lamp than in the full light of day. Alcibiades himself was clear enough, long-haired and brawny as he rushed naked from the flames with sword in hand. But the assassins on the right, scarcely visible in the gloom, made Keats wonder if his appreciation was at fault, or if they really were somewhat crowding one another, blocking each other's shoulders and limbs in awkward ways, as if it wasn't quite worked out who was meant to be in front and who behind. They were seven in all, some shooting arrows, some with hands raised against Alcibiades's sword, others retreating behind trees, and something in their composition suggested a bunch of children who wouldn't line up as they'd been told to, and who were not really fair targets for the hero's unclad wrath.

These were not kind thoughts, and Keats didn't claim to understand painting. He'd never questioned Severn's talent to anyone. He had once walked out of a dinner where some society painters were laughing at his *Cave of Despair* and making remarks on what the true cause for despair was. Even if Severn's assassins looked a bit like urchins and their arms hung a bit strangely from their shoulders, Keats was sure that if he didn't get his scholarship it would only prove the envy and hypocrisy of the Royal Academy. Anyhow, he told himself privately, in the half-expressed way of shameful thoughts, what harm was there in Severn continuing to paint, even if his talents were not perfect? Whose talents are perfect? Each of us struggles against fate, against his own limited powers. We have scarcely a sliver of a chance to reach greatness. It is best to be kind.

"Suppose I did go to Pisa?" he said.

"Pisa!" Severn's brush halted in his hand, and he looked over his shoulder. "But why? That is—" He took a breath and said more lightly, "Well, you know what I think of Shelley."

"On account of your disagreement over religion?"

"A disagreement, you call it?" He set down the brush and said plaintively, "Do you not remember? There we are dining at Hunt's, and him sitting bone-thin opposite us, eating his bit of vegetable supper like a moon-man, and he opens his mouth and says"—Severn pinched his voice unkindly, but not inaccurately— "'As to that detestable religion, the Christian—'"

Keats laughed. "I remember."

"You shouldn't laugh. My word, Keats, he declared he was going to write a poem comparing our Saviour to a mountebank, performing miracles like street-fair tricks."

"And when we were getting our coats to leave," said Keats, "that lady came up in a dither and asked you, 'Is that creature to be *damned*, Mr. Severn?'"

"And you would be his house-guest now?"

"I must be someone's. God knows, it is wretched to live at anyone's expense. But while I'm getting no money, I wonder if it isn't as well to be Shelley's expense and not yours. At least Shelley can afford it. Severn"—he lifted his hand—"you have your child. You have your painting."

"Well." Severn's face was slack with hurt, and his eyes would not stay on Keats more than a moment. "But you shan't leave me on that account? Why, you'll soon be writing again."

It was Keats's habit, when his writing was mentioned, to look inside himself, as if he might find his unwritten poems waiting in a dark cavity of his heart. But there were no poems there. They came from somewhere else, a borderland between himself and the outer world that his thinking mind was blind to. He didn't know where to look for this place, and lacking it, he peered into an empty well.

"I should be in London," he murmured, "prescribing digitalis and setting bones. Or I should be in the palazzi, teaching English to the daughters of marquesses. I don't know."

"You should be here and nowhere else," said Severn. When no answer came he tightened his lips, making Keats's silence an assent, and turned back to his work.

L'arco de lo essilio

HE HAD TO GET AWAY from Severn. Severn loved him too much. The thing was obvious once said, but it frightened him and left him at a loss for his next step. This apartment over the beautiful piazza, appointed with such care, was becoming a trap, and he had a horrible sense that Severn might be happy to keep him here forever, tending him and showing him off to friends like a tame falcon. The morning with the sculptor had acquired a bitter coloring in his memory. It seemed that Severn had only wanted him and the sculptor displayed to each other, that each had his place in Severn's collection. Even the sculptor's illness could be made into a charge: what baseness, to use a dying man so!

People came easily to love Keats. He'd been lucky past counting to fall ill among friends who were free with their money and time, and who would do the thousand things needed to get him to Italy. He owed them his life. And now that his life was restored, he wanted to get as far from them as possible. It wasn't ingratitude. He was angry because he'd been made helpless in the world, because he must pick and choose whom to depend upon. He wanted to be free; freedom was being obliged to no one; he would be happiest to live in the mountains, eating wild roots and imposing only on the sun and wind.

And who in the mountains—a clever voice in him asked—would read his poems?

Perhaps he wouldn't need anyone to read them. Perhaps he wouldn't need to write them, because a life without obligations would be a poem in itself.

He had to be practical. He was going to do a thing very unlike himself and leave Rome unannounced. While Severn was out

sketching he went alone into the sunlit piazza and found the corner where the vetturini lounged in workman's jackets against their
lacquered coaches, holding thin cigars in their mouths.

"Hi-hi!" they called when he came near. "You English?
Milord! Vettura for you, milord. How far?"

"Non io!" said Keats in his atrocious accent, "non sono
milord. Molto povero."

They laughed. A mustached man took the sleeve that Fanny
had hemmed and said, "Very fine. What coat, milord!" He shook
his head in reproach that Keats should lie to him. They kept speaking bad English and he kept speaking bad Italian; after the first few
words it became a contest. When he gave Pisa as his destination
they shook their heads.

"Better Firenze," they said. "Better Siena."

"Perché?"

"Pisa is very—" began one, and another broke in, "Very no
interest. Go to Firenze, see the Duomo. Michel Angelo."

Keats insisted. He would leave in *due notte*. They began to call
out fares, shouting over each over and edging closer to him; but he
had no idea how much a vettura trip ought to cost and felt suddenly endangered. He leaned into the mustached vetturino and took
his arm without knowing his price, only because the man was nearest and had spoken to him first. The vetturino waved his hand to
silence his fellows. They looked away, scowling, then turned back
into restful figures, smoking and spitting as they leaned against
their carriages. Keats's chosen man put a hand on his shoulder and
led him around the back of the coach, away from the smell of to-
bacco and horses' sweat, to copy down his address and fix the ap-
pointment. There would be a heavy trunk of books, said Keats,
lapsing into English; the vetturino waved his arm and said "non fa
nulla," and the thing was done.

He wrote a short letter to Pisa. He was grateful, he said, for
Shelley's generosity. He intended to take advantage of it only so
long as was convenient, and he hoped not to prove too dull a lodg-

er. The danger of living in bed in Rome, he said, was that one did nothing but chase sprites of the imagination.

Suddenly Severn was better to him than ever, as if knowing he had a new claim on Keats's guilty heart. He still did the cooking and washing up, though Keats was perfectly able, and now he said nothing about their expenses, or his own ambitions or troubles, or even the fame that he expected Keats to win. His painting, too, suddenly looked better. Perhaps the assassins weren't badly drawn at all, perhaps they were simply contorted in the extremity of passion. Had Keats misjudged everything? But when he thought of confessing his plans to Severn, and the pleas that Severn would make, and the half-truths he would use to justify himself, it all seemed cheap and cruel. In the evenings they read Shakespeare to each other, Severn in a fine clear voice much bolder than Keats's own.

Keats had chosen an evening departure because Severn was supposed to be gone that night, to a salon with Canova and other sculptors. But at the last moment the salon was called off and Severn installed himself for the night at his easel, humming bits of opera and waving his brush in time. Keats shut himself in his bedroom—he was writing, he said—and soundlessly took apart the tower of books that Severn had made, laying them in rows at the bottom of his trunk. His folded clothes went on top. He walked on tiptoe, pressing his boots gently to the tiled floor, and stopped cold each time a noise came from Severn's room. Every few moments he looked out the window to the piazza lying orange in the last hour of daylight. He had no idea what to do when the vettura arrived; if he could think of some pretext to send Severn away, he might try it, but only idiocies came into his head. And why the devil had Severn come home, just because his salon was canceled? Was there really nothing else for him in all Rome? Keats stepped back into the closet and in the faint light saw a shut door at the back, behind the empty armoire and water jar. He must have seen it before, without taking it as significant. Now it appeared to him as a portal in a dream, that comes into being only when needed. It must open directly into the entry, passing Severn's room by. He touched the latch and found it resistant; he pushed harder and it cracked in giving way, echoing off the tile. His arms froze in place. He heard murmurs from the piazza, the endless splash of the fountain, and Severn's voice in the next room, mumbling the same bar of Rossini as before.

Would he creep away like a thief? He would.

With his purse stocked for his fare, and lodging and meals for the road, he had a handful of British coins left over. He set them on the desk and scribbled a note beside.

I.O.U.

    Passenger fare, London to Naples

    7 days room and board, Hotel d'Inghilterra, Naples

    Vettura fare, Naples to Rome

    4 months room and board (incl full-crown dinners),

        26 Piazza di Spagna, Rome

    Hire of pianoforte

    Hire of horse

    4 months domestic service

    Physical and spiritual succour

    A lifetime's friendship

Less

    4/ 6d.

John Keats

Hoofbeats came from the window. He looked up and saw a dark bay trotting around the fountain with a black carriage behind. Hastily he wiped his pen, stopped the inkbottle, crept into the closet and swung the door wide. In the entry hall he heard the landlady and her daughter behind their curtain, raising a din of pots and boiling water.

The mustached driver sat in the open air, wrapped against the evening in a coarse blanket. Seeing Keats at the steps, he lifted his arm and shouted a greeting, but Keats shook his head and mimed a frightened glance at the window above, putting his finger to his lips. The driver nodded and laughed silently as he pulled the reins to stop. It was a scene out of opera buffa. Keats was Cherubino, trying to get out of Susanna's bedroom before the Count discovered him.

The vettura's door opened and a giant stepped out, dressed in rough canvas and enormous rope-soled boots. When he unbent himself his head came to the carriage roof. His hair fell short and thick over his brow, like a Roman bust. He started to speak, but the driver hushed him with a quick gesture and repeated Keats's meaningful look at the window. The giant nodded and lifted his arms over his great shoulders, showing he was to carry things. Keats beckoned him silently up the stairs; his soft soles made no sound, not even his breathing could be heard. Keats had him go first into the apartment—let them come out, he thought, let them hold me now! But the entry was vacant, the landlady behind her curtain as before. Severn was still humming. The giant ducked and folded his shoulders to get through the closet, and in Keats's bedroom he lifted the trunk so lightly and noiselessly that it seemed to hang like a bauble from his fingers. The books had etherealized, Keats thought, they had turned back into the minds that birthed them. And nothing of him remained in the room—only Fanny's things, he suddenly remembered, hidden in the desk drawer. He pulled it open, stuffed the bundle in his coat and followed the giant through the closet to the stairway. A giddy feeling took his feet as he shut the door, and he went after his trunk with charmed steps, almost dancing to see it so lightly moved. Out of doors his lungs felt the shock of open air, and the first stars hung free in the sky.

Fragment in a Vettura

ROME HAD NO STREET LAMPS and at dusk the entire city faded to murk. Keats sat facing backward in the vettura, his head half out the window, and watched shadows of roofs pass over the violet sky. Everything below was the faintest sketch. Nothing showed on the streets but the dancing orange tips of cigars; lit windows sprang into being like ghosts, waved their drapes and were gone. Keats leaned farther out and a breeze struck his face, smelling of cooking fires.

"It's so dark!" he called. "You don't fear bandits?"

"Not with Nino," the driver replied. The giant heard his name and smiled; he sat opposite Keats, head touching the ceiling and knees drawn close.

"And God protect us," said the driver. "We have priests."

"Priests?"

"They go to Firenze. We stop at the parrochia. Is all right for you, milord? Nothing to confess?" He barked a laugh. "No woman up the stairs?"

Keats pulled his head out of the wind. He would not sleep; he had craved motion for so long. His mind shot forward to starry landscapes, yellow hills and olive groves—but he pulled back on its rein, for he didn't want to think of arrival. His thoughts teetered and fell back to the room he had just left. Severn was still working peacefully, in the belief that Keats was beside him; or he had already discovered Keats was gone. He pictured him bent over the desk, reading the note, and felt a pang. But it had to be done.

Beguiling lady—

What was that? The phrase came from nowhere. But it had the old flavor Keats knew at once, the taste of poetry.

Beguiling lady. Subtle are her hands—

What is it then? A stage speech. A man watching a woman.

Beguiling lady! Subtle are her hands,
And sly her fingers parcel out the cards—

A card game. The lady is Dame Fortune and the players are a group of rakes, leering, making coarse jokes. The poet stands apart, watches the game and speaks—to whom? To his lover.

The phrases came up. He strung them like garlands from the ironwork of the meter. That meter was the one true clock, and though his mind could wander far in the dark—though he fell half asleep, dropping into lightless dreams that gave an obscure meaning to the wheels rattling under him—the lines held steady in his mind and time did not pass. All in a moment he arrayed his characters, gave them their words, and opened his eyes to find an early blue glow suspended on the landscape. The city was gone. He saw wheat fields, wooden farmhouses, a patch of weird gray shrubs on a hillside—one of them stood and grew a sheep's head. Nino was asleep with his chin on his chest.

The first good poem Keats ever wrote, his sonnet on Chapman, he had done after staying out all night. He'd walked home at dawn over London Bridge in the weird clarity of physical exhaustion; the shapes of buildings had pressed all their weight upon his gritty eyes. The sonnet too was perfectly sharp in his mind, each image laid alongside the last, though when it came time to write it down he was so groggy that he had to mark out the rhyme scheme in the margin.

His trunk was strapped above the vettura, but the pen and ink were still in his pocket, and he had to write now, before he lost

it. He reached into his coat, brushed the lock of Fanny's hair and
jerked his hand back, as if something had bit him; he'd forgotten it
was there. But she'd given him paper. He reached again and found
a sheet, flattened it on his lap, opened the inkbottle.

> *Poet.* Beguiling lady! Subtle are her hands,
>   And sly her fingers parcel out the cards.
>   Mark this: the hearts fall ever to her husband—
>   The others take the coins. Legerdemain!
>   A lie commands our love.

And his lover, who does not understand, finishes the line:

> *Lover.*   Believ'st in me?

The poet turns away. In his mind Keats saw Edmund Kean
playing Hamlet.

> *Poet.* How can I say? We know each other scarce.
>   We are thick-pelted things—we stretch our paws,
>   And one coarse hide but rubs against the next.
>   We are lonely.

She calls his name. Decide the name later.

> *Lover.*   ____, thou knowest me.
> *Poet.* Ay, what the world calls knowing. Feather'd locks
>   Thou hast, and eyes of jet, and cheek all snow,
>   And loving call'st my name—but here! But here!

He turns to her, and touches her eyes and brow.

> *Poet.* What is behind? How gross our human senses!
>   To know each other? Never, till we cleave

Our skulls in two, and from our furrowed brains
Wring out the thoughts.

Now what? Show the game, the leering rakes.

Dame Fortune. Say, what are you about with your fingers?
Rake. Nothing!
Dame Fortune. Don't stick your thumb out so, it's vulgar.
Rake. Ha! But see, the thing has such a particular physiognomy.

He looks down and points it still farther, waving the grotesquely fat digit over the cards.

Poet. I love thee as the grave.
Lover.   O horrible!
Poet. Nay, hear. 'Tis said that in the grave is peace,
    Peace and the grave are one. Be it but so,
    In thy soft lap I lie beneath the earth.
    Sweet grave! Thy fluted lips my passing-bells,
    Thy breast my burial mound, thy heart my coffin.

Again, that would frighten people. To relieve it:

Dame Fortune. You lose!
Rake. It was a lover's adventure. It cost money like any other.
Dame Fortune. Indeed? Then you declared your love like a
    deaf-mute, with your fingers.
Rake. And fitting it was. They say the fingers, of all things,
    are soonest understood. See, here I made a tryst with the
    queen; my fingers were princes enchanted to spiders; the
    fairy, Madam, was you; but the chance went ill. The lady
    was forever in childbed, each moment she birthed anoth-
    er knave. By God, I wouldn't have my daughter play this
    game—the lords and ladies fall so indecently upon each

other! And the knaves come close behind.

Keats laughed into his palm. He hadn't meant it to be bawdy, it was changing as he wrote. Suddenly the seat pitched under him and the vettura stopped moving; Keats fell forward against Nino, who opened his eyes and shouted something in Roman dialect.

"Mi scusi," said Keats.

Nino shouted again and pointed to Keats's arm. A dark stain wrapped his coat sleeve; another marked his breeches; shiny rivulets, coal-black, were racing across his seat. He grabbed the tipped inkbottle, flinging drops, and began to blot the bench with his paper, trying to keep the words clear though he saw them smearing under his fingers. Nino was calling something, trying to move, but their legs were tangled up and there wasn't room in the vettura for them both to stand. The carriage door gave way and Keats twisted his waist, clasping the filthy sheet to his breast, to find two white-haired men in cassocks staring up at him with pale, vulnerable eyes. A squat stone church stood behind them, and rosy daybreak on winter fields. The priests looked at Keats, then at Nino, then at each other, then back at Keats, then at the vetturino, who had come up behind with eyes scrunched shut and his hand over his mouth. He didn't seem to understand what he saw; his mouth was caught in a yawn and when he tried to speak, his lips quivered apart from each other and released only a groan.

"Colpa mia," said Keats, "tutta colpa mia. Please—"

"But your *coat*, milord!" the vetturino cried.

To Miss Brawne, Wentworth Place, Hampstead

MY DEAREST GIRL,

You will chide me that I have been so long without writing, & I will deserve it. I might plead my illness, & you will say, Shakespeare's Heroes run through with swords still managed fifty lines to their beloveds—I call up the rigors of travel, & you will answer with every three-shilling guide on Fleet Street—somehow those Gents & Ladies, going between the Carriage & the Inn, managed to write their volumes about columns, & Colosseums, & the depravity of Pope Horribilus the Whatth, who yet was Patron to the genius Whozzini, &c., not to mention the modern manners of the Italians. Only your poor Keats cannot make two poor Sheets—well the reason is simple; I have not seen the manners of the Italians. I have been four months in an attic room with only your Face before me. To write of the sights of Italy would but describe you to you. You "have o'erlook'd me and divided me; one half of me is yours, the other half yours." Really it has been a long dream with your Love or my hope of your Love the only thing to sustain me—could you know a thousandth part of my sufferings, which are not extractible from the Love that intertwines them. But my body is out of the sick-room, let me admit some light & air to the sick-room of the Soul. I will tell you natural things. The last two nights & days I have been in a vettura from Rome to Florence, & learnt my lesson, by the bye, about writing Letters in Carriages, for I upset the ink over the conveyance & myself and straightaway became a grimacing Boy of ten, holding out his hand for the Rod—but I was not struck. Even an ink smirched Englishman is a kind of Lord here. The vetturino has lent me a clean coat of his own, & I fear he wants to make it a gift. The generous Hearts of these people pass all report. I have two Priests for traveling companions—a giant out of Ariosto was our porter but he has departed us. The Priests are mild old signori & talk no English, but their speech is not so much dialect as most, so I understand them tolerable well & they me. They correct my Verbs for me when I confuse species of the Past, or try Conditionals on what may or may not be. My Latin is no help. You would fare better, talking French as well as you do. Why do you not buy a Grammar & study it? Supposing you came to Italy, you would be my tongue for me—'twould make up my fairest part. When shall I see you—I ache at the question—my sweet Girl, I wish I had hope of finding money for your passage, or of the Doctors releasing me to England. How long will we groan under this Division. I am out of practice with Letters. Italy is strange & I am strange to it. The country outside Rome is fit to be framed & hung in the National Gallery. They grow olives here, also wheat & the hills shall soon be golden, on the road one passes shepherds with their flocks, great gentle Dogs—but there are Wolves also, for this morning we passed a group of Austrian soldiers marching south to fight the Neapolitans. They were splendid & terrible in their white tunics & red trousers, with sabres and muskets at ready—one could hear the boots & horses' hoofs from far off, & they kicked up a great cloud behind. Rome is armed & everyone fearful on the road. I write from a guard-house at the border between the Pope's realms & the Grand Duke's, where we are detained while the Duke's soldiers ask questions of our driver. They have kept him near an hour. I was told that in Italy one deals most agreeably with official Persons by palming them a Coin, but

The guardhouse door swung open and the vetturino walked out, nervously brushing his shoulders. Keats put down his pen, stopping the inkbottle tight—this caused the priests to chuckle in a friendly way—and leaned his head out of the carriage.

"Do you see him?" asked the nearer priest.

"Yes," said Keats, "he is not yet coming. I think the guards are speaking to him."

"The government must be careful," said the priest. "With Naples fallen, who knows where it will end."

"È l'influenza del clima," said the other.

"Del clima?" Keats asked.

"A warm climate excites rebellion in the soul," explained the first. "That is why God placed the seat of His Church in the South."

"Ah," said Keats. "Vero."

"Like St. Augustine in Carthage," said the other. "Carthage, you know, was very hot."

"Davvero."

The priest gave him a narrow look. "You are a Protestant?"

"I am a questioner," said Keats. Both priests nodded, as if he'd given away the thing they expected, then softened their faces.

"Even so," said the nearer, "we are glad for you to be in the carriage. Soon to see Firenze!"

"La bella Toscana—" said the other, dreamily, and the carriage door was rapped. Outside stood a rifleman in thick side-whiskers and a bright white uniform in the French style, with sky-blue epaulettes and cross belts over the chest. He bent to look in the window and the height of his shako hat, fronted with brass badges and topped by a pompon, prevented him from getting his head through. His eyes moved around the carriage.

"Lei è il inglese?" he asked Keats.

"John Keats, di Londra."

"Please follow me," he said in slow, clear Italian, and pulled the door open. Keats was dazzled by his clothes and those of a second rifleman behind; they looked like children dressed for a pageant. Their faces, where not covered in whiskers, were pink and smooth. Their seriousness, too, was childlike as they watched Keats climb out of the vettura. The first rifleman pointed to the trunk on the roof.

"The trunk is yours?"

"Sì," said Keats.

"Bring it down for inspection, please."

"I am sorry," said Keats. "It is very heavy. Full of books." He ought not to have said that. The riflemen made faces and the first asked, "Foreign books?"

"Literature," he said. "Poetry."

"He says *very* heavy," said the other, frowning at the trunk, and with a dejected look began to move his arms, miming the actions that would be needed to get it down. The first lowered his brows, then raised them in sudden inspiration and peered back into the carriage.

"You were writing something inside?" he asked.

"A letter," said Keats.

"Very good! Bring the letter, please, and your passport."

The page lay on the carriage seat, half-dried and frail, and Keats felt he had to protect it. "But surely the trunk—"

"No, no," said the rifleman, "the letter is enough," and the other broke off staring at the roof and hastily nodded. Keats took the letter and was hurried across the road into the brick-walled guardhouse, where an older man in spectacles and the same blue-and-white uniform sat in front of a large ledger book. His plumed hat rested on his desk like a sleeping bird. As the riflemen stood to attention he ran his finger down the side of the ledger, fastidiously turned the wide page and at length, without looking up, asked for Keats's passport. Keats handed him the sheet with Lord Castlere-

THE WARM SOUTH ✎ 55

agh's signature, and the official copied out his name and nationality slowly, in a looping hand. "And your purpose in this country?"

"To visit the sights," said Keats.

"The sights?"

"The antiquities, and the landscape."

"There is nothing to see here," the official said.

"Ha." Keats made a cautious smile at everyone in turn. "Voglio dire—Firenze? Michel Angelo?"

"There is nothing to see here." The official carefully removed his spectacles, set them beside the hat and looked up. "You must have another purpose that you are concealing. Were you in this country in the time of Napoleon?"

"Napoleon? I was a boy then."

"You are traveling with priests. Did you go to Mass yesterday?"

"Beh—" said Keats, that being his Italian word when at a loss.

"Remember that we may confirm your account."

"No, I did not go. That is—I did not understand Mass was obligatory for travelers." His surprise past, he was becoming angry; but he also understood that this official was for some reason trying to anger him. The man leaned back, set his hat on his knee and lazily looked Keats over.

"What are your means of subsistence? It costs money to travel."

Keats huffed. "I am a poet."

The man raised his brows. "As you like. Still, it costs money to travel."

"I mean that poetry is my means of subsistence. I have published three volumes."

The first rifleman cleared his throat. "He is traveling with books, he says. And he was writing." He set Keats's letter on the desk. The official lifted it by its corner and frowned; then, letting it drop, he applied the frown to its author.

"That coat does not fit you," he said.

"No. I upset the ink—"

"He upset the ink!" shouted the official, lifting his gray brows higher, and held this fact out to the riflemen with open palms. "He upset the ink!" The riflemen smiled obediently, not seeming to know how much part they had in the joke. Out of doors their youth had charmed Keats; now it gave him a chill. Suppose you met a baby with a loaded musket in its arms and one fat hand on the trigger, and suppose it began to wave the muzzle in and out of your direction, smiling, with just enough force to make a discharge thinkable: well, you might do many things. You might shrink against a wall; you might hope to distract the infant into laying down its weapon—though carefully, carefully, with no alarming motions—but all the while you would surely be creeping backward, to distance yourself as soon as possible from the unreasoning threat. Pictures of Italian dungeons sprang into Keats's mind; he remembered Mrs. Radcliffe's galleries of medieval tortures and glanced back to see how directly the riflemen were standing between him and the exit.

"What is your destination in this country?"

Keats's legs shook. "Pisa."

"Do you have letters of recommendation there? Perhaps to a banker?"

"No. I will be a guest of—" Would they know Shelley's name? Was that dangerous? "Of English there."

"From where are you traveling?"

"From Rome."

"And you were there how long?"

"Four months."

"And during four months in Rome," cried the official, "you never had a banker?"

Keats's heart jumped backward. Could they see it? "Of course. Torlonia e Compagnia."

"Torlonia!" said the official. "Torlonia." He returned the hat to his desk and folded his hands. They had reached the end of an awkward road, said his look, at precisely the expected point, never mind Keats's efforts at diversion. "In that case," he said patiently, like a schoolteacher, "as an English client of Torlonia in Rome, you must have dined with him."

"Why, no," said Keats. "Not I."

"Never a dinner in four months?" he asked mildly. "Never a visit to the famous palazzo?" He leaned forward and thumped his hands on the ledger book. "And no memory, I suppose, of who else was at the dinner? Of what was said at table?"

"I was ill," Keats said desperately, "I couldn't dine. All winter I was ill."

"Oh!" said the official, and drew back. "You are in Italy for your health?"

When he had first come to Italy, they had kept him quarantined a week in the harbor. He'd thought they would never let him off the ship. "Why, no," he stammered. "It was the scenic interest. That is—la bella Toscana." These soldiers were not going to let him through. They were going to shut him in a sanatorium. "I had an attack in Rome, not serious. You may ask Doctor James Clark. It was the mind, the brain. Organic fibers—"

"You are in Italy for your health. Why did you not say so?" The official took his pen and finished out the ledger line. "Pisa—reasons of health—the first of March. Bene." He applied a stamp to Keats's passport and handed it back. "Fair travels."

"Grazie," said Keats, before he understood, and stared dumbly at the man's face. The threat had gone out of him. Now he looked tired and impatient for Keats to go away. "And—the letter?"

"What does the letter say?"

"It is a love letter," said Keats, flushing. "What it says is mine."

The official gave the letter a sad glance, folded it once and stuck it in a desk compartment. "We will keep it. You may go."

There was no questioning for the priests. With the sun sinking fast over the hills, they had just time to reach a roadside inn fronting a village of twenty huts, where the three travelers were given a back room with two beds and a writing table. The floor was straw and a damp breeze came in between the wall planks. The priests offered to share one bed, leaving Keats the other; they slipped off their cassocks and lay back to back like snowy angels, skinny legs protruding from under their tunics. Keats lit a candle at the table and unfolded a fresh sheet.

My dearest Girl,

You will chide me that I have been so long without writing, & I will deserve it.

The Loan Redeemed

AT FLORENCE HE PARTED FROM the priests, and while the horses rested through the afternoon he walked his empty purse around the city. The streets took narrow courses between rough brick walls and passed under heavy arches, so that the whole city seemed a kind of castle. Everything was cleaner than in Rome; there was no washing in the open, no spoiled vegetables. Cathedrals hid behind the corners and ambushed him as he went. He craned his neck and found fantastic spires hanging just over his head, too close to understand. In the huge, dark interiors he walked between the marble columns as if through fairy crypts. There were family chapels locked behind iron gates, dead kings with Latin on their coffins, huge painted Christs and saints and very few living souls other than the vergers tending rows of candles in glass jars. A few figures hid their faces in the pews. The paintings all looked flat and clean, from a younger world. Keats felt he didn't understand them and wondered what Severn would say. He needed no one to teach him the Italian landscape; the golden hills passed straight into his heart. But the works of man required knowledge. What was he missing?

"And where are you bound in Pisa?" asked the vetturino.

"It is Casa Galletti. Do you know it?"

"You mean Palazzo Galletti."

"Perhaps." Was Shelley living in a palace?

"Palazzo Galletti. Alla destra di alla giornata."

"Bene," said Keats, but only because the Italian language had failed him again. To the right of to the day?

"Also," said the vetturino, "in Florence are many shops for you to buy a coat. Ready-made."

"Thank you. I will have to wait." He slid the borrowed coat from his shoulders. "My old coat must introduce me to Pisa."

The vetturino clucked his tongue. "Signor, the stain is very bad."

"And if anyone tells me so," said Keats, "I will ask him: would this stain have shamed your Dante, or your Alfieri?"

"Ha!" cried the vetturino, and clapped Keats's shoulder in its bare shirt. "Have you not seen Dante in the paintings? He dressed very, very well."

Xenia

To REACH PISA WAS ANOTHER day's journey. Their carriage turned west and followed a narrow track through a sleepy, folded-up forest landscape where the river passed in and out of view between files of low trees. The same mountain hung perpetually on their right hand, though each time Keats looked up it had changed shape. His companions were now a young gentleman and lady who made a point of ignoring him and half whispered to each other in the dialect he'd first heard in Florence. *Casa* was *hasa* here, *amico* became *amiho*. Everyone said this was the purest strain of Italian, but Keats tried to imagine Dante talking this way and couldn't—not unless he dressed Dante in the same wasp-waisted coat and trousers that the gentleman had squeezed himself into. He looked out the window at the slow river and thought of the *Inferno*.

> ...sul passo d'Arno,
> ...something, something,
> ...cittadin che poi la rifondarno.

Drowsy after a night of bad dreams in a Florentine inn, he let his mind go slack with the current. The shifting mountain rippled its downward-pointing image behind the trees, and he felt teased with a thought about those lines, profound, elusive... the three-way mirror that was terza rima, that threefold reflection of sound, a structure inherent to the language—inherent how? Because it was inevitable. Because it had grown like a living thing from the vowels of the Italian language, assuming that sound is the soil of language and poetry is its fruit... for example the sound *Arno*, meaning in itself, what did it mean? A liquid word for the flow of the river, the flow of the rhyme, the recurrent and resplendent Arno reflecting Arno, Arno and again Arno....

His shoulders jerked, and he found that he'd slumped forward across the carriage, and that his head was in the lady's lap. "Scusi!" he cried, and pushed away, but the lady and gentleman were both staring out the window and wouldn't look at him. The wooly smell of her petticoat stuck in his nostrils and caught his forehead and ears on fire. He put his head out the window and the lady began to shake a fan over herself. Was she trying to clear the air between them? Was he such a blackguard in his blotched coat?

A maze of earth-colored rooftops rose from the plain ahead. In their center, looking delicate and very white, as if carved from shells, stood a group of domed buildings ringed by arches. The river swung from the countryside into the thick of the roofs, where it suddenly acquired bridges and an escort of flat-fronted buildings; then it swung again, silvering under the falling sun, into a blue haze that might have been land or sea. At the edge of the central group was a joke of a tower, slanted and hanging apart from its companions like a stage prop whose strings had half snapped.

Dear God, Keats thought. I shouldn't have come.

He was dazed and chilled at heart. As the carriage descended into the plain, passed outlying farms and what was left of the city walls, entered a desolate-looking street with grass sprouting between the cobblestones, stopped alongside the river and deposited Keats on the paving and called over a porter to pull his trunk off the roof, then rattled away with the gentleman and lady, who had not once acknowledged him, all he wished was never to have left Rome. No: never to have left England. Better to have suffered winter there. Blind fear had driven him out. So long as he was moving away from things, without thought of arrival, the movement had been enough—but what was he to do here? Did he think that poverty would sting any less in Pisa? That it would be any more tolerable to impose on others? And in an aristocrat's house! He hadn't seen Shelley in years and had complicated feelings toward the man, but just now he remembered only his fine fingers, his Cambridge accent, his indifference to money that came of never having had to think about it.

Well. He could not break down sobbing on the riverbank. It was evening and he needed a bed.

Low brick walls lined both sides of the ashen river. The air was cool, with a hint of sea. Keats and his trunk stood in the empty street and faced the bunched facades of three- and four-story houses, or palaces, or whatever they were. The nearest had balconies fronted in white stone and a marble doorway with two massive leaves shut against him. The lintel read

ALLA GIORNATA

So. To the right.

The neighbor building was another many-storied affair, with four identical doors set under half-moon windows. Did they all open to the same entry? Why, thought Keats, had Shelley felt the need to take lodgings the size of an opera house? He stepped up and rapped the nearest door, then bit his lip in the quiet and wiped his palms on his trousers. Across the river a child appeared from an alley, ran the length of a house and vanished. A latch cracked; the door swung open with a scrape of wood on stone, and a squat, round-shouldered fellow in a shabby footman's jacket leaned out and held a lantern to Keats's face.

"Buona sera."

"Buona sera. I am calling on Signor Shelley?"

"Shelley!" That name unlocked a smile. "But the signor is not here. He has changed his lodging."

"Not here?" Relief! All at once his fear melted away—if Shelley wasn't here, then nothing was decided.

"He hasn't moved far," said the footman. "Shall I show you?"

"No!" said Keats. "Thank you, no." He needn't do this. He could go back to Rome tomorrow; he could go back to England. "Could you direct me to a nearby hotel? With, ah, moderate rooms?"

"Oh, but he's so near!" said the footman. "The signor would hate to send his friend to a hotel—come, is this your trunk?" He set down the lantern, walked past Keats into the street and grabbed one end of the trunk. "Foo!" he cried. "Che peso! What have you got, signor? Shoes? English boots?"

"No," Keats said, hurrying after him, "please. That's not necessary."

"Or you deal in silver?" He was tugging at the trunk with such effort that he seemed about to injure himself, and Keats lifted the other end. But now the thing was out of his control; the footman set his shoulders and chest and began to pull it up the street with amazing force, obliging Keats to jog behind and try to keep his end from scraping the pavement.

"Really," he called, "I wish—"

"You'll see, it is very near." They were following the river and the line of palazzi curved gently ahead. A few windows traced yellow gleams around shutters. The only sound in the night was a chorus of faint voices, Keats couldn't tell from where, singing a melody he couldn't follow because his ears were full of his own ragged breath. O, that this too solid trunk would melt. It was ghostly, after the life of Rome, to see nobody on the street. Surely Pisa had ghosts to account for. The old medieval cruelties, siege and plague, starvation in towers. At a square corner the footman signaled that the trunk should be set down. Keats dropped his load and made to grab the man's sleeve, but he was already away, bounding onto the threshold and banging the knocker like an anvil. This building too had rows of doors along both streets and several stories of windows above. How could anyone live this way, carried from palace to palace on a whim?

The door was opened. A low Tuscan voice addressed the

footman and both men came out for the trunk. "This way, signor," the footman called, and Keats, seeing his things borne away from him, unhappily followed into the entry and around a square stair-well that kept throwing up confounding walls in the dark. After two or three flights came a burst of lamplight and voices, and he stepped quite suddenly from the landing into a dark wooden parlor outfitted with rugs and bookcases. The men were setting his trunk on the floor, and Shelley and Mrs. Shelley, along with an unfamiliar man, were staring in great alarm at the thing, as if they expected an animal to pop out. Mrs. Shelley had a child in her arms.

"But who *is* it?" Shelley was asking in Italian. "We aren't a hotel, you can't go bringing anything off the street." Mrs. Shelley lifted her eyes and cried out, as if she'd discovered a ghost. Shelley looked up and his jaw fell.

"Why, it is Keats!" he said in English.

He was older. Crow's feet touched his eyes and his chestnut hair was threaded gray. His child's nose and wide blue eyes no longer gave him his old ethereal look—a fairy creature, people used to call him, more spirit than man. He looked very human now, and tired.

"You see," the footman said proudly. "He asked directions to a hotel, if you can imagine. I know you wouldn't dream of it."

"Oh, the things *you* know," said Mrs. Shelley sharply, in a very good accent; as if someone Keats didn't know, a severe Italian woman, were talking through her mouth. She too seemed older, though Keats had never thought her young. Even at twenty she had been cool and ageless, with her low voice and high philoso-pher's forehead, her famous father's image masquerading in a girl's body. She was exactly Keats's height, but gave him the same wary feeling as a large man.

"I hope there has been no mistake?" he asked.

"No!" said Shelley, and smiled anxiously at his wife. "Natu-rally there is no mistake. Only, if we had known to expect your arrival—"

"I did write," said Keats. "Forgive me. It must have gone to your previous residence?"

Shelley blinked. "Forgive *me*. We have been so much on the move." He swept his hands wide in one of his old flourishes. "But no matter, I assure you. We shall make arrangements." He frowned at the trunk. "That is—if you wish to stay with us?"

"I'm sure I don't know where we might put him," Mrs. Shelley said.

"Mary, I did extend an invitation. We both did, some months ago. Is it not so?" He smiled again. "Of course things are altered. So many moves. Before Casa Galletti we were at the baths and our villa was flooded. We had to row from the upper story in a packet-boat." The smile widened, becoming the desperate sort of smile that is conscious of not meeting an answer. His hands gripped each other.

"I beg your pardon," said Keats. "Your invitation was gener-ous, but I perceive that it must be an imposition. I would be grate-ful if you could direct me to a hotel."

"But not at all!" Shelley cried. "Heavens, no!"

"Bene?" asked the footman, who hadn't followed the con-versation but understood it was time to leave. "Tutto bene?" He turned to Keats and bowed. "My pleasure to serve, signor."

A unpleasant silence followed and Keats realized he was sup-posed to give the man a coin. What did he have?

"Well, someone see to it," Mrs. Shelley said.

Keats flushed and reached for his purse, but Shelley was quicker and stepped forward with a glint in his fingers. "Thank you, Luca," he said, touching his palm; "you are a man of noble enthusiasms." Luca grinned and nodded, stepping back to the dark landing, and vanished from Keats's sight. Now he perceived everything he hadn't yet seen properly: the ruddy, curly head of the child in Mrs. Shelley's arms, and the man he didn't know, about his own age, who leaped nimbly around the trunk in tight dandy's trousers and extended his hand.

"Captain Thomas Medwin," he said, "your servant. You must blame me for the awkwardness."

Keats took the hand. "Surely not, Captain."

"Surely so! For I have already made claims on Shelley's generosity. He is my cousin, you know; he had no decent way to refuse me; but he has given me the only spare room in these apartments."

The man did resemble Shelley; or rather, he was like Shelley with all the unearthly boiled out of him. He had broad shoulders and a strong aristocrat's jaw, and seemed like the sort of man who could do maneuvers on a horse.

"I'm sorry," Keats said stiffly. "I have no experience in arranging palaces. From the street it seemed rather large."

"The palazzo is not ours to dispose of," said Mrs. Shelley.

Keats blinked. "I beg your pardon?"

"We have our bedroom with the child," she said, "and Captain Medwin in the upstairs room. That is all."

"You didn't think—?" Shelley asked, and brought his hand to his mouth. "To take an entire palazzo! Oh, we are not that rich."

"No," said Mrs. Shelley; "I should say we aren't rich enough for many favors you do."

Keats felt his shame turn upon her. No, he didn't like this woman. She might have learning, she might even have a kind of genius—one heard that said of women nowadays. But she had no feeling. He had a moment's fantasy of touching the skin under her clothes and finding it chill, like marble. She had embarrassed them into silence. Shelley was looking at the floor. Of course she was right; by any code of courtesy Keats ought not to be here. He should turn and walk down the stairs—but who would carry the horrible trunk? Only Medwin seemed not to understand and put out a beseeching hand.

"Please, Mr. Keats," he said. "Why do you not pass the night in the upstairs bedroom? I shall be very well accommodated on the settee."

"Thank you, Captain. In all decency, I can't."

"Come," cried Medwin, "you don't mean to commit a slander on the settee?" He set his jaw and thumped the back of the sofa. "I declare, 'tis a noble piece of furniture. Why, for one who has slept on the plains of Uttar Pradesh and the banks of the Sindh, it is a palace in itself."

Shelley seemed to wake from a trance. He smiled at Medwin and bent forward to rest his fingers on Keats's shoulder, saying, "Quite so. Mary would have it that I make a vice of liberality, and for aught I know she is right. But I feel I could never repent doing you kindness. Will you not stay?"

His eyes were like Severn's. This world demanding the right to love him—how had he earned it?

"Thank you," said Keats, and bit his lip against his flush. "I may be obliged to accept for tonight. Understand, it is only to save the honor of your furniture."

Medwin laughed raucously, Shelley more weakly. It was done; he had better not make himself sour now. He blew out a great breath, like pushing aside a stone, and turned to Mary. Her look was cordial now, with a touch of distance in her dark, wide-set eyes. Keats bowed to look in the child's face, smiled and raised his finger.

"Sir," he said, "you have the advantage of me."

The child blinked its eyes, pale and cloudy like its father's, and squirmed in its frock.

"Will you not tell the gentleman your name? He does speak very well," Mary assured him, in a softer tone.

"No!" squeaked the child, and followed with vague sounds. Was it Italian?

"In that case," said Mary, smiling for the first time, "allow me to present Percy Florence Shelley, who shall go now to his bed. Caterina," she called, and a young woman in tight black braids came to take the child in her arms. The serving man came as well and Mary gave instructions in Tuscan, pointing in series to Keats and Medwin and the trunk. The man made a face and took Keats's inked sleeve between his fingers.

"A battle wound," said Keats. But he couldn't say it in Italian. The man shook his head and pulled the coat from his shoulders; then bent his back, heaved up the trunk, swung it a yard and dropped it. He puffed his cheeks and repeated the operation. Surely Keats should help him—but nobody else was taking note. The trunk thumped away and Shelley waved him farther into the parlor.

"Sit with us," he said. "Are you tired? Have you dined?"

It occurred faintly to Keats, like an old memory, that he was famished. He couldn't think how to say it politely. But Caterina was back already with bread and sheep's cheese bundled in white cloth and a carafe of red wine. She set them on the parlor table and Keats was made to take an ottoman.

"I regret we have only peasant food," said Shelley. "Animal food we never have, which is obnoxious to some."

"To me, he means," Medwin said. "You have a beautiful soul, cousin, but I would not exchange you stomachs."

"And when you have eaten," said Shelley, "in the evenings we read aloud the day's work. Thomas had just begun us his poem of India."

"Then I intruded on it," Keats said, with the bread tantalizingly at his mouth. "Again I beg pardon."

"Not at all!" said Medwin. "It were worth a thousand intrusions to have the poet of 'Hyperion' as my auditor. For yes," he said, with a significant look, "Shelley has been a champion of your book. My own admiration will go without saying."

"I thank you again," said Keats. "I shall have to keep thanking you the next fortnight."

They fell silent. From the landing came the thump of the trunk going upstairs a step at a time. Keats bit his bread and the world narrowed around his mouth. It was crisp, faintly sour in the crust, soft and sweet within. He wet it with wine and it flowed like syrup into him. The cheese was firm, with the mild taste of Italian milk, and made him feel solid. The journey had worn him thin as paper. Medwin took some sheets from the table and began to shuffle them; Shelley and Mary went to the settee and sat apart from each other, their faces hiding their thoughts. When the bread and cheese were quite gone and Keats had wiped his lips and sat back, wine buzzing in his ears, the captain stood and cleared his throat.

"Sketches in Hindoostan," he said. "The Lion Hunt." He raised his finger like a conductor's baton and read, "O! The blood more stirs to rouse a lion, than to start a hare." He looked hopefully over the parlor.

"That is Hotspur," said Keats. "A true Hotspur line."

"Just so! But never did Hotspur meet a true lion. Scene: the borders of the Beekanair desert."

> There is a joy to vulgar souls unknown,
> There is a magic in that word—*Alone*!
> Though never in the fulness of its power
> Owned I its influence till this solemn hour.
> Is it—that in these wilds by Man untrod,
> More deep is felt the presence of a God?
> Or, that on Nature's sacred solitude,
> Sprung from the world, its fiends cannot intrude?

His elocution was superb. He must have practiced the lines aloud. Keats glanced at Shelley and Mary; both were looking at their knees. The poem worked through a long description of desert waste—birds, tigers, howling beasts, camels and Arabs, infinities of sand—before moving to introduce its hero, a man of good Christian blood, though sun-bronzed, who had turned apostate to Brahmanism, it seemed because of a bewitching Indian maid, though this part was quickly related and a trifle obscure. Meanwhile the thump from upstairs had stopped and the serving man had come back down with a different travel chest, which he swung into place behind the settee. The poem touched on a ruined temple.

> Was consecrate to Boodh—religion's wane—
> He flourished then, now Jug'nat has its reign.

"I should note," said Medwin, lowering his sheet, "that is an allusion to the expulsion of the Boodists from Hindoostan proper, in the eighth century. Jugnat, or Juggernaut, is he whose pagoda is now the favorite resort of pilgrims from all parts of India." He looked anxious and Keats nodded in an understanding way.

The poem resumed.

> Other Ata'ars may rise in after times—

"Ah," said Medwin, "and there I abbreviate the word *Avatara*, which signifies an incarnation. The Hindoos admit nine previous, you know, and expect a tenth to come, in the shape of a horse called Calki."

"I fear you may have to let some of this lore go by," Shelley said gently, "if you wish not to break the spell of your tale."

"Yes, yes; I intend to publish the poem with notes."

>   —in after times,
> Their very names unknown to other climes.
> But Nature's worship—changeless, chaste, and pure,
> Though these awhile may triumph, shall endure:
> And when their systems to the dust are hurled,
> Arise, new born, to reillume the world.
> But the night wanes; and yonder full-orbed moon
> Must yield her empire to Orion soon.

"Orion," Medwin added, "being the most brilliant of all constellations in the eastern hemisphere," and before anyone could break in, "But of course, of course, let the lore go by."

The hunting expedition got underway. Keats glanced at the Shelleys and for the briefest moment, while Medwin's attention was fully on his sheet, he saw a tight-lipped look pass between them. It was not consciously cruel, but had Medwin caught it, he would have been destroyed. Poor fellow! They were humoring him.

Mahouts and elephants paraded across the poem. The expedition crossed plains, ruins, pagan temples haunted by sinister hooting birds.

> Wondering that man should venture to intrude
> On this their silent reign of solitude.

Was it the second time around for that rhyme? There was a horrible joke in this, Keats thought, reflecting his own longing back at him. What did he desire if not solitude? What was the good of an Indian desert, if not to save him from sitting through poems about Indian deserts? Without intending it, he caught Mary's dark eyes and found the mocking look still there—not a communication to him, of course. Anyone might see it. No, this was unbearable. A bad poem he could tolerate, but not this sitting in the parlor and passing around glances. He touched his side and cried out.

Medwin stopped reading. "Mr. Keats?"

"Pardon me, Captain. I beg pardon of you all—I am a touch unwell."

"Oh dear!" said Shelley, with wide blue eyes, and half stood. "Unforgivable! I have not even asked after your health. We have an excellent doctor up the way."

"We need not disturb him," said Keats. "I fancy a faintness in the nerves is all."

"Believe me, I did not mean to neglect you. Your appearance

drove it clear from my mind—you look so well. What we heard from England had us fearing you half dead."

"So I was. Maybe more than half. But some Orpheus charmed me back up, I know not for what purpose. I think," he said to Medwin, smiling faintly, "I am only fatigued. Your incidents have proved so suspenseful, that to follow them may be more than my capacity tonight."

"But we haven't got to the lion," said Medwin.

"The lion shall wait for him," said Shelley. "We others will see the hunt through."

Keats stood, thanking them all, and Shelley and Medwin made anxious good-night wishes.

"You'll find your water jar not fit to drink from," said Mary. "The Pisan well is foul, and my husband has not yet contrived to send for fountain-water from the aqueduct."

"The vexations of moving house," said Shelley. "I would rather be wise as the snail, and keep only what I could carry. But that should lose me the pleasure of hospitality. *Xenia*—we must teach you Greek. Sleep well, Keats."

Released, he climbed the dark stairs. Behind a half-open door he found a lone lamp glowing orange and such a bed as he hadn't seen in months, twice the breadth of his Roman cot, with pillows and quilt and clean linen puffed delightfully upward in promise of soft dreams. His trunk was at the footboard, with the lid open to his books. His clothes had already been folded and hung in the armoire. His lone other possession, a handsbreadth stack of manuscript sheets, had been put on a writing table at the window. Easing back the shutter, he met a waft of night air and a faint view of the river's sweep under the palazzi lights.

He ought to sleep. But the sheets beckoned him and he took the chair. He hadn't looked over them since leaving England. Where had he been? There were so many unfinished things, all the pieces Brown had wanted him to write. The tragedy of King Stephen. His "Cap and Bells" that was supposed to outdo Byron as witty froth. The "Hyperion," that everyone so admired, he had twice failed to finish, and his publishers had finally put it out as a fragment. When he sounded its lines in his head, they no longer seemed like anything written by him. Someone else had made them, a younger cousin of his, and he didn't know how that person had meant to carry them forward.

No, he thought, turning over the sheets, he was not a real poet. He hadn't found his own style. He'd imitated Spenser's effusions, Milton's inversions, Dryden's lean couplets, and had tired of each. Nothing he had written would last. A few lines from "Hyperion," a few lines from the nightingale poem still sounded well in his head—but ten lines was no reputation. Suppose Shakespeare had written only "The Phoenix and the Turtle"?

At the bottom of the stack was the page he had scrawled in the vettura. It was ink-blotched from top to bottom and he had to read it slowly, with memory filling the gaps. But there was something there. It was a new style for him, a new theme. Was this his proper place? After so many false starts, was his real work beginning at last?

He slid the page under the others. Let it sleep there, a seed. He needed no more to hope on. Hope lightly clothed his movements as he stood, pulled the shutter to, undid his waistcoat and shirt and trousers and slid into the crisp embrace of the sheets. Fear no more the heat o' the sun. A consummation....

In the middle of the night he snapped awake. There had been a noise, some kind of blow, at the edge of his dream. He stared through the dark with a pounding heart and a red shimmer on his sight, but no second sound came and in a moment he had dropped back to sleep.

Vita nuova

DAY CAME IN THE ENGLISH style, sunless and cool, with a white glow that got inside things and made them radiate. Keats put his head out the window and sucked in the damp. For the first time in a year he felt no answering ache in his breast. The river was a crescent of smooth lead this morning, solid as the bricks along the bank.

The doctors might say what they liked. He was well. He must go.

And go where, and how? No sign came to him as he wet his hair and face from the water-jar, which had in fact an acrid smell. Shelley wanted him here and Mrs. Shelley didn't, but even had they both opened their arms, he would have shrunk back. Once again the offer came with too many conditions. Could Shelley even afford him? What *was* Shelley's income? He'd never thought to wonder. Past a certain threshold, and rather a low one, he saw all distinctions of wealth fade to a general white. There was having the money to take rooms—there was having the money to marry—and there was the opposite.

Was he to go back to Rome? The thought was lead. He would sit in the same carriages, sleep in the same inns, have some horrid scene with Severn. Well, go on and have it. After that no one would give him orders. He would book his passage to London. The old dark city billowed before him: cobblestones, hackney carriages, spires in fog, Hampstead Heath in flower. Fanny. His letter to her was stuck in the stack of manuscripts, not yet posted. It had gotten tied up with some disagreeable knot in his mind, and whenever his thoughts lighted on it they glanced away. He pulled on his boots and went downstairs. There was nobody below; the bookcases stood open and he looked over the titles. Godwin, of course. Wordsworth. Three shelves of Greek and Latin. Flanking them were a couple of half-size marble figures—Apollo and Diana, was it? These rooms might be small, but they were done up in luxury. A blue velvet curtain spilled along the window like a yard of ocean. How much did one pay for that?

He padded over the rug and looked into the back quarters. There was a dining table, a kitchen through one doorway and through the other, half open, a bright room with some kind of brown drape over a chair—it was Mary's head. He froze, a shy smile on his lips; but he was not seen. Shelley and Mary were both in the room, bent over adjoining desks. They were writing. He heard very clearly the scratching of their pens; one paused to dip his nib and the other followed. He should not be looking in. This must be a private hour, a sanctuary. To write with another, to know a love that encompassed this thing—he'd never thought of it.

Shelley stirred in his chair and stretched his hand to Mary's shoulder. It seemed a gesture of habit, not knowingly made. After a moment Mary shrugged off the hand and leaned away. Shelley pulled his arm back and his pen briefly stilled. Then he resumed writing, more slowly. Neither had looked at the other.

Steps came from the landing and Keats jumped back, as if caught doing something lewd. Medwin stepped in, followed by a figure of judgment. It wore a dark greatcoat and broad-brimmed hat, and its gloved hand carried a cane. It was enormous. It was death and the police.

"It's the doctor," said Medwin.

The figure pulled off its hat. Underneath was a head of iron-gray hair and an Italian profile copied from a sculpture gallery. That man belonged in this room, Keats thought at once; he was at home here, as the rest of them were strangers. He set his hat and stick in the corner and pulled off his thin gloves, one after the other, like the lord of the house coming home. Medwin seemed a child beside him.

"Signor Keats," said Medwin, and waved them toward each other. "Professore Andrea Vaccà."

This was planned, Keats thought. They had brought a doctor to give him a diagnosis and keep him in Pisa.

"Buongiorno, Professor," he said, taking the large brown hand; his other arm he kept at his chest. "Mille scusi, ma credo che—forse—ci sai un errore." Subjunctive with *credo*, yes. "Non sono malato."

"But I do not know who you are," said the doctor. "I am calling on Mr. Shelley."

He spoke English in baritone, with a good university accent. Keats pulled his hand back, confused, and looked to Medwin. "Shelley is ill?"

The rear door creaked and Shelley came out in his shirt-sleeves. Seeing the doctor, he rushed forward and took the man's hand in both his own, gushing Italian too fast for Keats to catch. His voice was strained; again Keats was struck by how tired he looked.

"And Mrs. Shelley?" the doctor asked.

"Mrs. Shelley has headache this morning. A very sublunary headache, she says, not worth a visit. Er—" Shelley gestured to Keats. "Here also is Mr. Keats, our guest."

"Yes," said Vaccà. "He tells me he is not ill."

Was the doctor mocking him? As he liked; it was Shelley that worried him. His lips were bloodless, his eyes bulged under puffed lids.

"What troubles you?" asked Keats.

Shelley swept his hand dismissively. "Oh, before *you* I am ashamed of it. The doctors could not agree whether I was consumptive, or nephritic, or what. They brought no benefit till we consulted Professor Vaccà."

"I did nothing but cancel the other doctors' treatments," said Vaccà. "Italy has much to learn in medicine."

"But you have consumptive symptoms?" Keats asked. "You as

well?"

"No, no," Shelley insisted, "simple annoyances. Nervous attacks, spasms in the side, that sort of thing."

"They prostrated him," said Medwin. "He would lie on the floor until they ceased. And he walks in his sleep. I heard you again last night, cousin. Did you collide with the sideboard?"

Shelley touched his thigh, wincing. "There must be some better way to dispose the furniture in that chamber."

Keats looked more closely into the thin face, the tired blue eyes. What had happened to Shelley these last years? A rush of sympathy took him; then he remembered himself and wondered if this would complicate his getting out of Pisa. It wasn't a matter of abandoning someone in need. Shelley couldn't possibly need him. But he couldn't resent the man while he suffered.

He looked to the open back door. "And Mrs. Shelley?"

"Nothing at all," Shelley said.

Vaccà bent to take up his bag. "Then the somnambulism continues. And the nervous attacks?"

"No, no. I shouldn't say so."

"Hm," said the doctor. "Shall we go into the back?"

"Er—Mrs. Shelley is in back, and the child. Perhaps the parlor is well enough? Our guests are cosmopolitan."

"I was on my way out anyhow," said Medwin. "I ride today. Get well soon, cousin; I want you beside me in the saddle." He shook Vaccà's hand, made a cavalry salute and departed.

"I'll leave you as well," said Keats. "My papers are upstairs."

"But do stay!" said Shelley, unclasping his waistcoat. "I have no secrets from a man who has read my poems. He has seen me entire." He threw the waistcoat over the settee and began to unbutton his shirt. "I wanted you and the professor to meet. He is a great man of science and letters, you know. A great friend to us."

There was nothing to do but stand at the bookcase while Shelley shrugged the shirt from his thin shoulders. Despite his graying hair his torso was still a young man's. He was Keats's senior by how many, three years? Not yet thirty. The ridge of his breastbone was clear, and his abdomen caved sharply under the ribs. The doctor took out the auscultation tube and held it to the mottled pink-and-white breast, making the medical man's face that Keats knew very well, that look of controlled compassion. He was seeking suffering and would interrogate what he found.

"Breathe in," said the doctor. "Out."

Shelley complied, still making friendly eyes at Keats, as if they were going to have a salon. Keats stuck his hands in his pockets and looked into Apollo's unfeeling face. He was getting into the thick of other peoples' lives, attending at their scenes.

"A curious phenomenon," he said, "somnambulism. I never experienced it myself."

A pause. No reply.

"Bell had a theory," he went on, "which might have interested you."

"Turn your back, please," said Vaccà, and as Shelley spun round, "It isn't Charles Bell?"

"It is," said Keats.

"At Great Windmill Street?"

"The same. You know the surgeons of London?"

"Why, I studied anatomy in London," said Vaccà, "many years ago. I was in attendance when Doctor Bell separated out the facial nerves." He looked Keats over with new attention; suddenly each had a place in the other's world.

"I was registered at Guy's for a time," said Keats. "I went to Doctor Bell's lectures."

"But are you then a medical man, Mister—? Forgive me."

"John Keats, apothecary. I did not study for surgery long."

"Absurd," cried Shelley over his shoulder, "an apothecary! Why, he is a poet."

"Really," said Vaccà.

"A poet," said Shelley, "and amongst the few such spirits in whom England may take pride."

The sculpture of Vaccà's face broke open in a first smile. "Well! A poet praised by Shelley is a rare thing. Otherwise I should have complained of the world losing a surgeon."

"The world did not lose a good one."

"Yet he remembers Bell on somnambulism," said the doctor musingly, "which I can't claim to know."

"It is a late theory," Keats said, "perhaps later than your studies. You must know Bell's prime contention, that the nerves of sensation form an organ separate from the nerves of motion? Well," he said, moved to go on, "it is natural to find certain cases, somnambulism among them"—he stretched out his hand, palm down and fingers open, as if groping in the dark—"where the separation is so perfect that the mind might be said to inhabit two worlds at once. The sensorium entertains the loftiest visions, whilst the musculature is driven through the earthly night."

"Ah!" said Shelley, "an allegory. The poet's condition."

"So I thought," said Keats, with a diffident smile. Shelley moved to stand and Vaccà placed a hand on his shoulder.

"Hold, signor; I have not done with you."

He began his palpations, efficiently pressing strong brown fingers against the pale body. There was movement in the far doorway, and Percy Florence tottered out in his frock, holding fat palms before him. Mary came after. A shawl was half pulled over her chemise, her hair fell loose and her mouth hung slack, without expression. Her eyes traveled back and forth very slowly, as if answering distant clockwork. Keats half smiled at her, but a chill took his back. Those were the Gorgon's eyes; they would petrify him.

Shelley called her name. His strained voice might have been a reproach or reminder. She did not answer.

Percy Florence crossed the rug, stopped at Keats's boot and grasped the buckle in his stubby fingers. He looked up, hanging open his wet mouth and making small noises. Keats knelt, put his hands around the child's middle and lifted him to his chest.

Mary's eyes stopped roving and fixed on him. With care he held the warm, sour-smelling body out to her, and after a moment she reached and settled him in her arms.

"Excuse me," he said. "We have crowded your quarters."

She looked to Shelley. In a low, malicious tone she asked, "What carnival have we today?"

Vaccà dropped his hands. They were a sculpture group: doctor and half-nude patient on the sofa, Keats and Mary to the side. No one spoke. From the quality of the silence, Keats felt that this scene must have happened before now. They were caught out of time. He must go.

"I am returning to Rome," he said.

The charm broke. Shelley looked up in wonder.

"Rome!" he said. "Have you not just arrived from there?"

"Pardon me if I speak plainly," said Keats. "I do it as I esteem you." He must steady his voice; dignity was at stake. "My health made me a dependent for a time. I have outworn that excuse. I kept to it only because I was sworn not to leave Italy, and because—if you'll forgive me—I thought you would find me a light burden. I see now that cannot be the case."

"But I don't understand at all," said Shelley. "Do you mean the bedroom? There are rooms to be had in Pisa; we'll find you one."

"And how shall I pay for it?"

"Why—" Shelley began a shrug, then caught sight of Mary's face. She returned his look without communication; then said, in the same malicious tone, "Keep him if you will. Make an endeavor of him. Have Claire back, and Jane and all; since I am not enough for you, nor is your last child."

She turned away, wrapping Percy Florence in her shawl, and walked to her chamber.

Shelley stared after her. His hands quivered in his lap, gripping each other. "I am sorry," he murmured, as if accusing himself. "Very sorry."

"Shelley?" Keats asked.

"Please!" he said, lifting his eyes, "don't heed her. Don't let her drive you away."

"I don't understand."

He threw back his head. "These years of travel have been so melancholy, Keats. We have lost children. She has letters from her father over money. An exile's life does not suit her. There are so few English in Pisa, we can't help befriending them. If they are women—"

The stream of his voice stopped up. He looked around, discovered his shirt next to him and pulled it on crookedly. He seemed a child in a man's garment, strangely touched with silver hairs.

"She is very jealous," he said.

Vaccà shifted from his kneeling position and placed a hand over Shelley's. The gesture was fatherly; his face was compassionate, perhaps reproachful. It tightened the knot around Keats's heart. He looked to the door where Mary had gone; it was open but seemed shut.

"Listen to me, Keats," said Shelley. "You don't wish charity, and that is well. Heaven knows I wouldn't insult you. But there are *recourses*, don't you know."

"I don't see what they are," Keats said quietly.

"Why, anything at all." Shelley raised a hand. "Lord Byron and I have talked of starting a periodical—yes, with Hunt, and others in your circle. Why should you not write for us?"

"As a hired pen, you mean? On your pay-roll, or on Byron's?"

"Well," said Shelley, and spread his hands with theatrical mildness, as if answering some attack on his character.

Keats shook his head in sorrow. "I don't doubt it would be a gift to the age. I can't work for you."

The light of hope left Shelley's face. He reached for his waistcoat and began to pull it on. Keats stuffed his hands in his pockets and several times cleared his throat to speak; each time his

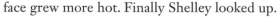

face grew more hot. Finally Shelley looked up.

"What is it?" he asked dully.

"I am very sorry. I must ask the loan of a few crowns. No more than will pay my fare from here."

"Oh." Shelley looked around the room, and asked in the same dull voice, "Where is Caterina gone?"

Keats pressed his lips together and shut his eyes. In two minutes he had brought them to the height of misery—how, when this was the last thing he had wanted in the world? He was unfit for the society of man. He belonged at the bottom of the river.

Vaccà stirred, coughed into his fist, and asked in his college baritone, "If I may?"

Keats nodded, despairing of speech.

"You say that you had registered at Guy's?"

"That is so."

"Then you attended lectures? And practical instruction?"

"I was there twelve months. I had a dressership."

"Indeed!" said Vaccà. "Then I don't suppose you'd wish another? We have not precisely the same system, but I perform regular surgeries at the University. I would have use for an experienced hand in the theatre."

The two Englishmen looked up as one. Was the doctor serious? In his dark coat and silver hair, with the bag at his side, he didn't look like a man given to idle offers.

"Why, Professor," said Keats, "that is very fine. But is it not irregular? Do your own students not make up the dressers?"

"There is always something for a student to do. Most are officially enrolled in theology, you know, and assist at services. In any case, for a friend of Signor Shelley's—" He opened his hands. "Non fa nulla."

There had been a night at Guy's when, the presiding surgeon being absent, Keats had had to open a man's temporal artery. The vessel was secretive, nestled under dermis and muscle; once the thing was begun it had to be immediately carried through, and

Keats watched an impersonal spirit take charge of his hand to guide the lancet, separating out the gory fibers until the pulsing artery wall showed through, was pressed with the thumb, bulged and slit open. Afterward Keats couldn't understand how he had done it. Somehow the will hadn't been his, and he couldn't imagine a career spent always in need of that outer force, requiring it to show up on every occasion.

"There is the question of lodging," he said.

"You may stay in my home," said Vaccà. "Please do so."

"But you shouldn't have to work as a dresser," said Shelley. "That's absurd. You should be free for literature, in the interest of mankind. Why not a subscription?"

"I thank you," Keats said. "I have been oversubscribed."

Try to imagine it. Vaccà as his host, Vaccà as his employer. The man was sober; he had almost an English manner, something like the surgeons at Guy's. Things would be done with reserve. But to go back to operating? After opening the artery Keats had gone to his guardian and announced he was giving up surgery for poetry. His guardian had declared he must be mad. Keats had said—what had he said?—that he was aware of having more gifts than most men, and that he was determined to make use of them. Something like that: something a young man would say.

"Professor," he said carefully, "your offer puts me in great debt. You may wish to revoke it upon seeing my work. I have not practiced in a couple of years."

"The hand remembers," said Vaccà. "The practice is engraved in the nerves."

Shelley brought his hands together. "Then let it be so! I am a thousand times grateful, Professor—should Keats accept, of course. I own I had never imagined him working his way here."

"Why, it is work," Keats said, stung. "It will do me good."

"Then you will stay?" he asked, and before Keats had assented, Shelley leaped up and began shaking his hand with verve, as if he had won a prize. A sober clasp from Vaccà was next. Was it so easy? It could not be; he ought to step back and start over. His gaze darted over the room, past the marble gods, the beautiful blue curtain, the forbidding door through which Mary had gone. Shelley's bright, tired eyes hung just before his own.

"We must make arrangements," said the doctor.

"My papers," said Keats, looking at the ceiling. "My trunk."

"They shall follow you," said Shelley. "Lift not a finger. You are under our care."

The doctor took up his stick and gloves and raised a dark brow at Keats. It was the turn of a wheel. He passed through the door after the doctor's wool coat and made circuits down the stairwell until they came into the early spring. The river's surface threw up white sparks; swallows circled in outline, carriages went back and forth on the far bank. How large the world! He stretched his hand to the sunlit brick wall and felt heat at his fingers. The doctor's black coat and shadow waited on the street, but he lingered on tiptoe in his boots, to touch the warm thing a moment more.

SECOND PART

To Mr John Keats, chez M le
Professeur Andrea Vaccà, Pisa

MY JOHN,

Buongiorno & Buona sera—e mille Buongiorni & so many
Buone sere more! You see I have got on. Ask me not how.
Only promise you shall marvel enough when I step on to
the Italian shore singing like a bird in my new language,
& it shall content me. I have half a dozen lines of Byron
to set down but I refrain as you disapprove of him—I <u>have</u>
been reading the Spenser you left me, but I will not quote
it. It is rich as Treacle & as slow. You will write poems of
Italy better than them all. O to be near you in that sun!
Wentworth Place misses you but you should not miss its
Weather—gray skies & rain pelunking on the Panes with
no change this fortnight. Mother & the family are very
well. I see less of Mr Brown now he is a family man next
door. We all of us wish we had more news of you when the
news is so singular—why were you so sudden in leaving
Rome? I do not say you had no reason but your Letter does
not say, and do not think I was sorry at your Letter for I
could read such a Letter every day and call myself Empress,
but you set us Puzzles. I have been in a cloud above a week,
dropping stitches & pricking my Fingers. It is some light
Fever in the spirit. Were it an easier thing for a Girl alone
to set sail, I would do such a thing as would set Hampstead
talking a twelvemonth. When I shut my eyes I see Curiosi-
ties—you know Italy for me is engraved pictures in Travel-

books, now I fancy my John engraved there with the rest. He has his Falcon-look to gaze over Columns & Colosseums, & his hand is out as if he would speak. Now tell me whom does he speak to? How do you live in Pisa? I have only a Letter from Severn that Brown showed me & that he did not show my Mother for that it was so full of fire & tears at your going as he thought to live with Mr Shelley, whom he calls degenerate—anyhow the family now thinks you a kind of Physician at the University there. Sam made a caper of it saying they would put you in a Frock-coat & shave your hair like a Friar & hang a cross of gold from your Neck. I would have you even so, if well & whole. Sam knows I will not pronounce on his tales of Romanism till I see the Country myself. Tell me what do the women wear in Italy? The new traveling-dresses from France are lower in the waist, with bunching at the sleeves & a great stuff of embroidery to three or four inches round the skirt hem—is it so in Italy, or do they keep to the high waisted style? You will oblige me with a prompt report for should it not please you John to see me debark from my Ship in the Italian mode, as a very Lady of the South—you must write often & write more—my sun is gone from England. Say you do not forget me. I will not write the thing I fear, I would not read it over again. Un (may I say) baccio from

YOUR FANNY.

In the Theater

IT WAS SAID ACROSS ENGLAND and in every city of the Continent, scattering one sentiment over half a dozen languages: no one likes a medical student. He has every vice of the young. He is arrogant, he is callous and impatient. At twenty-two he has comprehended the world. He is an opportunist, knowing the day will come when you give your body over to him.

His studies make a mockery of his religion. In the dissecting room he learns that God's image, the paragon of animals, is a faulty engine and may be pulled apart to its last cog. Just so his moral being is unstrung fiber by fiber. Soon he thinks it a rare joke to slap his fellow student with a detached arm, or to slip a cold kidney down an unwitting collar.

He drinks strong punch. He takes snuff and plays at faro. He goes about in a top hat and scorns to knot his neck-cloth. He promises the town girls that his science will protect them from dishonor. At night he shouts blasphemies in the alleys.

No one likes a medical student. Yet what is to be done with so many second and third and fourth sons? Even in Italy, the Church can't take them all; nor is there any use for lawyers in the age of Metternich, when across the realms of Europe—even in mild, enlightened Tuscany—the law is the monarch's word and no more.

Santa Chiara's bells rang for weekday Mass, and as a few pious citizens made their way to the cathedral doors, the larger crowd gathered at the hospital across the way. They wore narrow-cut coats with trousers and Goliard berets, bright red for the faculty of medicine; a few had on white-collared cassocks and laughed and whispered with the rest. Under the clamor of bells a rumor went back and forth: una operazione per il Professore Vaccà! Il Professore Vaccà sta per operare! The cluster of caps quivered and, one by one, the bright red spots were pulled within the dark hospital doors.

Of course a procedure by anyone was a thrill. For two or three minutes a human body would be brought to the peak of suffering, and life and death toss dice for the soul. But when it was Vaccà holding the knife—Vaccà who had studied in England and France, who declared in his lectures that Italy must become a modern nation, whom everyone knew to be under police surveillance for the foreign journals he read and the things he said at dinners—well, then a second drama was laid over the first, in which every student hoped to make his own part. Italy must catch up to the world in science. Pisa had possessed no modern medical school till Napoleon brought it. The operating theatre, with its descending circles of spectator rails—where the students now gathered standing, humming street songs, tossing wads of paper and shouting when a hat blocked the view—was a modern innovation, on the principle that observation was all. A slanted ceiling pane dropped a sheet of winter light on the bare table, a mere arm's span from the lowest railing. Every fold of muscle, every nerve and tendon would be seen. Perhaps other things too, depending on the procedure. Vaccà had delved in exotic techniques abroad. Today's operation, it was said, had required a foreign doctor, an actual Englishman from London, to be imported as an assistant.

The news ran up the circles and roused protest. Unpatriotic of Vaccà! If Italy was backward, the fault lay with its governments, not its people; certainly not with its young men, who would stand against any Englishman in matters of cutting and tying and stanching. Why, if Vaccà needed an assistant—cried one student in a cassock—what about we who have no positions, who declared for the theology faculty just to get room and board? Filthy Church robes—here he was drowned out by hisses and cheers, and some paper was thrown at him. Enough agitating; hadn't anyone seen the Englishman? Wasn't he very old? No, he was a child of genius, aged seventeen years. Nonsense! He was an army surgeon from the wars. He and Vaccà had met on the battlefield, in opposite ranks, and had joined hands to save the wounded. Then was it an amputation today? No, it was the English lithotomy; they would cut through the perineum to get at the bladder stone. The students smiled and grimaced, and cradled their hands between their legs.

Behind the operating table a double door spread its jaws. The chamber beyond was dark as smoke; one seemed to discover faint motions in the shadows, but no solid form till all at once a spectral limb appeared. A body stepped into the light, a pudgy senior student nobody liked much. He lifted his arms for silence and announced:

"The case is a tuberculous mass in the knee joint. Professor Vaccà will attempt excision."

Excision! Whispers rose. Amputation was one thing; many of the students had seen that already, some had seen it go badly. But to think of cutting the delicate joint itself, pulling out the fine structures—it brought shivers and a dark sweetness. The students felt tender for their own bodies. Each imagined the gentle run of blood in his limbs. The senior student stayed in the light till the whispers ebbed, then stepped back and joined a second apparition from the double door, this one taller and wrapped in a dark coat. That was Vaccà. He shrugged off the coat, came into the full light and rested his hands on the table, head bent as if about to give a soliloquy. But it was known that he never addressed the spectators and preferred to treat his operations as solitary struggles, as a mystic might struggle with God. He stared at his shadow as if looking the enemy Death in the face.

A third man came through the door, his arms loaded with canvas aprons and the dresser's box. Was that the Englishman? The students shifted and craned their necks. His face was pale under the window, as one would expect, and his light ginger hair, falling in loose waves, looked too as they had expected. But he was very young; at least his stature made him seem so. He hardly came to Vaccà's shoulder. He set the box on the side-table and held up the apron for the doctor to assume. This was an old Pisan garment matted with honorable stains, the pus and blood of many years. Tied into it, Vaccà took on the air of an artisan. He stood in meditation while the Englishman tied on his own apron, opened the box and set out knives of different sizes, the bone-saw, measures of hemp thread, screw tourniquet, forceps, eyed probes. The doors creaked wider and two boys came through, lugging a pail of steaming water between them. They set it under the table, left and came back with rags and sponges.

Another stepped though the door, a second student in his red beret. He held a bottle of brandy in one hand, and with the other guided a barefoot man who came haltingly in a white nightshirt. The skirt was cut away to expose one leg, shaved from the thigh down. It looked fresh and pink, like a boy's. Where was the affliction? At first no one saw, but when he was brought into the full light, the protuberance showed on the outer part of the knee. It bulged purple with stagnant blood, like a malformed second kneecap. Sighs came from the benches, then coughs and laughter as the students forced back their discomfort. "Hats below!" someone cried. The man looked around, wide-eyed, and his glance lighted on the side-table with its bright instruments and leather straps.

"Cristo!" he shouted, grabbing the student's arm, and made the sign of the Cross.

His voice had a country accent and the students quieted. They hadn't thought of him as coming from anywhere. Without clothes and shoes he had no history, he was nothing but his putrescent joint. But the voice came from a farm, and the students now saw his ruddy face, the thick gray hair falling in rustic fashion over his brow. Vaccà touched his shoulder and began to murmur in his ear. The man stared into the light, and as Vaccà drew back he made a beseeching look and took him by the arm, nodding. Vaccà spoke a few words to the assistants and the patient was helped onto the table. He took a large gulp of brandy, wrinkling his face, and lay back. The English dresser brought the tourniquet. The patient lay still as it circled his thigh, but when they moved to strap his ankles he sat up sharply, pulling back his feet. Again Vaccà had to murmur in his ear, while the man stared at his knee with a betrayed expression. Finally he surrendered his ankles and sat quietly, like a horse being bridled, until he was made to lie back so that his arms could be strapped as well.

The students understood that betrayed look. A laboring man, of the kind who ends up in the operating theatre, begins his life with four limbs like four children. He tends them and they give him service. Even if one slackens and gives way, he can make out well enough with three—so he imagines. But in fact his bad child, the swelling knee that hobbles him month by month, that oozes putrid matter and agonizes him at midnight with demands for impossible movements, has not simply abandoned him; it has gone over to his foes and become their captain. His tenderest defenses, the nerves and flesh, are breached from the start. The betraying child knows everything about him. It will take his work; more than that, it will take away the dozen small pleasures that made him a man, the dance steps at Carnival time, the old patched breeches that now torment him with chafing. Each day brings some new betrayal. But the father won't yet disown his child, he can't believe he is cursed for good, he has heartbreaking dreams of touching the knee and finding it as it was, joyful and obedient, full of healthy blood. Even at the last moment, strapped on the operating table, he can't quite despair of it. The tourniquet is slipped over his thigh and the brass key screwed tight. In the surgeon's eyes the separation is now made: above the tourniquet is the man, below is the problem. But the man knows better. The leg may be out of his power, it might be in China for all he can do. But he will know everything that is done to it.

The Englishman finished screwing the tourniquet and settled the bare leg in its straps. The limb was already turning livid from lack of new blood, faintly taking the same hue as the tuberculous mass that now seemed to crouch maliciously on the joint, a cornered spider. The students dipped their rags and sponges into the hot water and the Englishman took up the thread and forceps. Vaccà chose a slender ivory-handled knife and pressed the flat of the blade against his own neck; that was an artist's touch, to warm the steel. He bent forward, flourished the knife like an epée and in quick succession made three shallow cuts in the skin, describing a triangle around the joint.

The patient cried out. Some screeched, some bellowed like bulls; this was a low groan, choked before it rose too high. The audience saw the contortion in his mouth and jaw, the stiffness in his arms as he fought not to writhe in his straps. They shifted, stared over one another's heads, fought the sink in their stomachs as the Englishman's forceps peeled back flaps of skin. Without looking up Vaccà reached for the side-table, found a second knife by touch and neatly sliced through the yellow fat, then the ruddy muscular fibers. The knife left thin scorings in the flesh, hardly visible till the Englishman pulled at the cut tissue; then dark bursts of venous blood sprouted up and the students sponged them clean. There was no hemorrhage. The tourniquet was doing its work, holding back the mortal jet.

The patient gasped and rolled his eyes. They had been at work perhaps half a minute and already the thigh bone showed yellow-white under streaks of gore. Everyone recognized the knobbed joint from anatomical drawings and cadavers, but when Vaccà placed his fingers on the purple mass itself and pulled back a gobbet of flesh, an enormous abscess was revealed in the bone below. It was a foul brown color, darkening the surrounding tissue with rot. Vaccà pressed his knife-point into the brown matter and it gave way; the patient kicked in his straps and shrieked the name of God. The Englishman placed his hand on the man's neck and moved his lips. The patient stared at him with great white eyes. The audience shifted and grimaced; they wanted to believe in some kind of magic on the floor, in the Englishman's power to charm away pain. Under the window his white hand seemed cool, able to calm fevers, and his merciful whispers surprised them; for everyone knew that the English were heartless in their dignity, with no natural feeling.

Vaccà spoke a curt word and the Englishman let go the patient's neck and took up his forceps. The popliteal artery was half exposed in its nest of fascia. Vaccà cut back the gray fibers, pulled the yellowish arterial wall loose from the bone and sliced it in two. Bright blood welled out. The students wiped their sponges over the wound. The Englishman handed off the forceps to the senior student, who clamped it tight over the loose vessel; then he slipped a length of thread through an eyed probe, and in an instant had it looped under the artery and pulled tight. Vaccà had taken up the long saw and drew it over the bone to make the first scoring. Everything was moving quickly now, in the fusion that joined the surgeon's hands to those of his assistants as if governed under a single thought. Vaccà moved the saw with blunt carpenter's strokes, above the abscess and then below; under the two-note song of grinding bone the patient's face made a rictus, entering a suffering past motion. The assistants sponged blood, pulled back loose tissue, tied the smaller vessels as they were exposed. Once a gout of blood spattered Vaccà's apron; he spoke a sharp word and the junior student cranked the tourniquet a farther turn.

The worst was done. The abscessed extremity of the femur was pulled out and set like a barbarian trophy on the side-table. Now the sheared tissue and bone must be splinted together, the skin sewn up and the larger nerves cut back, lest they get caught in the wound and cause permanent pain. There was nothing more to discover. The months of convalescence were beginning, that no surgeon would ever see. The onlookers wandered in their thoughts, and some began to whisper about their examinations and girls in shops. There was a spark of interest when Vaccà cut a whitish nerve end and the patient twitched violently, but that was the last pale curiosity. There would be no hemorrhage, no spectacular mishap with the saw. The theater door swung open and shut, throwing bursts of blue light from the street, and before the sewing had started half the railings were empty. By the time it was finished and the serving boys had come to clear out the bloody rags and bucket of stained water, there was no audience left but the performers themselves, untying their aprons and rolling down their sleeves. The railings looked cold, as if nobody had stood there in years. Though midmorning light shone through the upper window, it seemed the end of a long day, time to reckon up one's doings and make peace. The patient had already dropped to sleep, as they always did, wrinkling his ruddy mouth as if to spit out the nightmare just given to his waking mind.

Doctor's Chamber

A HUMAN SKULL, PLASTER-WHITE, sat on the desk of Vaccà's study. Its lower jaw was missing and the upper row of teeth seemed to bite into the walnut veneer. The doctor's eyes would drift to it during pauses, and if the pause was long his hand would reach to stroke the hollow orbits. It was a theatrical gesture, but not false. Vaccà's knowledge of anatomy was real enough; so, it seemed, was his melancholy. His gaze on the skull was not a saint's or poet's but a natural philosopher's, who had reason to think that if only the arch from cheekbone to temple were less frail, the brain-pan differently formed, the apertures of the nerves more comfortably set, there might be an end to half the world's suffering.

Seated at the desk, with the brandy bottle from the operating theatre in his hand, he poured a thin measure into a glass.

"If the surgery goes well," he said, "I drink in thanks. If it goes ill, I drink in bitterness. In either case I share the patient's cup." He smiled at Keats, who stood before the desk. "Only a little, of course. Ne quid nimis. Do you wish any?"

Keats did wish it. He felt the gnaw in his throat. It was that strange feeling of lateness, tempting him to drink and end the day.

"I am not sure I deserve the patient's cup," he said. "I feel I should ask the patient."

"Hm." Vaccà tipped back the glass and swallowed. "You want to know if you did well?"

"I do, sir."

"You did well. You will face envy now." He set down the glass and his eyes drifted to the skull. "I have been twenty years at this university. When I started, surgeons were banned the use of the theatre. Only the philosophers were permitted to study anatomy.

To get cadavers at all was a struggle—and of course I had been abroad, I was thought too French." He tapped the skull's bony brow and raised his eyes. "Did you suffer today?"

"At the first cutting I did," said Keats. "And again, when the knife was pressed into the abscess."

"A young surgeon is aghast at what we do. So is an older surgeon. It is rare to find a man in his sixtieth year who still operates. I am forty-nine. We can bear it only in these middle years—perhaps two score of them. And we must enclose ourselves. Do you see what I mean?"

"I think so," said Keats. "I am ill enclosed."

The doctor sat back with the ease of someone who has sat half a lifetime in the same chair, with the same objects around him. On one wall was a windowed cabinet of medical instruments, not those used daily in the hospital but more precious assemblages of brass and mirrors, meant to be admired. Around it hung anatomical studies in red chalk, a man's portrait, a large gilt clock that was a gift from the Grand Duke. The window behind the doctor's chair showed a hint of street and river, with the same disorienting aspect as those old Italian paintings that placed their figures in the very near foreground and cast behind a far view of towns and hills in shadow.

"I was younger than you when I understood it must be done," the doctor said. "It was a conscious victory, to be won day by day: not to treat another's suffering as my own, and to treat my own suffering as another's. A spiritual operation on the heart, you might say, reversing the flow. I do not think it a natural thing." His heavy hand moved to his breast and hung there without pressing down. "You might do it, if you wished. Your friend Shelley could not. He suffers with everything, as he loves everything."

"Shelley is—" Keats cleared his throat. "I don't wish to say he is not my friend. I do not know him well."

"Shelley is mankind's friend." Vaccà smiled faintly. "I remember when I was like him. You see my bit of vanity." He nodded at the portrait, which in broad, romantic brushstrokes showed a young man with thick side-whiskers and a Roman brow and nose. A cockade of blue, white and red was pinned to his collar, and his face was so full of fire that Keats hesitated to identify him with the phlegmatic old doctor at the desk.

"I had heard that you studied in Paris," he said cautiously.

"I had a painter friend there." Vaccà gave the portrait an indulgent smile. "The man in that picture is all of seventeen years old. But he is bold enough to debate the French doctors in their own language. The vital principle as electrical fluid. A world without distinctions of birth. All choice by merit, the rights of man."

"You say those things as if you disbelieve in them."

"But I do believe. Even now they are all the creed I have. Aside from the vital fluid, which is a matter of dogma. We must observe. Always observe."

The doctor had been many people in his life; today he was a respectable Tuscan gentleman in dark clothes. When he was not treating the local nobles or the visiting English, he practiced the patrician arts of farming and horsemanship. He promised that Keats should see his villa at Montefoscoli, where he had vineyards and a stable of Arabian horses. But a decade before, he had gone with Napoleon's army on the Italian campaigns, performing battlefield amputations in tents; and before that he had gone to Charles Bell's scientific lectures in London; and here was this seventeen-year-old wearing the tricolor.

"The young man seems dressed for battle," Keats said.

"It was my painter friend who introduced me to the militia. All I did was to walk certain streets at certain hours—though there was the morning of the bells, of course. Do you know?"

"I have heard something," said Keats.

"All the bells of Paris rang that morning." With a wry face, Vaccà turned the skull so that it stared and bit the table in Keats's direction. "The militia was on the streets, handing out muskets by the dozen. There was no powder, you see. Everyone said powder was to be had at the Bastille—it was for that we went. I still remember the stock in my hand, so much heavier than a hunter's gun. I had never seen a shot wound in my life, except in birds and rabbits. We were thousands in the square. Three or four carts were on fire, the air full of smoke. Supposedly we had cannons, but I never saw them. Now and then a plank would be put over the moat, someone would run across with a message and the crowd would shout. One didn't know why. A man kept shouting, 'You whore, I'll break you up, you ugly whore.' I understood finally that he meant the fortress itself. He had a greengrocer's apron on. Everyone was dressed for work in the shops.

"In the afternoon the drawbridge came down and we shoved into the courtyard. Anything that resembled a box or a barrel we broke open. My empty musket was worse than useless, I was constantly bumping it on things. I thought that if I could only find powder, the gun would become an enchanted thing and protect me from harm. Yet I had no thought of firing it. I had decided, I think, only to fire into the air unless my life was in danger. But I found no powder, nor prisoners, nor an enemy. The guards were *invalides*, old men, and had been told not to fire on us. And the marquis, the garrison governor—"

Vaccà's voice had dropped in the telling. His eyes narrowed at the portrait, as if to make out a pattern in the brushstrokes; then he blinked and discovered Keats before him. "Pardon me. I must be telling a story you know."

"Not at all," said Keats. "I had a very menial education." He meant it lightly, but shame thickened his voice. "To me the flags of Europe are so many shop-signs."

"But you must know what became of the marquis?"

Had Brown told him? Or Hunt, or Frenchmen who used to visit the Brawnes? "Was it—the head was—?"

"You do know." Vaccà slid his hand under the skull and took it up in his spread fingers. "He had been killed already when I came back into the courtyard. What it meant to his killers I can't say. I was only a visitor, and they had passed their lifetimes under men like him. I saw them bent together, striking with swords and pikes at something on the paving, and between their legs I made out a wig and the back of a blue coat. I thought at first that they were striking an empty costume. Then they heaved it over and I saw the body inside. The body made up part of the costume, as it were. Everyone had joy in his face. Everyone laughed as if Christ had come.

"They had killed him for striking a man, and after the crowd broke from around the body, the one he had struck was brought forward. They talked nothing like the Frenchmen at the university, I scarcely understood them. But they gave him a sword. He was a fat man with a sheep's face, and after he took the sword one of his hands kept dropping to his stomach. The last living act of the marquis had been to kick him in the groin.

"He was a cook by trade, I think, but he was not a good butcher. The sword was dull and left gashes in the throat without making the decisive cut. Someone took it away and gave him a pen-knife. Someone else gave him a flask of brandy. They had put gunpowder in the brandy and were laughing about it. Everybody watched him drink as if they expected him to combust. It was as if we all were to blow up that night, leaving behind no France, and no earth. Then he knelt and began to work the pen-knife in the mess he had made."

Vaccà tilted the skull's underside toward Keats, showing the palate and brainpan, and chopped his hand beneath. "I had spent six months with cadavers and I saw what was his error. He didn't understand to introduce the blade between the vertebrae of the neck and disarticulate them. Instead he was trying to *saw* that tiny blade through the bone, turning his hands filthy, while the crowd boiled—" Vaccà grimaced and put the skull down. "The horrible thing was that it was done so badly. Had there only been more heroism. Had that cook been a cavalry officer, given to strike justice with his right arm." He made an ironic face and his eyes drifted back to the portrait.

"Had it been so," said Keats, "you would have rejoiced?"

"The universal joy might have taken me. I was young."

"And did they then—?"

"Once the head came off," said Vaccà, "they fixed it to a pike, just as you have heard. The bleeding head upon a pike." He sat back and his Roman face was mirrored in the cabinet of ancient blades.

"We must enclose ourselves," he said. "There is no end to pain."

"I have seen pain," Keats said shyly. "This morning was not the first time. But if everyone were enclosed—" He looked back at the portrait and found the eyes glaring their challenge from the frame.

"I have seen that face on Shelley," he said. "I believe it was yours as well. I am not sure it is mine."

"Oh?" asked Vaccà. "What face is yours, Mr. Keats?"

"I think it does not find itself in portraits." He turned from the picture. "You speak of pain, and I don't dispute you. But should we not also take some part of joy? You did well today, sir, and you flatter me that I did the same. A man came hobbling into the wards and he shall leave walking. Is that not miraculous? Ten years ago the leg would have come off at the thigh."

"He may leave walking," Vaccà replied. "Provided the wound is kept clean, and there is no shortening of the limb."

"If the legs prove uneven," said Keats, "he may walk a sloped hill, and pick flowers."

Vaccà leaned back smiling. "Very good. You are young, it is Carnival time. A ball is getting ready." He lifted his hand. "Go home, Mr. Keats. I shan't keep you all day in the wards."

Released into the stone hall, Keats met the busts of dead geniuses in a momentary terror, as if crossing a graveyard. But when he stopped and looked one full in the face, it was a genial old fellow with a bald pate and merry, deep-set eyes, who must have eased some jot of suffering in his time.

There must be an end to pain.

He straightened and stuck his hands in his pockets. Was that not his charm against the terrors of the flesh? For he had done well—Vaccà had said it.

He saluted the old fellow on his marble stand and walked on. He might be Doctor Keats. Doctor Keats, the surgeon.

He had done well!

A Borrowed Home

As far back as Keats could remember, all his ideas of careers, of cities to live in and the means of living there, had been born in ignorance. The less he knew, the more he loved. But again and again, he must reach into the mist of the future and grasp some solid form; and once grasped, it was future no longer. The page he had thought a perfect blank was already written over, front and back. He was in a fumy back room with fifty camphora pills to make up, or a shabby Westminster apartment with a pamphlet to review on the divine right of kings, and he knew a lifetime of any such task should scrape his heart dry.

How it was with women he didn't know. He'd gone to women now and then, like anyone. But in the real history of his heart there was only Fanny's name, and since fate—or some secret will of his own—had kept him from ever having her fully, the mist around her had never been dispelled.

He stepped onto the Lung'Arno, sucked in a breath of river and pulled back his shoulders like a bird stretching its wings. Carnival-goers had begun to gather at the café tables. Some wore domino masks, some full ghost-white faces with eyes and noses stretched to fantastic size. Their festival clothes glittered with colored sequins; they shouted at second-story windows and women in shifts leaned out to make mocking faces. Carriages went by with peacock feathers on the horses' halters and crape trimmings behind.

Keats had thought Pisa large, but really the streets of consequence were gathered in a tiny hub. The slanted tower seemed to follow him from across the water, looming sideways with a terrible intention of toppling; though Vaccà said it had leaned that way since the twelfth century, and must have already tipped during construction, since the upper levels could be seen making a vain effort to right themselves. Ahead was the brick-fronted inn dell'Ussero, with its awning advertising "Bevute e bigliardi" and café tables standing clear in the spring light. The space within darkened by degrees, becoming smoky and vague, until one reached the soft, smirched baize of the pocketless billiard tables at back, and the counter where the aproned proprietor moved back and forth to lay out cakes and ices, trailing fog from his cigar. The students came here in the afternoons to drink coffee and play the tables; they liked to crowd the penumbra, far enough forward that they could hail people on the sidewalk but far enough back that the person hailed could not see who was calling. Keats paused, peered inside, and a storm of applause met him.

"L'inglese!" came shouts from within. "The English miracle! The operator!"

A conclave of red caps emerged and surrounded him. In their dark robes they looked like a swarm of painted beetles. Most wore masks; were they real students, or impostors? A long-nosed Pulcinello, cap slung carelessly over a head of dark curls, caught Keats's shoulder and pulled off his own face. Underneath were the bright features of Leopoldo Vaccà—that was young Leopoldo, the doctor's son, sixteen years old and in his first year of studies.

"Kitsa!" he crowed, and pulled him into the thick of the crowd. "My friends, tomorrow's doctors. John Kitsa, di Londra—"

Tomorrow's doctors laughed. "We know him!" they said. "He operated this morning, you clod, with your noble father."

Keats spun around, bowing, and everyone told him in the same voice what matchless work he had done in the theatre. He had, in fact, met several of them before at the Ussero; they had told him the inn was named after a hussar slain in the Spanish war of succession, whose ghost walked the upper stories and possibly also the billiard tables, rattling his chains till Italy should be free.

"You undo me," he told the students. Was this envy? It didn't seem so.

"You operated today?" Leopoldo asked. "With my father? Dio caro, he tells me nothing."

"Why should he? Didn't you see it?"

Leopoldo swung on the student who'd spoken, but blushed bright pink under his wispy side-whiskers; for everyone knew he hadn't yet been to an operation. He had meant to do it months ago, he had told Keats, right at the start of his studies, but horrors kept taking him at the moment of entering the theatre doors.

"Shame, shame, shame," the students chanted, and closed around Leopoldo, joining arms. They traded a melody:

> *Won't see Father Vaccà*
> *Who invented the vaccinià*

"Not even true!" cried Leopoldo, and swung at his tormentor's cap. "You see, their blameworthy puns—"

> *Nobilissimo Vaccà*
> *With sculptures at his villà*
> *The bull fucks Europà*
> *Leopoldo fucks la vaccà*

And another returned:

> *Caro Leopoldo!*
> *Vaccinate that cow!*

making an awful gesture with his hips at which the circle broke into hoots. Leopoldo ducked free and collapsed against Keats.

"You shouldn't laugh!" he said.

"Your pardon," gasped Keats. "It's scarcely a month I've understood the puns in your language."

"You see," said a student. "He honors the Tuscan tongue!"

"That is no jest," said Keats. "It opens a door."

"A door? A sewer-gate," said another, who hadn't joined in the song.

"Oh, I am tired of you all," said Leopoldo. "I am leaving, and I am taking my Englishman with me. You mayn't torment me till the ball."

The students whistled farewells, and Leopoldo took Keats by the arm and led him onto the sidewalk. For a week he had followed Keats from one room of the palazzo to the next, had sat beside him at every meal, had to be asked to leave his chamber at night. He liked to show off his English, which was rapid though choked in accent, and he wanted to know things: were the cliffs of Dover really white, was London bright as day when the gas-lamps were lit, was it true that Protestant churches gave communion ale instead of wine, was Shakespeare or Dante the greatest poet, must Shakespeare be read only in English, was he or Milton more difficult, did even farmhands and cab drivers have the vote in England, was it true that English gentlemen read only Homer in school and boiled their food and never smiled? Keats answered as well as he could. It was a new duty. Till now he had always been the admiring boy in his own life.

A bend in the river, then its mirror, brought them up to the brick facade of the Vaccà palazzo, looking more sober than its neighbors, with no one hanging out the windows. In the parlor the family footman, white-haired and a head shorter than Keats, appeared from behind to grab the shoulders of his coat. He was an implacable old fellow who had dedicated his life to the principle that no outdoor coat should be worn inside, and Keats felt great admiration for him. Italian smells drifted from the hall: roasting meat, rising bread, tomatoes and peppers and garlic. Keats swallowed and Leopoldo reached into his pocket.

"Your pardon," he said. "I forgot you have a letter."

The paper was thick and browned, well worn in the fiber. It had come many leagues. The hand was Fanny's. He saw her fingers in the penstrokes, leading the quill in dance steps.

"Thank you," he said gruffly, and shoved it into his pocket.

"You won't read it now? I mean," said Leopoldo, with half-hid eagerness, "it looked like a woman's hand."

"A women does not like her hand stared at."

Leopoldo's confusion, the wound in his eyes, called up the face of his brother Tom. The dead before him! Keats shuddered and the image passed.

"I am sorry." He put his hands together, feeling awkward and very English. "Tell me, Leopoldo—haven't you courted? Have you a girl?"

"Ebbene—" The youth smiled; he seemed to want to say yes. "My mother is severe about it, you know. Father doesn't care."

"It is a difficult thing," said Keats. "I can't explain it. Every hour you have a new feeling. You crave, or you fear, or you are passionately indifferent. That is a thing you will not see in love poems: indifference as passion in itself. At least for an hour. We gather these in one word, as if they were a solitary thing."

Leopoldo made his curious face, lips slightly parted, as if taking in another fact about London. When he gestured to Keats's pocket, it was with reverence.

"And that is your girl?" he asked. "In England?"

"We are—promessi sposi, you say? Our English word is *betrothed*. Not in the world's eyes, but in hers and mine." He didn't quite know what he wanted to say, and getting at it was like pushing a boulder from its home in the earth.

"It is that word confounds me," he said. "A word old as Chaucer, meaning a promise, and money pledged between families—what am I to do with it? I am a world from home, Leopoldo. I came here thinking I should die." He half drew out the letter, then stuffed it deeper, out of sight. "What does it mean?"

Leopoldo looked alarmed. Perhaps he thought he was supposed to answer. He must know the core of love, Keats thought. At least he would know the desire that comes on young men like an angry god, driving them not outward but cruelly inward, toward their central aches. Perhaps he thought that was what Keats meant. He wouldn't know that at the end of youth the god slows and hardens, and starts to armor himself with connections, and promises, and money—always the hope of money. At sixteen you promise your life to another without thinking, as you would give it up in battle without thinking. What is anyone's life at sixteen?

They walked down a corridor molded in oak, with painted lions about to leap from the lintels, and came to a dining room spread with the wreck of a meal: empty dishes, bones floating in gravy, crumpled napkins, voided wineglasses and a servant's back carrying the last of something through the kitchen door. Sophie Vaccà sat at the head in a house gown, looking regal and fleshless, as if she had commanded the destruction of the meal without taking a morsel herself. Standing beside her was an Italian girl with dark curls and a black domino over her eyes.

"Ruin!" cried Leopoldo. "Mamma, Kitsa is hungry. Why didn't you wait?"

"Many things I know," said Signora Vaccà, "but not when Signor Keats will come and go. Giuditta, have them make up a plate."

"Cold mutton!" said the girl. "And water-weeds in your tea."

She was sixteen years old, born in the same hour as Leopoldo. The mask made her seem far off, like a character in opera, but she had her brother's ruddy cheeks and the same slight build in the shoulders. When they stood together they were like young cats or foxes. She threw Keats a sort of invented salute and went back into the kitchen.

"Now she chooses your punishment," said Signora Vaccà.

"I would appeal it!" said Keats. "Your husband kept me in conference."

"He gave a private lecture, you mean to say?"

She made an arch, French smile: a tiny victory for Keats, since he was afraid of the silver-haired lady of the house. He hadn't charmed her and didn't know what she thought of his charming her children. Leopoldo, who had never imagined that his mother might be frightening, threw his arm over her shoulders and asked if she wasn't ashamed to be such a hostess; dear God, look at poor thin Keats, who had come all the way from England only to be entertained by a Frenchwoman.

"Don't be blasphemous," said his mother.

"Sayest thou! Madame anti-cléricale!"

"No punishment," said Giuditta, coming back with a plate. "Only a test." She set bread and sliced fowl before Keats, with roast chestnuts on top, and a tumbler of white wine. "You were in conference with my father? I shall tell you what he did and take a chestnut for each right guess. First he showed you the skull on his desk."

"You are cheating," said Keats, with a smile. "But it is so."

"I am wise. Next he showed you his French portrait. And then he told you about the Bastille." There were three chestnuts in her mouth and through them she said vaguely, "You keep the one, signor."

"She knows nothing," said Leopoldo. "Women aren't allowed in the college."

"No more than young monkeys," she mumbled, "with bad beards on their cheeks!" Her eyes flashed against the domino and she swallowed.

Signora Vaccà rapped the table. "Very good, both of you. The carnival evening is not begun." At once they stepped back and drew together, embarrassed at behaving like children.

"You cause them to perform," she told Keats. "One would think they'd never met with a foreigner."

"I very much hope I am the worst they ever shall meet," he said. "I thank you humbly for this bread I have not earned. Perhaps I had best take it in my room, before the long evening?"

"Be released, signor Keats."

He had a large upstairs chamber given over to extra furniture:

there were two beds, two writing tables, two armchairs and water jars. It was comfortable, drowning in cushions, but the doubled things gave him the feeling of an invisible companion. Once he was alone with his meal, the lamp lit and a cheerful hearth driving out the spirit of March, he took the sealed letter from his pocket. It was gunpowder; it would summon Fanny, and she was a jinn who couldn't be commanded once she was called up.

He set it on the desk and turned it so that his own name faced him. His cheeks warmed. It was all very well to think of her as a far-off anchor, guiding him true, as in Donne's poem. But if she mentioned seeing Brown next door, or going to the Hampstead dances where one met Frenchmen, he would have no sleep for a week.

Coward! He cursed himself, slit the letter, unfolded and read. Then he read a second time.

No. There was nothing to offend. It was herself, in her familiar hand. She sent sketches of home and she missed him sorely. He knew it because she told him so, and because her every other line was a question, asking after his ideas and impressions so far away. Her image came up in fragments; her eyes flashed and her fingers leaped in slim gestures, all steeped in an animal comfort that he chose to call love, lacking another word.

What distressed him? Why was his mind a boiling kettle, a cup slipping from its saucer?

"She is a dear girl," he said aloud; "a dear, sweet girl."

He circled the thorn in his heart without lighting on it. It would take far worse tortures to make him admit, or even form the thought, that the image he now saw in fragments would, months ago, have come up living and whole. He did not think of his love as changeable. The pledges he'd made! The joys and sorrows he'd known!

They are watery things, joys and sorrows. Once they are given names and stood up as the pillars of one's existence, they vanish from sight. They will give no hint of transforming underfoot into rock, losing their liquid spirits drop by drop until nothing remains but their skeletons—that is, nothing but the pledges that came with them. Keats would have denied in shock that such a change was possible. He would have answered with his fist anyone who whispered that he might recoil from a love letter because its gestures and caresses seemed all to take place on the other side of a stone wall, and touched him only through the hand of duty.

Masques

Night leaped from the Arno, unfolded in the sky like a priest's cassock and dropped to blot everything at once. The buildings, the bridges, the hills and slanted tower all winked out, and formlessness took the world. Shadows reared and melted against the streets and river. A stray lamp in a window, a candle in a wanderer's hand floated free of all ground and lit up fragments of grotesques, long-nosed masks and hoods pulled over faces. "Be killed!" they cried, and sprang on one another, trying to blow out the candles. The murderous calls echoed before and behind, and blind objects whipped through the air.

It was the depth of historical night. Remember the Middle Ages; imagine the old barbarities come up from centuries of burial. The sun of enlightenment had set on Italy before it ever had the chance to dawn.

Across the blind river and down a blind street, walls splayed suddenly outward to a piazza ruddy with torchlight. Burning brands lined the yellow face of the opera house, rising like an ocean rock against the null sky. Lanterns with colored screens decked the doorway. A row of carriages was created from the murk; each sent forth its passengers and was unmade; and all passed through the open portal into light and sound, a spitting of trumpets and sawing of viols, a wooden dancing floor under five, six, seven stacked circles of private boxes, each filled with characters in costume, escaped tonight from the stage and given the freedom of the house. The women hid their eyes in sequined dominos, pointed or dressed with feathers to give them the look of cats or long-legged birds. A gentleman had cut asses' ears from felt and tied them over his head. Pulcinella was everywhere, and sad Pierrot, smirking Harlequin. A few of the dancers in ball gowns had mustaches and hairy arms, and some of those in coats and cravats were smooth-faced, with long hair spilling down their backs. The mock men and women moved freely among the true ones, took partners by the elbows and spun them around in country figures. The guests at the doors puffed thin cigars and tossed back tiny glasses of lemon liqueur.

Foreigners were here, of course, to see the spectacle. An English or French eye found it a barbarous show—the superstition of the Catholic South! Its pagan gaudiness! But the blazing chandeliers cast light on the soul. In every corner the talk was of revolt and liberty. *Napoli*! was the whisper; hadn't the Neapolitans met the Austrian forces yet? Wasn't there movement in the mountains? Were they evacuating Rome? The campagna was ancient Italian terrain, the Austrians didn't know it. It would take just one victory in open country, just one puppet king sent packing... but of course just as many took the Austrians' side, especially when a police informer came near. Everyone knew who the informers were, without it causing hard feelings. One simply curbed one's tongue on meeting them and exchanged bows as with anybody. The city governor and his wife sat in their official box on the second terrace, waving blessings upon all below.

The music hit a flourish and stopped, and a man in a red frock coat jogged to the front of the stage. He called out his own introduction, with a hopeful look of getting the crowd's ear; he was an improviser, but not one of the famous ones, and nobody paused to look at him, even when he began to read their suggested themes off scraps of paper. The opinions of Lorenzo de' Medici on the Tuscany of today. A Christian girl raised by Turks. A husband cuckolded by an entire literary academy. The liberty of Naples— here someone shouted and clapped, and suddenly the whole crowd roared to life. The improviser beamed, as if he'd already delivered his masterpiece. But a rhythmic thump sounded under the cries; the Grand Duke's soldiers were striking their musket stocks against the floor. The voices fell. They were one more costume party, these soldiers, in their blue jackets and white cross-braces, and tonight one might miss them entirely, except that their guns struck as solid things. The man in the red coat gave a long look at something offstage and announced that he would improvise on the Christian raised by Turks.

"We deserve no better," said a man in a fourth-terrace box, in French, and turned his back to the stage.

The Grand Duke would want this box under watch. It was packed close with pale Englishmen and other doubtful exiles, and the man who had made the remark was Professor Andrea Vaccà, liberal and presumed freethinker, whose wife was French. He wore no costume, but everything had the look of a costume that sat on his shoulders. The same frock coat that wrapped him in melancholy at the medical school now gave him the look of an entertainer—a stately entertainer, to be sure, say the conductor of an orchestra. His eyes gleamed. Signora Vaccà wore gloves and a domino, and a peacock-tail headdress that waved as her head turned. The young foreigners had got themselves up as some kind of revolutionary army; they had mismatched officer's jackets and hats decked with the carbonari cockade in blue, red and black— they even wore swords at their sides. How had they gotten into the opera house like that? The tallest of them, continuing some earlier remark, said in French, "But we *should* obtain guns!"—just as the back curtain opened and the two Vaccà children pushed their way into the box, followed by an indigent English poet, or someone dressed as an indigent English poet, with ink all over his coat.

"Here he is," said Leopoldo, in Italian. "I know we are late, I met friends on the floor."

"Parlons français," said Vaccà, "il y a des invités."

Greetings flew around the box like escaped birds. Keats bowed to Vaccà and his wife, to Shelley and Medwin in their soldier's hats and jackets, to a third soldier he didn't recognize, to Mrs. Shelley looking chill and elegant in a black gown, and to a strange, small man in a turban and long Eastern beard who sat in a corner chair.

"Bon soir," he said to everyone, "très bon soir."

"Or perhaps English," said Vaccà.

"Bless me!" said Keats, "is my accent so bad?"

On stage the improvisatore waved his arms and threw out couplets, moving his lips very fast with a thudding accent on the rhymes. The words came in a strange order or were strangely used; Keats couldn't make anything of them, except that the man thought it permissible to rhyme *Turchia* with *Italia*. God, that was as bad as Byron. Someone on the floor made a catcall.

"But what do you mean about obtaining guns?" asked the third soldier in a heavy accent, taking Shelley's arm. "It is not a partridge-hunt, is it?"

"Guns?" asked Leopoldo, his eyes brightening. "What's this?"

In a calming tone, Vaccà said that Signor Shelley was following his fancy this Carnival night and did not mean to offer a serious plan.

"But I am serious," said Shelley, shaking his arm free, and turned to the newcomers. "Hear me out. The principality of Lucca, which I understand not to have changed since Dante's time—"

"It is a duchy since the congress at Vienna," said Vaccà.

"It is a hive of priests and tyrants. Like its neighbors, it is squeezed breathless in the fist of Austria, and now a man is to be burned at the stake! For heresy! Can you conceive it?"

"I scarcely can," said the third soldier. "I should not have mentioned it. Suppose it is untrue?"

"Of course it is true," said Shelley; "of course such villainy is abroad in these times. I propose we free the man."

The soldier ducked his head to Mary. "I am sorry," he said with a rueful smile. "You have a claim against me now. Never again shall I tell your husband the day's news."

Mary bent her head, her face warming like a lamp. Keats had never seen her look so upon anyone—who was this? He must be a southerner or easterner of some kind; he was sharp-nosed and dark, with a chin beard and a mustache like a cat's tail. The soldier's costume sat on him more plausibly than on Shelley, or even on Medwin. He smiled brilliantly, there was foreign sun in his vowels. Keats disliked him.

"I asked that you hear me out," said Shelley. "By sea Lucca is a short journey. My boat would carry a small party to some near harbor, and provide us a means of escape with our captive. I don't propose an entire campaign."

"You have a boat?" asked Keats.

"He has turned sailor since we came here," said Mary. "He thinks one cannot understand the ancient poets without it. Modern Pisa knows only a madman would sail the canal to Leghorn and back." The party laughed—everyone but Keats must know this already—but Mary wasn't looking at him. She addressed everything to the easterner, whose smile brightened till it seemed about to catch his beard on fire.

"I didn't know," said Keats. To the easterner he said, "Nor do I know you."

"Forgive me!" said Shelley. "Prince Alexandros Mavrokordatos, nephew to the Hospodar of Wallachia." He indicated the easterner, then the turbaned man in the corner, who blinked at them. "And here is the hope of English poetry, John Keats."

"Oh!" said Mavrokordatos. "The author of," and made a sound something like "ee-per-yawn."

"I beg your pardon?" said Keats.

"He means your 'Hyperion,'" said Shelley. "That is his conception of authentic Greek." He spoke lightly, but Keats saw that he disliked the prince as well.

"It is Greek as we Greeks speak it," said Mavrokordatos; "that is all."

"And you signori shall free the heretic?" asked Giuditta. "God help him! If you must rescue someone, why not stay in Pisa and free the governor's daughter?"

"Giuditta," said Signora Vaccà, and her peacock feathers waved in warning.

"I'm telling no secrets." She spoke in Italian, with one hand at her hip, and pointed over the balcony. "Do you see the marquis, in the box with green curtains? He keeps his daughter locked in a convent."

Shelley squinted his blue eyes. "He with the side-whiskers? A jailor?"

"Ah," said Vaccà, "perhaps a more moderate word for our governor. It is not uncommon. While they seek a husband for the girl, her education is given over to the sisters."

"Education!" said Giuditta. "You're such a diplomat, Babbo, I could slap you."

Leopoldo snorted in laughter. "What a pity we never sent *you* to a convent," he said, and grabbed for his sister's shoulder. "If they could pack an ounce of it in your head—" She slapped his hand and he lunged over the crowded box, falling against Keats and Mavrokordatos.

"Oh now!" cried the prince, in high humor. "Dear children!"

Giuditta drew herself up, hair curling wild and flint in her eyes. But Vaccà and Leopoldo shared a moment's smile—so that was it. They indulged her. Her anger, like her youth, wasn't quite her own; it was a showpiece.

"The girl is jailed," she said, "whoever the jailor. For four years she hasn't set a foot outside Santa Anna, unless it was to visit her father's house. Not even at Carnival."

"Is that so?" Shelley's eyes kindled and he lifted his hand as if to sketch a path. "Santa Anna lies on the river, does it not? A stone's throw from the city? A boat could draw up, under darkness—"

"What, are you become a shipping line?" Still full of mirth, Mavrokordatos cocked his head at the balcony. "And what's the matter below?"

The catcalls and whistles had come up louder, and the improvisatore had fallen back from his downstage post and edged nearer the musicians. He moved his head in slight circles, as if trying to wind up a piece of clockwork, and his couplets came sputtering between pockets of empty air. The party listened a moment and everyone burst out laughing at the same time; Keats too, though he'd missed the joke.

"*Are* there volcano mountains in Turkey?" asked Leopoldo.

"It's his plot forcing it upon him," said Shelley. "He over-composed it as he went, and now the stitching won't mend. Any poem will stumble, I fancy, that so depends upon story and incident. They are low allurements."

"You are divine!" said Mavrokordatos. "But not everyone is—ah, metaphysical as you. How should you have treated the Christian among Turks?"

"I should have chosen my own subject. I never suffer a man to give me another."

"Superb! Pray name it."

"Well." Shelley made a regretful face at the improvisatore, then stood to his full height, pulled straight his jacket and hat, and swept his arm over the ball like a strategist marking out terrain. "Why go abroad? Take the subject around us."

His eyes had a martial gleam; there was something Napoleonic in his attitude, if not his person. Suppose Napoleon had been born tall, and fair, and an aristocrat, and hadn't needed to fight his way up from under every disadvantage of nature.

"I would evoke a masque," he said. "Not a masque such as tonight's, in which men and women put on the faces of spirits and demons to lose themselves in an hour's revel; but the contrary masque of our waking hours. I mean that in which disguise and person are turned about. The demons of our age, Murder and Fraud—have they not put on the smooth masks of men? Do they not walk among us robed and sceptered, as if our laws and hallowed institutions were theirs by right?"

Medwin laughed and slapped his thigh. He was out of place in this company; all evening he'd been about to speak, but either he couldn't turn the conversation to a congenial matter, or else Mavrokordatos was taking all his lines. Now he knew something and wanted to show it. "Cousin," he said, "you've already written that poem! You don't mean to give us a sham improvisation?"

"I don't mean to give any poetry at all," said Shelley. "I am describing our age."

"No, no, dear Shelley," said Vaccà; "you are found out. There must be a penalty."

"For shame! Pray make it a light one."

"Only that you surrender this poem, if it exists." The doctor held out his palm. "Surely your gifts have better employment than to make armed raids on our neighbors?"

A hiss came from below and a storm of confetti shot from the floor to strike the improvisor's raised arms. "Maledetto!" he cried, and braced for a stand, but another volley answered him, and he turned on his heel and fled. Muskets thumped the floor, the orchestra began to play and Shelley sank into his chair.

"Really, it were better that Mary give you a reading," he said. "She is writing a novel of Lucca."

"A novel!" said Keats. He hadn't meant to speak aloud. But Mary's attentions to the prince had stung, and he wanted her to look at him.

"Indeed a novel," she said. "Or mayn't I enter upon this academy?"

He laughed nervously. "You have a seat already, to be sure. I simply didn't know we should call you a novelist, as well as a philosopheress." He meant to say it warmly, but a mocking strain had gotten into his voice.

"But you must know Mrs. Shelley's 'Frankenstein?'" asked Mavrokordatos.

"Her what?" Keats looked around him; everyone had a half smile. "The ghost story?"

"No," said Mavrokordatos, "I should not say a ghost story."

"I thought there was a ghost story of that title. I had heard—" He faltered. Was he making another joke of himself? "Shelley, I thought you wrote it."

"People think as they will," said Mary. "There was design in publishing anonymously. In any case," she said, turning to Vaccà, "I can read nothing to this party. It is not an art like poetry; the words are not so few as to be carried about in one's head."

"I regret it," said Vaccà. "But the argument is worthy. The penalty returns upon Shelley."

"She undoes me!" he cried. "She won't put on a Carnival costume, she won't read."

"No costume?" said Giuditta. "That is easy, signora; I'll find you a domino."

Mary threw an icy look at Shelley, who smiled back with blind good humor. Did he not know he was provoking her?

"Thank you," she said to Giuditta, with an atom of forced warmth. "I am who I am."

"Nay!" said Shelley, "say rather with Iago, *I am not what I am*—wise words from the malefactor. Break the lock of the self! Tonight of all nights, none here is who he is. No, nor who she is. Why—" He half rose from his chair, enthused out of measure, and swept his arm again from the balcony. "Those men and women below, those who exchanged garments, understand best of all. Spirit is one; it is not to be found in trousers or a gown. Plotinus! In that whitest light, even the distinction of sex is a vanishing shadow."

"Ha!" said Mavrokordatos.

"You have no costume, Mary? Well, Keats too has come in his daily dress." Shelley faced them and opened his hands.

"Oh, no," said Mary.

Keats's neck turned hot. He clutched the lapels of his coat and stared back at Shelley's sparkling eyes, not quite able to ask what he had in mind; nor to assume the scandalized, half-hidden smile that the rest of the party was throwing back and forth. Giuditta was the first to break out laughing.

"You English," she cried, "how I adore you!"

Mary shook her head. "That is enough, Shelley."

"But it is exactly right!" said Mavrokordatos, taking her arm.

"If you had resided longer in the South, you would know everyone wears a costume this night. Whether you will or no. Should it not be a costume you have chosen?"

"I rather think it's been chosen for me." But her voice to him was softer, and with a yielding air she turned to consider Keats. Their eyes were exactly on a level. She dropped her lashes and glanced over his boots, his breeches, the shoulders of his coat. It was a frank appraisal, closer than courtship; he was being measured out. He saw freckles dusted on her neck and forearms where the sun had touched them. As for her black gown—he ran his eyes over it, pressed his lips and looked aside. The party closed around them in a half circle.

"You will do it?" Shelley asked.

Keats bowed to Mary. "If you consent, I do the like."

"But you are shirking a task," Vaccà told Shelley.

"Not at all!" Shelley put his hand to his heart. "If they exchange, I will read."

"But exchange where?" asked Mary, looking skeptical still, and Keats knew she would refuse him. Mavrokordatos went to the balcony, undid the curtain sash and pulled the cloth inward, tassels trailing, to screen off an arms' breadth of space in the corner. He grinned as if he'd carried off a magic trick, then did the same with the curtain opposite; meanwhile saying something in Greek to his uncle, who stood with his meditations and shuffled aside. Keats and Mary were surrounded. She was pulled slowly back from him, pressed into the far corner as he was guided into his own. A hand drew the curtain and hid him from the general gaze.

He shrugged back the coat that Fanny had hemmed for him. He threw off waistcoat, shirt, shoes and trousers, and passed them one by one over the curtain. Each thing met applause as it was snatched away. For a short while he stood on his thin shanks in stockings and drawers, with the soft curtain brushing his shoulders. Then came a rustling, and the gown descended on him like a great black bird. He caught it in his arms and turned it about. Everything was velvet folds, powder and spice; he couldn't tell which way was up, and it grew larger and vaguer as he moved it. It would smother him. The curtain shrugged aside, Giuditta stepped in and he shrank back, pressing his skin to the wallpaper.

"Don't fret!" she murmured. "We thought you should like help."

"I am *en déshabillé*," whispered Keats. "Are your parents not here?" The box was hushed past the curtain, waiting.

"My parents are infamous liberals." She took hold of the gown. "Let me have it."

He let it go. She pulled the cloth back from his, as he thought, sorrowful-looking breast: broad enough in the shoulders and ribs, but the skin drawn close and pale over them, with flat teats and a scrub of ginger hair. It was the breast of a man who had been shut in bed a long time. Giuditta spun her finger in a circle and he turned his back. The skirts fell over his head and shoulders, and inch by inch were worked down till they wrapped his legs. The bodice brushed his chest, then tightened its embrace, and he felt Giuditta's fingers fixing the laces at his back. Blood prickled hot in his forehead and cheeks, and followed the touch of her hand up his spine. He was not ashamed. His breath came fast. Closed up in the ladies' dressing room, he felt himself very much a man, enveloped in a woman's velvet, her second body. The cloth was warm and kindled a low fire under his image of Mary, turning it about. She had always been cold in his mind.

"This is firm velvet," murmured Giuditta. "Silk pile, silk backing. Lucky for you! If it were muslin, you'd have to wear her petticoats as well."

"Petticoats!" he whispered.

"Else your entire estate, signor, would be on show." She gave the bustle a purposeful tug, setting it straight. "Stand away. Let me see you."

Keats turned, legs moving free in the skirts, and pressed himself to the wall. Giuditta considered him. "I would do more, with more time," she said. "Your hair should be dressed. And I would powder you here." She waved where his breastbone came up pale and knobbed from the bustline, like something that had grown on a tree. Then she looked up and laughed.

"Now don't look sad!" she said. "You're a fine girl."

"Ciabatte!" called someone. A pair of ribboned shoes was passed over the curtain and Keats held his foot out; but they were minuscule, made for a child, and Giuditta put them aside.

"You'll do well enough in your stockings," she said. "Are you ready?"

He made a foolish smile, opened his arms and nodded. Giuditta swept back the curtain. The box came back into being; it was the second half of the magic trick. Everyone—Shelley, Mavrokordatos, Vaccà and his wife—wore the same expression, bright-eyed and very faintly smiling, as if they didn't know what was allowed. The opposite curtain dropped away and the image of Keats appeared. From his blue coat and boots, his white shirt with its rakish open collar, a woman's fair face looked out—fairer, truly, than she had ever appeared in woman's clothes. Her delicate chin and cheeks, her drape of russet hair made a better picture of Keats than he himself. A lifetime of looking into mirrors had shown him nothing. There he was: quick-eyed, half-starved, a bird's spirit in bright, shabby clothes. His brass-fastened boots had a faint military look; the whole costume was a kind of armor, wrapped tight at the waist but flamboyantly loose at the neck, lifting the body from the ground as it shrank the figure into a narrow channel. She towered over him in his stocking feet. Whether it was that towering expression in so slight a form, or simply the end of the moment's surprise, she broke loose the party's laughter. Leopoldo's cheeks puffed as he touched his lip; Medwin and Mavrokordatos made mock salutes. Shelley threw back his head and let out a peal high and clear as a bell. One would think it the laughter of angels, were there pranks in Heaven.

Mary stiffened and her face turned white. But Keats bent his head low, held his skirts aside and dipped in a curtsy. That changed everything. He was the woman; he took her shame on himself and gave the man's part up to her. She understood. She brought her arm to her waist and bowed.

Shelley placed a hand on the shoulder of each. The touch was warm and dry, and Keats shivered; he'd never gone so exposed into the world. For the first time he understood how one became naked in these gowns. Shelley guided them away from the balcony, smiling, and stationed himself in their place. He straightened his soldier's jacket and hat, clasped his hands behind him, swelled his breast and spoke.

> As I lay asleep in Italy
> There came a voice from over the Sea,
> And with great power it forth led me
> To walk in the visions of Poesy.
>
> I met Murder on the way—
> He had a mask like Castlereagh—
> Very smooth he looked, yet grim;
> Seven blood-hounds followed him:
>
> All were fat: and well they might
> Be in admirable plight,
> For one by one, and two by two,
> He tossed them human hearts to chew,
> Which from his wide cloak he drew.

He kept his eyes on the ceiling as he recited. The verses did not seem learned by heart; he might have been making them up on the spot. From Castlereagh, whose name he pronounced with a superaddition of venom, he carried on through the British Cabinet. The figure of Fraud, in a gown like Lord Eldon's, wept tears that became millstones to shatter children's brains. The specter of

Hypocrisy, riding past on a crocodile, was clothed like Sidmouth in the light of the Bible.

> And many more Destructions played
> In this ghastly masquerade,
> All disguised, even to the eyes,
> Like Bishops, lawyers, peers, and spies.

It was past great. It was genius. This was Shelley the metaphysician? Shelley who wrote poetry like fog, each line blurring over the last? These outlines were clear. He had worked magic with the names of those hated ministers—names that, when they came up in conversation, caused Keats an inward groan. Not Eldon again; not Castlereagh again. Of course they were monsters, but there was no getting rid of them. How could anyone get pleasure from another evening heaping calumnies on their heads? Shelley made one forget those evenings. One knew the men for the first time and thrilled to rage.

> Rise like Lions after slumber
> In unvanquishable number,
> Shake your chains to earth like dew
> Which in sleep had fallen on you—
> Ye are many—they are few.

> What is Freedom?—ye can tell
> That which slavery is, too well—
> For its very name has grown
> To an echo of your own.

God, what a call! Keats's soul rallied but stopped short of abandon; a weight held him back. Was he annoyed? Well, yes. Shelley was producing an effect and he envied it. The box was still as a church; the sounds of the ball seemed to float up from underwater, far distant. Were the verses that good? He glanced sideways and saw everyone making the same prayerful face, with lips slightly parted as if to sip the words from the air. How had he never managed to bring about that face? How had he never written like this?

He wanted Shelley's poem to stumble.

No—damn the wish! Poetry is fellowship! Where one triumphs, so do all.

He gripped the thought and felt an uneasy satisfaction. Shelley's call came at his point of climax, as the figure of Hope, a defenseless maid, threw herself before the murderers and monsters. An unnamed shape took form in her wake. As its words rang out, lo, the nightmare figures fell lifeless to earth.

But its words continued to ring out, long past what the scene required, and Keats began to suspect that the scene was not coming back. The celestial voice was starting to grow specific in its complaints.

> Paper coin—that forgery
> Of the title-deeds, which ye
> Hold to something of the worth
> Of the inheritance of Earth.

Paper money? That was matter for a poem?

Well—said Keats's generous angel—it was doubtless a serious subject. Was it not the livelihood of men?

No. The crystal hush was lifting from the box. The suspense had ebbed, the spell watered away—and it was not noble, but Keats was glad that the poem was coming down from heaven to earth. If it was turning into a sermon, he could wrestle it.

The men of England were addressed, rallied against their oppressors.

> And then if the tyrants dare
> Let them ride among you there,

Slash, and stab, and maim, and hew,
What they like, then let them do.

With folded arms and steady eyes,
And little fear, and less surprise,
Look upon them as they slay
Till their rage has died away.

Against his will, Keats was caught again. Fight without fighting. Answer force with peace—why, it was Christian! Of course it was unreal. Surely no tyrant in history had been brought down in this way. But that image of steady-eyed men, neither moving nor blinking as their fellows were cut down, made his eyes prick hot. Silence dropped over the box like a glass bell, and Shelley's voice, ringing in their ears unhindered, closed this scene with the same call as the last, now transformed in sense. Rise like lions after slumber. Ye are many, they are few.

"Maestro!" said Medwin.

Shelley ducked his head at the applause and waved his long fingers before him. So bashful, for a man with the carbonari colors on his hat. Keats clapped with the rest, forcing out bitterness through his palms. Shelley had won.

"Do stop," he said. "Thank you. Stop."

"Sublime!" said Mavrokordatos. "If you will give us such a song every time this gentleman puts on a gown"—waving to Keats—"he may never wear trousers again. I will send for a full wardrobe from Paris."

The box laughed and Keats bit his cheek, lest he spit out an answer. But Shelley stretched an arm to him.

"Say not so," he told Mavrokordatos. "You have not heard *him* sing. He outshines us all."

Shelley's look was frank as truth. Was this a new move in the contest? Or was he so selfless that he saw no contest at all?

"Such praise, in such company," Keats murmured, and

dropped his head.

"Modest maid!" said Mavrokordatos. "I die at your blush. Say, where is Carnival tonight?"

"You are within it," said Vaccà.

"Then where is the dance?" And before Keats could pull away, the prince had grabbed both his arms and begun to wheel him over the box. The mustached smile spun before him, fruity eau de Portugal caught him in the nose—what was he, a tavern-wench?

Well, what must a tavern-wench do when Falstaff grabbed her? Cuff him! Kick his shins!

He wrenched an arm free and the whirling stopped. He found himself set before Mary.

"It is time to dance!" said Mavrokordatos.

"Ha," Keats gasped. "I know not how."

"No more does Mary," Shelley said. "You shall do very well."

She stood over him like a slender tree, her face tapering from her high forehead. As he smoothed the gown against his sides, he saw a kind of waxing wonder in her eyes: she must see her own image in him, as he saw his in her. Realizing that, he felt the hard edge of sex break loose and had to adjust his skirt again.

"One feels the cold in that gown," she murmured.

He forgot the box around him. A smaller box was built around them alone. He held out his arm to her, but that was backward. She must hold out her elbow in his inky coat sleeve, and he rest his bare forearm on hers. So joined, they found the way clear from the box and passed under the back curtain to the corridor behind.

Walking down a dim stairway, gently shoving past other revelers, Keats couldn't find the floor with his stockings. Mary's stride held him. As they stepped onto the open floor of the opera house, she looked down and said, "I *have* read your last volume, Mr. Keats."

"Have you?" he said. "Then you know how far short I fall of your husband's praise."

"Poets!" She rolled her eyes. "You are all thus: you beg for compliments, then you refuse them. I do admire the volume. Let it be said and done with, else we shall dance about it all the evening."

"You honor me."

"Not as you wish to be honored. I don't say you are Milton. You don't sit on the peak of Parnassus."

"I would answer with a complaint against novelists. But I know only one, and she surprises my expectation."

He hoped to get a smile, but her mouth barely eased. "I suppose a novel is beneath you?"

"I am not so prejudiced!" He pressed her arm. "Why, I began to read *Clarissa* on the voyage to Rome. I found it—"

Now she did smile. "Well?"

"I found it very long," he admitted.

"Then you lost much instruction on Mr. Richardson's idea of virtue."

"Of Mr. Richardson's ideas I can tell you nothing. I know he described a great lot of furniture. Also the clothes worn by his personages, and the gardens about their estates, and their carriages. There is so much *stuff* in a novel—such a need of objects to get the plot under way. Your husband said it above; it is a minor interest. It seems to me that is the fault of prose."

"Of course!" said Mary. "Imagine some tedious novel concerning—oh, suppose a lion hunt, in Hindoostan. Would it not be wholly refreshed and quickened, simply by putting it into verse?"

Keats looked down. "I know. Would that it were."

Mary shrugged in her coat. "Some things are stillborn. I can't recommend Mr. Richardson to you. You ought to read Madame de Staël."

"I should like to read you, Mrs. Shelley."

She was pleased. She held out her arms in a girlish pose, to see how the sleeves hung. "Is it true you cannot dance?"

"Entirely so."

She took his arm and guided him onto the floor, between the masked couples spinning in time with the orchestra. They found themselves stationed at an awkward distance, each lightly touching the other's elbows. In this stiff circle they began a slow revolving motion, like one of Hooke's snow crystals tumbling through the night. Anyone watching from the balconies would laugh. But the position had an advantage; each had a clear view into the other's face and saw strange eyes and lips framed in one's own clothes, as if holding a magic mirror in one's arms. It was a philosopher's dance. Keats felt like confiding things.

"It is genius what Shelley gave us," he said. "I've never heard the like from him."

"He would be glad of hearing that from you," said Mary. "Not from everyone."

"And the sentiment is true? He would see a revolution in England?"

"As would I, being my father's daughter." Her husband's passion came into her voice. "We have such hope from Naples. You see the state of Italy; how centuries of tyranny have degraded the race."

Keats looked over the floor. "These about us are degraded? Do they know it?"

"Here you see society. I speak of the common Italian. You hear how they use their women! Shut for years in convents, till they are sold in marriage? Yes," she said hotly, "I do call that degraded. I will call it so to anyone."

In fact these weren't the sun-darkened faces from the streets. The bare shoulders and necks, the cheeks showing under dominos, were all indoor things, very pale, with an un-English olive tint. People had begun to sweat garlic into the air. Everyone laughed who caught Keats's eye. One could always laugh at a man in a gown.

"I met a sculptor in Rome," he said, "who claimed the Italians were not ripe for a republic. He said they had no experience of free birth."

"They want a leader. One essentially noble, above the com-

mon run, who will not become another Bonaparte." Her look softened, becoming dreamy. "Likewise the Greeks—they have fallen
from what they were. They wait for their Washington. Their Boli-
var."

Keats guessed whom she meant and said sharply, "It seems
Shelley does not much like Prince Mavrokordatos."

Mary tilted her head. "No more do you. Because he is dark?
Because he is a prince?"

"Why—" He wondered what else she saw in his heart. "I don't
know," he confessed. "Only that you seem to like him very well."

"He is not the sort to please everyone. He has excellent qualities enough. Shelley will not consider them. Sometimes with men,
it is like bringing two dogs into a house."

"I suppose women are never jealous of each other?"

She frowned and loosened her hands from his elbows. Why
had he said that? They continued to roll their awkward circle about
the floor while other couples swung past at twice the speed, in time
with the bright viols. When the song ended, neither moved to let
go.

"If you would know the truth," said Mary, "Shelley is tor-
mented that he cannot like Mavrokordatos better. He so believes
in universal sympathy, that he is confounded when it fails in the
particular."

A fanfare snaked up from the stage, coiled around them and
spun them into the next turn. This was a slower measure, and as
they wheeled near the floor's edge Keats saw the two men standing
together. Shelley was in discussion with a bearded Harlequin who
was waving at his carbonari hat, and Mavrokordatos stood behind
with his own hat tucked under his arm. When his glance struck
Keats and Mary, it became a sulk. Keats dropped his eyes, thrilled,
and grasped her arms tighter.

"I am sorry my own sympathy fails me with Shelley," he said.
"I know he means well."

"No man living means better."

"But he has what I haven't, and he makes generous offers without thinking. It's easy to despise a man for that."

"You don't hide it," she said.

"Debt is a wretched thing, Mrs. Shelley!" He felt sudden, choking pity for his old clothes, and with a sob-like convulsion pressed his hands to them. Her slim middle was beneath. She stiffened at his touch, and they slowed and halted, like a boulder coming to rest at the bottom of a hill. He let her go and she drew back, saying, "You are not the first who carried a light purse."

They stood upright among the swaying dancers, like rocks in the ocean. "No," said Keats. "But my own purse is on such familiar terms."

He didn't sound witty in his own ears. She was right; here was no place to pity himself. He offered a modest hand.

A shout came from the floor's edge and the Harlequin's arm flung up at Shelley, who was suddenly bareheaded. His fiery hair fell around him as he lunged after the masked figure, but Mavrokordatos caught him by the arm. The Harlequin leaped away, throwing his plaster smirk indifferently over the hall, and slipped into the crowd.

"The blackguard!" Shelley cried, putting a hand to his costume sword. Was it only a costume? "Let me loose; I'll requite him."

"You won't know him," said Mavrokordatos.

"I know the sneer in his voice," he said, "all Tory and Austria in one—hello, Mary. I've been insulted."

"What did you do?"

"I spoke the truth! And I wore a hat with an emblem the fellow didn't like."

"*You* did not like what he said about your heretic. Come," Mavrokordatos said, laughing, "you must own he is not much of a heretic after all. Would you call it simony?"

"What a merry man you are," said Shelley, and bent to pick his hat up.

"We had some words over the case in Lucca," said the prince. "It seems Shelley's heretic is in fact a priest, who stole a chalice from the sacristy. He was caught trying to sell it."

"And they would burn him at the stake for that?" asked Keats.

"Not this week, I think. He has escaped to Florence."

"That is the man's story," said Shelley. "If you would believe—"

The letter X marched up, banded in white on the chests of three soldiers, and a hand clapped Shelley's neck. He stiffened and rolled back his eyes. Mavrokordatos became suddenly agreeable and began to speak in soft Tuscan to the soldiers, who, in between glowering at Shelley, gave him negligent glances from under their brims. In their shako hats they seemed eight feet high. They were older than the soldiers at the border, with rough, sandy faces folded in small lines.

"Our friend is leaving this moment," Mavrokordatos said. He pointed to Keats. "This lady will see him out."

"Certo," Keats said.

"After all, avarice is a sin." And when Keats frowned, the prince gave him a railleur's look and said, "You have been hoarding Mrs. Shelley! She must be spent."

Incredibly, that made the soldiers smile. "Outside, then," said one, and casually shoved Shelley forward. Mary reached after him, but Mavrokordatos checked her by linking his arm in hers. Together they stepped back into the dance, rapping boots in time like a pair of officers on leave.

Shelley's face fell. His tall frame came apart like a heap of wire, and he let Keats take him away without a word. Only at the outer door did he stop and peer back at the whirling dance with sad, marine eyes.

"We've lost her now," he said.

Keats followed his look but saw nothing. "Shelley," he said in a passion, "are you and she—?"

"Yes?"

Keats shook his head. The piazza outside was empty of carriages and the torches cast orange heat on their faces, making them squint. They walked farther into the square and found the air cold, the flagstones bare and the torchlight skewed behind them, throwing spidery shadows forward in the gloom. They shrank from the glow. Shelley took a colonnade into a crooked side street, where dark walls framed a downward slope into nothing: the invisible river, yellow points of candles. A gust came up, lifting the sweat from Keats's shoulders and back, and he shivered.

"Shelley!" he called. "It matters not! Do you know it matters not?"

The tall shadow halted. "Matters?"

"A tyrant may eject you from a ball! But your poem—" He hurried forward and found Shelley's profile cut sharp under a lit window. "The masque you gave us is more than I have heard from anyone. Truly, from anyone now living."

Shelley's head dropped. After a long silence he said, "If you take pleasure in my poor poem—"

"Please! Don't dissemble, Shelley, or you'll hurt me. I shall think you not open. I don't know for myself, but I think a masterpiece must come away from you as you write it. You must be sure of it ever after, as a thing apart in its perfection."

Shelley's eyes lifted and he began to walk again. The street ended suddenly at the Lung'Arno. A half moon had come up and hung low on the water in gray and silver, under a city of stars. They passed whispering figures with candles and came to a ledge overlooking the current. Shelley rested his elbows on the stone and looked down at the silvered skin of his hands.

"I must apologize," said Keats.

Shelley glanced aside. "To me?"

"For some lines in a letter. You may not remember them. Hunt had given me, as from you, a copy of your 'Cenci,' and I answered with some talk of God and Mammon—that a modern work perhaps must have a moral purpose, but it were better for you to curb that purpose and be more of an artist. I was full of advice that day."

"Your letter was frank," said Shelley. "I suppose I took it as a signal of respect."

"So you should have. But I was wrong to write it."

"If so, that was because you spoke against your own angels." Shelley smiled in the gloom. "After all, your letter came in company with a volume. And as I read in it, I came to think your advice not sincere. Your 'Hyperion—'"

Keats shook his head. "I beg you, not again."

"Come, was not that poem a revolution? The war in Heaven? The tyrants cast out by Apollo?"

"No, no." It was a blow to think his poem might have been like Shelley's. "You forget Apollo cast out nobody. That was to come in later books. Those you call tyrants, I called suffering hearts, mourning their empires. I was not tactician enough to bring off a revolution."

"The fault is not yours. You had reviews that might have killed a man."

"Not me. I care not for reputation."

He rested his elbows beside Shelley's and watched the silver and black rippling of the water. From the far bank came an echo of the night's murderous call, then high laughter.

"I am doubtful of endings," he said. "Supposing I hammer a last line onto my poem, it simply returns upon me as a question. A revolution is something. What is the day after a revolution?"

"The first day," said Shelley.

"That is not enough. It was just the hitch in your 'Prometheus Unbound'—if I may say so. You ended the contest too soon. For two acts you had nothing but singing in Heaven."

Shelley bowed. "I wrote it knowing it should not be for many. Few have read Dante's 'Paradise.'"

Keats wrapped his arms over the gown's empty bust. "I have not read Dante's 'Paradise.'"

They became embarrassed in their silence. Shelley pulled in his shoulders and Keats felt he'd been cruel. "But your masque!" he said. "It deserves the world. Will you not print it?"

Shelley shook his head. "It can't be published. Hunt has assured me of that. They were my personal reactions only, on hearing of the riding down in Manchester. Defenseless souls!" An ember flared up in his voice and faded. "None will read it."

"It will be read forever," said Keats.

Shelley tilted his head, then put his hands on Keats's shoulders and brought him close. They faced each other inches apart, and seeing Shelley's bright eye and fine brow so near in the moonlight, Keats understood why people described him as an angel. He heard the flicker in the other's lungs; he was held in a flame of fire. Abruptly Shelley let go and stepped away.

"Forgive me," he said. "I had a fancy."

Keats shook his head, awed. "It is well."

"It was your clothes. For an instant you really looked like Mary. I mean Mary as I used to know her."

Shelley sank back, resting his forearms on the ledge, and gazed a while into the brittle light of the moon.

"I wish she had your passion now," he said.

De vulgari eloquentia

SPRING OUGHT TO BE A time of lean harvests, but food out of measure weighed down the Vaccà table. Artichokes spilled in bagfuls, bean pods burst with grape-sized morsels; there were yellow tomatoes, Tangerine oranges, ruddy squashes and crumbled sheep's cheese, a tang in everything of vinegar and pressed olives, and always a beaker of cool wine beside.

Keats was seldom alone with his hosts at table. The palazzo at suppertime was a common haunt and word might be given to set a dozen places, setting Keats beside a doctor or German professor—he did well enough with these, talking science in bad French—or else the big-bodied chief of a manufacturing concern, whose enthusiasm at meeting an Englishman would cool when he found Keats could tell him nothing about London commerce. The Grand Duke's government and army went unrepresented. Sometimes a priest joined them. Vaccà had good relations with several and would talk no politics. They ate with pleasure, praising the Tuscan soil, and wiped their mouths neatly when they were through.

On private evenings the great table was pulled from the dining room by a pair of broad-backed, sweating boys and a smaller oval piece installed in its place. Sitting next to Signora Vaccà in the honey-colored lamplight, Keats discovered that she was an anchor. The doctor leaned farther back in his chair with each glassful of wine, and his speech too became oblique, unspooling in long paragraphs about his memories of Paris, or the news from Vienna and Rome, with no conclusion in view until his wife, who never slanted a degree in her seat, put down her fork and said, "Yes, Andrea, and Danton is dead, and Consalvi has not yet written you for advice."

Leopoldo, a more errant planet than his father, rocked back and forth and said, well, Consalvi *ought* to be writing his father. Perhaps there was no helping wickedness in government, but at least their stupidity might be cured. His mother smiled at this and took up her fork.

Giuditta was governed by no laws of motion. She would hang her head over her plate for minutes at a time, then look up and exclaim something, rubbing her fingers together. Keats sat beside her and saw her low-buckled black slippers swinging back and forth throughout the meal, chasing each other in circles and figure-eights. Occasionally she caught him with an enigmatic look, as if still wearing her domino.

A few mornings after Carnival night, the white-haired footman came into Keats's room with a wrapped packet and a murderous museum piece of a paperknife. Keats was shaving; so the footman sliced the wrapping himself in two strokes, deft as any surgeon, and brought out three thinnish volumes in plain paperboard. A note was folded at top.

> You find here a Story which I own is full of <u>Stuff</u>—but perhaps you will discover among the Stuff some Matter. Will you call some afternoon & read Greek with us? It is not a charitable offer.
>
> M.S.

The volumes declared themselves the tale of "Frankenstein: or the Modern Prometheus." It must be a household article, that mythology. In place of an author's name, the title page had two lines from Milton and a dedication to Godwin. Keats smiled, hefted the modest weight, toweled off his cheeks and went downstairs.

The Vaccà library was the largest he had ever seen in a private home. Cloth and leather spines ran between wooden pilasters in all sizes, red and white and sorrel, stones in a riverbed ten feet high. On his first introduction he had turned round very slowly and said at last to Vaccà, "There was a time when I thought ill of professional men with pretensions to literature. You will smile."

Vaccà had nodded, but made no smile.

"I mean that I had to measure myself against that man," Keats said. "He had a livelihood and I did not. I would tell myself: this man has bought lifetimes of poetry, but poetry is not in him. Words are his toys. He might as well be playing at whist, or shooting rabbits."

"It seems to me you describe the thoughts of a young man," said Vaccà.

"Beside you I feel very young, Professor. My ideas are falsified. The barrier cannot be so steep between literature and life."

Vaccà had taken the compliment with grace, and Keats had felt himself made gracious by it, his first bright morning in that beautiful home. This morning his spirit was otherwise. He half reclined on the library sofa, took his fearsome knife to the first page of Volume One and expected, without giving it thought, that he would be amused. What an odd creature was Mrs. Shelley, with so many ideas in her head—how in heaven would they shake themselves together into literature? The brief author's preface, with its talk of Dr. Darwin, and physiology, and German ghost stories, and the *Iliad* and *Tempest*, had him smiling already. What was she after?

She had a bit of contention on her chosen form.

> The most humble novelist, who seeks to confer or receive amusement from his labours, may, without presumption, apply to prose fiction a licence, or rather a rule, from the adoption of which so many exquisite combinations of human feeling have resulted in the highest specimens of poetry.

Very well, madam! Those are the stakes. He settled deeper into the sofa.

Women write novels because they are weak draughts. If a

poem is a crushed flower, and each word bears a drop of essence, then a novel scatters a handful of petals along a desert road. The poet is the heart. The novelist crawls over the skin, and finds nothing there but conversation and costume. A certain woman talks all afternoon. Another woman makes it her business to represent people talking all afternoon. In either case feeling is mimed from a distance; it is not known. One can hardly blame the authoress, whom nature and society have not fitted for the passions that make up poetry. Still, if she takes the gambit of making her narrator a man and has him declare on the first page that

> I also became a poet, and for one year lived in a Paradise of my own creation; I imagined that I also might obtain a niche in the temple where the names of Homer and Shakespeare are consecrated.

—it is hard to avoid a tightened lip. A novel about a poet—is that really the aim? Thank God, Keats saw, in the next sentence the narrator confessed his failure in literature and resolved to go to sea instead. Very wise.

He felt secure that Mrs. Shelley had never been on a Greenland whaler, nor to St. Petersburg or Archangel, nor mounted an expedition to the Pole. Her inventions were lively enough. Her imagined ship drove itself into the gray north, was bound in ice and met with a series of haggard travelers passing improbably over the edge of the world. He was tugged, and found himself cutting and reading more quickly. Was this skill? Well, it was an effect brought off. He did want to know who was the stranger discovered on the glacier. That was the novel's one recourse to beckon a reader down its barren road: the child's question, what comes next.

Biography. Birth and education, friends and sweethearts. He recognized their shape and passed them over. He might have been tempted to drop the volume entirely, but that its picture of a dying madman wrapped in furs at the pole had run him through. He would have to keep reading and suffer through the whole of the madman's novelistic youth, only because he had to see how the one became the other. Apparently it was going to happen by way of a medical education—which was a perfect fog, since Mrs. Shelley did not know anything about physiology, or if she did know anything she kept it close. Probably that was intended. One couldn't narrate his school-days lecture by lecture, after all. The parts of the ear in order? No, the character was already turning a little mad. That was the trick; the outer world was not worth describing against the personage's inner flame. So the chaff of the novel fell away. No more costumes, no more carriages! It was—well, it was poetry, in a way. But God, what she had given him for a ruling passion: grave robbing? Torturing dead flesh? He hadn't thought her so ghoulish. Strange, pale woman.

The house cook came into the library with toast and coffee, and asked if the signor would be dining at home tonight. Keats said that he supposed so, and reached for the cup vaguely, without looking up, because the dead flesh was waking. Christ. Arteries and nerves. He clutched his arm with a shiver, as if his own flesh were dying on his bones. All at once he was back at the bottom of his illness, imprisoned in sheets with his mouth hung open in a dead gasp. One shapes a thought slow in the brain, over midnights, feeding it blood. It gathers flesh to itself, pulsing. It drops like fruit. The face of one's thought laid open on the dissecting table has black lips, opening and closing in gasps. A yellow eye blinks and rolls upward, the dead eye of one's thought seeking the thought that made it.

It lifts its hand.

God! Flee!

Keats looked up and found he was alone in the library. His coffee cooled untouched on the table. He had turned his back to the wall and a high window lit the page he was reading, but the library was full of dim spots and his eyes kept making shapes in the corners.

That horrible face. It might come from anywhere.

It was late afternoon when he closed the third volume. He lay on the sofa with shut eyes and felt the beating blood in his neck. Fear and horror had drawn him through the book, like thread following a needle, and had dropped him nerveless on the far side. Only a small clock remained ticking in him, turning over a question. Was it a masterpiece? Was it not a masterpiece?

Some pages should not have been there. The prose was not perfect. But the ticking clock whispered to him that these were quibbles, and that this was the second masterpiece he had found in as many days. He thought of his own Lamia, his Saturn. Were they as sublime as Mrs. Shelley's monster? They were not.

Oh, why did it matter! Why always measure himself against others?

He was vain and his ambition devoured everything. Mrs. Shelley's madman was his portrait. He had forgotten the taste of life. All he did was toil at it, trying to make literature. Even his horror and pity at her book—were they true horror and pity? Or was he not rather bending his mind to them, like a mechanic, to see how the work was done? It drew from a deep well. The articulate monster, made innocent, made cruel: what was that? The fear of monsters engendering each other: what was that? He thought of Vaccà and his skull, the heads on pikes. The masque of destruction. Shake your chains to earth. The ghost turns in the burning flesh, locked within the bones. Misery made me a fiend. The yellow eye, once made, looks back into the eye that made it. A deep well….

Keats was still splayed over the couch, his hand resting on the shut volume, when they came to call him to supper.

Cospiratori

MOST AFTERNOONS ONE FOUND A dozen students or more in back of
the "Bevuti e Bigliardi" café, making a circle of shoulders around
the table where papers were spread out. The journals printed
in Naples were smuggled through border crossings inside coats
and trunks, and ended up in Pisa as rolled tubes or many-folded
stars. The students bent over the smudged lines, overlaid with the
ghosts of the words they had been packed against, and read passages aloud. A dwarf is as much a man as a giant; a small republic
is no less a sovereign state than the mightiest kingdom. All royalty
must be exterminated!

In Naples the carbonari had accosted the old Commissary of
Police under King Ferdinand, torn him from his supper, stabbed
him in the heart and left him to expire on the cobbles with the
number 1 pinned to his lapel. A number 2 must follow. The fled
king, returning in back of the Austrian army, was addressed in a
column:

> *Traditor*! From the moment
> In which thou brok'st thy covenant,
> A hundred knives, O *traditore*,
> Point full eager at thy *cuore*.

"But that is lust for blood," said Leopoldo, whose side-whiskers were starting to fill in; "it is the wrong sentiment."

"Wrong?" cried the student in Church robes, who had read
the poem. "Say rather, they do not go far enough."

"They do wrong to concentrate on enemies," said Leopoldo.
"Ferdinand is a clown, a nothing. What of the future? The broth-

erhood of man?"

"You talk like your English poets," said another. "They give us forty stanzas on the brotherhood of man, and nothing on the English ships in Naples harbor. Neutral, they say!"

That was light innuendo, since Keats too was at the table. He made a tragic face and said, "Alas, my carrion-bird government. Alas, Castlereagh."

"Come, Your Holiness," said Leopoldo to the robed student. "You have no thirst for blood. If I held you a dagger to Ferdinand's heart, you would not drive it in."

The students looked rueful. It was true they didn't have the makings of assassins. Their project, apart from reading the newspapers, was a play for the puppet theater that everyone knew couldn't be produced. A traveler from Florence was shipwrecked on an isle of apes and taught them the system of monarchical government; following his teachings, the most apish ape of all was named king. Professor Vaccà came in one afternoon to hear it read, and sat in his black coat with a glass of grappa while the students leapt between chairs, making ape-hoots and bellowing about divine right. Afterwards they crowded him to get his opinion, though in private, Keats knew, they laughed at his manners and called him "The Consul" or "Lorenzo de' Medicina." But it was not easy to make Vaccà answer a question, and after a quarter hour of conversation he managed to depart without giving the young authors any assessment of their work. Later he said to Keats that, literary merit aside, they were certainly brave lads. Probably the Buongoverno had five informers in the café that day.

"However," said Leopoldo, "this is not to exclude other endeavors."

A look of conspiracy divided the table. Half the students became suddenly curious and alert; the other half scowled, and one elbowed Leopoldo in the ribs. "Omertà!" he said. "The English!"

"I want Kitsa to help us," Leopoldo said. "My noble father trusts him."

He puffed his cigarillo, enjoying himself, and the others cupped their hands around their saucers. Keats gave him a careful look over the illegal newspaper.

"Am I to understand that you wish me to take advantage of that trust?" he asked.

"It is nothing. A very small thing. You need only detain my father a minute or two, whilst I retrieve an item from the college pharmacopeia."

"An item! I thought you were renouncing murders."

"It is a packet of quotidian sulphate," said Leopoldo.

"Your pardon?"

"Young Vaccà," said another, "who has not taken his pharmaceuticals course, means to say a sulphate of quinine, compounded against quotidian fever."

"As it may be," said Leopoldo. "Some Frenchmen discovered it and sent a quantity here, as we have such pestilential marshes. We have had it above a year, kept locked in a cabinet. The Buongoverno will not approve its use."

"Why not?" asked Keats.

"It comes from France," replied a senior student. "And what is French physic, if not sedition and regicide? Our noble lords still think that Napoleon's vaccinations were a poison plot."

"It falls to us to give it use." Leopoldo leaned forward and explained in an enthusiast's whisper that last month he had borrowed the pharmacopeia key from his father's desk, alienated a quantity of powder from the cabinet and delivered it to a marshy village along the Arno. A certain Don Niccolò was physician there—a genuine hero, said Leopoldo, an old classmate of his father's and a thoroughgoing radical whose practice the authorities were sworn to extinguish. They would sooner lose all medicine from Tuscany than see him supplied.

"That is infamous," said Keats. "Why not tell your father?"

Leopoldo made a pained face. "My father weathered the change in governments well. You've seen his dinners. He won't compromise himself with the college."

In the end it was the illegal newspaper that won Keats over. Its crest was a crude drawing of Minerva's helm and the type must have been smudged even before it was wadded up for its journey. Such a flimsy thing, to spit in the teeth of statesmen. Years ago he had wondered about Shakespeare's manuscripts. What was the look of the page where the bard had written, say, "I come to bury Caesar"?—surely just such a scrap, fit to wrap a fish. The students gave him the crumpled sheet to keep, and he had it still in his coat pocket when he left for the hospital next morning.

His duty once a week was to help Vaccà carry off some spectacular procedure in the public eye; the rest of his time was passed in the wards. He inflicted pain on the souls in the beds. A swollen shoulder needed a vein slit and a leech stuck under the arm. Sciatica required a steaming plaster on the thigh, to raise a red blister and draw the serous blood away. The scarificator's blades sliced ribbons of blood across the belly and perineum, the lit torch and glass cup sucked the flesh outward and caused new inflammations to bloom. The patients never asked why these things were happening to them. They winced, and out of pride tried not to wince visibly. The kindest thing Keats could do was to work quickly and force his mind into his hands. It seemed a scant mercy. Yet that morning a red-capped student caught his elbow and asked if he would come to the next ward over. A lung patient needed a blister, he said, and was saying that she would have it only from the English doctor with the red hair. Once he had done it, and caught Vaccà's elbow at the appointed time, the doctor asked him whether he had considered becoming licensed as a physician in Tuscany.

"Here?" Keats asked. "I hadn't thought it possible."

"I can arrange for you to sit the examination," said Vaccà. "It is not difficult."

"But I could not do it."

"You are doing it every day. I understand you are doing it rather well."

"I don't mean the work." Keats smiled tightly at the medical busts. A high window caught the sun and threw it over the hall, picking out points of glint in the granite. Robed and capped students went back and forth on the checkerboard paving, their steps echoing from the arches above. "Life here is very beautiful," he said. "It could not be mine."

"You seem certain of it."

"I have duties in England," Keats said shortly.

If the doctor had any curiosity about those duties, he was too courteous to show it. He lifted his hands in a gesture of understanding, and Leopoldo turned the corner and came strolling down the file of busts with his hand stuck ostentatiously in his pocket. He greeted his father with a collegial nod and Keats followed him into the sunlight, where the lad suddenly whirled around and flung his arms around Keats's neck.

"Fire!" he whispered. "Snatched from heaven."

He drew back and held open his coat pocket to show an unsealed packet of brown paper. A fistful of fine white powder rested at bottom.

"That is all?" Keats asked.

"The dose is nothing. That is the miracle. Ten such packets would heal the country."

Leopoldo shut his pocket and, taken with his own words, cast a far-seeing gaze over the white city. Then he shook Keats's hand, made an esoteric sign surely invented just at that moment, and leaped in his boots back up the college steps, two at a time.

Reflections on the Revolution

DIOS PLAGAN EKHOUSIN EIPEIN,
parestin touto g' exik—

Mrs. Shelley's voice hung on the consonant and she bit her lip. Keats bent his head beside hers and squinted at the accent marks sprouting like grass from the lines.

"Exix—" he said.

"Exi-hnefse," said Mavrokordatos, smiling.

Mrs. Shelley repeated it. The half-known script shimmered at them, rising and falling. When a passage was read out, a sense of marble would catch the air in the room, beckoning them to a place where all time conjoined. But there came a snort from the next room and Shelley leaned his head through the doorway.

"Really," he called, "that is not Greek; that's a sneeze!"

Mavrokordatos looked up and laughed. For him Shelley was always the same joke, one he never tired of. "Thank you," he said. "Some millions of Greeks will disagree."

"They are wrong," said Shelley. "You people shall never come up to your ancestors whilst you go clotting Aeschylus with efs and afs. The upsilon is a clear stream. Why choke it? It stays open till the verb ending falls. *Exikhneu-sai!*" He cut the air with his hand. "The knife-stroke of the aorist! A singular blow in time."

"You're not helping us," said Mary.

"Oh!" It never occurred to Shelley that he wasn't helping. He made a sour face and pulled his head back through the doorway.

These clashes never outlasted the moment and left no marks of their passing. Mary began the strophe over again in the same hushed, cool voice, and Mavrokordatos listened with the same tight smile under his mustache. Everyone had accepted that the ground beneath them would erupt every hour or two. Only Keats was shaken. If this were his marriage, he would never dare step into his own parlor.

Aeschylus was a strange creature. He wasn't like the Romans, who seemed always to be winking at you from between their hexameters; nor was he a frank spinner of yarns like Homer. He was spare and slow. So far as Keats saw, he used no variation in gravity. His people were solemn as priests from the first line, declaiming their harsh language packed with consonants like a landscape of stones. And the vowels were cold springs. It was divine enough. It had that trick of stilling the air, like the most awful parts of Milton—perhaps more than Milton. Certainly it suited the character of Agamemnon, yoked like an ox to his curse and stumbling toward it, thinking it a crown. But he was a granite statue, and if the statue were spun round it might prove thin in the back. When Mary came to the end of the strophe, Mavrokordatos applauded and Keats sat with folded hands.

"The strangeness in this play," he said at last, "is that Agamemnon is a dead man."

Mary smiled and lost her masked look of reading Greek. "His fate is to die. Is it strange?"

"Fate in Greece is a terrible goddess," said Mavrokordatos. "Remember, the audience at the foot of the Acropolis know all the while who Agamemnon is, and what shall come to him."

"Homer's audience knew the same," said Keats. "If you know nothing else of Achilles, you remember the tender spot in his hide. But Achilles is alive till the moment he meets his death. This Agamemnon—" He frowned. "Everyone in this play speaks as if he knows himself dead already."

"The chorus do not know anything," said Mary.

"The chorus are like people in a nightmare. They are made to sense the thing that is coming, and then to find they knew it all the while."

"A nightmare, yes," said Mavrokordatos. "It is meant to terrify." He made the same grin he was always making at Shelley. These English, who didn't know what a tragedy was!

"The terror I understand," said Keats. "It is like sculpture; it lives out of time. I see that. I think I should have been more in sympathy with it before my illness."

A look went between Mavrokordatos and Mary. Was the surgeon's assistant finding fault with Aeschylus?

Keats smiled shyly. "It is only a human taste I miss. Chaucer's pilgrims, or Nick Bottom stumbling through the woods with loam on his boots. What is humble."

"Iphigenia," said Mary.

Keats raised his brow. "In this play?"

"No. She is not in this play. That is the tragedy." Her long finger pointed into the book. "What weighs most is the thing that happened ten years past. Everything is the working of a curse, and the curse persists because this man killed his daughter to get his warships out of the harbor. That is the seed."

He looked into the book. "Perhaps."

"You watch the men in these plays and you see only sculptures. The women you don't perceive, because they are shadows cast by the men. Without them nothing is understood."

Perhaps she was right. She really did talk like a schoolmistress sometimes. But Mavrokordatos answered in high cheer—yes, it was just so—and the unmeaning grin leaped right from his face to hers. Ludicrous! She ought to see herself in a mirror. Was she really in love with him?

Her book he hadn't known how to broach at all. For a day or two he had kept silent, and when his silence began to seem significant he said, "You were frank in admiring my work. I ought to return you the compliment. Your book was—"

A masterpiece? Genius? They were empty words. She'd laugh.

"I thought it a skilled piece of work," he said. "It was very unlike a novel."

"Then it had no skill," she said, "for a novel was intended."

"No, no," he said, blushing. "I mean that it frightened me. It played on my passions, and it had more meanings than it expressed in plain words. I call that poetry."

She narrowed her eyes. "Since it is you who say it, I must think it praise, and not the starting point of an argument. I thank you. But tell me," with a teasing smile, "what significances did you see in my book?"

"My children," said Keats.

The smile dropped.

"My poems follow after me in a train," he explained. "They ask why their creator sent them imperfect into the world. How is he such a bad God?"

She relaxed a fraction and he shook his head.

"You should smile. Of course I have no child. I am not in a position to marry. Some in my circle had children by mistresses. I thought it awful as Milton. All in a moment to shape a new universe, and bring about a new heaven or hell? How to determine which? I have watched my friends fight in the courts for their children, as if that were security—"

But he had outrun what he meant to say. "Forgive me! It is not Shelley I mean."

"Everything is sadness," Mary said tightly, "that relates to Shelley's first marriage."

"I am sorry. I know you have had losses—in this country—"

"Tell me what more you see in my book."

He turned to look over the titles on the bookcase. At length he said, "As your book is a poem, you know what the making of poems is. We rob from the dead, thinking to put Milton's tongue in our own mouths. But supposing our made thing carried its own spark of life, and moved its own limbs—" His fingers hung in the air without completing the thought. "I suppose Christ's words had that power. And Rousseau's. Doctor Vaccà has told me his stories of Paris."

"The doctor enjoys his stories."

He looked into her sun-crossed face. "I have not written since my illness. It changed me. I wish different things now."

Her brow lifted, inquiring.

"I should like to make something that speaks as your book does, or Shelley's masque. Something that joins artistry to purpose. The freedom of England—the freedom of men—is not a matter on which I would be silent."

The words took him up, and he was surprised at the throb in his voice. But perhaps Mary mistrusted it; her brow was still lifted. He looked down and said the humiliating thing. "You may say I am seeking an education."

"One is ever seeking it," she said, and pulled a volume from the shelf. "This book is my mother's. It is on France—a reply to Burke."

Keats shook his head. "I have read little philosophy by the Tories."

"Burke was no Tory."

Yes, a schoolmistress. But he took the red morocco volume and turned a few pages. The Rights of Men. The Rights of Woman.

"Burke was a disappointed Whig," Mary said, "and he misunderstood France. Yet he foresaw there would be more killing. He suspected that, in the end, some popular general would take power and make war on Europe. My mother despised him."

"Because he was in the right?"

"He was *not* in the right. He made his prophecies, but about the deeper thing—about liberty—he was wrong. Liberty is not a gift from Lord Liverpool. It is not inherited like a set of spoons."

Keats looked up, expecting a speech, but she had dropped her eyes.

"My mother did not live to see what became of France," she said quietly. "I never knew her."

"It is a great loss."

"And now all is done, and France has a king once more. So I must hold these things together in my mind. That Burke foresaw everything, and yet that he was wrong, and my mother was right."

She was talking almost to herself. Perhaps she was talking to the book. Keats felt himself suddenly superfluous in the room, or rather that this room was her mind, where he had not been invited to step.

"And that task," he said carefully, "is why you wrote your monster story?"

"I don't know why I wrote my monster story. Everything I am is in my mother's book."

In the dusk hour Shelley stepped from the back room in rumpled shirtsleeves, abstracted, with the day's writing behind him. Often he held Percy Florence in his arms, and when Mary reached for the child, drawing them both to her breast, Keats felt himself a lonely particle in space. It was incredible, he said to Shelley, that anyone could compose poetry with an eighteen months' child in the room.

"A child is most improving company for a poet," said Shelley. "He shows you the birth of speech at first hand. A bird sings out the window, he answers the song—he is Adam! He has named it."

Medwin, arrived in the meantime, would repeat something he had read about the relation between the Sanskrit and the Greek, and how German scholars had found out the original language of mankind, at least to a few words. Mother, father. One horse, two horse.

"Well, those are Percy Florence's words exactly," said Shelley. "We all might return to nature with him."

"Must we follow nature in all things?" asked Mary, peering into the child's face. "The male animal is stronger than the female."

Very true, said the men, and talked of the subjection of women. Shelley had begun to call on the governor's daughter locked in her convent outside the city, though Keats didn't understand how he arranged the visits. The girl was a captive bird, said Shelley, caged by native barbarism. Keats shifted in his seat, afraid that Mary would become angry, or else that Shelley would decide to kidnap the girl in his boat. But all that followed were theories of society. In ancient Greece, said Shelley, women were degraded nearly to slavery; surely it was this insult that had turned Greek men to their particular practices.

Medwin giggled into his palm. Mavrokordatos scowled and said that Shelley must be thinking of the Romans, the perverse Romans. "There is Aphrodite," he said.

"Aphrodite is an ideal," said Shelley. "We know they found their usual beauty in the male."

Medwin pressed his hand tighter against pink cheeks, and Shelley insisted that he meant no base imputation. "After all," he said, "no one knew precisely what was the amorous practice."

"Why, I know what was the practice," said Medwin.

"The literature is silent!" Shelley insisted. "Read Plato's *Banquet*, or any of the highest productions, and you will see such a height of feeling as could never be coupled with any—ah, painful and horrible usage. If one considers those physiological experiences that come at the dawn of manhood, in sleep—"

"Oh, yes?" Medwin asked with a great grin.

Shelley lifted his blue eyes to the ceiling and said in his unassuming boy's voice, "The satisfaction must have been innocent. Perhaps it was a mere clasping of arms."

Medwin slapped his knee. "Then who washed the linen?"

Keats stood, and expressed regret that his hosts would expect him at home for supper.

Medwin gave him a sly look. "And who would not dine at Casa Vaccà? That wine cellar! And that daughter!"

"Mr. Keats chases no one's daughter," said Mary.

He left the palazzo with embers in his heart. But his joy was always an overfull vessel, always wanting to flip over and void itself. After walking a block the spark turned sickeningly bright, and he had to shut his eyes and steady himself, pressing his hand to a sun-warmed wall. At the Vaccà house he found father and son smoking cigarillos in the sitting room. The moment he stepped in, Leopoldo leaped up, grabbed his arm and began to declaim something that seemed to be the middle of a speech, full of the word *rivoluzione*.

"What, here?" Keats looked past the drapes to the sunny street, quiet as a painting.

"In Piedmont! Turin is free!" Leopoldo swung back to his father. "Tell him, babbo—the carbonari flag over the barracks. Blue, black and red! The charcoal flame!"

"What I heard this afternoon from the governor's aide," said Vaccà, "and it is not certain, is that Victor Emmanuel has given up the throne to his nephew. There is talk of a constitution. I suppose it will be the same that the Neapolitans have imposed."

"A constitution!" crowed Leopoldo. "Our Grand Duke shall quake in his breeches."

"Ebbene," said Vaccà, sucking his cigarillo, "don't confuse the Grand Duke with the Bourbon kings. Our duke is not a bad man. His advisors thrust the worst policies upon him."

"Oh, babbo, you too? The advisors, the advisors—how can you be so naive? All because the fellow gave you a clock!"

Keats looked down, considering. "If the Austrians sent an army to Naples," he said, "I suppose Turin shall have the same?"

"I suppose," said Vaccà.

Leopoldo bit his lip, and from the front hall came the laughter of women.

"It's arrived!" Giuditta cried, and came half running through the doorway with her arms thrown out. Seeing Keats, she put her hand to her mouth. "Oh! Wait, mother, he's here."

"Ought I to be elsewhere?" Keats asked.

Vaccà stood. "We have a gift."

"For me? No."

Signora Vaccà stepped into the room bearing a brilliant red

emblem. It ran the height of her body to the floor, and there billowed into the sleeves and tail of a coat. Keats dropped his eyes to his own stained sleeves. Fanny had hemmed the cuffs in fine fingerwork, nearly invisible; only he saw it.

"That is a good Tuscan red," said Vaccà. "The Guelph lily."

Keats shrugged back his old coat in a slow convulsion. The white-haired footman, who had come in behind Signora Vaccà and had probably been long awaiting this chance, took it in his spotted hands, flipped it over his arm and bore it from the room.

"Don't destroy it!" Keats cried.

"He shall not harm a thread that is yours," said Vaccà.

The new coat was a cotton velvet as thick as the other, with the same angled cut at the skirts, and lined in burgundy satin. It had gilt buttons like crushed stars, three to a side. Giuditta held it to his shoulders. He slid his arms into the sleeves, straightened his back and turned slowly in the new embrace.

"You want only a sword," said Leopoldo, "and you are a soldier of Italy."

Giuditta kept pace behind him, her small fingers tugging at his shoulders and settling the line at his waist. "Just so, Mother," she said, "a fine fit for our little Englishman." She leaped back with a feline grin, knowing she stood at the edge of cruelty.

The Captive

IN OPEN COUNTRY EACH MORNING came brighter and warmer than the last, and cypress and pine dipped their boughs over the river like retreating shadows. The current ran quick in the center; at the reedy bank it slowed and skimmer insects went dancing on the slight, ductile membrane that the water raised against the element of air. Dragonflies glinted the blue of burning gas. A scattering of pepper grains in the sky became a flock of starlings that fell upon the cypress, for a minute or two traded leaps among the boughs and grassy bank, then rose in a storm and winged downriver. A mossy smell hung on the water, and a hint of brine from the west, where a last bend hid the river's mouth.

The convent, set on a rise above the bank, was the only work of man in the valley. Its low tower of medieval stone was joined to a circuit of newer walls capped by curving ironwork that ran along the cells and eating hall, about the chapel with its bell of weathered green bronze and back again to the grove of dark trees that spread over the garden. The bell had rung at dawn, and women's voices risen in chanting. Now there was only wind in the leaves. From the top of the tower one might have looked down and seen the sisters moving about the grounds, pulling weeds and drawing water from the well. From below one saw only barred windows, and clumps of wild grass gone to seed.

A craft came from upriver, oblong and slight, skimming the surface like a fallen leaf. From a distance its hull resembled tarred wood, but at closer range one saw that it was only canvas, stretched over a lattice of warped laths to form an oval cup. There were three inside, one at fore with an oar in his hands and two seated behind. The pilot was Shelley. Leaning forward, legs in a wide crouch, he dipped his blade into the green water and held them in the main current—though his gaze kept drifting from the river to the sky and hills. Returning to earth, he made sudden correcting strokes and threw up splashes. Keats wiped his wet brow and hummed *Rule, Britannia.* Mary said that they might have been in a sailboat with a tiller, in which case they would have had Shelley steering with one hand and trying to read Plato with the other.

"To read and steer is no difficulty," Shelley said. "The one is an intellectual operation, the other purely mechanical."

"Till you turn the page," said Keats.

No one took boats on the Arno. The water was so shallow that only a craft as tiny as theirs could get draught. The Pisans thought it a perfect English madness; that morning Shelley had rowed almost to the Vaccà doorstep, and Keats, coming out to meet them, had found a small crowd leaning over the river wall, whistling and shaking their heads at the canvas bowl that shivered with every ripple.

"Ma va per la vita!" they said.

Two bends in the river wiped Pisa from view and the modern age with it. The forest valley might have been prehistoric; or, allowing for the convent, they were at least in the time of Bocaccio. Under Shelley's steering the boat stuck in the reeds ten feet from shore, and he leaped out in canvas boots. Keats's own boots were borrowed and much too large, but he helped to drag the craft through ankle-deep water to the bank. Mary came out leaping, so as not to catch her pelisse on the rim, and tightened her hood around her face as they started up the slope. It gave her a secret look. Suppose this was a tale out of Bocaccio: any traveler they met on the road would ask who were these three, what mystery bound them together.

They climbed through ankle-high yellow grass until the convent showed an arched door. Shelley marched ahead, the breeze lifting his hair, and Keats went gingerly behind. Water had gotten into his right boot and his stocking squelched. At Shelley's knock a panel swung open to reveal an iron grille, and a moment later the whole door gave way. He bowed to two forms within, robed nuns with pink faces like flowers pressed to a white page. They seemed to know Shelley and greeted him with girlish voices, smiling, like shopwives flirting with a customer. Did they know this was the town atheist?

Keats had never been inside a convent and had an idea that they would be questioned about their errand, or that he might have to profess something, or be splashed with holy water. His wet boots were awkward on the threshold. But the nuns simply turned back in the corridor, and the one in front clapped her hands.

"Teresa!" she shouted.

"Come," whispered Shelley. "We'll have her presently."

Keats squinted in the dark. "Did you not say her name was Emilia?"

"That name I chose for her. It names her soul."

Shelley lifted his fingers to his lips and peered down the corridor. Mary stood apart in her hood, strange as a painting. Icons were set in the stone walls, some painted and some carved, all very small and in a flat medieval style that seemed, to Keats, to say that human life was very simple. A few penstrokes would tell everything. A chorus carried down the hall, rising as a door opened, then faded as one of the icons came walking toward them. It was a pale woman, young, in a plain dress the same cool gray as the wall. Her white face and hands moved around it as independent things. Her black hair, caught up behind and falling over her shoulders, reminded Keats of the pictures he had seen in Florence. Catching sight of Shelley, she laughed and came up running, past the nuns who had shrunk to either side; then she collected herself, made a curtsey, and held out her pale hand for his kiss.

"Dear brother!" she said.

Keats felt constrained before beautiful women, and the Contessina Teresa Viviani, whose soul was named Emilia, was very beautiful. Her black-and-white profile, with green eyes and a faint rose in the lips, was so regular that it hardly possessed its own features. It was the ideal face. And if she were only an ideal, and not a living girl who would look at Keats and form an opinion of him, he might breathe easier.

"Another English poet!" she said to him. "I meet so many now."

"Alas," said Keats, "then you know we are not all Shelley."

She laughed. "And were you also driven from your native land? I think exile must be the bitterest thing."

"Oh, mine is not a poetic exile. I keep finding myself in the wrong carriage."

"We are all of us exiles on earth," offered Shelley, "all seeking our spirit's home."

"So we are!" said the girl. "Often I have thought it." She gave Shelley a look as if to ask how he had read her mind, and he answered that it was natural for sister spirits to share such inspirations, never mind their differences in native clime.

"Tell Keats the infamy you suffer," he urged.

She sighed. It was weary to hear, she said. She had lived four years in the convent, ever since her father had taken her stepmother to wife. She had refused the first suitor her father chose her. In two months she must marry the last. She might not refuse him, nor stay the appointed date.

"I am sorry to know it," said Keats. "Perhaps you should say no more."

The Contessina blinked and looked to Shelley.

"If it is weary to hear," Keats said gently, "it must be all the more so to tell. Even these walls"—he gestured to the file of icons—"seem to have only sad messages for us."

"Oh!" She smiled. "You are not a tragic poet. You love life. We should go into the garden."

She led them down the hall. The nuns had gone through a side doorway, and as they passed the opening Keats saw women at desks and a sister at front leading them in a monotone chant. Were these the nuns of the convent? No. They wore gray dresses like the Contessina's and their hair fell uncovered over their backs. The Contessina herself walked very near Keats for a few paces, glancing sideways at him, but he had nothing to say and she withdrew, falling into step with Shelley.

"Do you believe," she asked the taller poet, "that such inspirations come to us from former lives?"

They went through another arched doorway, Shelley holding the door open, and came to a stone porch from which a half dozen steps led down to a sunlit green diamond enclosed by pines and yellow walls. A cobbled path wound among beds of purple and white blossoms: thyme and basil, verbena, some strange flower in bell-shaped clusters. Sap hung thick in the air. Shelley went down the steps together with the Contessina, talking quietly of Plato's myths of the soul, the insults and abuses that love suffered in this world and the reward it must find in the next.

"I believe the loving soul leaps out from creation," said the girl, "and creates a world for itself in the infinite."

Keats hung back and searched out Mary's face under her hood. Had she fallen into the look of the Gorgon? Was she going to shout at Shelley?

No. She was peaceful. She looked at the flowers and smiled at nothing.

The Contessina pointed to an iron gate in the back wall. "That is not latched. We might pass through and walk to the river."

"Is it permitted?" Shelley asked.

She smiled mischievously and glanced behind her. "I think for a short time. Perhaps if someone remains—"

"Provident escape!" said Shelley. "A faery gate!"

The two of them crossed the garden. Without quite glancing back to confirm that the others would stay, Shelley swung open the portal. The daughter of Pisa's first family led him through, speaking of love, and the gate closed behind them.

"A faery gate!" murmured Keats. "He thinks that?"

Mary bent her face over the flowers. "You think otherwise?"

"I think this place is no prison. It is a school. The girl has been telling stories."

She kept her face in the flowers a long time, and at last pushed back her hood. "Certainly you wished not to hear them."

"I am sorry for the forced marriage. On my honor, I pity her. But do you not think there are ways of telling it? Did you not see the other girls at their lesson?"

"I saw them." Her face was calm, shut to him. Did she not understand he was her advocate?

"I own," he said, "I know not what it is for a girl to spend four years in this place. I suppose she might play a part without knowing which drama it comes from. She might get others to play alongside her. But a grown man must know better."

Mary had turned away and wandered among the violet blossoms, holding her shawl close.

"You don't suppose there is going to be a rescue?" he called. "That having quit the garden, Shelley is escaping with her in his boat?"

She spun round. "Next to Shelley," she said, "every man in the world is fatally hard of heart."

He winced under her cold brown eyes. He remembered what Shelley had said of her suffering, the dead children, and it came to him that he might open a channel to her heart. The morning after his father's carriage accident, they had rushed him home from school before first prayers. A gray handkerchief lay over his father's face, and he supposed a devil had snatched the face from under the cloth; but his father was only dead. His mother took to her bed. Her red hair fell in tangles around her eyes, and her eyes followed the bowl in his hands. When he brought the spoon to her lips they would not move to take it.

But it might be wrong—it might be egoism—to speak of these things, merely to open a channel to her heart.

"Why does Shelley bring you here?" he asked softly. "To

come alone would be kinder."

"All love is one. That is his gospel." Her voice was stark, conceding nothing.

"But that is untrue."

"Is it?"

"Love can't be one. It takes so many objects. Why—" His voice rang hollow in his ears. There must be some argument to convince her. "There is the sparrow that picks about the gravel. A line in a book. The old book itself, worn in its corners. A bassoon."

"A bassoon?"

"Entirely! Its particular tone, how it strides—you know that is a bassoon, and no trumpet or clarinet. You are the bassoon whilst you recognize it. That is the half of love. The other half is a blessing, I think, or a holy will. But it is never apart from its object. So I say love is not one."

She gave him the same dark, inquiring look she had given the flowers. He could not sustain it. Their gazes broke and went to the shut gate, at rest in its sunlit wall.

"If Shelley could but *see* with his philosophy," Keats said. "If he did not wear it like a blindfold—"

"Don't attack him!" She made a gesture as if to push him away.

"I mean no attack."

"You understand nothing! I am the lack in him, I drive him to seek others. Why do you speak of love? I know it not."

"Mrs. Shelley. Your pardon."

"He ought to be with that girl. With anyone. His first wife could not please him—he came to me, but see, how far worse am I! Love is free, he says, but only he has the goodness for it."

She was trying to repel him. She spoke coldly, as if compelled by reason, but he saw that anger made her reason far harsher. She stood among the flowers with burning eyes and dared him to accept her words.

"I have wished to die," she said.

What had he unlocked? "Many have wished it," he said.

She lowered her voice. "You are a medical man. Is it not possible, in this country, to procure the essence of bitter almond? Is it not only a drop?" She came closer, bringing her pale face to his. "I wish one thing I might take as my own. One atom that depends upon nothing else. If I could but hold it in my hands and say, this much none may have from me—no one's property—"

"I am engaged," said Keats.

She bit her lip and stepped away. Her eyes dropped and she took a few steps among the flowers, the shadows of boughs flickering over her shawl.

"I have not heard you speak of it," she said.

"Often I cannot think of it."

"She is in England?"

"She writes from Hampstead. And I write to Hampstead, when I can compel myself. I wonder if I am a monster."

She made a sudden, bitter laugh. "It is not monstrous to wish freedom from an attachment."

"Freedom!" he exclaimed. "Did I say that?"

"Perhaps. What is she to you?"

He gave her a long look and said, "She is my betrothed."

"Oh!" She dismissed him with a wave. "If it is the betrothal, and not herself—"

Quiet settled on them. The sun traced each thing in the garden and froze it where it stood. A spotted thrush burst from under leaves, gained the back wall and left them. Time in the garden turned rocky and still, shored against the moment when the gate swung back open and the Contessina stepped through, followed by Shelley with his face warm and pink. He spoke fast and low, out of breath, and she shook her head.

"I must go," she said. "We've been too long."

"Say it to Mary," Shelley begged, "that thought you so well expressed."

She gave Keats and Mary a sideways look. "You may leave

through the back gate. No one need dismiss you."

She broke from Shelley, clutched her gray skirts and hurried up the stairs. As she vanished, Keats turned to find Mary already gone through the gate and Shelley trailing after, casting backward glances. He followed slowly with his head down. Outside the gate he asked dully, "Had you a pleasant walk?"

Shelley sighed in answer. "Pleasure and pain," he said, "not to be disentangled."

Mary was halfway down the slope, her hood drawn up and her skirts sweeping the grass behind her.

"How the girl suffers here," Shelley mused. "And yet the beauty she goes in, garbed herself in beauty, along the noble river—"

He could talk that way, Keats supposed, without engaging the cerebrum at all. His lips and tongue did the work on their own. As they walked down the slope Shelley fell into a hymn on the sun and trees and water, and the old roads of the Florentine merchant-kings. His cheeks and temples were ruddy with sun and the slight wrinkles at his eyes stood out in white. Keats trudged beside him, helped him push the wet boat off the bank and held it steady as Mary stepped inside. She settled herself on the struts with her arms folded, still as a carving, and together they towed the craft back into the weedy water. All at once a caprice of the current took up the craft and spun it rapidly out from shore. Keats started and leaped after. He landed behind Mary, his boots trailing in the water, and the craft rocked as if lifted by a hand. Shelley stumbled at fore, pitched forward and vanished.

Mary stretched her arm. "He can't swim!"

Keats pushed himself from the deck and dropped into the water. The river slapped his face and its cool muscle pressed him down. He was not a strong swimmer. But he could hold his position by splashing and soon enough discovered an impediment to the splashing, which was Shelley beside him. The body rested face down in the water, weightless, neither floating nor sinking. Keats gripped his waist, tumbled his legs beneath him and kicked back to the boat. Mary caught the limp arm and pulled it, and as they lifted him from the water, dead white and dripping from his hair and clothes, he coughed in a sudden convulsion. Eyes shut, he began to laugh.

"Are you all right?" Mary cried.

"Divine," he said, and coughed again as they laid him on his back. "In the water—such peace. I might have stayed forever."

"You would have stayed three minutes," said Keats. "Did you never swim as a boy?"

"Swimming?" Shelley's eyes opened and he made a wry face. "I have read of the practice."

He began his laugh again. It was a high, unworldly sound that seemed to descend from the sky and expressed nothing but mockery for the three of them in the boat, tied to their wayward bodies. It was indifferent to life and death. Mary cradled his head in her hands and stroked the wet hair at his temples, but the laugh would not stop, and her fingers fell away. She looked up at Keats and he gently touched Shelley's shoulder. He could not read her gaze but felt they had contracted an alliance against the man between them.

Quinine

The Vaccàs kept their carriage house north of the river, on a deserted street fronting the slanted tower. At first light Keats and Leopoldo passed beneath its shadow, turned on the grassy cobbles and found the stable doors already thrown open to the street. A pair of horses stood in the low sun, being harnessed by the angry student who had to wear Church robes for his scholarship, and a senior student Keats knew from the café, and also Giuditta, who was moving around in the shade of a broad hat and a man's jacket much too large for her. Leopoldo stumbled when he caught sight of her, and threw out his arms.

"How are you here!" he cried.

She waved her hat at him. "Good morning, fratello mio! Are we not bound for the marshes?"

He rounded on his colleagues. "Who brought her?"

"None," said Giuditta; "I determined myself. You talk very freely at home, O conspirator."

Leopoldo arched his brows. "Oh, you are an acute girl. I laud your perspicacity. Get home."

"Gladly!" she said. "And mightn't I stop in the hospital, and tell Father your brave errand?"

"But you make us too many," he said petulantly, and his brows collapsed. "We won't fit in the phaeton." He peered into the carriage house, where the sport car sat teetering on its high wheels.

She laughed. "You, driving Father's phaeton? Into the first bog?"

Keats put a hand on Leopoldo's shoulder and said, "Come, you can't be too angry. She is doing just as you would have done. You know she is precisely you."

"Grazie," she said. "Listen to your Englishman."

"The barouche will hold five," said the senior student, "with one as driver—should you trust me with the reins, madam."

She bowed, dipping her hat. "Let someone have brain in the medical school."

Leopoldo reddened, reached into his coat and stood with the quinine packet in his fist. The barouche was rolled out and its shafts hitched into the harness. They left off the top and started past the first fields under a clear sky, now lightened to dusty blue. Giuditta sat beside Keats and adjusted her hat against the morning sun. In the opposite seat Leopoldo measured pinches from his packet and dropped them back in. The angry student, having nothing to be angry about, smiled in his robes and might really have been a young priest going into the country.

They climbed from the fields into the folded hills, took a northward turn and dropped into a sunless valley of pines. Ivy ran thick under the boughs and they rattled among dark tendrils until the sun popped up and all at once they came to the water's edge. The river, shaking free of the hills, spread in a silver mirror across a floodplain dotted with marsh grass and yellow clumps of reed. The road ahead sank to a loamy track between slimed-over pools. A light brimstone smell hung in the air.

"These are pestilential marshes?" Keats asked.

"Every marsh in Italy is pestilential," the driver called back. "The malaria from here to Naples."

He slowed the horses. Yellow mud dripped from their wheels and water welled up in the tracks behind. At the top of a buckthorn a pair of jackdaws blinked gray eyes and cackled. They passed houses walled with irregular slats, in places only sticks, and thatched with bundles of reed grass. Most had no windows and their crooked entries were without doors. A fence circled a muddy stock pen where bristly black pigs lay at peace. As they neared the walled town ahead, a larger structure drew apart, built from brick and ruined from front to back. Its entire length stood open to the sky and a pale carpet of weeds ran over its floor, dotted with seed tufts and yellow flowers and swelling here and there in suggestion of a structure beneath. Outside the walls lay several rectangular beds of earth, overgrown and broken in their lines. To Keats the whole affair had the look of a tomb. It was more sinister than the ruins at Rome; it seemed a recent death, the blood not dry.

"The old gunpowder works," murmured Leopoldo. "From the wars."

They stopped beside a livestock pen and goats came trotting to stretch their necks over the fence and sniff the horses. As the party climbed out, Leopoldo grabbed Keats by the shoulder and slapped his neck. He pulled away a palm smeared with bright blood and the small, dark wreck of a mosquito.

"Diavolo," he said, wiping it on the grass.

A group of brown men leaned against the fence, axes and long knives at their feet. They were naked to the waist and sucked blue smoke from their pipes. Giuditta wrinkled her nose and said that it smelled like burning tar.

"Would you rather smell the goats?" asked Leopoldo. "Or the marsh? On my honor, I don't know why you're here."

He made a gallant nod at the men, who stared back without interest, as if watching birds go by.

They climbed a hill to the town's open gate and passed through into a narrow piazza. Past the church with its plaster Madonna they found a broad stone building with eaves slanted so low that one had to duck to pass. A half door hung in the entry, under a slat on which a rod of Asclepius had been scored with a knifepoint. Leopoldo rapped it and a grunt answered. It did not sound to Keats like a welcome, but Leopoldo had already pulled back the door. The dimness within was broken by blue light from a ceiling trapdoor, under which a thick, young-faced man sat naked to the waist with a half-raveled splint around his forearm. A woman in a peasant kerchief stood behind him and a dark old fellow with a wild gray beard knelt before. At Keats's entry he looked up and showed a face marked with red whorls from beard to hairline. His left socket, missing eye and brow, was folded over in a compression of scars.

"Who's that?" he barked.

"The quinine," said Keats.

Leopoldo put a hand on Keats's shoulder and begged to introduce his great friend, a doctor visiting from London, to Don Niccolò di Natale.

"Oh, it's young Vaccà," said the man, and relaxed. "Don't call me Don. Who are the others?"

They came squinting through the door and Leopoldo began his introductions, but Niccolò's eye went to Giuditta in her oversized hat and jacket. "And who is that? You don't mean to say Pisa has women in the medical school?"

The students laughed. "God preserve us!" they said.

"Thank you," said Giuditta, bowing. "I should rather be an actress. Then I might be a doctor, and a soldier, and a lady at court, all in the same night."

Niccolò snorted. "They have a different kind of play at Pisa now. Will you act a nurse and fetch me that wheat-paste?"

He unraveled what was left of the splint and exposed a pair of snapped planks that had pressed welts into the man's forearm. Giuditta handed him a clay pot of viscous white and he began to soak a fresh strip while checking the line of the planks. It was all too much for two hands, and without thinking Keats tossed back his red coat and stepped in to take the patient's arm at the wrist. The limb was swollen—he could see it had been a bad fracture—but it was well set and the line of bone ran true. Niccolò gave him a curious look, but allowed him to hold the planks in place as he began winding the strip.

"You should have come on pharmacy day, young Vaccà," he said. "I've nothing to give out but camphor and laudanum. Is your Englishman not deceived about that powder?"

"Why no," said Leopoldo, brightening, and dropped the

packet on the bench. Niccolò hefted the weight and made a wry face.

"All he can spare, I suppose. How is your father?"

"Ever my father," said Leopoldo.

"Lorenzo de' Medicina continues his happy reign," said the student in Church robes.

"Ha!" the doctor said. "It was a puppy Lorenzo I knew. He hadn't yet gone to France and become a genius."

"Are the quotidian fevers common here?" Keats asked.

Niccolò looked at him as if at a dull child. "Of course the quotidian fevers are common. I have them. The women have them. This fellow on the bench is sure to have them, if he hasn't already." He wiped the paste from his smallest finger, poked it into the powder, touched his tongue and spat. "It tastes evil enough. Do you know a dose?"

"Grana duo," said Leopoldo, "sexta quaque hora sumenda."

"Thank you, Cato. A fine lot of Latin we speak out here. Nobody has so nice a measuring spoon. I told you the last time, if you want to be useful you ought to make up pills."

"We might do so now," said the senior student. "Have you materials?"

"There's a balance. Flour and tallow will have to do for your binding. Go ask the neighbors—let young Vaccà ask. They might open their fists." He grinned, showing yellow teeth, and gripped Keats's elbow as he made to stand.

"Not you. You've started the job."

The students skirted the stove and cot and wooden trunks, ducked their heads under the sausages hanging from the rafters and filed back outside. Giuditta stopped at the door, fixed her dark eyes on their work and cautiously made to return. She had never seen Keats in practice; nor, it occurred to him, would she have seen her father. He held the planks to the patient's arm and the doctor wound the bandage, dripping paste over the bench, till the binding began to cling to itself and the wood drew firm. The young patient sat motionless, looking into the corners through the hair falling over his brow. Giuditta spread her skirt, knelt on the earth floor and asked his name.

He bent his neck in a sort of bow. "Zenzo, signora."

"May I ask how you were hurt, Zenzo?"

"Beh, signora—our horse—"

"Don't you blame the horse!" said the old woman, and began to talk in dialect. She kept repeating the word *aratro*, plow; it seemed the lesson was that a plow handle must be held in a certain way and not another. *Stupidotto, stupidotto*, she said, making Zenzo wince, until the doctor held up his hand.

"It's not the lad's fault that he's a blockhead. No one ever taught him to plow."

"Primo taught him," said the old woman.

"Primo with the clubfoot?" The doctor shook his head. "This is what happens to us," he told Keats. "The lad is a child during the wars. His father and brothers are off in someone's regiment and never come home. So who's to take him into the fields but women and old men? He takes a plow that he can't hold, and hitches it to a team he can't drive, and he gets his forearm snapped. That's how we go hungry in the spring."

"I suppose the marsh soil is poor?" said Keats.

"There's land enough down the river. It was the wars. A generation ground into meal so that Bonaparte could settle a score with the Habsburgs. Or the English settle a score with Bonaparte. Pray you tell me which."

Keats smiled. "If you will throw my nationality at me, please do remember that I come in a gang of university students, republicans all. I will give Bonaparte his due. Did he not vaccinate the country?"

"Vaccinia." The doctor sighed. "I know the students set much by it. And by the quinine powder, and whatever else they get from the university. We can't eat any of it."

"It is not only the university," Keats said. "They read the news from Naples, and from Turin."

"More Napoleons," said Niccolò, "more wars. God blind me if we need them. All the swamp out there," he said, waving at the door, "was farmland in the time of the Medici. It's never been drained since. Ours is the dark age."

He wrapped the last strip, smoothed the paste and swung the bound limb over to Giuditta.

"Help the lad out, if you will," he said, "and save him from politics. This must keep in the sun till it dries."

She offered her small, white hand to Zenzo's good arm. He turned his head shyly and rose from the bench, at which the old woman thrust her arms under his shoulders and impelled them out the doorway under the shadow of Giuditta's hat. Niccolò wiped his hands on a rag, took a stone jar from the stove and began to scrape the unused paste back inside. In a gentler voice he said, "I'm glad of the powder, young doctor. And don't think me ungrateful to the students. I would caution their hopes. Today it seems to relieve the pestilential fevers. It may not do so tomorrow."

"I see," said Keats. "You are a skeptic in all things."

"Only in what I do not understand. Physic is an accident. We find it to work once and use it blindly ever after. Tell me, how do you imagine the powder combats a pestilential fever? What is a pestilential fever?"

"Surely—a fever provoked by pestilence?"

The doctor grinned sharply. "Your pardon," Keats said, coloring. "I can only give the general opinion. The infectious principle is carried by vapors, on the damp."

"It can't be the damp alone," said Niccolò. "And I won't be answered by your calling it an infectious principle. Did you never see the play with the quack, who said it is the dormitive virtue that brings about sleep?"

Keats shook his head, pained to think that even the browned doctor might exceed him in learning.

"Why does the quinine work only against periodic fevers,

such as we have in the marshes? I tried it on other things, you know. Puerperal fever, for one. The woman died inside twelve hours."

Keats shut his eyes; he would not dispute over the dead. The half door was thrown open and the students came tramping back in, laughing about an answer that a peasant woman had given Leopoldo when he asked for tallow. But they had gotten it, and flour as well, and dragged out a water jar from the corner. The sections of the brass balance came from under the stove and were screwed into an assemblage that dipped back and forth in judgment. They squeezed the binding to muck in their palms, forced it through the channels of the mechanical roller and diced the strips into gray spherules. Faces had started to show outside, peering over the half door.

"Thirty apiece," Niccolò called, "no more, and I don't promise it will work. Come tomorrow for examination."

He and Giuditta handed paper bundles over the door, Giuditta lingering with a couple of farm lads and telling them something that made them blush under their sunburns. She laughed, enjoying her superiority. Once the heap of pills had thinned out against the bench, the visitors thinned away likewise and the students passed around a rag to wipe their palms. Flour streaked everyone's sleeves and collars. Niccolò put a hand on Keats's shoulder.

"Tell me truly," he murmured, "what are you doing here? What business have the English in our bogs?"

"I work with Professor Vaccà," Keats said. "I study, if you like."

"An Italian goes to London to study," said the doctor. "Never the reverse. Not even Andrea Vaccà could get himself an English student."

"You must believe my circumstances are complex."

The doctor harrumphed. "So must I. But I remember the grand-touring English before the wars. Those were useless gentlemen. If it isn't your government that sent you here, you might do some good."

The sun was buried and the light falling fast as their carriage climbed from the marsh back into the pines. Giuditta sat beside Keats with her jacket wrapped tight against the wind, her hat in her lap and her black curls flying like a banner. Keats took the Neapolitan newspaper from his coat pocket and could make out only Minerva's helm and a few words in the headlines. Giuditta's and Leopoldo's hands held it alongside his own. The dusk showed no difference of shade between their skins. It came to him that he would like to slough away his Englishness entirely, down to his lips and tongue.

"Does Italy have many such in the marshes?" he asked.

"Don Niccolò is an exile," said Leopoldo. "He was banished from Pisa for what he did in the wars. Did he tell you none of it? How he lost the eye?"

"I would not have asked."

"It's no secret. That gunpowder works was his. He made powder for France against the Austrians. You ought to have had the story! It happened in the late campaigns, when saltpeter couldn't be shipped in on account of the blockades. He requisitioned a farmhouse and turned the whole estate into a factory. They laid out manure and brewed it with ash and straw. Genius!"

"Then he's well used to unholy smells," said Giuditta.

"They shipped powder by the ton. It was used all over the north. If it had held, who knows but we would have kept out the Austrians for good."

"Then it did not hold," said Keats.

"My father told me. There were mills to mix the charcoal and brimstone. Don Niccolò was always in the works, refining the recipe. The mixture changes depending on the damp in the air. He stayed nights, all alone, or with just one man to help. Everything was secondhand, of course, put together from grindstones and plough-blades and I don't know what. There were metal parts that should have been stone, or the other way around. There were always sparks. In the winter there came a very cold night and the mists didn't rise off the water as usual. The whole works caught fire. It was divine luck, said my father, that Niccolò was not himself turning the mill just then, that all he lost was the eye and some skin.

"My father and I went to see it later. It was like now but fresh, with black timbers and brick thrown everywhere. You could just see the shape where the hall had been. The last campaigns were started—probably the Austrians were over the Alps already and into Lombardy. They declared the peace and set up the marquis as our governor. My father did what he could, but there was no question of Don Niccolò ever again practicing in the city. So he declared that he'd go back where the works had been, and make it a ploughshare."

In the roadside grass, a gray smear against the last purple of sky, Keats saw explosions, and threw up his hands as yellow-green lights shot past his head. "Guns!" he cried.

"Lucciole!" Leopoldo knocked for the barouche to stop, and he and Giuditta climbed to stand on their seats, stretching their arms to the floating sparks.

"They're early," Leopoldo called. "A warm night."

Giuditta lunged and a star vanished in her cupped hands. "Turn your palms," she told Keats. "So."

She released the light between his fingers. It winked out and back again, filling the tiny chamber of the animal's back parts. The feelers of the head, the articulated legs trembled against his skin, and after a moment's breath the oval-cased wings shimmered and carried the star back into the night.

It was wholly dark when they reached the city. Keats jogged along the hushed river in back of Leopoldo and Giuditta. "What shall we tell Babbo," asked the children, "whatever shall we tell him?" At the palazzo steps they cut their voices to whispers and crept up, breathing hard, in hope their absence had gone unnoticed—but the lord and lady of the house were standing in the front hall, dressed to go out of doors. Both had looks of sadness that turned sharp with surprise when they discovered Keats and the children at the door.

Keats drew breath, ready to take responsibility for everything. But Doctor Vaccà was not looking at him. He held out a printed sheet and Leopoldo stepped forward to take it.

"The date?" Leopoldo asked.

"Two weeks ago," said Vaccà. "It is the last."

The crest was that of the *Minerva Napolitana*. The headline escaped Keats. That word *campagna*, was it a campaign, or the countryside? Love freedom, hate tyranny. There was something about the defense of the city.

"The battle in the mountains?" he asked.

Leopoldo shook his head. "It is over. The Austrians will be at the gates of Naples."

"They will be through them," said Vaccà. "Ferdinand is king again."

"So soon?" Keats asked. No one answered. A quarter hour later came a second paper, a pair of lines that somebody—one would never know who—had scrawled on a ripped corner and folded tight for a journey. The Austrians had won the day at Novara. Turin was taken as well.

"It is finished!" Leopoldo cried, and dropping to his knees began to weep. His father and sister took his shoulders.

"It has happened before," Vaccà said gently. "It is not so hard for you. No one will banish you from the cafés, or take away your books."

"But Turin—but Naples—"

There was nothing to tell him. Keats too laid a hand on the lad's thin shoulder and left it there, knowing full well that no consolation can be given to a young man weeping over what he has read in the newspaper.

Epipsychidion

THE SUN CAME UP BLANK, an indifferent god, and threw laughing light on the water. The Shelleys' palazzo seemed defeated by it. The bricks squatted around the doors and confessed their failure to be more than dumb stone. Keats followed the footman's coat up the stairs, revolving dark thoughts: what a bother was a stairway, how many hours of life one spent climbing it, how soon that labor would be lost if one chose to topple out the window. He had come to a house of mourning. Vaccà had turned very quiet after giving the news from Naples, and Leopoldo as well; it was Giuditta who had paced the hall, spitting curses at Metternich. Keats was surprised that she knew who Metternich was. Watching them grieve for their nation, he had felt his presence to be an imposition and had retired early to his room. With the Shelleys it would be otherwise. Italy was theirs by adoption, and the claim needed constant renewal; their wound would be shallower but keen.

He was shown into the parlor. Mavrokordatos stood at the hearth, reading aloud—was it Greek?—a newspaper he held before him. In the other hand he swung about his costume sword from Carnival night. Shelley stood just outside the blade's circuit, with a strange grin on his face and eyes full of weary fire. Catching sight of Keats, he leaped over the ottoman, and Mavrokordatos dropped his sword to follow.

"Poetes fileleftheros!" cried the prince, throwing out an embracing arm.

"Hi," said Keats, swamped in eau de Portugal. "You've had the news?"

Mavrokordatos showed a fierce, bearded smile. "Greece is free!"

"Greece?"

"You don't know!" Shelley and the prince began to talk over each other. There had been revolts in the Peloponnese, and other Eastern-sounding places that Keats hadn't heard of. Ypsilantis had given a proclamation, which Mavrokordatos began to read from his newspaper, attempting a translation as he went.

"But I knew nothing," said Keats. "I meant the news from Turin, and from Naples."

"Extremely sad," said Mavrokordatos.

"I believe it an unwavering principle," said Shelley, "that when the torch of liberty is extinguished in one place, it must be kindled in another."

"Doctor Vaccà and his family are greatly distressed."

"Of course they are! It cannot but be distressing to be abandoned by history. So often is human progress too subtle for earthly eyes—one discerns its orbit only from afar. Naples and Turin will have their day. Today it is the isthmus of Corinth."

"And the day is for deeds, not talk," said Mavrokordatos. "This morning is my adieu."

He bent to pick up his sword and dangled the naked point over the hearth rug. The blade was broader than Keats remembered. Perhaps this wasn't the costume sword from Carnival; or perhaps that sword had not been a costume.

"You go to fight?" he asked.

The prince bowed. "My uncle and I will take ship from Marseilles. Everything is arranged. Prince Ypsilantis—" His voice dropped. "Sometimes one hears things that are not true, but I am told he asked after me particularly."

He was not boasting. Standing at full height with his beard and strangely lettered newspaper, in a jacket and cap of yellow silk, he was revealed as a man of importance. It seemed that his time in Pisa must have been a parenthesis, and his true life now resumed.

"God bless you!" said Keats, and clasped the other's arm.

"We must go directly," said Shelley. "Our man is getting up

the coach."

"And Mrs. Shelley?"

"In back, writing."

The prince twirled his newspaper and sword and walked out to the landing. Keats was left alone in the parlor. The hall stood open behind him, and with the sense of a repeated dream he silently crossed the rug to the place where he had last spied on the Shelleys writing together. Today the study door was shut. He might peer through the keyhole; but he paused in his crouch, for he heard a sob from the other side. He raised a fist and rapped twice, very lightly. A gasp answered. He touched the door, found it stubborn, pushed harder and loosed it with a tremendous crack that caused her to bolt from her writing table, scattering sheets, the child in her arms.

"Your pardon!" he said.

She stood with an empty face. Her hair fell in tangles; her eyes were red-rimmed over wet cheeks. She was the Gorgon again. Without breaking her look of stone, she lifted one hand from the sleeping child and waved it slowly over herself. The meanings were many, if he would follow them. He had seen too much of her suffering. It was weakness; it shamed her; but the greater fault was his for stepping unannounced into a closed room. There was a tightness at the corner of her mouth, hinting at some caustic amusement that ran far below the surface of her suffering, a river under ice.

"I will go if you wish it," he said.

She folded herself around the child's body and dropped into the chair, hair falling forward over her face. He ought to go. But a fine impulse, perhaps the surgeon in him, encouraged him to probe the wound.

"You had a last interview with Mavrokordatos?" It should have been a question; it seemed to accuse. "The freedom of Greece? Or—" She rocked from side to side, swinging her hair over Percy Florence's head, and Keats understood it had nothing to do with

Greece. It was the grief for Italy that he had thought to find in this house, that Greece had overshadowed. He put his hands behind his back.

"I am intruding," he said in a lower tone. "I came in sympathy. Last night I had the news from Naples. I was with Vaccà—"

"Oh, God!" she cried. One hand patted madly at Percy Florence's curls; the other flew over the sheets on the writing table. "Must you see it? Will you not rest till you've seen it?"

Keats stood dumb. In sleep the child's features were softer than anything human. The head was flung back, the wet mouth open over the white throat, the shut eyelids veined blue and fringed with gold. Above the writing table hung silhouettes, the faces of older children with stronger features and thick hair. Those were the dead.

"You must be at the bottom of everything," said Mary. "My day's work." She thrust half a dozen pages at Keats. "He would have me write out the fair copy."

He smoothed them and turned them upright. The lines were in Shelley's hand. They were written in haste, heavily canceled, and titled:

> Verses Addressed to the Noble and Unfortunate
> Lady Emilia V—, Now Imprisoned in the
> Convent of —.

> Her Own Words—

A transcription followed of the thing Keats remembered the girl saying at the convent, that the loving soul leapt out from creation. At top was a word he had never seen.

"Epiphys—" he said. "Psych—"

"You may translate it," said Mary, "as a soul that has grown upon another soul, as if it were mistletoe. A parasite."

What could one do with these verses? He could not read

them as poetry. It was a forest of exclamation points, addresses to
the girl—sweet Spirit! Poor captive bird! Seraph of Heaven!

> Would we two had been twins of the same mother!
> Or, that the name my heart lent to another
> Could be a sister's bond for her and thee,
> Blending two beams of one eternity!

"Ah. He has household plans." There was a mocking lilt in his
voice, not natural to him; he wanted to touch the bitter laughter in
her. "Would you have such a sister?"

"The sun and moon cannot be sisters," said Mary.

He paused, unsure of her meaning, and she rapped the paper.
"You are not reading."

He must ignore her lowered face, the ungroomed smell of
her body; likewise the cancellations and crabbed hand on the page.
The poet seeks the spirit of beauty. He wanders. One stands in his
path who seems to be the sun, but is in truth

> The cold chaste Moon, the Queen of Heaven's bright
>   isles,
> Who makes all beautiful on which she smiles,
> That wandering shrine of soft yet icy flame
> Which ever is transformed, yet still the same,
> And warms not but illumines.

In a cold bed the moon's face shines upon the poet. His being
grows bright and dim as she waxes and wanes; a death of ice en-
gulfs him. All comes in a dream. Among a forest of budding thorns
the poet is given to meet Emily, the sun.

Twin spheres of light, who rule my earth of love, join in my
heaven! Do not disdain each other! Govern me by turns, day and
night! A ship is floating in the harbor. Wilt thou sail with me? Our
breaths shall intermix, our bosoms bound—I pant, I sink, I trem-

ble, I expire!

Keats blushed and dropped the sheet with a sudden feeling of having looked through a keyhole.

"At least you have a place in the solar system." The lilt was still in his voice. Mary rocked her head back and forth, and as the child stirred she laid a finger across the shut eyes.

"On parasites," Keats tried again, "I believe Doctor Vaccà advises a treatment—"

"The parasite is I," said Mary.

He reached for her shoulder and she started away. He sank kneeling on the rug, bringing his face to hers, and she twisted her neck to hide herself.

"Mary," he said.

"You see me naked, Keats," she said. "You see the black thing I am."

"A fit is speaking."

"Were she mistress of his body, I should not care. It does as it will. But that he must go seeking his twin spirit—" She spoke with awful clarity; she was irrefutable as Euclid. "I am the darkest spot in his life."

"No," said Keats.

"I shall never be worthy of him, nor of his child. I would be erased."

"No."

Again he touched her shoulder. Her neck untwisted and her dark eyes, swollen under their drape of hair, sought his. She rocked forward, paused, bent nearer, and as his hand slid from her shoulder to her nape she laid her dry, warm, half-closed mouth against his lips and let it quiver there, a captive insect. He pressed back and she retreated, came to rest on his cheek, again darted away and moved the insect of her kiss from his cheekbone to the corner of his eye, his temple and ear, the bend of his jaw, the side of his throat. Her nose and eyelashes brushed his face. He touched the shifting cords of her neck. Her arms were caught under the child and he imagined them moving together in a confined space, their limbs held fast. He remembered Paolo and Francesca. They embrace in the whirlwind, arms and lips given to each other. Yet they are locked in Hell.

A noise came from behind and Keats fell on his haunches. Shelley stood in the doorway, his eyes fixed on the space of air where their faces had joined.

"Why!" he said.

Keats pushed against the rug and tottered to his feet. His body had fled its reins, his knees escaped him. Something possessed his tongue and stuttered, "I am at your disposal."

Shelley squinted. "Your pardon?"

A high hiccup of laughter escaped Mary. "He won't *fight* you—"

Percy Florence kicked in her lap, screwing his eyes shut, and began to wail. Shelley stepped closer and Keats, discovering his legs beneath him, made a desperate stagger for the open doorway. He collided with a chair, pushed away, stumbled past the books, the drapes, the blank marble eyes of Diana and Apollo.

"I say!" Shelley cried.

Keats gained the landing, the child's shriek still pursuing, and tumbled down the stairs. The flush of love touched his cheeks, and a rising sensation far worse, a nausea that poisoned his blood. He had made a false step. The thread of time had spun only a moment. Yet he could not spin it back—he could not retrieve the moment before. As he burst onto the threshold his elbow was seized, and he was spun round to face Shelley's delicate brow and exhausted angel's eyes.

"Keats! Stay!"

"I shan't," he cried. "I can't ask your pardon. I know not what—a thing of a moment—"

"But love her!" said Shelley. "Why should you not?"

His face shone. He would offer the heart from his body.

"Wake her soul," he implored. "It was awake once, years ago.

I have lost the way. Her misery, Keats! Do you know what it has been, to live years with that misery?"

Keats stood dumb. Shelley clutched his shoulder and whispered, "In the mornings a chill comes from her side of the bed. I swear it. I dare not open my eyes. I am afraid to look on her, to see whether she smiles or frowns. In the waking hours we move under such weight. I can scarce lift my face to her. I fear her."

"But, Shelley," said Keats, "you do it to her. You are killing her."

"I?" His face went blank and he shivered. By terrible degrees his spirit fell back from his eyes into an inner pool, and his hands dropped listless. Very quietly he said, "Keats, you know scientific persons. Is there no one capable of preparing the prussic acid? I cannot ask Vaccà. But to hold that golden key in my hand—"

Keats shook his head. "No."

"All I have desired is beauty and liberty. I have acted from no other principle. Each good impulse but compounds the evil. We are chained in this life."

"Shelley!" Keats seized the taller man's shoulders. "What will you? The stars?"

His spirit broke the surface of the pool and peered out.

"You woke her soul once. Be constant. No one must die."

His golden lashes blinked. He tilted his head, furrowed his brow in strange inquiry and, moving very close, pressed his lips lightly and chastely against Keats's closed mouth. For a heartbeat he hung silent, as if waiting on a question, then spun about and went at a soft tread up the steps.

The river pulsed at Keats's feet. The sun hung high. He would be expected at the hospital.

The *Minerva Napolitana* was in his pocket. He tore off a corner, scribbled a note with a sliver of pencil and found a boy on the sidewalk to whom he gave it, together with the Grand Duke's head on a copper. He turned his feet from the river and walked up a crooked lane, the sort of free walk without destination that he had taken long ago, when he was not yet in love, and not a poet in anyone's eyes—only to two or three young friends as untutored as he.

His heart tumbled after itself. What had he done? Nothing—that was the mercy. How he might have tangled his life!

Why live?

One lives to work.

His unwritten poems closed like specters around him. He had not touched them in months. God only knew what they were. This was a terrible task. It was beautiful too, a golden stairway. He must climb it alone.

All that had happened at the Shelleys' was a dream of warning. He dare not take a wife.

At a tiny, signless wine-shop huddled under a nest of brick arches he asked for a bottle, and for pen and ink, without knowing what he would do with them. Something that might have been a couplet beat wings in his head, but he could not pursue it till he wrote Fanny. His penance had come. My dearest Girl—though I have no right to call you so. How shall I speak of my Fear & the Task before me—no, he could not say that. It was grandiose. She deserved something she would understand. But though he knew every sentence to be true, it would come out false from start to finish. Nothing separated falsehood and truth but his burning task, and his fear of losing it, that he had no gift to express. He poured another cup of wine—it was dark purple, tasting of burn alone—and shifted the paper on the table. No one else was inside but the shopkeeper at his casks. The sun did not reach past the threshold.

The stark Truth is, I have no hope of Income equal to a wife, to say nothing of children, even in the meanest Style of living. I am bound by Duty, by every moral & social Consideration, by my own Heart (though the Heart break asunder)—no, it was not true. It spoke neither of his task nor of his fear. But it bore at least some relation to her world, and did not commit the fault of placing itself at an absolute remove.

If I remembered anything of Honor, I should own there is none in this. I cannot ask you to be comforted that our Attachment was not in the World's eyes—nor ever to forgive, no, thrice never—only to remember me later in Life, when you are at Peace & happily disposed, as one who saw far too late his Unworthiness of you & to the best of his Ability acted with his last Shred of Virtue.

Pisa rose and fell under his feet. He did not feel drunk. His awareness sat low in his body, filling the extremities. He perceived with great clarity the crooked forms of old paving stones, the tufts of grass breaking from between them. That good ground was always underfoot, shrugging off the follies of cities. He turned his back on the spires and walked until the paving gave way to dust, past outbuildings and stables into the wide vestibule of the country. Fields ran over the hills, plowed in ridges or waving with grass, up to the dark line of forest. He came to a broken wall no higher than his knees and sat against it, amazed to find himself a part of this order. There was no doubting the force that moved him. He looked into the divine clarity of the sky, felt a warmth in his limbs, named it exhaustion and fell asleep. He woke in colder air, under a violet sky with the first stars faintly picked out. Winter had fled north, but the days of summer were not yet come.

He found the Vaccà house entirely dark but for a single window in the lower story. There was no dinner tonight; the family must be paying a call elsewhere. The old footman, who answered the door and took away his grass-stained coat, only shrugged; the wanderings of Keats were not his charge. He walked the dim length of the hall, the painted lions invisible above him. The senses were sharp in his hands and feet. The library was lit and as he came squinting to the doorway, Giuditta sprang from her seat with an open book in her hand.

"There!" Her eyes burned in the lamplight and a smile hung on her lips. "I thought you should never come! I have waited—"

His pulse shook his fingers. She set down her book and

stepped across the room. It came to him that he could answer her purely, without entanglements. Everything was easy; it was like stepping into a golden pool, into the poem where he had so long wished to dwell. She led him up the shadowed stairs. He whispered that there might be pain and she dug her fingernails into his arm.

Later, in the dark, he thought of boasts that other men had made. "I shall never do you dishonor," he said.

"I know." Moonlight silvered the curtains and glinted in her eyes. No trace of mockery remained in her voice.

"We will make our home here," he said. "I cannot promise you wealth or society. We will live in the country, with books, and heal the sick."

"Then get to your own bed," she said, pushing him away in sport, "and tomorrow we'll tell my father."

He went down the hall in bare feet, boots and clothes bundled in his arms. In his own borrowed room, with its too many chairs and beds for a man alone, he sat at the writing table and lit his scrap of candle. He took the letter he had written from his waistcoat, read over it and found that it said everything badly. But he folded the sheet tight and dripped the candle over the seam, resolved that he would not alter a word. He felt it was honesty.

THIRD PART

Leghorn Harbor

FOR THREE DAYS AND NIGHTS Severn had existed in carriages and wretched Tuscan inns; knowing the ship was expected today, he had gone at first light to the harbor; but the waterfront was empty, even the sea barely consented to move, and for hours he had paced the planks alone in the marine cold, with a sting in his left heel from the boot he could not afford to replace. Sunlight touched the water and turned it the particular glass green he had never been able to fix on canvas. He stood in the shadow of the storehouses and was not warmed. He had hardly slept on the journey. He was sure that too much had been asked of him, but when he tried to reason out the error, he could not make his thoughts follow one another.

He stuck his hand into his waistcoat and touched the edge of a letter already worn soft by his thumb. The horizon drifted with white specks, phantoms that would not turn into substantial ships. Even when a speck did persist and steadied into an actual sail, it only gave his reverie a more painful focus. Brown must know what to do. But supposing Brown did not know—it was too much for a man alone in a foreign place.

A small crowd had collected on the waterfront, dock workers and foreigners talking English and French and waving their hats at the approaching ship. Among the bright dots waving back from the deck, Brown was easily distinguished. He was taller than anyone, thicker too; the speck of his arm swung up and down so lustily that Severn fancied he saw the familiar old grin, in fine miniature, long before the face was really visible. At perhaps fifty yards the ship seemed to halt and remain in place, quietly growing larger, while the crew ran about the deck doing things with the rigging. Voices were heard, waves slapped the hull, the sailors went below and oars were thrust out. A second, smaller head appeared at Brown's shoulder and Severn craned his neck, amazed, to see if he really had a child in his arms. He hadn't believed Brown would actually get it out of England. Despite himself he grinned in admiration: no, one mustn't underestimate the man.

Ropes were thrown out, a plank extended, and the Grand Duke's blue and white policemen marched on board to check passports. Before Brown would debark, he made way for a bird-faced youth beside him, who tiptoed along the plank, leaped onto the pier and loitered there, annoyingly within earshot, as Severn came up to the water. Brown's smile was tight and tired. The child was barely awake, his lashes half shut against the day.

"Look at him!" Severn cried, and took the larger man's arm. "I could not have dreamed it."

He looked over the delicate brown hair, the blue-veined forehead, and felt threatening tears. It was a year since he had seen his own son in London. He might not recognize the boy at all.

"I am glad to see you, Severn, and to see land." Brown's voice was the same full bass, but he had less hair at the crown and a mournful sag pulled at his eyes. He shifted the child into the crook of his arm and unfolded each leg in turn, stretching his creased trousers.

"To take him on so long a journey," said Severn.

Brown chuckled morosely. "I cannot lie. It was an endeavor." The sun touched his eyes and he squinted. "I trust Italy is beautiful. We must rest."

"Of course," said Severn, and then remembered it would not do. "No. I am sorry; we must go to Pisa directly. I must tell you—"

Brown screwed up his face. "Five minutes, if you please. I will not kiss the ground, Severn, but I would eat." He opened beseeching eyes. "As you love me, is there food in Leghorn?"

"We cannot stay in Leghorn. It is Keats."

"It *is* Keats!" Brown turned to the bird-faced lad, who had followed them off the pier and was, Severn realized, listening to their every word. "Five minutes. Our things are not brought ashore."

The lad made a comradely sort of smile. Was this a companion, then, and not a stranger? He was very young, not grown to full height. His jacket was an impressive green, cut slim, and a neat bowl of black hair fell under his broad-brimmed hat. Severn was disturbed by him. He had forgotten that Brown, dauntless as he was, could not be relied on for practicalities; he followed his appetites, he brought in strange confederates when you were expecting a conversation alone.

"Brown," he muttered, "it is a grave business. I've had a letter."

"Indeed!" Brown's eyes twinkled. "Just so have we."

His mirth struck Severn with horror. "Then you know what he has done!"

Brown's smile did not shift a fraction, but his eyes darted to the black-haired lad in a look of warning. Deliberately, as if commencing a prologue, he said, "Severn, do you know whom you speak with?"

"I beg your pardon."

"You recall Miss Brawne?"

"The girl?" Severn shook his head and wished that Brown would stop his irrelevancies, and that the lad would go away. "I met her. I don't know. Keats told me nothing till we had left England. It scarce matters now."

The twinkle returned to Brown's eye, but with a forced aspect, not quite detached from the warning look, as if he were begging Severn not to upset things. With something more of the actor's look he extended his free arm to his companion. Under the dark fringe of hair a startling pair of blue eyes met Severn's, and the smooth cheeks lifted in a shy, nearly coquettish smile.

"Brown!" Severn cried, his heart leaping. "You did not!"

Brown laughed aloud. "You must believe the fault was not mine. It came out of Shakespeare."

"Stuff!" said the black-haired creature, in a fluting voice. "Master Brown will allow me no ideas of my own. He thinks I have it from *Cymbeline*."

Severn stared into the blue eyes. Such things could happen on the stage, he supposed, but not here, not on a material harbor where he had come to complete an errand. No, he had not slept enough. Brown had a jesting tone now and was explaining something about Kemble mounting an antiquarian production at Covent Garden. "And Imogen took such a fright of what Posthumus might be about in Italy, that she insisted on the very same."

"Insisted on—" Severn shook his head. "Antiquarian?" He frowned at the bowl of black hair. "She cut it?" he asked feebly.

He was ready to weep. He had placed all his hopes on Brown's arrival. Now to find that Brown had done this infinitely stupid thing, the kind of thing you discover yourself to have done in a nightmare and spend the rest of the dream repenting—it was nearly as stupid as what Keats himself had done. And if Keats had only written a week or two earlier, before Brown set sail! Miss Brawne—for he did recognize her face now, cut and pasted like a cartoon illustration into this senseless clothing, and the postcard Italian harbor—tilted back her chin, slid a gloved hand under the black bowl and pulled out a ginger curl.

"The clothes I sewed myself," she said.

How old was she? The garments were well turned, impractical for travel: that green jacket, tight trousers.

"Why?" he asked.

"I must be thought Brown's nephew," she said. "Else I am his mistress, and the mother of the child."

"The hardship should be mutual," said Brown.

"But with no warning!" Severn said. "You sent no word."

Brown looked abashed. "The word should not have arrived before we did."

"Does her family know? Does anyone?"

Brown frowned more painfully in his beard, as if disadvantages were only just occurring to him. Miss Brawne took a folded envelope from her jacket and Severn, seeing in it the same letter he had been worrying all morning, felt a cold finger at his back. Brown held up his palm.

"Not that," he said; "not yet. I promise you, Severn, all shall be explained. But some food, I pray you. Some Continental fare. We have had our fill of floating islands. Anything but salt pork; anything that does not come out of a barrel."

Under the eaves of an osteria—which Severn claimed, falsely, to know well, for it seemed imperative that he show knowledge of Italy—they had their trunks piled against a railing and ordered soup and cheese and roast quail. In passable Italian Brown called for bread and milk for the child and white wine for himself, and Miss Brawne handed Severn her letter to read. The writing was not Keats's. It was by the younger Keats, the brother in America, and written months ago. Apparently letters were an age in coming down the Ohio. There was only one sheet, but it was cross-written and full of finance and law and allusions to parties Severn had never heard of. He had to read most of it twice over before he understood.

"There is money?"

"Not a fortune," Brown said. "Not an independent living. But imagine—even one hundred a year, for eight or nine years. What a beginning for Keats! It is not yet what we hope for him. But surely it is more than he ever hoped for himself."

Severn frowned at the sheet, bit his lip, paused as a waiter shoved a bowl of soup between his elbows. "I don't understand. How could such a thing be lost in Chancery?"

"You don't understand Chancery if you don't understand that. Keats is an orphan. The scribblers, and the magistrates, and the dog-men after their scraps, have not made it their business to look after him."

His voice ran hot with bitterness and Severn remembered their common love for Keats: that young, questing, falcon-eyed lad, who deserved so much better than he had ever got.

"He had no one to tell him that he had a portion from his grandfather. I don't suppose his guardian ever knew. The intelligence came to his brother by chance. But the short of it, Severn, is that he is saved."

"It is enough to marry on," said Miss Brawne. She was tearing at scraps of bread and rolling them into tiny pellets. So far she had put nothing to her lips. "He must have told you?"

Severn felt his throat squeezed. "He told me something."

"We were always sure of our hearts," she said. "Where we should find money, we never knew."

He dropped his spoon. "Brown," he begged. "Will you come across the way with me?"

Brown raised his eyebrows, set down his fork and shifted the yawning child into Miss Brawne's trousered lap. Severn led him by his large hand into the street, past the warehouse gates, the dogs sprawled in the sun and halted carts with donkeys nosing for grass. His heart beat fast with what he had to say. He hated muddles, hated quandaries of all sorts. He could not keep this one locked another moment in his soul.

Translations

IT WAS BROWN WHO HAD first received the letter, in Hampstead; and it was Brown who had read it aloud to Fanny and her mother, explaining the contents as he went. At first she had no idea what it meant. Then she understood: the hand of heaven was opening. But what an affront, that the hand of heaven should come in through this big, balding, winking, sometimes indecent neighbor of theirs, who ordered in quantities of liquor and had gotten the Irish cook with child.

Of course Fanny and John had not married, of course everyone thought of Brown as the soul nearest him. It was Brown and not Severn who should have gone to Rome in the first place, but he had been delayed in Scotland. Now he talked of nothing but his lost chance.

She had never believed that John was dying. It was a false report, a dream. When word came of his recovery, she had felt very light. Her feet had floated up from the floor. And she would go on rising; this letter from George would lift her out of the world. That John would die was too cruel to believe. That John was poor—how could he be otherwise?

Brown sat in their best chair, light from the garden picking out motes on his jacket, and explained how it had happened. Yes, it was possible. Yes, Chancery really might lose a man's livelihood and discover it again after twenty years. Here was the document to prove it, and himself to serve as the document's interpreter for as long as Fanny and her mother required.

"Then it is sufficient to marry," said Mrs. Brawne.

"It is sufficient for Keats to live as he likes. His wants are few. He exists for his art."

Brown blinked as he spoke and slumped his big body forward in the chair. All night they heard his infant crying next door. He must wish that he too could exist for his art. He hadn't liked to see John courting Fanny, and found ways of saying it that were not quite uncivil.

"Does he know?" she asked.

"He cannot know," said Brown. "His brother will not have found him in Pisa. This cannot go by letter. I am leaving directly, and will tell him myself."

"Directly!"

"Next Saturday week." His face softened, as if looking on the sun. "To be with Keats, in Italy—I tell you frankly, I have long wished that happiness."

"And I—" said Fanny, but no one was looking at her. She hadn't said it aloud.

"I wish you joy of it, Mr. Brown," said her mother.

He could talk; she was in a fever. She had been studying Italian from a primer. She could write beautiful long sentences to herself, but was afraid to speak them aloud. At night she wished for a magic mirror—just to know how John sat in his chair, what things provoked his smile. He had gone for no comprehensible reason to Pisa, to the disreputable Mr. Shelley, and that was months ago. There had been no word since.

Brown too must have been confused, for on his way out he did a thing he had never done before, which was to make the Brawnes a social invitation. *Cymbeline* was mounted at Covent Garden. He was taking Abigail, to show her culture. Would they come?

Later he would repent and say that everything had been the play's fault. Of course that was nonsense. They weren't innocents; they had read it before. Only none of them, somehow, had thought ahead of time that they should have to see Imogen and Posthumus married in secret, and Posthumus banished to Rome, and Imogen pining after him in England, hearing rumors of his inconstancy—well, it was awkward. Abigail's cheeks turned pink. Conversation fell off and from the second act their row was stone still. Not even Jupiter and his eagle, dropping suddenly on wires from a hidden pulley, could startle them from their constraint.

It was John who was jealous, not Fanny. She couldn't imagine him courting another woman. With her he had never been a gallant. The only gallant was Brown, and what disturbed her was to think of Brown standing over John in another country, one hand on John's shoulder and the other behind his back, talking about some carved head or other and bearing down with dark influence.

On stage, Imogen put on a man's disguise for her journey: tunic, hose, a hood.

A marriageable girl at home is something like a flower and something like a sideboard. She is looked at and admired. Others in the house, coming and going, will drop things upon her without thinking. She stands in such a way that she hardly feels the weight. But if she were to move out of place—imagine! A structure years in the building would topple.

She had never tailored a man's suit to order, but she knew how the pieces fell. Since John had left, she had worked many evenings past sundown. Her mother would not lack for bills to collect.

Saturdays Abigail tied a bonnet under her chin and went to market. Fanny waited till she had disappeared down the lane, then went and knocked next door. The door opened a few inches and Brown's sleepy, suspicious head appeared in the gap. He seemed already to be peering out from a ship's berth, as if his half of Wentworth Place were floating down the Thames to open sea.

"Miss Brawne!" said Brown. "You find me at my worst. I thought it was the fellow with the coffee."

"May I come in?"

She smiled and traced artless circles with her hands. She had to charm him. It wasn't only that he seemed, as she stepped into the dim room, to be twice her size. She needed to know what he knew, how one could simply determine to leave the country and be gone in a week's time. She remembered when this place had been full of poetic disorder, pamphlets and wineglasses. Now there were shirts piled at a washtub, pots on the gridiron, the writing desk stacked with dishes and a bottle half full of milk. Shoved behind them, like remembrances from a different home, were pen and ink, and a few written sheets.

"Pay those no mind," said Brown. "I once had the fond idea that one might write with a child in the room. But my duty—"

Young Charles knelt at the unlit hearth. He spoke in birdcalls to or for the toy he was pushing back and forth, a wooden horse on wheels. He was nearly two years old and in the last months had lost the impersonal, rounded, rose-and-blond look of the Christ child and come to resemble his parents. When he was frightened, his lower lip shrank to the same pink knot as Abigail's. But his father had all his love. He took the horse in one hand, clapped it against the other and squealed till Brown smiled on him.

"A sacred duty," said Fanny.

Brown bent his head.

"But I thought you were to write in Italy?"

"As I am able. Hunt wants me for his periodical. He wants Keats as well."

"And you are taking young Charles with you."

He narrowed his eyes, but Fanny answered his look in all innocence and he went back to looking merely sleepy. "You've spoken with Abigail."

"She told me all. Please accept my congratulations—privately, if you prefer it."

He shook his head. It was no use asking a woman to keep quiet. "I suppose you do not find it natural to think of me as a family man. Had anyone told me what was entailed in having a child—what one should have to give up—I cannot say if I should choose it." He smiled. "I know you will say I never did choose it, that it came by accident."

"I beg your pardon," said Fanny. "I should not have pre-sumed." This was the difficulty in talking to Brown, that he moved so easily from banter to perfect frankness and back again.

"One never *could* choose it," said Brown. "That is my mean-ing. Everything has become more difficult, not only the writing. Nevertheless—" He shrugged. "With you I will not pretend. As a man of letters I shall never be what Keats is. I turn my ear to the same gods, but they do not whisper the same songs. I have only my child. He has my name. I will own him before anyone. And yes, it is impossible that I should leave him behind."

There is a certain kind of rake, Fanny thought, who survives very easily the translation to a family man. He takes his new au-thority for granted, as he once took for granted his charm.

"You did not call to hear my sentiments," said Brown. "What can I do for you this morning, Miss Brawne?"

"No more than you have done in the past. You have rendered me so many assistances as a neighbor, and as a friend to John. I have not always received them graciously."

He laughed. "I am not accustomed to this tone in you." But he pulled out a scuffed chair for her and sat in its partner.

"I would ask a particular favor," she said. "It is my mother who will object. She will suffer no actual harm, I promise you, other than the surprise of—well, of my absence. For a time."

Brown was sleepy, uncomprehending; then a smile showed. "Oh, very good. I see what you're about." He shook his head. "Now, how should I—"

"It is not money," she broke in. "I have that. But as for the other things—"

"Other things!" Yes, he was amused. It was a fine joke that she knew so little, not even what to ask after. "Miss Brawne," he said kindly, "how should I ever play such a trick on your mother? Your Keats will not be in Italy forever, I promise you."

"And how long will *you* be in Italy?" she asked. "And how long young Charles?"

He shut his lips. A creak came from the hearth: young Charles stood on tiptoe and was leaning over the grate to grab the bellows. Brown grunted in annoyance, reached out and scooped him up around the middle.

"Abigail did not tell me her feelings on your taking the child to Italy," said Fanny. "But it is very far away, is it not? I suppose a wedding—even a hasty wedding, without witnesses—must have given her peace of mind."

"Now you *do* presume," said Brown.

"I do not know the law. But are you certain a Catholic wedding gives her all the protection she believes?"

He grasped the child's shoulder. "If you have filled her head with fears—"

"Not a word."

He smiled. The smile meant nothing, and when he saw Fanny unmoved he leaned back in his chair and let young Charles go free on the rug.

"I am not sure what to say," he said. "You do not know half so much as you imagine. Please be assured of that."

"Perhaps you don't know the half of what I would do for John."

He frowned at her.

"We have been too long apart," she said, "and I do not wish others near him when I am far. Is that strange?"

Young Charles, once free, had run directly back to the grate and gotten the bellows by its handles. His hands parted and joined; the device wheezed and a storm of ash struck him full in the face.

"In the name of Christ!" Brown lunged into the plume and came out wrestling a powdered white thing, kicking, bent like a bow. He got the bellows loose and flung it to the floor, and the child shrieked and twisted so that Brown was forced to drop him. Everywhere he had been touched, over his face and frock, the white ash was smeared gray.

"Why *do* that?" Brown shouted. "Why do it?"

Fanny dropped to her knees and tucked her arms under the small body, stiff as a spring. The moment she took him up, the catch loosed and he keened, flinging his face into her neck. She clucked her tongue, humming, till he stopped to listen; then she passed her hand before his face. His blue-gray eyes fixed on the silver glint of Keats's ring.

"You calm him as soon as Abigail," said Brown. "I haven't the trick."

"I have a brother and sister," Fanny murmured. "Did you never care for anything weaker than yourself?"

"I had dogs."

"A dog has strength," she said. "Is he not loyal?"

She did not want to be unkind. Rocking the child had brought her back to the time of children, the moment hung free. Young Charles circled his fingertip over the ring, and Brown stood and watched.

"Why must it be without your mother's knowledge?" he asked at last. "She might consent."

She shook her head. "I will not have *might*. I will not ask permission of anyone."

"But how in God's name do you expect to do it?"

Fanny smiled and wet her hand at her mouth. She wiped ash from the child's face, took his smeared frock under the arms and held him up to his father.

These Mortals

SHE HAD PLANNED TO MAKE the entire journey in disguise. But Brown shook his head and explained that a sailing ship took its passengers as cargo, and would place them in berths the length and breadth of their bodies with only a bit of curtain to separate them; and further, that the close stool below deck would respect no disguise. If he hoped to shock her, he failed, but she admitted the point.

He would make arrangements, and in return she would help with the child and give herself out as his sister. That would be nodded at even if it was not believed. Yet the passport, which he got in her absence, was made out to one Francis Brawne, a *gentilhomme anglais*; he had heard that a man would face fewer questions at borders. She asked if Brown had actually seen Lord Castlereagh sign it. He shook his head at her naivety and explained that the Foreign Office kept a stack of signatures ready.

Young Charles shared her berth. He slept badly in the close air, with strange beams creaking above and waves slapping the hull below; only if she lay on her back and curled him against her shoulder would he be still. He drooled on her gown, she sweated under his weight, his movements jerked her out of dreams. The Italian sun waited for her. The orb took shape on her eyelids, picking out that corner where John had hidden himself. She would touch his shoulder and his eyes would lift to her.

After a day's time, young Charles called her "Auntie" and would have no other company. She felt the ship's crew also in love with her, perhaps some passengers as well. A prank was afoot, she gave them to understand, and when Leghorn harbor finally came in sight they all watched her go below and come back up the ladder in a man's jacket and wig. It was like putting on a suit of armor or mounting a horse. She could not move her limbs as she was used to, and everything seemed barred by a visor. Yet she had a sense that new motions were possible, outside her accustomed range.

How low the sun, how bright! It was not the ghostly orb she had imagined in her berth; it was a cauldron, it flattened everything. To keep her eyes open made her thirsty, but she could not shut them. Anything might happen. Young Charles was still in her lap and the chair seemed to rock beneath her, still floating at sea. It was strange to see waiters bringing dishes to the table and carrying them away, just as in England. For all she knew, Italians ate in some entirely foreign fashion; for all she knew they breathed through gills.

"Auntie, horse."

There was a donkey cart across the way. A pair of broad-chested men leaned against it. The donkey dipped its dark head after sprigs of grass, and the Italians too were chewing something. Young Charles tried to squirm from her lap and she held him back.

"Not in that road. See, how dirty!" Her voice was low; she did not want the men to catch sight of his fair hair, his rose cheeks. She was hardly less afraid for Severn and Brown. But they were returning now, stepping over wheel ruts as they rounded the loose-planked waterfront.

"See," said Fanny, surprised at her own relief. "It's papa."

The men had their heads down and their hands at their backs. At the railing Brown looked up with a distracted smile and bent for the child.

"Was he obedient?"

"He is always obedient," said Fanny.

They sat. Brown stared at his soup and wine, and said at length, "Mr. Severn had news for me."

"Yes?"

"I had not thought—" He turned to Severn abruptly and said, "The error was mine, of course. To think he would remain still, whilst we moved about him: a child's error. Had I been here to hold him down! Truly, Severn, had you no power?"

"Why no," said Severn, shaking his head; "you know I had none."

"Gentlemen?" said Fanny.

Brown took a breath. "Keats has—absented himself, I should say—from his former connections."

"What connections?" She frowned. "He is not absent from you, Severn. You have his letter."

"That is true," said Severn. "The letter is unusual."

"As Mr. Shelley is unusual? He has made an atheist of John?"

"Keats is no longer in Pisa," said Brown. "He has gone into the country."

"To work," Severn added quickly, as if that were reassurance. "He practices as a village doctor."

"A village doctor!"

"I suppose he saw no other way to earn a living," said Brown.

"He sent a few coppers with the letter. For his debts, he says. I think it is as much as he earns."

Fanny forced a laugh. "Well, *that* need not go on. We shall deliver him. Shan't we?"

"If he wishes deliverance."

"If?" They would not meet her eyes. "What more do you know?"

"I would not for the world alarm you," said Brown. "Severn, will you read somewhat?"

"Aloud?" Severn asked.

"A portion," said Brown, with emphasis. "On nightingales."

Severn reached into his coat and pulled out a bundle crossed over with John's writing. Fanny's heart leaped, but the men made guarding faces and she felt a foreboding, as if some cruel ritual had begun. It was an old feeling, to discover herself part of someone else's stratagem.

Severn read.

"My friend, never did I dream a heart already in its twenty-sixth year might entertain such revolutions. I blush for the youth I was in the spring. It is very nearly too late that I have learned what it is to answer a duty. I do not mean duty as the schoolmaster conceives it, not to the family or the Crown or the parish relief society—you understand that. I think we who came to Italy have struck out our names on those contracts. There is the duty to nature, and there is the duty to pain. Those are the same. Do you understand? It comes as if revealed—I grow short of breath when I think on it, the pen dries up in my hand. The duty is to tell no lie. I would say through a trumpet that we have all of us committed the blackest falsehood, ever and often, to deny ourselves among nature—her pleasures and poisons—it is the poison always in her right hand, for the last draught. I do not mean a simple pessimism. It is not Dr. Johnson's lesson in classical couplets. This truth is deeper. It is the hawk upon the sparrow—this year it is the moving of armies. That is the turning of one wheel, and we are hawk and sparrow alike. Shelley's Plato and Plotinus say only this, if they mean what they say. Aeschylus too, though Aeschylus expects too much of his gods. I read Lucan in the country and think he is the poet for the age—we have nothing in English poetry, not even Lear, to show how we may be so insulted in our flesh. That is the duty to pain. The duty to nature is explained if I say that I have altered my thoughts on nightingales. 'Immortal bird' was the lie. We have only the mortal thing to treat with, the frail thing, in all compassion. But it must be done quietly. Should quietude give way to coldness, it may be the coldness is only seeming, as comes of painting in the colors of truth."

Severn's voice gave out and he lowered the sheet.

"Is that the Keats you remember?" Brown asked.

"I never knew John by his philosophy." Fanny held out her hand. "Be so good as to let me see the rest."

"It was addressed to me," Severn said, returning the sheet to his coat, "and I think not meant to be shown about."

"Delicacy is wanted," said Brown. "I will see for myself how it stands with Keats. I promise I shall not be slow to tell you. There is a gathering in Pisa, where his play is to be read."

"What play?"

"He has written it for Hunt's periodical," said Severn. "Some Italians have the reading. On my honor, I know nothing else—it is secret business. Hunt and Shelley know something more."

"Mr. Hunt is here?"

It was the whole literary circle from London, then. They had all followed after him; she saw them stationed around him in a ring, facing outward with crossed arms.

"I could have it delayed only till Brown arrived," said Severn. "I know Keats would want him there. Since no one—your pardon, Miss Brawne—expected you—"

"You will lodge in Leghorn tonight," said Brown.

"You are not serious!" she said. "For what do you think I made this journey?"

"For what, indeed!" Brown replied. "We must see how things stand. If Keats is altered, how do you suppose he should receive you, with no announcement whatsoever, in some corner of Lord Byron's house—"

"Lord *Byron* is a part of this?"

Severn held up his hands. "It is not as you think. Really—extremely awkward—you must think it through."

She put a hand to her lapel. "Haven't I my incognito?"

Brown smiled tightly. "I *think* our Keats should penetrate that stagecraft."

"Be reasonable, Brown," she said, and felt her cheeks warming. "I give you my word, I shall keep back from the action. I shall not get in the way of your investigating. Let me but glimpse him."

"You know that is not possible," said Brown.

"But *glimpse* him," she repeated. "For the rest you may do as you like. Disregard me utterly. You may tell Hunt and Shelley anything at all—only do not say, there is one who crossed the ocean with me, that I have placed in a Leghorn inn for the night, for that was the prudent thing."

"This is not a parlor game," said Brown.

"I never won at one," she replied.

Whatever the answer for which he opened his mouth, it struck him suddenly as not right, and his eyes slid away. Severn would give no struggle. She would claim this victory as she had claimed those before. And it was a dizzy thought, that only a month ago she had been a seamstress in her mother's house, unworthy even to receive a letter. Brown and Severn grimaced and she smiled in answer, recognizing the childish face that a man is sure to make when he fails to get his way.

Trovatella

IN THE SPRING THEY WOKE hungry, ate morning cakes of maize and grass seed and went out to the fields before the sun had burned off the mist. Lilies covered the swamp and poppies sprouted on the fallow land. The air was rich and rotten, with a salt burn that caught in the throat. It was a week's job to hack out the scrub and drag a board piled with stones between the hedgerows, a day to run tracks behind an ox and plow and two weeks to dig the furrows down to their full depth, going foot by foot with a spade. In the hills the soil was yellow and full of stones. Nearer the water it was soft and black, but the mists hung late, and if the rains were heavy the swamp would creep outward to drown the green shoots.

At midday the air cleared and a light smell of brimstone blew off the water. They sat under olive trees and squinted at the yellow hills. Someone's daughter came from a farmhouse with a water jug; they chewed more cake and ate boiled eggs from their pockets. Their hunger was not gone, but it was quieter. At dawn it had pierced them; now it rested on their stomachs and asked them to sleep. So long as they worked, the work would blunt their feelings, but they were not ready to start again. They lifted their eyes to the red-roofed farmhouses and thought of the cool insides of their homes. The women would be hanging spindles from their fingers, sifting seeds, milking the animals and holding pouches of silkworm eggs to warm against their breasts. They dropped mulberry leaves into reed baskets by the stoves. The worms twisted on the warm weave, ate morning and night and filled their enclosures with pebbly droppings and vacant dry skins.

That spring the family from Lucca kept their younger daughter, the sharp-faced one, indoors. No one saw her in the vegetable garden or going to soak hemp in the marsh. When she went to Mass, she wore a gown of loose homespun that could have had a horse underneath for all it showed. The family were strangers, only three years on their plot, and no one was friendly enough with the mother to ask about a confinement. Everyone told the priest, of course, but he was a young priest and timid, and wouldn't go to houses as the old priest had done. One afternoon they heard screams coming across the fields. When they realized which farmhouse it was, they sent a boy to the castello for Don Niccolò. By the time the doctor arrived in a mule cart, the house had fallen silent. He asked how long it had been and rapped the door with his stick. The mother came out sweating, with her sleeves rolled past the elbows.

"She had stomachache," said the mother.

"I'll see her," said Don Niccolò.

"She's resting," said the mother, "and we haven't money for your fee."

"I'll see her," Don Niccolò said again.

"And the nations of the earth behind you?" asked the mother.

The doctor turned to the men. "All right," he said, "you called me, I'm here. You can go back to the fields."

The men left and the doctor went inside. No one saw how long he stayed, but some of them met his cart going back to the castello that evening.

"Well?" they asked.

"She had stomachache," said the doctor. "Tell the priest."

Next morning, the first patients in the consulting room found a red infant sleeping in a reed basket under the table. It was a girl, with a few tufts of flax on her head and a twist to her lip that made her look clever. A Maria from outside the castello wall came as a wet nurse. It would go to the Ospizio dei Trovatelli in Pisa, like all such babies, but that would have to wait till the medical students made their next visit to drink Don Niccolò's wine, and in the meantime it had no place save under the table. That must have been the reason it ended up going home with the doctor's assistant, the red-haired Englishman. Some said the foreigner was mad; but the action was not ugly as madness was, it was too odd for madness to explain.

The Englishman had been there a few weeks, since the start of clearing season, and outside the consulting room he and his young wife kept to themselves. They were setting up house in the old gunpowder works, which had one or two rooms with enough roof to keep them dry. With some extra boards and straw it might have been pleasant, but they hadn't asked anyone in the village for help, and unasked no one would offer it. As a physician he had skill. Don Niccolò trusted him and everyone trusted Don Niccolò. He had helped with Zenzo's arm. Pills rolled from his fingers looked no different from those Niccolò made. His lancet never cut past what was needed to open the vein. He spoke a few words at a time in his heavy accent; his hands were so pale that their touch seemed to cool the skin like water. Yet his eyes were bright.

The wife was a city girl, pretty and weightless. She paid visits about the castello but never stayed long; she gave gifts of coffee and chocolate but ran out after a few days. The first time she saw silkworms in a basket, she screamed. She had planted a vegetable garden in front of the gunpowder works, in a place that got no sun. They installed a cradle in their dwelling and brought over the Maria as wet nurse, and paid her a good rate; and the family from Lucca kept on at their farmhouse down the hill, with no more friends than before.

The first night the child cried till dawn. On the second night the Englishman and his wife were heard shouting. On the third night came a shattering noise, easily heard over the castello wall, and anyone who looked out from an upper story would have seen the Englishman's shadow striding out the door in a nightshirt and swinging the infant back and forth in his arms. He shouted in his own language and then in Tuscan.

"Zitta!"

He was a man and his voice broke like anyone's. The moon was out over the grass, and off the dark marsh the bad vapors were rising that no one could see. The doctor stopped swinging the infant, held it close and began to sing.

The air was foreign. In a faster time it would have been gay, but the doctor sang it slow, like church music, and his weak breath could scarcely be heard under the infant's crying. One would have thought the vapors had already eaten his lungs. He wasn't dressed for the night. But he stayed a long time in the damp air and continued to sing even after the infant gasped and fell quiet. He seemed not to know he was out of his own bed. He was thought better of after that.

Pilgrims

BEHIND THE CASTELLO, WHERE NO visitors came, a slope of canary grass ran from the outer wall down to the marsh. A brief attempt at a brick quay traced the shore, with five or six old cannons stuck in muzzle first as moors. The Grand Duke's factor had forbidden fishing the marsh, a rule that meant nothing since no one could tell what was marsh and what was open water. Weedy passages were always opening and closing, and the river was so shallow from bank to bank that nothing but fishing scows could be expected to range it. Certainly no one was expecting the twin-sailed schooner that now appeared round the golden headlands and came dancing up-river, light as a pond skater. Men in the fields straightened for a better view and scratched their heads.

Two sails were too many for a boat so light. The wind was careless with it, rocking the hull forward and back; the foresail dropped, then the main, and the double-masted outline began to drift, turning its prow like a sleeper shaking his head after a dream. A pole was extended from deck and the boat slid toward the quay, forcing its keel through weed mats until it knocked against the scows and came to rest.

There were two on board, both in broad hats and white canvas jackets with the afternoon glaring off their backs. They jumped from deck to shore and started uphill arm in arm, the tall grass swallowing them to the waist so that they looked like bits of sail-cloth blown free. Those in the castello were just waking from siesta; they heard voices from a strange quarter, opened their shutters and saw a man and a woman nearing the gate. Their accents were unfamiliar and they laughed like holidaygoers, in this place where no one had ever come on holiday. In the tight stone lane past the gate, they looked around after something that was not there to meet them. Nothing moved but a few dry leaves gusting past the piazza's empty fountain.

The buildings had not opened their doors for the afternoon, but the cobbler's shop had an open window. The man stuck his head within and asked something in high-pitched Tuscan, and the cobbler's mutter answered.

"Grazie!"

They walked on to the piazza, where a lone door stood open under Don Niccolò's stone arch. A slant of sun picked out the English assistant within.

He was bent over a table at the edge of the light. He wore no jacket; his sleeves were rolled past the elbows, flecked with dry blood, and his hands at work drawing pinches of something from a jar. Copper streaks glinted in his long, loose-bound hair. Sunlight had reddened and roughened his arms and face, and a growth of russet whiskers lined his jaw. On the shadowed table a patient lay face up, shoes pointing toward the door.

The visitor touched the door knocker and the assistant looked up from his work. The jar dropped from his hand, cracked against the floorboards, bounced and rolled away. A plume of sunlit powder rose in the doorway.

"Your pardon!" said Shelley.

Keats stared like a fox surprised in its den. His eyes darted between the spilled powder, the man on the table, the shelves and sacks heaped about the room. His dusted hand dropped. A narrow golden band circled his ring finger.

"Well," he said. "I am discovered."

"You cannot have meant to hide," said Shelley.

"Was it Leopoldo told you? His father?"

"Say a word if we impose," said Mary. "Say half a word, and we will go."

"Say it not," said Shelley.

"We will go," Mary said.

Keats slowly bent his knees, keeping his eyes on the doorway, and sent his hand in search of the fallen jar.

"You had better come in. Is it not hot out of doors?"

Their white jackets, the brightest things in the room, seemed to glance moonlight over the dingy brass instruments. Shelley's arm was out as if to throw over Keats's shoulders, but he was shy of direct approach and after a moment of confusion took off his hat and stepped sideways toward a cabinet of ointment jars. Mary held a paper parcel under her arm.

"You catch me at my trade," said Keats. "This room has no hospitality."

"We ask no inconvenience," said Shelley.

"Yet you are here." He took a large stone jug from the floor and tugged out the cork. "Cool yourselves, if you wish. I must beg your indulgence while I tend this man."

The patient had not moved; his stocky legs, slung over the table's edge, were still. Over his face and hands were scaled lesions, cinder-colored where powder had been applied. His heavy eyes, the lone live things in the rubble, darted toward the visitors and away. Keats took another pinch of powder and began to rub at his cheekbones, and Shelley sniffed the mouth of the jug.

"It is wine?" he asked.

"Very weak," said Keats. "Children drink it. The water is foul here."

Mary caught Shelley's eye and shook her head. He set the jar on the ground and they took a slower look around the room. Notebooks and yellowed papers stacked against the walls; sacks lay humped in corners, bellies full of secrets. The patient's wounds clustered on his knuckles and face, outlining his nose and cheeks as if cast there by a malignant light. Between the scales, raw patches wept an amber crust. His eyes darted back to them; they looked away and Shelley put his hand to his own cheek, as if he felt an irritation there.

"What this man has is not a leprosy," said Keats. "It touches none that live within the town walls."

"What then is it?" Mary asked.

"I do not know. A maize-eater's disease, it seems, but those who eat maize within the town are not afflicted. We cannot say what is the poisonous agent." He looked to the jar on the floor. "I pledge my reputation, it will not harm you to drink that."

Mary was still incredulous, but Shelley picked up the jar and drank off a large mouthful. The patient's face and hands were now coated in gray, and Keats helped him to climb from the table. The man put one scabbed hand on his breast and held out a copper in the other, speaking in dialect too thick for the newcomers to understand. Keats refused the coin several times and finally the man dropped it on the table, took a battered hat from the door and walked barefoot into the piazza.

A smile had touched Keats's lips while he spoke the foreign language; alone, he lost it. He shifted on his feet, looking for a place to put himself.

"You look a Continental madman with those whiskers," said Mary.

He touched his cheek and half smiled.

"And your sleeve!" she said.

He looked at the bloodstains and shoved his cuff past the elbow. "I beg your pardon."

"Why, Keats," said Mary, "we have not come to find fault."

"No! You come out of solicitude, is it so? I do not merit it." Light caught his green eyes and he seemed once again the man who had climbed their palazzo steps in the spring. "You have penetration. You must perceive that I could not bear to live at the expense of others. I would not impose further upon you, upon Vaccà."

"We never thought your company an imposition," said Shelley. "As for Vaccà—"

"Do not say you come to speak for Vaccà!"

There was the wound. "We would not do it," said Mary. "We were given no errand."

"He has hardly spoken to us," said Shelley.

"And why should he speak to you?" said Keats. "He is proud and he will trust no English poet now. I had all of ten minutes' audience with him. *I have seen the world, and I know why a man goes from a rich country to a poor country. Lives are cheaper here. My mistake in you, Mr. Keats, was to believe you honorable because you are poor.* And he shut his cigar box with a click—so," miming the gesture.

"And Giuditta?" Mary asked.

"Giuditta is like me. She wished independence. I have tried to give her it." He held up his hand. "On the way out her father's door, she decided she was owed a parting gift and took rings. We have been to the priest—all of it."

His voice was tight, and the guests did not feel that congratulations were expected.

"You have our apologies that we come unannounced," said Shelley. "We knew not how to send word. Perhaps some courier—"

"I am ashamed!" Keats cried, pushing himself from the table. "It is shameful to be discovered here, at work with my sleeves rolled up. I am ashamed of my conduct in Pisa, from beginning to end—that it began with an uninvited knock on your door, that it ended without a farewell."

"No, Keats," said Mary.

"It was so strange!" he said. "I was strange. The city appears in my dreams, you know, as if upside down. The baptistry dome, the slanting tower. I do not know who I was."

His feet were spread like a pugilist's; he might have been giving a challenge. A tramp sounded on the threshold and a large man with a white beard and scarred face came through the door. He nodded to Keats and dropped his bag on the table in a way that showed him master of this disordered room. The white-clothed visitors he ignored till they stepped forward, begging pardon; then he raised his brows, widening one good eye and a whorl of scars where the other was not.

"Who's that?" he said.

Shelley took up the Italian language like a tool he did not quite remember how to handle. Keats dropped his boxer's stance and, looking embarrassed on Shelley's behalf, laid a hand on his shoulder and introduced the visitors in much better Tuscan than he had commanded that spring.

"Oh, they're not patients," said the large man, and turned away. "I was at the factor's wife again. Pains in her fingers, pains in her feet. She wants to be told she has the wounds of Christ. She hasn't a basin fit to wash in."

He shoved his bag aside, went to a squat washstand in the corner and busied himself with the soap and water jug as if there were no one else in the room.

"You have met Niccolò," Keats said over the splashing, "who refuses surname or title, but has permitted me to work as his assistant."

"You wash as well," said Niccolò. "Isn't that powder on your fingers?"

"He thinks a physician ought always to be cleaning his hands," said Keats. "I have told him, a surgeon in London would not stop to do it before opening your abdomen."

Niccolò laughed gruffly. "A surgeon in London does not know what he does not know. Our priest will not give out bread and wine to the superstitious without his *lavabo inter innocentes*—is it too much that I address their bodies with clean fingers?"

He went past with the full basin in his arms and pitched water and suds out the doorway.

"And how do the patients take this ritual?" asked Shelley.

"You have seen a patient," said Keats. "They take all things in silence."

"The consulting room is no place for talk," said Niccolò. "They're a bad-tempered lot anyway. Rimuginano."

"I beg pardon?" said Shelley.

"They—stir in the head," said Keats. "They brood."

"On the money they don't have," said Niccolò. "On a marriage refused. And I too must be silent. If I speak the name of Tomasso in Matteo's hearing, he'll spit on the floor, never mind that their quarrel was fifteen years ago."

"Stubborn hearts," said Shelley.

"So they are," said Keats. "Yet any night in London, I remember, a man might stumble into the wards with a broken nose or slashed arm, and no story to explain it. Not here. They have no will to injure each other."

"You mean you don't see those injuries," said Niccolò, "because they know to keep them out of my consulting room. Haven't you seen the dead mice along the cartroad, that the children catch to twist their heads?"

"I have seen that elsewhere."

"And what of your infant girl? You don't suppose she was the only one! My Londoner, you have not been here long. If you've left me nothing else to do, I will have that"—taking the wine jar from Shelley's feet—"and upstairs."

He shuffled to the back stairway and his patched boots carried him out of sight.

Shelley rubbed his lips and blew out. "Perhaps to you, Keats, that decoction is weak as water. I take wine seldom."

"An infant girl!" said Mary. Her voice was light, but Keats was startled back into the fox look.

"There are orphans in the months before harvest," he said. "We have taken one in. That is all."

"You and Giuditta both?"

He tightened at Giuditta's name. "Call it an experiment in hope. I had a younger brother and sister. She never did. We ought to have experience of a child—" He shrugged and looked away, the phrase not finished.

"Why, Keats!" She laughed aloud, wide-eyed at the thing she guessed; but she was shy also, and put up her hands. "Pardon us, if you are not giving it out."

"Well, you will want to come and see her now!" There was hurt in his voice and something that edged on joy, hesitant and bounded. He crossed the room before Shelley's startled face, which had not quite divined the secret, and took his jacket from beside the door.

"I mean I am inviting you to supper," he said, and beckoned them into the sun.

A cenar teco

THEY WENT DOWN A RUTTED cartroad and Keats pointed out everything in their path. The grass on the high slopes was for pasturing sheep. The lower growth was green hemp. There were stands of mulberry trees, farmhouses with fenced orchards. The honey-colored fields were wheat that the padrone sold abroad. The pale green stalks were maize that he sold back to the contadini who grew it.

"*The* padrone?" Shelley asked. "Is there only one?"

"It is the Grand Duke," said Keats. "The village is his personal property, though he little attends it. You may see his factor within the castello—a fox-faced man, who twitches his nose at the window and writes reports to Florence."

"Hateful," said Shelley, "that an institution should pervert a people's love for the land."

"They do not love the land here," said Keats.

"Have they forgotten their nature so?"

"They hate the land. They call it *la miseria*—the work they do so as not to die."

"But if their condition were altered."

Keats looked sideways at his companion. "Forgive the impertinence, but have you no lands of your own in England?"

"Certainly I have. Or my father has them, which comes to the same thing."

"Well."

Shelley looked with pain over the fields. "They shall be differently disposed one day," he said, "if I live so long."

The earth was dry, fragile with cracks; their shadows glided over it. A woman walked among the stalks below, baskets slung from a pole over her shoulders. The quay came into view, and the twin masts of the schooner rising past the fishing boats like a heron among sandpipers.

"Our *Ariel*," said Shelley.

Keats considered it. "I have never seen a two-masted craft of that size."

"It is to give her speed," said Shelley. "She goes like a witch."

"But do the high winds not strain her?"

Shelley shrugged. "She is for the shallow rivers, the canals. We should not take her on the open sea."

"And you fear no storm?"

He held out his palm and shook his head. "There is no rain now. Perhaps tonight, when we are safe in bed, the heavens will open."

"If her sails were up, you would see the insult," said Mary.

Keats burst out laughing. "Forgive me," he said. "Leopoldo was here and told me of something Lord Byron had done. I thought it was perhaps an invention."

"It is fact," said Shelley. "Don Juan's name lies across the foresail. We have tried turpentine, spirits of wine, buccata—every remedy in the lore. I shall have to cut the cloth out entirely, and put reefs."

"Will his lordship not take offense?"

"As he pleases," said Mary. "Lord and poet as he is, he cannot be allowed to make a coal-barge of our boat."

Keats went on laughing and Shelley shook his head. "It is a childish business," he said. "But you must not disparage Byron for the figure he cuts. I have brought him round to admire your 'Hyperion.' You and he cannot go forever without meeting."

"No?" Keats asked. "I am away from the world."

"Byron says the same of his life in Pisa."

"Then he too wishes to meet no one. I am not surprised. What I read of the 'Don Juan' gave me the most horrid idea of human nature, that he could have exhausted the pleasures of the world so completely that there is nothing left for him but to laugh and gloat over scenes of human misery."

Shelley looked to Mary and hemmed.

"In any case it should mortify *me*," said Keats. "Do you know the first sonnet I penned as a boy was one 'To Byron'?"

Mary laughed. "Is it so?"

"*Still warble, dying swan*! It was atrocious." And rounding on them, fearful: "You shall not tell him!"

Shelley placed his hand on his heart and swore he should not.

"If Byron cannot tempt you," said Mary, "suppose we told you Hunt is arrived, with his family entire? He has been a fortnight in Pisa and cannot understand why you have left town."

Keats's face opened, boyish for a moment. "But if he cannot understand, rumor must inform him. And he will want to come here." He frowned at the afternoon sun, stewing in marsh haze. "He should wish another species of countryside."

"He wants you for the journal," said Shelley. "I should say we all do—it is unanimous. Your name is grown bright in Pisa."

"Then I am glad it stays in Pisa," said Keats, "and does not come here to dazzle me."

"But you do not only tend blisters here? You do write?"

"I write," said Keats, and bit his lip in repentance. "At any rate I divert myself."

Roofs were scattered between the garden patches, some well laid with shingles, others heaps of boards. "Those houses—you go into them?" asked Mary.

"Very seldom. It is improper, you know, that I visit a house of women while the men are out, even if the women be none of them younger than sixty-five. That is why Don Niccolò has his consulting room."

"How do you endure the smell?"

"I have not perceived it in months." Keats shrugged. "Hunt will not like what I am writing."

"Anything from your pen," said Shelley.

Keats smiled darkly, as if at some bitter epigram, and Mary held out the parcel she had been carrying under her arm. "If it makes amends for our surprise, we have an offering."

"For me?"

"We thought you might want for reading."

He took the parcel and bowed. "See, even here you teach me."

Revived, he led them down the cartroad. Ahead rose an outbuilding of brown brick, or something that had once been an outbuilding, with a fallen roof and walls thrusting jagged teeth at the sky.

"Our ploughshare," said Keats. "It was a gunpowder factory during the war."

The guests smiled in disbelief. But washing was laid to dry on a wall and beds of earth sprouted among the fallen bricks. There were corn stalks, fennel, tomatoes on stakes.

"I do not understand," said Shelley. "Do you sleep like field mice, in the open air?"

"We do better. Come."

He led them round to a portion of wall that still supported roof beams. Fresh thatch had been laid around the flue and a door hung open in a new-hammered frame. They entered a high, bright chamber paved with loose stones, under a sloped roof and clerestory open to the sky. Food hung from ropes, crates and slats had been draped with cloth and made into furniture, one wall was taken up by an enormous hearth that might have done for a mess hall. It had the look of a sketch from the far East, of a British company making camp in a pagan temple after having blown it apart.

"Giuditta!" Keats called. "See what has come on the breeze."

She was bent over a boiling pot at the hearth. Her feet were bare; she wore a bonnet and a brown peasant dress draped the heavy curve at her waist. She squinted through the steam and held the dripping ladle outward like a weapon.

"He is not here!" she said.

Her voice was sharper than before, her movements quicker.

Her cheeks were drawn in. Shelley raised a greeting hand; she halted, and with a sudden shrill laugh lowered her arms and curtsied, a gesture from a life in city rooms.

"Signor Shelley, Signora Shelley. In white clothes! I thought you were some army."

"Are you visited often by armies?" Shelley asked.

"No one visits," she said. "You look divine."

She came forward, extending an arm for balance on which veins stood out, and embraced them in turn. They kissed her flushed cheeks and congratulated her, the Italian language returning to them. Mary touched her belly and asked after her health.

"Oh, let us not speak of it," said Giuditta. "I live with a physician already."

"But do you keep house alone, in your condition?" Mary asked.

"Condition! You mean I look like a kitchen maid." She glanced at her bare legs streaked with soot. "Or like a case for the Daughters of Charity. Well, the fault is not mine; no one warned me of guests."

Shelley said that she looked a perfect genre scene, and named several painters. But she did not want to dwell on her own aspect. She touched their sleeves. These were sailing jackets? Truly? And they had come the length of the river? They must show her the vessel—but were they not hungry? Polenta was boiling in the pot, and next to the hearth was a board stained crimson with fish guts. The creature itself rested on the gridiron, as long as a man's arm, one blackened eye gazing up the chimney flue.

"That is animal food," said Keats.

"What of it?" she asked.

Shelley shrugged and said, "I never wish to be troublesome."

"We should have done very poorly in Italy, did we refuse to share tables," said Mary. "We were grateful"—she paused—"at your father's house, and are no less so here."

"We will salute its great spirit, as the savages do." Shelley joined his hands and bowed to the sizzling fish. "I did not know they grew so large in these waters."

"We have many monsters," said Giuditta, and began to worry it with a poker.

"Oh," Mary said softly, almost in pain. She was looking at a small bottle set to warm on one side of the hearth. Giuditta nodded and with a slight gesture directed her to a corner set back from the fire. A low cradle rested on the paving and a flaxen-haired infant lay within, half awake on her back, swaddled from the neck down with one red fist worked free and ruminatively stuck in her mouth.

"I call her our Minerva," said Keats, hoisting her in his arms. And it was true; her shock of hair bristled like the plume of a helmet.

"She has owl eyes also," said Mary, and moved her finger for the dark orbs to follow.

"A foundling?" asked Shelley.

"Just so. There was no one else to care for her till she went to the Ospizio."

"And she will not go to the Ospizio," said Giuditta; "I will not give her up now. But we must decide on a name, Gianni. I do not think they will baptize her Minerva here."

"She would complete our circle at Pisa," said Shelley. "The Hunts have eight children, but none so small."

"What circle is that?" asked Giuditta.

"Oh, we have a bounty of English—a nest of singing birds, Mary calls them. There are friends of Keats, and others besides. Lord Byron is with us."

"Lord Byron!" She rounded on Keats. "*He* is your friend?"

"Ha!" said Keats.

"Oh, you will have principles." She sighed. "Signora Shelley, you see him?"

"No one sees him overmuch," said Mary. "We rented him a palazzo and he sleeps indoors till two; then he rides and shoots till dusk; then he comes home to drink. He must write when no one is looking."

"Lord Byron," Shelley said, bemused, as if expecting to find more magic in the name. "Of course we have known him a long while. He feels his exile here."

"My father will give him a second home," Giuditta said with conviction, "as he has done for so many. Now come, Gianni, you never told me you had such friends in London! Do *they* know Lord Byron?"

"Not everyone finds the knowing of Lord Byron a distinction," Keats said.

"Pf, you disapprove. Do you know," she asked the Shelleys, "how much in the great world Gianni disapproves of? You may tell me of your singing birds. What are the English like in a party?"

"It were better to come yourself and meet them," said Shelley. "To go down river is easier than up."

"I can visit no house in Pisa," she said, "be it ever so congenial, while my father's is closed to me."

His face softened. "That is yours to say. I think you give yourself too hard a penance."

She smoothed her dress over her belly and Keats touched her shoulder. "We are glad you call on us," he said.

They showed the home they were making. Keats's study was a crate draped with burlap, on which were laid books, pen and ink, a candle. They cooked small meals in the enormous hearth. The open ceiling was no hardship in the summer; it was rather a boon, as the chimney was blocked. Of course they would have to make repairs before winter.

"Do no vapors enter at night?" asked Shelley.

"Niccolò mistrusts the idea of pestilential vapors," said Keats. "Our science has not well described them."

"Yet Niccolò has not cured all the fevers," Giuditta said, and put a hand to her belly.

Shelley walked from one ruined wall to the other and marveled at their height. He felt like one of the cats in the Roman forum, he said; Keats must write something titanic here. Mary stood apart and asked Giuditta if she did not find rustic life, without servants, to be incommodious.

"Incommodious?" said Giuditta. "We have mice in the thatch. They are the devil's acrobats, and if I hang the flour from rafters they crawl down the ropes. Pray check your chairs for spiders."

"I am surprised there were no rooms to let within the castello," said Mary.

"Gianni did not wish to ask favors."

"I did not wish to live better than those around us," Keats said. "Those in the castello are not friends to those in the fields. They collect the rent and eat the bread. I did not think I could write among them."

He spoke with conviction, but he was vulnerable; he knew he might be condemned. Giuditta took a broad knife and used it as a peel to draw the smoking fish from the fire onto a plain board. She bit her lip, stuck the blade fast in its back and began to pull toward the tail fin.

"Then you do write here," Mary said. "If not for Hunt, for someone."

"He writes late," said Giuditta, parting the fish. "Sometimes he leaps from the bed in the middle of the night. It is like living with a night heron—bent over that crate, with his quill and his candle, laughing to himself."

"You laugh?" Mary asked.

"At times I laugh," said Keats.

"The laughter of the possessed," Giuditta said, "three hours before dawn. I have told him, caro sposo, you may stop laughing, or stop writing."

"The fault is yours," he told the visitors, "both of you. I read Dante's 'Paradise' because I was ashamed of not having read it— because you half convinced me that a modern work is duty bound to imagine a heaven. I should not have come to such ideas on my own."

"That is your endeavor?" Shelley asked. "A heaven?"

"Hardly!" said Keats. "How should I start? That is the trouble with heaven; it has no beginning. It is too solemn to treat with solemnity. I am making a play."

"A philosophical play?"

"An historical play. Perhaps it has a moral. But I have no spleen for satire, and I will not point out in advance who are the clowns."

"You ought to open your parcel," said Mary.

He discovered it still in his hands. It was weighty and square, and he tore back the wrapping to find a beautiful binding in green morocco from the Shelleys' library.

"I do not know if it is to your taste," said Mary. "But we had spoken of France, so I bring you Monsieur Thiers's history."

"You guess well." He opened it to the title page. "Very strange."

"Are you going to give them your secrets? He will not give them to me," Giuditta said.

"I hardly know the argument," Keats said. "France compels me; very good, but why? It would be easier if I were an historian, like Monsieur Theirs. Then I should talk of causes and the present day—this country but five years at peace, our own childhoods under blockade."

"You are thinking of Bonaparte?" asked Shelley.

"I am *not* thinking of Bonaparte. There is nothing dramatic in a monster of egoism. You cannot make him surprising. The earlier names, the names in this book, are otherwise." He shut the cover and held it up. "The minds that moved over a kingdom, casting shadows."

"Now he is going to talk about Danton and Robespierre, like my father," said Giuditta.

"Your father remembers more than Danton and Robespierre," said Keats. "He saw the hungry people. One needs both—

Shakespeare understood that. The princes speak in verse, the commoners in prose. We must touch the earth. To live in this country and treat fevers—"

"He wants to write for the contadini who can't read!" said Giuditta. "I have told him, he might go to their huts and explain it line by line; they will not understand. They are born to the dirt."

"A man I blistered yesterday told me that the rich are like the poor in two ways. Their, er, *faex* smells the same; and they die."

Mary curled her lip. "That is a proverb," she said, "but I doubt it is poetry."

"Before we learn anything, we learn the insults to our flesh. My patient has never left this hillside. Yet we both of us know that hollow in the stomach which would set us to scraping for crumbs, or for grass. *He would fain have filled his belly with the husks that the swine did eat: and no man gave unto him.* That is not Paradise. But Dante's Ugolino is poetry also."

"Dante's Ugolino is bad poetry before supper," said Giuditta. "Will you dine?"

She had quartered the fish onto plates, heaped an earthworks of polenta around it and poured wine into stone cups. Now she was trying to gather up everything at once in shaking hands. Shelley hastened to her, but she shied back and would have fallen entirely had he not caught her in his arms and relieved her of the dishes one by one, setting each on the draped board that served as a dining table.

"Sit," he said, "I beg you."

She shook her head, and her teeth chattered.

"Keats?" asked Mary.

"Ask him not," Giuditta said. "He is too much my physician already." She drew herself up, pale but steady. "Thank you, Signor Shelley. I am weak at times."

Gray clouds had clotted the strip of open sky, leaving the hearth fire to light the room. A black burn mark lapped the circuit of the upper wall. The infant Minerva, who had nodded off in

Keats's arms, was laid back in her cradle. They sat on uneven stools and Shelley lifted his cup.

"L'acqua fa male," he said, "il vino fa cantare."

They drank. The wine was sour and stuck in their mouths like syrup. The visitors coughed and, finding no water on the table, reached for the bread. It crunched with grit and turned papery as they chewed.

"It is different from town food, of course," said Keats. "We use what the land gives us."

"And very properly so," said Shelley. He cut a morsel of fish and brought it to his mouth. At once his face drained of expression, as if he had fallen asleep.

"Is it all right?" asked Giuditta.

"Hrm," said Shelley. Mary looked as if she were about to spit.

Giuditta dropped her fork. "A fiasco!"

They looked at the thing they were eating. It was thick and charred, half raw within, heavy with grease and marsh water. Shelley reached for the sour wine, gulped and swallowed.

"Please," he gasped, "I esteem what you do. It would be a great poverty always to have the same dish on one's plate."

"Gianni likes to make excuses for me," said Giuditta. "Do not you start as well."

"It is no excuse. You are heroic to make this life for yourselves."

"Everyone must buy bread from the factor's oven," Keats said. "Sometimes there is grass in the meal; sometimes they deny it; but it scarce matters when the people are hungry enough to go out and eat the grass unbaked."

"That is medieval," said Shelley. "Truly, I think of historical accounts—" and Mary touched his shoulder, and he broke off.

"When caught young," said Keats, "the fish is really not unpleasant. Only when larger—"

"Mercy!" Giuditta slammed her palms on the table and stood. "You do not need me. I will go to the castello and get you something better."

"But do not trouble yourself on our account," said Mary.

"I will get something better from the castello," said Giuditta, striding for the door, "and then I will go and drown myself."

She slapped a hanging sack aside and it swung back and forth in the doorway, stuttering daylight on the insulted fish.

"Well, go after her," said Mary.

"She does not want me."

Mary tapped Shelley's arm. He lifted his brows and, seeing that Keats kept still, stood and walked from the room. The moment he was gone Keats dropped his head low, forelocks brushing the table.

"We have no secrets," he said. "You have seen all."

"Keats, my friend," said Mary. "They are secrets no one keeps."

He looked up through his hair.

"It happens in any home. My parents condemned all marriage. I have sometimes thought they were right, that we should better seek companionship or solitude day by day, as we require it. But truly, I cannot imagine that world. More courage is asked for."

"You are courageous." He thought a while. "Will you permit me to apologize for my conduct in Pisa?"

She made her wry smile.

"Do not force a story from me," he said. "I tell you, I know not who I was there. And you and Shelley came today from nowhere, like ghosts in a storybook—I thought, what shall I be made to answer for?"

"If you asked Shelley that question," she said, "he should say the same as I; that you called us to ourselves, and have our thanks."

He looked full on at her pale skin, thoughtful brown eyes, high forehead. Those last weeks in Pisa there had been a brightening of the air whenever he saw her, as if from a hidden sun. Now she was herself again. If that sun was not entirely faded, it no longer troubled his breath.

"Let me say a simpler thing, in friendship," he said. "On the day I saw you last, you were troubled by matters that were no affair of mine. I had no right to intrude, but I am sorry to have left you in that state."

She thought and, remarkably, she laughed. "Well, as I say, no one keeps those secrets. All is over with Shelley and the contessa. Do you know it was just as you said? Her imprisonment, her rescue was a fable. She is married to a baron now."

"Is it so?"

"Shelley was stricken to the heart. Not because he did wrong; because he was deceived."

Keats tried a smile and found that it was safe, that they could share the small gesture without harm. "And no other contessa visits him?"

"You read his poem," said Mary. "Do you not remember, his inviting her to live with him on an island?"

"I remember the poetry was fine," said Keats.

"It came from the heart. All he wants is that island life. And he is disappointed again and again. Not because there is no such island; because he can find none worthy to dwell there with him."

"I should say that comes to the same thing." He lifted his hands and laced his fingers together. "A love song—Raleigh's shepherd, say—has much weaving, much embroidery. The flower cap, the kirtle of leaves." His fingers drew tighter. "But when two are wound so close, one might say each has a boot on the other's neck." His hands dropped to the table. "It is that most hateful of things: a contract! And the terms of the contract are resubscribed every morning, when I choose not to take myself to the highway."

"You have thought of leaving?" asked Mary.

"I have thought of everything," said Keats. "But it must be just. That is the Fury that pursues us, that we must always render each other justice. So if she exhausts herself carrying water, or burning a fish on the gridiron, then I must count the coppers I bring home from the consulting room. Everything is to have value!

That is what I fled from; I wanted no more coins with the Grand Duke's face on them. But if I write while she sweeps the hearth, at how much of her toil shall I rate a verse?"

"You call this a hardship of living as man and wife. I would call it a hardship of living without servants."

"And who made them servants? As I say, universal justice is our Fury."

"Not even Shelley would have dreamed that." Mary shook her head. "You should not live here."

"I should not live anywhere," Keats replied. "I sit in this room and think of Dante's heaven."

Mary followed his eyes over the burn mark that wrapped the wall. "I see the mark of hellfire."

"You must look deeper. The heaven Dante gives is not happy." He fixed her with his green eyes. "There is joy in heaven, of course, but no happiness. The blessed would not understand it. Their being is duty, the praising of their creator; their reward is to be dissolved in that duty. It is like looking at the sun. But they are hard lessons. It is in heaven, you know, that Cacciaguida tells Dante of his coming exile, that he will eat salt bread. It is no figure. You tasted it tonight."

"I do not remember you such an enemy to pleasure," said Mary.

"I am not! Upon my soul, I am not. Say rather, I would not have pleasure stand in the way of love."

She cocked her head, curious. "Love of what, Keats?"

"Humble things. Particular things. This spot of earth. These dozens of contadini."

"You say the contadini do not love this spot of earth."

"Well."

"Do you love it?"

"Solitude has its uses," he said. "No one has laid claim to this place. It will be cold in winter, but the factor does not think to charge us rent."

Mary thought a while. "I remember the night that Shelley and I left my father's house. I was hardly older than Giuditta is now. One cannot speak of regrets—my life was made that night. But they were sad years. We were poor, often friendless. The worst was estrangement from my father."

"But the sadness ended?"

"The variance could not last. My father had made me what I was. To seek beauty and liberty was all his teaching, and I had done it as best I knew. Vaccà will forgive you, Keats. He does not wish this parting."

He drew back. "You are not sent on embassy?"

"He is too proud to ask it openly. But if you go to him, he will open his door." She took his arm. "Keats, Giuditta is not well."

"You see it also." He shook his head. "She is angered if I say it—she does not want me as her physician. Her only illness, she says, is to be with child."

"Did you not say this was a feverish land?" Mary asked.

The infant Minerva coughed in her cradle and began to cry. Keats leaped to his feet. "Damn me," he said, striding across the room, "the bottle! She never had it."

It was still at the fire, not overwarmed. Keats picked up the child and tipped the bottle between her lips till she began to suck, snorting through her nose.

Voices sounded from outside. They went together through the doorway and found Shelley and Giuditta at the crumbling wall. His face was bent before hers, hands on either side of her bonnet. He spoke urgently and low; she nodded, keeping her eyes downcast, but Keats saw the flush of tears.

"Shelley?" said Mary.

He let go Giuditta's bonnet. "We must sail," he said. "The light is going." And it was true; the clouds above them had darkened to granite.

As they descended the hill Giuditta's steps faltered, and when Keats reached for her elbow she stiffened, trusting him with none of her weight. He felt a shudder in her arm and understood that she no longer wished to hide it, that it was a reproach. The breeze had died and the grass stalks stood in still expectation around white stones yielding the day's heat. Fireflies winked down the slope; the *Ariel* or *Don Juan*, whichever it was, waited motionless at the bank.

Giuditta pulled her arm free and turned to Shelley. How far was it, she asked, to Pisa by river?

"No more than an hour," said Shelley. "We go with the current."

"It seems another world." Her voice was breathless from the walk. "And to think there is an ocean beyond—France, and even England—"

"I cannot doubt you will see them."

"Be still."

She leaned forward and slapped her palm against his neck. He started back, and she opened her hand to show him a crushed mosquito in a smear of blood.

"Many monsters!" For a moment she seemed about to swoon.

Shelley leaped aboard and extended his hand for Mary to follow. They undid the moorings, lifted the sails, and Don Juan's name showed in proud black letters along the backstay. Shelley moved between the masts like a dancer, tugging the ropes in such a way that the air, which seemed to hang dead around them, nonetheless filled the sails and drew the boat slowly from the bank. He and Mary waved, became smaller, and soon could not be distinguished from the unquiet motion of the sails themselves.

"And what did Shelley say to you?" Keats asked.

"No more than anyone might see." Giuditta wiped her brow. "That I am not happy here, and ought to go back to Pisa."

"And go back how?" He turned his back on the water. "I suppose he is disappointed that he has never yet managed to rescue anyone in his boat."

"And what should it be to you, if he did?" she asked. "Tell me you would not be happier here alone, with your books and pen, and the horrible bread, and no one to task you with earthly things." Her forehead was very pale, slick with perspiration. "Do you think Shelley asked me alone? He wants you as well; he wants to stage your play, he and all your other friends that you will not see. But you must stay in a gunpowder works, and ruin yourself."

Keats shook his head. "They misunderstand. It is not the sort of play that can be staged."

"You are impossible!" She trembled and stepped backward. "You make yourself my legs; I may not move without you, and this is a marriage. How long till I see town again? How long, if you please"—a string snapped in her voice—"till I buy a cake of lemon soap?"

He could strike her. The thought came unbidden.

"I am afraid, Gianni. To have this child—"

The soul flew out of him. His soul was everywhere around him: in the clouds over the marsh, the brick quay, the shifting water, only not in himself, not in this body of desire. Her teeth chattered, her eyes moved back and forth as if in a dream, and he took her hot and shivering in his arms.

"I see the future," she murmured.

"I have not been looking after you, Giuditta. Childbed is soon, you must rest."

"It is not childbed. It is the years after. Days and days, no different from the days now. I see the future, and it does not change."

He drew back and saw thin streams of tears running from her eyes.

"Your life could be well disposed, surely, if I were not in it?"

"Such a thing to say," he whispered.

"You should live here, with your books, and heal the sick. In the evenings you should read and write, with none to stop you, none to whom you felt obliged. Is that not what you want—not to be obliged?"

He threw an arm around her shoulders, steadied her elbow and began to guide her up the hill. The marsh was wrapping itself in night, and insect lights winked on and off, indifferent as heaven.

"It seems cold," she said dreamily, "but yours is a cold country, I have heard. Your cold hands—touch my forehead."

He felt her fever and knew what chord in him should vibrate in answer. But it was stopped up; he was a husk. Such must be the embraces of the damned. And with that thought his deathbed in Rome, a deathbed which he had perhaps never left, took form around him: the smell of old sweat, the bloody burn in the throat. A blight touched all things. He clutched Giuditta tighter, as if to take all her weight upon himself; it was too incredible, too cruel, that he who had dwelt so long on death's doorstep should not yet have seen all its faces.

Casa Lanfranchi

LORD BYRON, THE CYNOSURE OF Europe, was used worse than a dog. Lord Byron was a wanderer, welcome in no country. Lord Byron's politics were identical with Christ's. The governor of Pisa, imagine, had sent round myrmidons with daggers to beat at Lord Byron's door and tell him that he was not allowed a shooting gallery in back of his palazzo. As if there weren't a thousand worse things! Lord Byron would do as he liked. The threats of a petty satrap were so much wind to a man who had just armed the spring revolts in the Piedmont, who had made his Venice palazzo a storehouse for muskets—

"Oui, oui," said Severn, "formidable."

The Frenchman in yellow trousers bowed at the interruption and drew breath to go on.

"But have you no word of others?" Severn asked. "Of Monsieur Keats?"

The Frenchman touched his mustache. "Kits?"

"Whose play is to be read."

"Eh bien—" He laughed and lifted his shoulders. "Lord Byron entertains singular persons. A physician, is it, who makes his home in a marsh? That is not one's usual set. No more than these other animals," and he winked at the stairway.

The pink and white marble hall stretched so wide that it required an extra row of pillars across its middle. The guests were gathered to one side under lamps; opposite the glow, where dim stairs rose to a half landing and broke into tributaries, was the province of beasts. A narrow-hipped bulldog sat panting at the balusters. Shadows of cats slipped behind. Someone had seen a fox—Severn fancied he smelled it—and two white monkeys lifted their tails and begged figs of anyone who passed. The birds were troubling. A peacock and guinea hen chased each other in flurries up and down the steps; nor did Severn trust the strutting crow, nor the falcon that perched on a shutter and condemned them all with great black eyes. A painted stork, as Severn supposed—*pas du tout*, the Frenchman corrected him, *une grue égyptienne*—stalked the corner on splayed claws, spreading and stowing the great black and white emblems of its wings. When it stood on tiptoe and extended its neck, its golden crown came nearly to Severn's own. It was perilous, a spear on stilts, and he found himself moving so as to keep the Frenchman between him and it.

"Lord Byron wrote an exquisite verse on a dog," said the Frenchman.

"I beg your pardon," said Severn, "I must find Monsieur Keats," and left him standing with the bird trained on his vitals.

No one at this literary evening knew the author of honor. Why were they here? It was only that Lord Byron's doors were at last open to the town. Everyone knew that some kind of amateur theatrical was going up tonight, but they had come for the menagerie.

A curtain in yellow silk, ugly against the pink stone, screened off the salon, as it was being called, where the stage had been constructed. The fabric billowed as people went past; now and then someone peered around the edge but did not linger. Everyone had come in evening dress, the men in tall hats and the women in gloves that they pulled tight before plucking canapés from the sideboard. Between their dark heads and backs flashed the occasional English face, a pink fish breaking surface. Severn made for one of those apparitions; it turned its head and flung out a crown of ginger curls, and he stopped aghast. It was the Brawne girl! She hadn't stayed in the carriage; Brown has been a fool to trust her; she was a whirlpool.

No. The figure was too short, its coat sky blue. It was the eldest Hunt lad, along with four or five of his brood. They all wore bright clothes and were diverting themselves by swarming nearby Italians, circling their waists in a train and winging back to their mother's taffeta skirts. Mrs. Hunt stood among them like a leafless tree. Her eyes drooped, and every time a child knocked against her she reached for her husband, who took her hand while his warm blue eyes darted after every other thing in the room. He had not lost the habit, Severn saw, of seeking out the most important person in any gathering. No one really blamed him for it, any more than they would grudge a cat its choice of lap; but since Lord Byron was not yet present, nor any other large quarry, Severn might borrow him. He caught Hunt's eye and instantly gained a delighted smile, as if Severn above all was the man he wished to see. He remembered the stories of Hunt in prison— how he had painted clouds on the ceiling and played battledore, how his jailors had not been able to refuse him a pianoforte.

Hunt took his arm. "How now, Canova?"

They had not seen each other in a year. Severn bowed to Mrs. Hunt and to any of the children who would pause for it; they named their common friends and began to disburse their news. Brown was accounted for; there he was at the curtain, talking with a tall sort of scarecrow in a patched coat—heavens, Severn realized with a pang, that was Shelley the atheist. He asked about Hunt's journey, though he knew the story already. Yes, Hunt said, the rumors were true, they had been nine months traveling. Foul weather had held them at Ramsgate, then beat them up and down channel till they put in at Dartmouth, Marianne so poorly that they must winter at Plymouth—

"Now pray do not test his patience with Plymouth," said Mrs. Hunt.

"To pass over her health is Marianne's privilege," Hunt said. "And what of you, Severn? All the way from Rome to see our play?"

"I thought it was Keats's play." He could not keep the strain from his voice. "No one here knows where he is. No one knows who he is."

"They shall know both," said Hunt. "He will not show himself before the performance. He is backstage in meditation, as he calls it—I say he is fretting."

Severn looked to the curtain. "I have not seen him since Rome. I had a letter—Hunt, I do not know what to think."

Hunt smiled kindly. "But why think anything?"

"He left without warning! I could not imagine he would take up with Shelley," lowering his voice, "and this matter of a Pisan girl—"

"Of course." Hunt brought his face near Severn's. "But is it not to be expected? Keats is of an age to form attachments, and he brings no family to ease his exile." He gave a sideways nod to Mrs. Hunt, who seemed to understand she might join the conclave, and to decline the honor. "Once he was well again, and felt a young man's blood beating in his veins, he must have wished to root himself."

"Then was he quite unattached, in London?" Severn asked.

"Quite," said Hunt.

"Oh forgetful!" said Mrs. Hunt.

The children had left her and she brought her tired face close. "Do you not remember all summer, when he lay with fever on our couch, who brought the cloth?"

"The cloth?" Hunt took her elbows. "Well, of course the neighbor girl was there. I do not say Keats was an anchorite. I am speaking of an attachment such as carried us together here, through endless storm—"

Mrs. Hunt straightened suddenly and shouted, "Thornton! John!"

The boys had left off chasing the Italians and were now holding out figs for the monkeys, pulling them out of reach every time the creatures leapt up. They crouched low, clacking their jaws, and thrashed the tufts of their tails.

"Did Keats tell you, then, that he felt the beating blood?"

Severn asked. "That he must be rooted?"

Hunt seemed surprised at the question. "Well, what has he said to you? You say you had a letter."

"I do not understand the letter. Hunt, I understand nothing." Guests were still going past the curtain, introducing their heads between fabric and wall, and Severn envied each of them; he envied everyone who saw more than he. "I have not read his play."

"Nor I, nor anyone," said Hunt. "No one has seen a line of it, save the players."

Severn blinked. "I thought you were to publish it."

"So I am. It is Keats!—let him write what he will."

His face softened with love and he seemed to lose sight of Severn before him, of his wife shooing the boys from the monkeys. Severn shut his eyes and wished that he were not an artist, and all his friends not literary men. They would never attend what needed attending. How had they ever managed to collect the money and documents to get Keats to Italy before he expired?

"Severn. I say, Severn."

Hunt's hand was on his shoulder. "I am told," he murmured, "that Keats has a legacy. Is it true?"

Severn started back. "Who told you that?"

Hunt looked hurt. "The question is indelicate. I beg your pardon."

"I beg *your* pardon," Severn said; "this is why I must find Keats, to speak with him—"

"And before or after you speak with Keats," a firm voice broke in, "he should die of shame, hearing his affairs discussed so. Severn, may I have your ear?"

It was Brown. Hunt stepped back with a shy nod, and Severn saw he was not offended; he was ashamed. Of course—it was Hunt who had lent the greater part of Keats's traveling money.

"You know Shelley, I believe."

Severn took the pale, long-fingered hand that was offered him. It was many years since that dinner at Hunt's where Shelley had called the Savior a mountebank. It all seemed remote and comical now, down to the bit of broccoli Shelley had been eating, and Severn was prepared to be generous so long as this tall apparition did not prove yet another barrier.

"Shelley has been kind enough to tell me what he knows of Keats's present mode of life," said Brown, "which is a great deal."

"You mean his life in the marsh?" Severn asked.

"He is in the marsh no more," said Shelley in his high voice. "They have returned for diverse reasons, above all his wife's health."

"Wife! Must we use that word?"

"Where is the Brawne woman, Severn?" Brown asked. "No, do not squint; I have told Shelley everything."

"She is waiting where I told her to wait," said Severn, "out of doors in the carriage."

"And she knows nothing of Keats's connection?" asked Shelley, his delicate face tightening. "How long do you intend to keep her in suspense?"

"I will not yet mix the sulfur and saltpeter," said Brown. "See, the native is here."

The girl who would steal Keats from England sat on a window bench, eating cake. Her complexion was the golden sort that suggested darkness without actually being dark; her hair was ink-black. A couple of young men stood beside her, and Severn stared at them as if expecting proof, from across the room, that she was a coquette. She did not look at them. She buried one hand in her hair and tucked her ankles beneath the seat. The forward bulge at her waist was plain.

"Keats has become entangled," said Brown. "We must free him."

Shelley frowned. "The entanglement is rather advanced. Do you conceive that Keats would do something dishonorable?"

"What they are calling marriage," said Brown, "is some bit of Popish farce in a barnyard, is it not, without witnesses? I cannot see that any English society need recognize it."

Something tugged Severn's coat and he spun round to find a monkey's wrinkled face peering at him. Its paw was out, and he saw with revulsion that its small black eyes were fixed on the bit of candied orange he had taken from a side table. He threw the morsel down; the creature pounced, tail whipping, and the Hunt boys laughed. He heard Brown's deep chuckle also—did no one find occasion for gravity this evening! Angry and blushing, he turned to the parqueted entry where a footman was taking people's coats, and there he saw the Brawne woman. There was no mistaking her this time. She stood alone, still in costume, and swept her eyes over the room.

"Brown!" he hissed. "Brown, stop laughing—see there."

Brown followed Severn's eyes and took a breath. "Well! You had better go to her."

"*I* had better! Are you not her chaperone?"

"She will hear nothing from me. My God, Severn, can you not take her in hand? I am quite occupied here."

He turned to Shelley and began deliberately to speak a shade too low for Severn to hear. Severn opened his mouth and shut it, but Hunt and Shelley bent away from him and he had no choice but to break from the group. He lifted his chin to draw Miss Brawne's attention; as her eyes passed over him, his knees lost a jot of strength.

"I say," he called. Try as he might, he could not infuse his voice with Brown's firmness. "I say, there."

De cape et d'épée

FANNY REALLY HAD INTENDED to keep her promise and stay in the carriage, but she had not counted on the darkness of this Tuscan town. There were no lamps in the street, the moon was shrouded away somewhere and the only light came from the door of Lord Byron's palazzo, blocked every so often by the cloaked outlines that stepped into its aura—some single, some arm in arm—and hesitated a moment before mounting the shallow stairs.

Young Charles lay beside her on the carriage seat. His breath moved in sleep and the faint light through the window picked out the haze of his eyelashes. She felt ripe with power, as when the dreaming mind becomes almost aware that its surroundings are a sham and, without quite pronouncing them unreal, knows it might conjure anything into being.

She leaned into the night, spoke a few Italian words to the driver and opened the carriage door.

At the top of the stairs she met a forest of lamps and candles. Marble gleamed white and pink like a dessert, too rich to live in. A footman was taking coats; she remembered her disguise and shrank toward a stand of jessamine branches. In the dark she had quite forgotten what she was wearing. Now she found herself staring full face into a mirror, and for two moments fell in love with the young man in the frame. His shoulders were wrapped close in the green jacket; under the black bangs his eyes shone an unearthly sky color. There was an unreality to him, neatness and smoothness carried a touch too far. She smiled, was encouraged to see the smile returned, and a red-faced Severn appeared behind the young man's shoulder.

"For God's sake, Miss Brawne!" he whispered. "You said you

should keep back from the proceedings."

"So I am," she said. "Nothing is proceeding in the flower arrangement. Where is John?"

Severn shook his head and said something about a yellow curtain that he would not stoop to look behind. She took his elbow and compelled him to conduct her into the hall. There were children skipping among the suits and gowns—animals too, roaming ungoverned. A white, shaggy, dog-size beast with long forelimbs and a flattened human face was trying to snatch something from two older lads with chestnut locks.

"I know them!" she said; "those are the Hunt boys."

"Yes," Severn murmured, "you might consider they will know you as well. What have you done with Brown's child?"

"I did nothing. The driver has him. Now, I see Mr. Hunt and Mr. Brown—who is the tall man?"

"That is Shelley himself."

"Severn! You said he was a demon. Why, he looks very fair. He only wants his collar starched."

It was not a question of his collar, Severn said. Beside Shelley stood a severely handsome woman, not tall, bare-shouldered, hardly older than Fanny herself. Was it Mrs. Shelley? She cast an unfeminine, knowing smile at something Shelley was saying, and without warning turned to Fanny herself, picking her out from across the room. She shrank back and let go Severn's elbow.

She had better take her part seriously. A young man ought to keep his head high, his shoulders loose. The wig itched her temples; she held back from scratching. He must have a lazier walk. His eyes might fall on the women. The Italian gowns did not affect high waists after all—perhaps their history made them suspicious of French fashion, or perhaps such fashion had never reached this place. The fabrics were stiff and cut high at the neck, like something Fanny's mother would have worn when Fanny was a girl. Some even had ruffs at the collar. But the younger women wore white flowers in their hair. One of them caught her eye;

Fanny offered a half bow, playing the libertine, and the girl colored and turned away.

"Suppose we keep apart from the crowd?" Severn asked. "If we go nearer the stairs—I am told Lord Byron is coming down presently."

"I have not come to see Lord Byron."

Yet Fanny could not keep from glancing at the staircase. She had seen Byron's likeness in engravings, and remembered him not for his handsomeness—anyone might be handsome in an engraving—but for his clothes. In one pose he wore a dark cloak and open-collared shirt with a brooch; the other was in Eastern dress, with a turban falling past his brow and a sword in his arms. Fanny had met enough poets to know poets did not dress like this, not even the fashionable ones. They were clothes for a stage player. Early on John had condemned her taste for Byron, and she hadn't explained the truth of it, that one loved Byron as the player first and the poet second, that the clothes were needed no less than the verse.

They passed a row of pillars dividing the room. A gathering at a window bench, from which Severn urged her sharply with his elbow, had a girl seated at center wearing no ornament but the white flash of her teeth. Three or four men stood in her glow and made brief sallies at which she smiled without looking up. Her gown was drawn up in front as if to conceal her waist. That was hardly a disguise, Fanny thought; no one could doubt her condition. None of her quick fingers wore a ring.

She had looked too long. The girl felt her gaze, and her hands slowed as she tried to make out who was the foreign-looking young man across the room. One of her companions broke in and asked something that Fanny almost understood, about the girl not appearing in the play. She dropped her eyes and the man asked something more, having to do with the play's author.

"Cattiva," said the girl. That meant her health was bad.

Severn pulled at her wrist. "You don't understand the language?"

"I begin to," Fanny murmured. "May we not—?"

"Decidedly not! It would be thought rude," and with an ungentle tug he pulled them onward.

"Severn, who is the girl?"

"I have not been one night in Pisa. I know no girls."

"But she knows the play."

He shook his head. "What a girl claims to know—"

"What, the painter!"

A handsome fellow in an officer's uniform blocked their way to the staircase. "Your pardon if I interrupt your conference," he said genially. "I fear you must look out more closely for the beasts. Why, I once saw a bird very like that"—pointing out a long-necked, long-legged, beaked form in the shadow of the banister—"leap onto a man's shoulders in India, and all but take his eye."

Severn attempted a laugh. "Thank you. I dare say we shall not confront it."

"If you are given to choose!" He laughed richly. "Oh, they are noble creatures—the natives say that if one be killed, its mate will never pair again. Certainly I have heard the survivor calling all night for its lost companion, and I never could shoot them since. Captain Thomas Medwin, sir," offering a hand to Fanny, "good evening."

"Pardon me, Captain Medwin," said Severn. "Er—Mr. Francis Brawne, nephew to Mr. Brown."

"Brawne and Brown, Brown and Brawne." Again came the rich laugh. "Everything has its drop of poetry tonight."

"A pleasure, Captain." Fanny took his hand, ignoring Severn's tap at her elbow. "Have you met with many poets tonight?"

"Oh, poets are like birds, and not to be startled. But I have seen some few. My cousin Shelley is at the curtain, and I fancy Lord Byron will soon show his colors. If you happen to know Mr. Keats, of the 'Hyperion'—"

"Do *you* know Mr. Keats?" Fanny asked, and Severn bit his

lip.

"I cannot say *know*. I had the honor to meet him but once, at my cousin's."

"But he has a reputation here? He is thought a worthy poet?"

"Why—" The good humor in his face seemed to pass beyond sure territory. "No doubt he has a reputation of some sort. I am told to expect something singular tonight—something altogether modern, you know, after his change of life."

"Change of life?"

"Captain Medwin!" Severn exclaimed, "you dishonor yourself! You have not included your own name among the poets."

Medwin laughed again, bashful and pleased. "Well, I cannot claim to stand in their rank. But it is true, Mr. Hunt and his brother may see fit to offer something of mine to the public, the profit of my sojourn in India."

He began to talk of lions, and did not notice that Fanny was ignoring him, staring Severn down. She knew that he and Brown had kept things from her; they knew that she knew; yet the magnitude of the deception was perhaps not clear.

"There is a joy to vulgar souls unknown," said Medwin. "There is a magic in that word—*Alone!*"

A brash, baritone voice broke in from above. "What is he for? Why, he sees to it that no Cockneys shall come up the stairs."

A bulldog descended the steps, muzzle lifted, nails rapping the stone. A step behind came his master, dangling the leash negligently from one hand. He did not look like an engraving. His form was too broad, too vague in the face. But he wore black in the evening, as Brummell would have done, and there was no question but that the laugh had been his, and that he was addressing the crowd instantly collected at the base of the stairs.

"Very good," said someone, "but the Cockneys have your salon"—to suppressed laughter.

"I grant concessions to those I esteem," said the dog's master. "Does Shelley desire that I stage a play in my house? My door and my wine cellar are open to him. On this occasion."

Fanny had imagined many things of Lord Byron, but never that he would be fat. Only knowing him in advance could one recognize the famous nose and brow stationed over wide cheeks and a heavy jaw. His hands were thick and covered in rings, like a bishop's. Yet he was not grotesque. He was not even unhandsome. Somehow he wore this suit of too much flesh to advantage. He could not now be the sorrowing wanderer of his poems, but he could be someone older and more formidable, the master of a house. Gliding along the stairway, he turned one knee inward, favoring his foot so that it hardly rested on the steps; his shoulders and neck kept level and independent of these maneuvers, as if something were balanced on his head. It was like seeing a giraffe come down a staircase—or as if the long-legged bird, which had vanished from its corner, was here transformed.

"There," said Medwin, satisfied, and turned his back on Fanny and Severn to join the crowd.

As Lord Byron stepped to the floor, his foot gave beneath him. He ducked with an automatic gesture; the invisible object slipped from his head and he grimaced. But whatever demon drove him to cut this figure straightaway took hold of him, pulled him upright and balanced itself upon him once more. He was still dressed in black, he still held the leash. His hair, falling in ringlets, was almost completely gray. He started across the room and the crowd went with him, catching Severn and Fanny in its circuit.

"I do not know," he said, answering someone; "I have hardly met the man, though I am giving him my house tonight. Hunt has been our intermediary, and the Italian players honor me with their visits—the son of that doctor, for one, who jumps about like a kangaroo."

He carelessly pointed out a man at the pillars, presumably the doctor, who stood wrapped in a black coat, with iron-gray hair and a hawk's nose bent gloomily down. He rested both hands on the pommel of a stick, as if standing outdoors in bad weather. His eyes were fixed on the pregnant girl in the white gown.

"I know nothing of the piece," Byron was saying, "save that its première has been again and again delayed. The last I knew we were waiting on some arrival from Leghorn; but here are the authors of the scheme."

Brown had gone elsewhere to gather clues, and the group at the curtain was reduced to Shelley, Mary and Hunt, bent together in close conference and unaware of the approaching cortège.

"The players are Italians," Shelley was saying, "but they are not to represent Italians. He is cannier than that. The history is French, the dramatis personae likewise."

"Cosmopolitan, I am sure," said Hunt. "But is it not sad, that he has lost his England? He told me he should trade away all Virgil's pastures for a solitary dog-rose."

"I think he shall not have lost England, so long as he writes in his native tongue," said Shelley.

"And history is perhaps easier drawn abroad," said Mary. "He would not do as Shelley has done, and address the killings at Manchester."

"Even so," said Hunt, "'The Death of Danton'—as a subject, it seems to take liberties. Events that our fathers remember, that I very nearly remember myself—"

"Very good!" said Byron.

They turned and gave good evening a little bashfully, as if unsure of the propriety of their discussion. Byron smiled in pleasure at catching them unawares.

"Whatever the young playwright's subject," he said, "I hope you will agree that matters not a whit, if he has not reformed his style upon some more correct model."

Hunt straightened, aware he was being particularly baited. "And the correct style, my Lord—?"

"The classical," said Byron, "which is no extraordinary opinion. I claim nothing for my own judgment; only that it is not so diseased as to hold we must throw out everything we have inherited." He smiled tolerantly and ran his hand over his gray temple. "Pray, how should a fledgling from Whitechapel think himself equipped to throw over Pope, and soar to heaven on his pinfeathers? We may admire the Satanic pride, but never the want of understanding."

His speaking voice was deep and gentle, and Fanny did not immediately grasp the depth of the attack. Someone coughed and suggested that the younger poets did not universally disdain the old.

"We may try it," said Byron. "Who is young here? Not you, I fear"—to Hunt—"I must excuse ladies"—to Mrs. Shelley—"you are altogether *too* young," discovering the oldest Hunt boy behind him; and Fanny shrank, foreseeing that the lord's wandering gaze would finish on her.

"You, sir."

"I?" she asked.

"You are the judge of Alexander Pope. Does he live or die?"

Fanny bowed. "I know only that he is no favorite with Mr. Keats."

"*Mister* Keats." Byron pursed his fine mouth, as if tasting a sweet. "Well! Open a book of Mister Keats, which is supposed to contain poems, and see the company he chooses! Yes, yes," he said, waving off an interruption, "the 'Hyperion' is fine enough. But his other offerings, and in the book before—why, in some lines he puts eight syllables, in some twelve. That is organic measure? Bosh! English is not Greek; I daresay it has no feet to stretch. A defective line is a defective line." And he looked to Fanny—curious, it seemed, if she would answer.

"The poetry is beautiful," she said, "in many places."

His mouth curled. "In many places. That is your defense?"

"How many can say so much?" asked Shelley. "How many have written ten immortal lines?"

"Perhaps there are ten immortal lines out of four thousand," said Byron. "I had not patience to find them out. He has versified

Lempriére's mythology. Why write such a thing over again?"

"But there is originality," said Fanny. "He adapts the argument—the two women."

Byron looked confused, and she colored. Why introduce the argument of the poem, when she herself did not approve it? To catch the hero between two women, and at the last moment make them out to be one and the same—of course it was a cheat. One was a fair goddess, one a dark maid; it was something about earth and heaven, an allegory, John had said when she asked. She knew what that meant.

"I am astonished that you discerned any argument whatsoever," said Byron. "I could make out nothing through the exhalations of the style. It is a kind of mental—hrm, let us say he is viciously soliciting his ideas into a state which is neither poetry nor anything else but a"—he lifted his hand, conjuring the phrase—"a Bedlam vision produced by raw pork and opium." He spun round on his strong foot. "And you, sir," leaning over Fanny, "you are cool towards Pope?"

His eyes glinted like coins. The circle was silent.

"Surely every man has his style," she murmured. "That is— must they all contend? Till only one remains in the library?"

She could not give a line of Pope if she were asked. Byron drew himself up, once more the dangerous bird, but he did not strike. He considered her costume, laying it aside piece by piece till he apprehended her as she was. His generous mouth, that so delighted in the taste of things, smiled in one corner.

"Good lad," he said. "Good Ganymede."

He reached out a hand. She shrank away, and he laid one thick finger on her cheek just below the eye, grazing her skin with the cold band of his ring. He chuckled, spun again on his foot and glided from the circle, which instantly broke apart.

Flushed, Fanny turned to the gathering at the curtain; she would read by their faces whether she had done well. But there was no curtain, no gathering. Servants had pulled aside the yellow silk and lanterns were being lighted in the dark space beyond. The stage was a platform knocked together from slats that might have been pulled out of barrels or packing crates. Footlight lanterns picked out bent heads of nails. Guests were walking in from the bright hall; they squinted, held out their arms and bumped into the velvet backs of chairs. Fanny joined their current, holding her breath in case John was to be seen, but the lamps were scant and someone's head blocked her view in every direction. To be in the thick of the audience seemed suddenly perilous. She worked her way to one side until she reached a wall, where the molding gave her a handhold against the press of the crowd. Her heart lifted. Now was the revealment and struggle; she felt keen, ready to claim her own.

The Death of Danton, Act One

AS THE GLARE DRAINED FROM the spectators' eyes they saw players already on stage. Several figures sat close at a table: gamblers, their lank hair tied back with ribbons, and a woman dealer in a red gown. A man and woman stood at the corner opposite. The man's head was turned aside to watch the card game, stock still with his chin in his fist. His collar was open, his cloak had an oval brooch at the shoulder. The literary folk in the crowd were quickest to work out what the pose meant, and soon everyone was whispering to his neighbor; everyone had seen that engraving of Lord Byron somewhere.

Was it Danton, posed this way? Was that the joke?

There was a cough in the dark, and Lord Byron's own voice came deep and strained: "A monkey—a monkey!"

Some of the guests laughed. Danton did not turn his head, and as the audience continued to look for chairs, or gave up on finding them and settled against the walls, he ran his hand through his hair and began to speak.

Danton. Beguiling lady! Artful is her touch,
   And sly her fingers parcel out the cards.
   Mark this: the hearts fall ever to her husband—
   The others take the coins. Legerdemain!
   A lie commands our love.
Mme Danton.   Believ'st in me?
Danton. How can I say? We know each other scarce.
   We are thick-pelted things—we stretch our paws,
   And one coarse hide but rubs against the next.
   We are lonely.

Mme Danton.　　　　　　Thou knowest me, Danton.

Danton. Ay, what the world calls knowing. Feather'd locks
　　Thou hast, and eyes of jet, and cheek all snow,
　　And loving call'st my name—but here! But here!
　　(*He touches her cheekbone, her brow.*)
　　What is behind? How gross our human senses!
　　To know each other? Never, till we cleave
　　Our skulls in two, and from our furrowed brains
　　Wring out the thoughts.

His rhythm was good. His Italian accent was murky as the stage lights. His countrymen in the audience recognized him, as they recognized the faces at the card table; some were students, some the sons of respectable families, everyone had seen their amateur theatricals at the café. But they were speaking a foreign language now, and more shocking, the daughters of Pisa were on stage next to the sons. Did their mothers know?

The surprise of the Byron costume past, the English audience decided it was a caprice and best ignored. The lines themselves were no puzzle; everyone had heard imitations of *Hamlet* before.

The cards were dealt. A young man in rouge and a wig took a pinch of snuff and made an obscure gesture, and the dealer rapped his hand.

Dealer. Say, what are you about with your fingers?

Hérault. Nothing!

Dealer. Don't stick your thumb out so, it's vulgar.

Hérault. But see, the thing has such a particular physiog-
　　nomy—

The card players laughed: the solitary sort of theatrical laugh, in which the audience does not join.

Danton. I love thee as the grave.
Mme Danton.   O horrible!
Danton. Nay, hear. 'Tis said that in the grave is peace,
    Peace and the grave are one. Be it but so,
    In thy soft lap I lie beneath the earth.
    Sweet grave! Thy fluted lips my passing-bells,
    Thy breast my burial mound, thy heart my coffin.

Fanny's scalp prickled; for she had heard those very words, or words near enough, from Keats himself.

Dealer. You lose!
Hérault. It was a lover's adventure. It cost money like any
    other.
Dealer. Then you declared your love like a deaf-mute, with
    your fingers.
Hérault. And fitting it was. They say the fingers, of all things,
    are soonest understood. See, here I made a tryst with the
    queen; my fingers were princes enchanted to spiders; the
    fairy, Madam, was you; but the chance went ill. The lady
    was forever in childbed, each moment she birthed an-
    other knave. By God, I wouldn't have my daughter play
    this game—the lords and ladies fall so indecently upon
    each other! And the knaves come close behind.

Someone in the audience laughed: a surprised burst, quickly choked back. There was muttering. Who, again, had written this, and under what provocation?

A young man strode through a side door and gained the stage. His flowing black wig declared his character; his coat shimmered blue in the lantern light, excepting one sleeve that was thoroughly smirched with ink as befit the genius of polemics. Under the costume of Camille Desmoulins someone recognized young Vaccà, the doctor's son, and cried encouragement from his seat. Everyone liked the young Vaccà.

Fanny recognized the sleeves she had hemmed a year ago, and her heart leaped.

> *Hérault.* A frown, Camille! Didst tear thy carmine cap,
>   Or blotting rain obscure the guillotine?
>   Did the gutter crowd press close, and give no view?

Young Vaccà threw out his smirched sleeve, a gesture only somewhat compromised by the paper in his other hand, at which he had to glance before speaking.

> *Camille.* Time was, Hérault, to play at Socrates,
>   And mock Alcibiades in his sulk;
>   Now give ear, classical republican!
>   Your guillotine romantics have the day.
>   Another twenty are made sacrifice—
>   We were deceived. The Hébertists are slain
>   For want alone of system in their crimes,
>   And that the faction after Robespierre
>   Quake for themselves, lest any men should seem
>   More merciless, more swathed in blood than they.
> *Hérault.* We are become antediluvians.
>   Saint-Just would bend us naked to all fours,
>   That Master Robespierre might raise new men
>   Upon the Genevan watchmaker's design:
>   Lectures and dunce caps—and a clockwork God!
> *Camille.* Five hundred heads for peace; so said Marat.
>   They swell his tally with a row of noughts.
>   How long have we to sprawl like newborn babes
>   'Midst blood and filth, with coffins for our cradles
>   And heads for baubles? Progress! Clemency!
>   The banished deputies must be restored.

He read well, the doctor's son. He was certainly better than Hérault, who did not seem to understand which were the important words in an English sentence. The play was starting to seem less like *Hamlet*; perhaps it was *Henry*. And daring as it was to ground a *Henry* play in living memory—one could not stage this in England—it did explain certain points. The indecent Hérault must be a Falstaff. That was comprehensible, if not quite forgivable.

> *Hérault.* The Revolution has attained the age
>> Of self-remaking. Forthward must it cease,
>> And in its stead the Republic commence.
>> We shall exchange our principles of state:
>> For duty, right; for virtue, happiness;
>> For penance, preservation. Let each thrive,
>> Let each unfold his nature. Be he sane
>> Or madman, true or base, rude or urbane,
>> It touches not the state. We are fools all;
>> Let none impose his folly on another.
>> Let each seek pleasure in his fashion, save
>> That none may gladden in another's harm,
>> Nor choke his neighbor's wellspring of delight.
>
> *Camille.* The shape of state must be an airy veil
>> To cling skin-close upon the people's form.
>> Each pulse of artery, each tightened nerve,
>> Each longing quiver must be there transcribed.
>> The figure may be fair or hideous;
>> That is its right. Authority have we none,
>> To cut a frock in any shape we please.
>> And to them who would throw a nun's constraint
>> Upon the naked shoulders and soft throat
>> Of France, our well-beloved sinneress—
>> We rap their hands! Nude goddesses, Bacchantes,
>> Olympic tourneys, sweet melodious lips:

These things we crave—O warm, limb-loosening Love!
Let Robespierre's Romans, if they will,
Sit them chaste in the corner, and cook beets;
They shall give gladiator games no more.
Let divine Epicurus, let thrice-fair
Venus of shapely buttocks be installed
In place of dead Marat and Chalier
As saints to our Republic. Ho! Danton!
In the Convention shalt thou lead the charge.

Hérault had risen from his chair and stood close by Camille, in that near embrace so often seen at the Ussero: young men, in love with the world of their imagining. Danton left off his hungry, meaningless peering into the eyes of his wife, and showed his face as if waking from a dream.

Danton. I shall. Thou shalt. He shall… if we live all
　To see the morrow… as old women say.
　An hour passes. Threescore minutes flown.
　Is it not so?
Camille (*uncomprehending*). That much explains itself.
Danton. Ay, everything explains itself. And who
　Shall bring to pass these sundry lovely things?
Hérault. We will, and honest men.
Danton.　That "and" between—
　A fair wide word! It distances its neighbors.
　The road is long, your honesty may lose
　Her breath, ere ye join hands. Faith, honest men!
　You may lend them money, stand their christenings,
　Or wed them to your daughters—but no more.
Camille. Wast thou, wise man, who didst commence the fight.
Danton. Those Romans raised my hackles. Never I met
　With any prancing Cato of their stamp,
　But I gave him a kick. That is my nature.

(*He turns to leave.*)
Mme Danton. Thou goest?
Danton.　They flay me with their politics.
　　'Twixt post and portal will I prophesy:
　　The cast of freedom's statue is not poured,
　　The oven glows, we may yet burn our fingers.

He swung his bulk about like a boat tacking its sails and walked out through the side door. The card players stood, collected their table and chairs and tramped off stage with the rest of the company. The spectators tried to catch one another's eyes in the dimness. What should they think—was it a bad play? Probably the students were stammering out abominable lines, but the stammering made it hard to judge. One hesitated to declare anything sooner than one's neighbor.

A man and woman shuffled on stage. They were graying, with sunken faces, and nobody knew them; they did not look like performers, nor like people that one could take any pleasure in watching. Their clothes were patched. Suppose they were street characters, who had simply happened in through the open palazzo door?—and without warning the man raised his hand and slapped the woman's face. She clutched her cheek and dropped to one knee.

Man. Puttana! Dose of mercury! Bewormed sin-apple!
Wife. Ohimè! Help! Help!

They spoke Tuscan prose. Were they comedians? Some in the audience laughed, taking it for a Pulcinella show, but those in the front row wondered if they ought to get up and stop it. Three men, sans-culottes in shabby jackets and work boots, strode through the door and pushed their way on stage. Battered cockades were pinned to their hats; at their waists were daggers.

Citizens. Pull them apart!

Man. Stand off, Romans! I'll dash this carcass to her bones. Thou Vestal!

Wife. I, a Vestal? A fine day that should be.

Man. From off thy shoulders do I tear the cloak, and hurl thy carcass naked in the sun. Whore's bed! In each folding of thy body is fornication.

He made to seize her again and the citizens pulled them apart.

1st Citizen. What's the matter?

Man. Where is the girl? No, girl she is not—maiden!—that neither. The woman, the wife?—no, nor that—only one name may I call her! It chokes me, I have no breath for it.

2nd Citizen. Good, it should smell of brandy.

Man. Cover thy bald pate, old Virginius. The raven Shame sits upon it, and gouges thine eyes! Romans, a knife! (*He falls.*)

Wife. He's a good man, sirs, but he can't keep up with his brandy. It gets him in the legs.

Man. Thou art the vampire tongue that laps my warm heart's blood!

Wife. Leave him be, 'tis come time for his bawling.

1. Cit. What's happened here?

Wife. Sirs, I was sitting on this rock as you see it, in the sun to warm myself, for we have no wood, sirs—

2. Cit. Not even your husband's nose?

Wife. And my daughter was gone to the corner, for she's a good girl and keeps up her parents.

Man. She owns it!

Wife. Judas! Would ye have a pair of breeches to pull up, except that the young men pull down theirs? Shalt thirst, brandy-cask, if the fountain dries up? We work with every other part, why not this; thy mother employed it to bring thee into the world, for all it pained her; shall the girl not furnish for her own mother? Thou criest for pain? Dunce!

Man. Lucretia! A knife, Romans, give me a knife! O Appius Claudius!

1. Cit. Ay, a knife, but not for the poor tart. What has she done? 'Tis her hunger goes begging. A knife for them who buy the flesh of our women! Woe to them who whore with the daughters of the people! Ye have wind in your bellies and they have fat stomachs, ye have holes in your coats and they have warm furs, ye have welts on your fists and they have velvet hands. Ergo ye work and they do nothing, ergo they stole what ye had by inheritance, ergo ye would have a pair of coppers from your birthright and must beg and whore for it, ergo they are villains and their heads forfeit.

3. Cit. They have no blood in their veins save what they sucked out from ours. They said, the aristocrats are wolves, and we hung the aristocrats from the lampposts. They said, the king's veto devours your bread, and we struck down the king. They said, the Girondists starve you, and we sent the Girondists to the guillotine. And each time they stripped the clothes from the dead, and we went naked as before. 'Tis time their fat thickened our soup. Death to anyone with no hole in his coat!

1. Cit. Death to anyone who reads and writes!

2. Cit. Death to anyone who flees!

Citizens. Death, death!

A young student, one of the card players, ventured on stage and was seized.

1. Cit. He has a handkerchief! An aristocrat! To the lamppost!

Student. Monsieurs!

2. Cit. There are no monsieurs here! To the lamppost!

Student. Mercy!

3. Cit. We show more mercy than thou. 'Tis but a curl of hemp to kiss thy throat, and that but a moment. Our life is death by toil, our sentence sixty years to hang and quiver, but we will cut ourselves loose. To the lamppost!

Student (gathering courage). You will see no brighter for it.

1. Cit (laughing). Bravo! Let him go!

The moment the student's arms were loosed, he turned to flee and nearly collided with a small man in a periwig and cravat. He had taken the stage unseen and stood at center with his spine straight and nose lifted; his gray jacket and waistcoat were brushed clean, the ruffles lay crisp on his shirt. Two attendants, women in clogs and soft caps, stood in his train. The student shrieked—no one could doubt who this figure was—and made for the opposite door. The apparition in the wig watched him go with a passionless grimace and raised a hand to the crowd.

Robespierre. What's the matter, citizens?

3. Cit. What do you think? August and September's drops of blood have put no red in our cheeks. The guillotine is too slow. We want a thunderclap.

1. Cit. Our children cry for bread, they shall have aristocrats' flesh. Death!

Citizens. Death! Death!

Robespierre. In the name of the law!

1. Cit. What is the law?

Robespierre. The will of the people.

1. Cit. We are the people and we want no law, ergo there is no law, ergo death!

1. Woman. Silence, let Aristides speak! Silence for the Incorruptible!

2. Woman. Hear the Messiah, come to choose and to judge.
He will strike the wicked with the blade of his sword.
His eyes are the eyes of election, his hands the hands of
judgment.

Robespierre. Poor virtuous people! Your duties ye discharge,
Your enemies ye offer. Ye are great.
In thunder and in lightning do ye storm.
But strike not your own body in your wrath,
O people, murder not yourselves. Ye rise
Or fall by your own force; this your foes know.
Your legislators watch with tireless eyes
And would guide your inevitable hands.
Come to the Jacobins. 'Midst brothers' arms
Shall ye hold blood tribunal on your foes.

He spoke better English than the others, and needed no sheet
in his hand. It seemed almost believable that the citizens would be
stayed by his words, and their hands drop from their daggers. He
started off stage and one by one the crowd joined arms and followed, the women bringing up the rear. The old couple crouched
at the platform's edge where they had been dropped.

Man. Woe! I am undone. (*He tries to stand.*)

Wife. Here! (*She helps him.*)

Man. My Baucis. Thou heap'st coals upon my head.

Wife. Stand up!

Simon. Dost turn away? Ah, canst forgive me, Portia? 'Twas
my madness struck thee, not my hand. O, Hamlet does
it not, Hamlet denies it; his madness is poor Hamlet's
enemy. Where is Susanna, where is our daughter?

Man. There, at the corner.

Simon. Best of wives, let us go to her.

They left shuffling, as they had come, and the stage was quiet.

From her post at the back wall, peering around the heads of those nearer, Fanny had not understood everything that was shouted. But the core of it was plain; he was trying to do all of Shakespeare at once. What was more, he was leaving in the ugly parts of the plays, that any decent company would have struck out for a staging, and making them uglier than before.

Hunt and Brown whispered to each other; Hunt's voice at least had accents of complaint. Did they see what Fanny saw? John might as well be standing before her with his falcon look, gripping his manuscript in both hands. No play could be made of this revolution, he would say, unless it be cruder than Falstaff and blacker than Lear all at once. Hunt and Brown might call it bad work; they could not deny it was deliberate. John would do nothing in half measures.

The sans-culottes marched back on stage, now wearing red caps and carrying the length of an enormous red flag between them. They stretched it wide and suspended it, blank and monitory, from the rear wall. How, in Pisa, could one get a flag of that size without raising suspicion? The Jacobins took the stage, men in breeches and cocked hats, women in bonnets and Robespierre at their center.

Speeches commenced, again in English verse. After the native prose they seemed more awkward than ever. Yet suppose it was premeditated; suppose that even in the awkwardness there was design. Did it not suggest some truth about the historical actors? Had not each of them mimed an alien part, and fumbled his weightiest words?

> *Robespierre.* I would speak.
> *Jacobins.* Hear the Incorruptible!
> *Robespierre.* Oft have I said, the people's enemies
>   Divide into two camps, and under flags

Of diverse emblem, by most various tracks
Pursue their prey. The first camp is no more.
A mockery was their affected zeal…

"It's copied!" Byron's baritone sounded from the floor. "Be damned if the entire scene is not a copy from start to finish!"

Hunt murmured a reply.

"Not at all," said Byron. "To have versified Lemprière is one thing, but Monsieur Thiers's history book, and a half-remembered pamphlet?—so far as he troubles himself to put them into verse."

"But even Shakespeare—" Hunt broke in.

"My dear Hunt! If I thought you were serious in likening this scissors-and-paste job to Shakespeare, I would bring up the lights and put an end to the performance this instant, promises be damned."

Some of the Jacobins had begun to clap, and one by one all joined in, loudly and out of rhythm. The sans-culottes cheered and stomped their feet, and Robespierre's words were lost. All left stage; the last to go pulled a knife from his belt, seized the red flag where it hung and sliced it up the middle. With a pair of silk ribbons he tied back each half in turn. They were red curtains now, and when he took up two of the footlight lanterns and placed them behind the cloth, they became significant curtains, casting scarlet invitation on the room. The workman stepped down and gave place to a young woman in a thin red gown and stocking feet, carrying a bedroll under one arm. She laid the bedroll on the bare stage and herself on the bedroll, and the audience held its breath; some shifted for a better glimpse of the face half concealed by a bare arm. Who was it? She must be known to someone. What family would permit its daughter here?

Danton came in, bulky, arms out and grasping. He half pounced on the bedroll and the girl rolled easily out of reach. Someone in the audience gave a bawdy laugh, but those on stage were not smiling.

Girl. No! Leave me so, at thy feet. I'll tell thee a story.
Danton. Thou couldst put thy lips to better use.
Girl. Leave me, I say.

Her voice was sweet and untrained; it came weak off the stage, a raspy Tuscan that might be the sound of the fields or streets but was not the language in Fanny's primer. She strained to follow.

> *Girl.* My mother was a wise woman. Purity was a virtue, she told me. People came to our house and talked of things, and she sent me from the room. When I asked her what they wanted, she said I ought to be ashamed. If she gave me a book to read, I had to skip pages. I might read the Bible as I liked, everything in it was holy, but there were things I didn't understand. I mightn't ask anyone, I had to brood. Then came spring, and everything went on a bit ahead of me, I hadn't a part in it. I ran into a particular air, it nearly choked me. I looked at my limbs. Sometimes I thought I was two, then I melted back to one. A young man came often to the house, handsome, a talker, I didn't know what he wanted, I had to laugh. My mother told him to come oftener. It pleased us both. We didn't see why lying between two sheets wasn't as well as sitting on two chairs. I liked it better than his conversation. Why should I have the smaller thing and not the greater?

Again Danton reached for her; she pushed his hand away and he grinned. That last night with John, when after his mournful talk of squeezing their brains, he had suddenly held her to him—withhold no atom's atom!—he was still constrained, shy of his own desire. It was not a lover's assault; she had felt no danger. He was like a cat teasing at something in himself, which did not quite extend to her. There was something of the same feint in Danton, and Fanny understood that the Byron costume was a dodge. This Danton was a story that John was telling about some part of himself. She blushed and under the blush felt a chill. What remained to be shown?

> *Girl.* I was like a sea swallowing everything, digging deeper. I couldn't see any difference, all the men melted into one body. It's my nature, who can help it? One morning he came and kissed me as if to choke me, he clasped his arms at my neck, I was unspeakably afraid. Then he let me go, laughed and said he'd almost pulled a stupid prank. I didn't know what he wanted. In the evening I sat in a pet by the window, there was a feeling between me and everything, I sank into the sunset. A crowd came down the street, the children ran ahead and the women watched from the windows. They were carrying him along in a basket, the moon was pale on his forehead, his hair was damp. He had drowned himself. I had to weep. That was the only break in me. Other people work six days and pray the seventh, on the New Year they think things over. I don't understand any of that. I don't know any division. I'm always one, wanting and touching, a glow. My mother died of grief. People point their fingers at me. It's stupid. It all runs to the same thing, how people have their pleasure, in bodies, saints, flowers or baubles, the feeling's the same, your delights are your prayers.

The room answered with laughter and a street whistle. The girl ignored them. And well she might, Fanny thought, since they fell so wide of her words. They were trying to make merely indecent something that was far worse. It was a nakedness of the soul; her knees were drawn up, her thin arms hugged her shins, a stellar cold pressed her gown. It hardly mattered whether her words were true—were delights indeed prayers, could anyone be a swallowing sea? The trick was in how she was made to speak.

> *Danton*. How is it, I cannot take thy loveliness
> 　　Within me whole? Not compass thee entire?
> *Girl*. Danton, thy lips have eyes.
> *Danton*. I should be transformed into atmosphere,
> 　　To bathe thee in my flood, and break upon
> 　　Each wavelet of thine undulated form…

No, she hated this Danton. She could not imagine following him through an entire play. Hadn't he had a wife in the first scene—what had become of her? They had gone offstage and she had been wiped from his consciousness. He would speak to one woman about the brain, to another about the body; all was exchangeable.

The doctor's son entered in his blue coat, and Fanny bent forward, expecting a reproach. But no; he simply looked down and addressed Danton as if the girl were not there. Robespierre had been to the Jacobins, he said, and had made threats.

Danton, the lout, lounging on his bedroll, hardly attended.

> *Camille*. The people's misery is a mighty lever,
> 　　Weighted with blood. Do lighten it one drop,
> 　　And to the lamppost Robespierre is raised.
> 　　He wants ballast. He seeks a heavy head.
> *Danton*. I know. The Revolution is Saturn,
> 　　And devours its children. (*Pause*.) No; they will not dare.
> *Camille*. Danton, thou art a venerated saint;
> 　　No relic does the Revolution heed.
> 　　It strews the limbs of kings about the street,
> 　　Tears statues from cathedrals. Dost thou think
> 　　To remain standing as a monument?
> *Danton*. My name!

Camille.   Thy name! Thou art a moderate.
   Another am I; and Hérault the same.
   They call us rogues. In sooth, they are not wrong.
Danton. You dream. They have no courage but in me.
   The revolution's course is not full run,
   They keep me whetted in their arsenal.

The girl leaned against Danton, now that he no longer pursued her, and toyed sadly with his hair.

Girl. Thy lips are cold. Thy kisses choke in words.
Danton. So much lost time!
   (*to Camille*) Tomorrow will I go to Robespierre.
   I'll anger him, and break upon his silence.
   Good night, my friend.
Camille.   Good night, Danton. (*Murmuring.*) Beware.
   A girl's thighs are thy guillotine. The mount
   Of Venus shall be thy Tarpeian rock.

More whistles; someone hooted, others gave affronted coughs. The actors stood and walked offstage, Danton carrying the bedroll. That last phrase hung in the silence. But the coarseness did not matter now, Fanny thought. It was black as intended, and no more could be done.

What had been John's life here, to turn him against his own sense of beauty? He must have done it from some deep hurt—a painful thought. She knew what cruelties he had faced: the world's neglect in his illness, the guardian who had refused him support. But he would have restitution and more. Her hand went to her pocket and clutched at the folded letter, just enough to feel the give of the paper. That much was real. The rest waited to be put right. In the meantime Danton and Robespierre must take the stage and confront each other, the one gesticulating and enormous, the other standing prim and firm in his shadow. Not one innocent has been struck down, Robespierre declared, and Danton took his leave. Robespierre slumped forward, as if he had required the other's resistance to stay upright, and rubbed his hands together as one chilled.

> *Robespierre.* Must he go? They will say, his giant's form
> O'ershadowed me, I called him from the sun.
> If it be so?

He cast a glance over his shoulder, as if suspecting a watcher behind.

> *Robespierre.* My every thought upon its neighbor spies.
> A mockery… and yet…
> (*Pause.*)
> Assume the robes of dead aristocrats,
> Their leprosy contract. He quits me not!
> Ever he points, with bloodied finger: there!
> With swathe upon swathe-band I stanch the wound;
> The stain beats through.
> (*Pause.*)
>   I do not know,
> What thing in me gives the lie to the rest.

He went to the edge of the stage and mimed a gaze out a window at a city asleep.

> *Robespierre.* Night dances on the earth. Thoughts without shape,
>   That crept off shy at daybreak, form assume
>   And steal into the silent house of dreams.
>   They peer from lightless chinks; they open doors,
>   Possess warm flesh. They murmur at the lips,
>   And soft the limbs stretch outward in the dark.

So in our waking life, that brighter dream,
Does the spirit not conceive more in an hour
Than in a year the body might commit?
All sin is in the mind.
(*Startled.*) Who's there? Lights! Lights!
Saint-Just. Do you know me?
Robespierre. Saint-Just!

It was a handsome man who came in with a lantern, almost a boy, though the light hardened the lines of his face. In his other hand he held a newspaper.

Saint-Just. You are alone?
Robespierre.   It was Danton left me.
Saint-Just. I met him in the palace, red of face,
    Crying epigrams to the sans-culottes.
    Grisettes ran at his calves, the people swarmed,
    Each mouthed his phrases in his neighbor's ear.
    We shall lose our advantage.
Robespierre.   What will you?
Saint-Just. The committees call
    To formal session: public safety, law.
Robespierre. Much ado.
Saint-Just. So great a body we must bury deep.
    We'll lay him in his armor as a king,
    And slaughter horse and slaves upon the mound.
    Hérault-Sechelles. Camille.
Robespierre.   Camille also?
Saint-Just (*handing him the newspaper*). See what he writes!
Robespierre. He is a child, he was laughing at you.
Saint-Just. Read!
Robespierre (*reading*). "Upon his own Calvary, between in-
    famous thieves, the blood messiah Robespierre cruci-
    fies, and is crucified not. The prophet Saint-Just declares

his master's Apocalypse to the Convention, carrying his
head like a monstrance."

Saint-Just. I will make him carry his like Saint Denis.

Robespierre (*reading on*). "Is it so? Is this Messiah's clean shirt
the death-shroud of France?"

(*He looks up.*)

Et tu, Camille? Enough. Away with them!

Only the dead return not. What is the charge?

Saint-Just. You have pronounced it, at the Jacobins.

Robespierre. That was to raise fear.

Saint-Just.   It shall do for more.

I'll make a banquet of it, course on course;

You have my word, they will die of the meal.

Robespierre. Then swift, tomorrow! No long agony!

My spirit pains me these days. Be it brief!

The handsome boy nodded and carried away the light. Alone
in the dark, Robespierre gripped himself, in the same chilled attitude as the barefoot girl that Danton had toyed with.

Robespierre. So be it. Let the blood Messiah come,

Who crucifies, and is crucified not.

He redeemed them with His blood, I with their own.

He made them sinners, I assume their sins.

His was the passioned, hurtful ecstasy,

The hangman's horror mine. Who suffers most?

Yet in these thoughts is much frivolity.

Why must our eyes turn ever to that One?

The Son of Man is crucified in all,

Each spills his lifeblood in Gethsemane,

And none redeems another by his wounds.

My Camille! They are gone from me. All gone.

Gone. All is desolate. I am alone….

Curtain Call

THE WORLD AROUND ROBESPIERRE WAS extinguished, the man himself a shadow. Under his cloudy wig the pale oval of his face was hardly to be seen. His hands quivered like moths. Shadows crept and stumbled behind him, the next scene getting ready. A trample of feet sounded from the main hall and Tuscan voices called for the proprietor.

"There is no proprietor. Il milord—"

"What milord?"

The curtain was pulled aside. Lantern light shot in from the hall, striking Robespierre square in the face, and he blinked his small eyes. Was it the Directory come for him already? What had been in the front hall was now tramping in front of the curtain, many and towering; dark protuberances swayed like a forest on the march and were revealed in a last ripping away of the curtain to be the tall hats of policemen. There were a dozen of them, all in the white-on-blue uniforms of the Grand Duke's gendarmerie. The footman of the house came running alongside the captain and Byron rose from his chair.

"Your pardon, milord," said the footman. "His Royal Highness—"

Byron put his hands on his hips and looked down at the captain, whose face beneath the towering hat was somewhat lower than his own. "I have breached no edicts, sir," he said in an Italian lazy with Venice. "Tear apart my palazzo, you will find no shooting gallery."

"You will accept my personal apology," said the captain, and pointed his baton at the stage. "You present a theatrical entertainment?"

"I do not *present* it," said Byron, his voice rising in pitch. "My house is borrowed."

Hunt rose and encouraged Byron backward with his arm. "Sir, if anyone is to be named responsible, let it be I. The performance is to benefit a journal I am organizing. Lord Byron is imposed upon only for chairs and a roof."

"A journal?" said the captain.

"My God, man," Byron hissed in English, "do not talk of journals to these people."

"My charge is to halt the performance," said the captain. "The matter is reported to be seditious."

"Reported!" cried Byron; "who reports it?" He turned on the room. "I am informed upon!"

Shelley stood, ignoring his wife's hand at his elbow, and placed himself shoulder to shoulder with Hunt.

"Captain, I pray you," he said. "None of us will deny his convictions, but I cannot agree with the charge. This is pure poetry."

The captain was speechless a moment, and pointed at last to the stage where Robespierre stood blinking, now joined by Danton and the doctor's son in the Camille costume, all of them shuffling like schoolboys in front of the torn red flag.

"You deny the play is seditious?" asked the captain.

"Its author is a perfectly benignant spirit," said Shelley.

"I thought this man was the author," pointing to Hunt.

"No, no," Hunt said. "The author—"

On stage the costumed students looked askance at each other. Behind them a slender shape in a bright red coat stepped into the light. Fanny started, heart drumming—it was him, it was not him. Of course it was him. Who had told him to affect that beard, the long hair tied back with a ribbon? He came forward slowly; a familiar shy hand brushed a lock from his forehead, and his eyes roved the chairs in the front row. He was seeking out his friends, of course, as he would at any reading. He wanted to know what they thought.

"Signori," he said, fog in his voice, "you must lay blame upon me."

"The play is yours?" asked the captain.

"The defects are mine. What is objectionable?"

"In my house!" said Byron. "Shelley, Hunt, you shall do me a thousand penances for that I allowed this to go on here."

"Your lordship, I hope you do not take the costume amiss." Keats put a hand on Danton's shoulder and smiled slightly. "It was a *jeu d'esprit* upon the aspect of a revolutionary, no more."

The captain nodded at his men and the two foremost moved for the stage.

"I supposed a schoolboy prank was meant," Byron said coldly, "and I might give some very direct criticism, had the outcome not been so very nearly fatal when the *Quarterly Review* attempted it last."

"A rumor and a lie, I think," said Keats. "Have you a judgment?"

"I must be thick indeed," said Byron, "for I can make out nothing. Danton is drawn as a mere monster."

"I supposed I had drawn from life." The two gendarmes mounted the stage; the other actors stepped forward and Keats waved them back.

"Life!" said Byron. "I see you did your reading, but how is the smell of the lamp to cover the smell of the gutter?" He turned to the captain. "Sir, whatever your informant has told you, I cannot be called to account for it. What does he give Camille to say—nude goddesses?"

"I do not count myself among Camille's party," said Keats.

"But Robespierre is not the hero!" cried Byron. This was not repartee; he was really angry at what he had been made to watch, and he was not alone. Murmurs came from the chairs around, and even Shelley and Hunt, boldly as they faced the police, turned sad when their eyes fell on Keats. He had not given them what they wanted.

"It is not a question of heroes," said Keats. "Signor capitano, if the Jacobins concern you, I promise you that they all have their heads struck off at the end."

"The performance is ceased," said the captain. "You must answer questions." He made a sign to his men and they took Keats by the wrists.

Fanny shrieked and straightaway clapped her hand to her mouth; but she was unobserved. The whole room was moving and calling, Shelley pushing his way toward stage, the hawk-nosed doctor and his daughter on their feet. The doctor reached for the girl's elbow; she ducked him, knocking a chair on its back, and leaped onto the stage with her belly before her. Keats shook his head, but she dove across the platform and managed, before a policeman pulled her away, to brush his face with her fingers.

Fanny pushed into the general press. The throng was unsure whether it wanted to go forward or back, and she forced her shoulders past one spectator after another until she reached the footlights, where her path was blocked by the captain himself, a short, broad man with waxed mustaches and pale eyes on a level with Fanny's own. Several more gendarmes had gained the stage; one of them struck the doctor's son a blow in the face, and he fell back. Others had wrapped their arms around the unresisting Keats and were pulling him down to face the captain, who alternated a searching look between him and Fanny and, struck with sudden insight, reached for Fanny's wig and tore it loose. Her hair, fire-colored in the lantern light, spilled over her eyes.

"O heaven!" said Keats, and would have fallen backward, were he not held in a net of arms.

She pushed her hair aside. The captain's men were all around her, the evening's spectators in a farther ring, Severn and Brown, Shelley and Mrs. Shelley, Lord Byron himself. Keats stared from among the grasping hands, blood beating in the hollow of his throat.

"A ghost," he said. "A vision."

"John, no."

"But—" His voice cracked. "To pursue!"

For months, since the start of her journey, she had imagined the moment of unmasking. He would be dumbstruck, no doubt, and if she surprised him with arms about his neck—in her mind's eye she had always leaped so to embrace him, never mind who was looking on—he might freeze a moment till his spirit caught up with his eyes. Even circled by police she might have done it. But she had never thought he would show fear at the sight of her. He was truly frightened, as the gendarmes had not frightened him, nor the sparring with Lord Byron.

The captain hefted the black wig as if seeking something hidden inside. "You are not one of mine," he said to Fanny. "Whose are you?"

"No one," said Fanny.

Her months of studying the language had forsaken her. The pregnant girl was pulled forward, her hair loose from its dressing and streaming about her face.

"Who is that, Gianni?" she asked. "Another English friend?"

"She was in London," Keats said. "She was to stay."

In his panic he was nearly childish. No one could perceive his wavering voice, his shifting eyes, without suspecting an unworthy trick. The pregnant girl's eyes turned cold—and if a ghost was anywhere, Fanny thought, it was here: an apparition in a gown, half dark and half pale, bearing a claim of suffering. She spat like a peasant at Keats's feet.

"You are false!" she said. "I knew you hated me. I did not think you should be false."

"That will do," said the captain. "These three, and the actors."

"Take him," said the girl, "and put him to breaking rocks."

She tore one hand free, grabbed at her own throat and pulled out a chain on which a gold ring glinted. Her hand was caught; she thrust her arm sideways, the chain snapped, the ring flashed in the air and was gone. The doctor's son was back on his feet. He shoved against the joined shoulders of two gendarmes, and when they did not yield he pulled his costume sword from its belt.

"Bloody tyrants!" he cried, and swung the blade.

His opponents ducked back. Was the thing able to cut? Fanny was let go; the doctor shouted at his son and Byron pushed for the door. Shelley made a sign to the doctor's daughter over the heads of the crowd.

On stage, one of the gendarmes drew a short rapier from his belt, and after a moment of sparring knocked the hilt from the young man's hand. He fell sprawled on the boards, stretching for the weapon that had landed out of reach, and his adversary bent forward and ran the tip of his rapier into his lower breast.

The captain made a cutting motion high over his head. The gendarmes joined shoulders and began to move in formation, pushing the crowd from the room. Fanny saw a glint between her feet, and as the press of shoulders knocked her back she ducked and closed her fingers on the fallen ring. All was shouting, the smell of bodies in close air. Behind faces and coats the stage was entirely hidden, the fallen boy not to be seen. The red flag still showed, sliced in half on the rear wall.

FOURTH PART

Darkling

THE NIGHT HAD FALLEN CLEAR as glass, and for many hours the great and little bear, the bull and charioteer, the hunter and his dogs had turned steadily about the pole, each silver point quietly aflame over a river so calm that if one stood at the bank, one saw mirrored stars rising from the depths. Those stars in the river were first to mark the change. They began to blur and dart, and one by one were snuffed out, together with their parents above, by a growing patch of darkness in the west. Damp gusts whistled along roofs and batted leaves up the pavement, and at the door of Casa Lanfranchi the torches were blown out. Those who had been guests in the house stepped outside and were shrouded. Blind calls crossed the street, muffled in the thick air: where was Professor Vaccà, where was his son? Where was Lord Byron? People stumbled against each other and laughed in panic when they recognized the other's voice. *Sirocco*, they said, and whistled low.

Fanny sat in the darkened carriage with her forehead in her hands and young Charles curled like a cat beside her. She had pulled off the green jacket and her hair fell loose around her face. A screw turned in her breast, forcing tears into her palms; she gasped and the thick air pressed her back like a mother's hand.

Severn's voice was at the window. He had been up and down the street, asking questions. Professor Vaccà had carried his son to the hospital; Keats was taken to the Palazzo Pretorio. Tomorrow a party must go and meet with the commissary of police, or whoever was in charge. His voice carried a hectic note of consolation, as if to ease Fanny's troubles by reminding her of his own.

"You knew," she said.

"Upon my soul," the hectic note rising, "I am entirely in the dark."

"You knew, all of you, and told nothing! Two words were enough—but you must make me a fool."

He made a noise of minor despair and receded. Fanny shut her eyes and dropped her head forward, on the brink of a plunge. There was no more journey before her and she had not come to its end. She had found John and had not found him. The dim figure that she had seen on stage, sunburn and whiskers, sat beside the ache that for a year had clothed itself in his face and voice. She could not fit the one into the other. Foolish, foolish, to have followed so far.

Wind beat the curtain, and the horse nickered. Brown's voice was at the window now, asking where was his boy, and who had been watching the boy while Miss Brawne was adventuring indoors. It was a risk and an expense, he said; he had just made an ocean voyage, as yet he had got no paying work, he could not keep a coachman as nanny to sit up hours with a sleeping child.

"But it was you told the coach to stay," said Severn; "you wanted Miss Brawne stationed there."

"And fine fruit that bore. What is his fee?"

The curtain jerked aside to show Brown's head, lit from below by a lantern. "Miss Brawne, are you within? We must take rooms for the night."

The weeping died in her breast. It was a cold habit from their journey, that she could not permit herself to appear impractical before him.

"Which rooms are those?" she asked.

"Rooms in the palazzo. Hunt arranged them."

"I will not pass the night within that house," she said.

Brown snorted and withdrew. "I pray you, Severn, don't look a fool. Hunt! I say, Hunt!"

Children's voices had come up, Hunt's diffident tones beneath. Fanny knelt on the seat and put her head into the night. The lantern rocked, swinging shadows about, and Brown leaped upon Hunt, who had just raised an arm to ward him off.

"How could you allow this?" he cried. "What is this scandal, this thumbed nose, you had him write for your journal?"

"I never did," said Hunt, pushing him away; "I never saw a line."

"I see your stamp! You always exercised too great a power," and he actually raised a fist; but Hunt's children were all around. "Well, this Michaelmas parade has got hold of Keats now. Must we go to the consulate?"

"There is no British consul in Pisa," said Hunt, brushing off his coat. "You should have to go back to Leghorn."

A shape in a gown floated between the children and into the light; it was the woman Fanny had earlier taken for Mrs. Shelley. She bent her severe young face to Severn's and murmured something.

"The place is a mausoleum." Brown looked into the lightless sky. "That Keats should forsake his friends and come to the ends of the earth—he deserves to be locked up. I shall tell him so. It cannot be Shelley who made him pen this thing. Do the Italians write in this manner?"

"I cannot tell you what the Italians write," Hunt said. "But if Keats is truly arrested for this, we shall sell three times the copies."

"Copies!" said Brown; "will you talk of copies when he is sent to Elba?"

"They will not send an Englishman to Elba. I have enjoyed police custody myself, Brown, and mark my words, I can make Keats a proper reputation from this. He has had bad reviews, to be sure, but he has never cast a tyrant in the teeth."

Mrs. Shelley took Hunt's arm and asked if he had not seen Shelley leave the salon.

"What!" said Hunt. "Shelley missing also?"

"I do not know. Please," turning to the others, "did no one see how many the police took with them? How many were hurt?"

"Mr. Shelley was not hurt," Fanny called. "He left after Lord Byron."

They squinted in her direction. Mrs. Shelley took Brown's lantern and stepped forward, holding it high. Fanny pushed open the carriage door and came into the street. Face to face with Mrs. Shelley, her heeled boots raised her half a head higher. Up close Mrs. Shelley was older, with a sober cast that reminded Fanny of her own mother.

"You saw them?" she asked.

"Lord Byron went first into the crowd. Mr. Shelley followed after."

"And God knows if they are locked up by now," said Brown, "or on the highway to Rome. Come"—he reached for her shoulder—"the police may yet return. You ought to be indoors."

Over all the weeks of their journey together, he had never made bold to touch her. "I will not!" she said, thrusting back his hand. "I will walk to Leghorn first."

"Mr. Brown," said Mrs. Shelley, "surely her strength is tried enough this evening?"

"I advised her to stay in the carriage," said Brown. "I advised her to stay in Hampstead."

"Yet someone has persuaded her across an ocean."

Brown shook his head. Mrs. Shelley frowned and applied the lantern light to Fanny's boots, her shirt and trousers, her face.

"Well," she said, "this is the forest of Arden."

"Frances Brawne." She put out her hand.

"I know who you are. Not by name; Mr. Keats was not indelicate." She passed the lantern back to Brown. "If it is Lord Byron that has Shelley, he will keep him a long while, asking for penances. Perhaps, if you have nowhere to stay, you might best come with me."

Fanny hiccuped in surprise. Brown scowled—of course he did not want her loose in the city. But she could quit him; she could be quit at once of all these men and their panting contention over John's shadow. Her heart began to race again, as when she had stood before the stage.

"You oblige me greatly," she said. "I should not presume so far."

"Ehilà," Mrs. Shelley called to the carriage driver, "you will deliver her things," and pointed out the curving way into the darkness between palazzi and river.

The cobblestones seemed to rock under Fanny's feet, but she did not stumble. The street was deserted and a few lit windows shed just enough light to pick out the paving at their feet. Warm wind snapped at their clothes and splashes echoed past the river wall. It seemed to Fanny that she was once more on the ocean, the lights of strange ships passing above.

"I thank you," she said, and found her voice stilted. "I do not know what I should have done."

"You could not have known," said Mrs. Shelley. "How old are you?"

"Twenty-one."

"Does your family know you are here?"

"Not yet."

"And the scheme was all yours? It is quite an Arabian story."

Fanny put her hands into her pockets.

"I mean no reproach," said Mrs. Shelley.

"I did what I must to come here," said Fanny.

"And why must you come here?"

"My life is here."

"Mr. Keats is here, you mean," said Mrs. Shelley. "That is perhaps an end of life, but you must not confuse it with life itself. It would be terrible if that were so."

Her voice was sad, not scolding. The walkway narrowed and their shoulders nearly touched as they passed through an arch. A lone pine in a courtyard lashed the sky with its crown.

"I was younger when I left," said Mrs. Shelley, "not eighteen. England seemed narrow, the world wide. That Shelley was married already—we thought it should mean very little once across the water. Perhaps it would have meant little enough, had he not left children behind. I am sorry if these are old tales."

"Not at all," said Fanny, and waited for more, but Mrs. Shelley had fallen silent. A fleck of water struck her cheek.

"You say you know me. Did Mr. Keats speak of me, then?"

"He would not spool out every thread," said Mrs. Shelley. "The fault was partly mine; I was jealous. I thought him another of Shelley's romances."

"Mr. Shelley—romanced him?"

"Mr. Shelley might romance a patch of blue fresco in a church, and I would be jealous of that also." She spoke with warmth. "Mr. Keats came with nothing and hated to be a dependent. It was like feeding an orphan fox, that nips your fingers."

"He is not poor now! I came to tell him."

"Is it true?" asked Mrs. Shelley. "I could not understand what Hunt told me."

"He has not a fortune. But it is more, so much more, than we thought we might marry on." She caught her breath, again on the brink of a plunge, and must have betrayed it in her step, for Mrs. Shelley took her arm.

"I do not know all his story," she said. "I know that he thought a marriage in England beyond his expectations."

"You mean that he has practiced economies, and made do with the cheaper article."

"That is unworthy," Mrs. Shelley said sharply. "Even if she were not Signora Keats, she should deserve better."

Footsteps and laughter—was it students, carousing late?—sounded across the water. A lit ember, someone's cigarillo, approached on the sidewalk. Fanny shivered and stepped aside to let the shape pass. It coughed; Mrs. Shelley reached for its sleeve and it protested in Lord Byron's voice.

"My lord!" she said. "What are you about? You are looked for at home."

He withdrew his arm and brushed at his cuff. Fanny could not see Byron's face, but imagined him frowning. "You flatter me," he rumbled. "I cannot be looked for in earnest."

"You left without warning. Did Shelley not go with you?"

"What did I leave? All the city insinuate about my house, drinking my wine, and none ask after me. It is Keats they want."

"And you so begrudge it that you left your own house?" asked Mrs. Shelley.

"I left because the scene was unpleasant," said Byron, "and because I have a footman for such things."

"But Shelley did not go with you?"

"Who else is here?" Byron held out the ember of his cigarillo so that smoke caught Fanny in the nose. "Oh, it is Ganymede. You love him also."

"Whether I will or no, my lord."

"He can spit in the Grand Duke's face," said Byron, "he can get himself thrown in irons. It matters not."

"To him it matters," she said, "and to me."

He laughed. "You think me petty, that I begrudge him the world's love. It is not so. I know where I stand in the rank of men." He straightened, drew on the cigarillo and flicked his fingers to dispatch it to the river. "I am admired," he said, "as a man admires a costume, that he wishes to steal and wear for himself."

A rattle came up on the paving and Fanny's cheek was spattered. She had felt no rain since leaving England.

"When Hunt speaks Keats's name," said Byron, "or Shelley, or anyone, I hear love as if for one's cousin, one's child. I do not understand the trick. But it communicates even into his verse—his mawkish, extravagant, ill-formed verse, which is yet sustained on that quality." His voice drew inward, debating with itself. "Suppose—it is not impossible—that when I and my works are quite forgotten…."

"We must go in," said Mrs. Shelley. "If you meet with Shelley, I am waiting for him at home."

Byron's shadow sank against the wall.

"Good night, my lord," she said.

"Forgive me, Mary. I could not dissuade him."

"Dissuade him? What from?"

"I do not know; I could not make him tell me."

"But he left—" and her voice turned hard. "Was he outfitted for travel?"

"It was dark," said Byron, "perhaps twenty minutes past, at this very wall. More I know not. He said no one must fear. But he would not have me compromised before the police—and the police cannot know, he said, where we are bound."

"We?" asked Mrs. Shelley.

"He and the girl had some definite place in mind, where she should be protected. Of course I advised against it," his voice turning urgent, "in the strongest terms I could command."

"You advised him!" said Mrs. Shelley; "and you expected advice to be sufficient?"

"I tell you I could not dissuade him. He believed he was acting in the right."

"He always believes he is acting in the right!"

The wind heaved and thick drops began to pelt. Mrs. Shelley moaned and broke into a run along the river wall, her shoes slapping the paving stones.

"Good night, my lord," said Fanny, and started after in her men's boots. Two or three blocks on, Mrs. Shelley's shadow halted in front of a white palazzo with a single lantern glaring through the rain. She leaned over the river wall and looked up and down its length, the outline of her hair swinging wildly before her.

"His boat!" she said.

Rain battered Fanny's shoulders; she wiped hair from her brow. "I see nothing."

"It was here."

A break in the wall opened to steps and an iron post at bottom, where ropes might be secured. No rope was there. Mrs.

Shelley shook her head at the vacant thing.

"But where should they be bound?" Fanny asked.

"How can I know?" Mrs. Shelley cried, "I, who was always slowest to chart those winds!"

Rain streamed over Fanny's eyes. She blinked it away and on impulse bent forward to grip Mrs. Shelley's arm, for fear that she should tumble into the water. Was it wrong that her heart was opening only now, in the moment of disaster? Mrs. Shelley returned her grip, and after a moment let go the river wall and began to walk with her, neither leading nor following, toward the white palazzo. From the halt in her step, Fanny guessed she was little accustomed to walking side by side with anyone.

"This is your home, Mrs. Shelley?" she asked.

Mrs. Shelley stopped before the palazzo's arched door as if facing it for the first time. The small flame of the lantern, enclosed against the storm, shaped a ring of light in the falling water.

She shook her head. "I knew we should never keep a home. I asked that we be cast about the earth together."

Palazzo Pretorio

THE STRAW PALLET SMELLED OF piss, sweetish and rotting, and cloyed Keats's throat however he turned on it: curled on his side, or crouched head to knee, or flat on his back with his crown pressed to one wall and his feet to the other. A taller man could not have stretched his full length. He could make out nothing by sight and had no courage to explore by blind feel; crawling things touched his neck and arms and he slapped them away, not knowing if they were really there.

An aperture let in the sounds of storm and a warm spray that was instantly chilled against his skin. He had tried knocking his fist against the wall, but no one would perceive it under the wind. His heart sang at a pitch it could not sustain; he would end by doing something mad, by dashing his head against the wall just to prove it harder than his bones.

After the first pass of panic he lay emptied, as he had lain so many nights in Rome. The bare sense of space girded his body from end to end; inside him was the tick of time. And time deceived. With no other thing to measure against, it came loose from its track and chimed the same instant again and again—perhaps it had been doing so a very long time. Perhaps Rome had never left him. The old walls and furniture still kept guard. The basin on the floor waited for him to bring up the black bile. Around the corner Severn and Doctor Clark conferred in whispers, and the fountain sounded from the window:

> As you are living, all your better deeds
> Shall be in water writ, but this in marble—

A gray handkerchief lay over his father's face. It was a devil that had snatched the face from under the cloth. His mother's red hair fell in tangles around her eyes.

Deep in the earth, where the dead had their courtroom, a white hand showed across the crowd. Keats shoved among shoulders and reached for the pale fingers. When at last he took them in his own, he found them damp and hot; the color had deceived him. He tugged the hand and the arm came weakly after, wrapped in a jacket sleeve. The form he had thought a woman's was a boy's. It was his brother's face: clear blue eyes, a spume of bright blood at the lips. Keats made to wipe it away, but Tom tightened his grip and pulled his hand down to press it in line with his lung, bending Keats forward in a motion that met no resistance and tipped him off balance. His frame jolted and water struck him in the face.

He was looking up at a small stone room in stormy light. A high, narrow strip lined with bars gave onto clouds. The walls were mud-colored, slick with damp; a lone cobweb in the window glinted raindrops and a trail of moss ran beneath. Rough scorings marked the stones, patterns that might have been messages from captives before, but when he lingered on the shapes they ceased to suggest letters.

He had wished for solitude, and it had been given him. It was an ending Dante might have conceived.

The tide of dreams ebbed and cast ashore the happenings of last evening, solid and sharp, in their proper order. Giuditta—the apparition of Fanny. It had been no dream. Even now they were somewhere beyond these walls, breathing.

He shivered and scrambled from the pallet, limbs aching with cold, to face the door. Heavy wood bolted over with latches, a grille that could not be opened from the inside. He knocked and the boards thudded. He tried again, harder, and might have kept hammering had some instinct not pulled him back, warning that it was dangerous to let loose so soon—he might be here a long time. His possible actions must be rationed out. Supposing his friends were in cells nearby; and he remembered Leopoldo's shudder on the stage boards, and water touched his bones.

He sat on the sweat-stained covering of the pallet. In this half day it was no easier to mark time than in the night, and he fell into an uneasy doze. The latch gave a thunderous click; his heart stuttered and he scrambled into a crouch. Was the door being battered in? It creaked loose from its frame and two men stepped inside, dressed in gendarme's uniforms and tall hats. In the narrow cell they had no space to stand side by side.

The man in front gave commands in a voice dull with routine, matched to gestures: stand up, face the wall, arms forward. A clumsy set of manacles was fastened about his wrists. The cold iron pinched bone and served as a yoke to pull him into the hallway, one guard before him and one behind. There was no light, but the guard at fore had a lantern that glinted on the latches and grilles of the doors they passed. When Keats lifted his eyes, terrible shapes appeared—the gibbet, the axe—before breaking apart on approach into further doors. Of course they could not do it, not in peacetime. But there were island prisons. He had seen the captives at St. Peter's, laying flagstones. The Austrians had their mountain keeps.

They climbed steps to an antechamber with a chessboard floor and narrow, mullion-crossed windows in file. In the rainy light Keats saw the gendarmes clearly for the first time; they had the same smooth-cheeked, childish aspect of the border guards on the day he had entered the Grand Duke's realms. They led Keats through a side door into a small, badly lit room full of drawers spilling papers, where three men sat behind a scuffed table. The first wore a cap and black robes and must be a magistrate or priest. The second was smaller, spectacled and bald but for bushy sidewhiskers, in a policeman's jacket with epaulettes, medals and sash. The third was young, stationed to one side before an open ledger.

Keats was compelled onto a low stool and the guards stepped back. The magistrate nodded at the captain, the captain nodded at the clerk, and the clerk turned his ledger to a fresh sheet and inked his pen.

"John Keats of London," said the magistrate, "no fixed residence or profession."

The clerk scratched. Keats cleared his throat and began to say, in a voice soft with disuse, that he practiced as a physician and resided at present with Andrea Vaccà. The captain struck the tabletop with spread fingers, shaking his head, and the magistrate continued to speak in a slow Tuscan, wheezy and dry, with the accents of an older generation. He was narrating the actions of John Keats entirely in the subjunctive—a usage that the Keats on the bench had never encountered, and that seemed to evoke some elaborate fantasy or prayer. That John Keats had entered the Grand Duchy on the first of March by the Rome–Florence road, giving reasons of health as his occasion for travel. That John Keats's table companions at Pisa had been the liberal Vaccà and the atheist Shelley. That John Keats had stolen a deadly French poison from the university pharmacopeia and fled the city in order to deliver it to Niccolò di Natale, an agent of sedition during the wars. That John Keats had invited numerous English to Pisa after him, including that Lord Byron who had supplied guns to the Piedmont revolt and wished to install a shooting gallery in back of the Palazzo Lanfranchi. That John Keats had associated with university students at the inn dell'Ussero, where foreign newspapers were read and indecent plays put on. That John Keats had himself authored a play, which performance at the Palazzo Lanfranchi had last night incited riots, its subject being no less than the French regicide.

"Your pardon," said Keats, "in the play was no regicide."

The magistrate's brows went up. The captain spread his fingers to strike the tabletop once more, and Keats said, "Your lenience, signori; am I to answer this account?"

"You are to answer the questions put to you," said the magistrate. "How many now at Pisa are in the employ of the British government?"

"The consulate is in Leghorn," said Keats.

The magistrate's face darkened. The captain smiled under his whiskers and waved at the clerk to stop writing.

"How many now at Pisa," the magistrate repeated, "other than yourself?"

Keats frowned and glanced behind him. The two guards stood rigid, staring with discipline and boredom at prescribed points in the air. He had been ready to admit all he had done, but the prospect of being made to admit entirely different things seemed to open a trapdoor where he sat.

"I have no knowledge of my government's activities," he said carefully, "beyond what is common."

"Who was intended as the target of the stolen French poison?" asked the magistrate.

"That is no poison; it is physic."

"You are sure of that? There is no deadly dose?"

"If it is medicine," said the captain, "why steal it? Why transport it in secret?"

He seemed truly curious. Perhaps he was the reasonable man here, open to appeal. But Keats had no answer. The scheme had been Leopoldo's and he would not smirch Leopoldo's memory.

"We were only cautious," he said.

"Cautious!" said the magistrate.

"He does not deny it was stolen," the captain murmured to the clerk.

"Let us have more of your caution," said the magistrate. "What became of the guns in Turin?"

At this Keats looked quite blank, and the magistrate explained in annoyance—surely Signor Keats knew this already—that numerous guns used in the Piedmont revolt, including those known to have been supplied by Lord Byron, had not been recovered by the Austrian army and might at present be in any imaginable cellar or warehouse across northern Italy. The mention of revolts struck the captain with sudden insight, and he leaned abruptly forward to ask who was number two.

"Number two?" said Keats.

The captain's face reproached Keats for his mulishness. The police commissary in Naples, he said, found dead with the number one pinned to his chest. In a different room Keats might have laughed, but the magistrate was growing angry.

"If you are so perfectly ill-informed," he said, "perhaps you will tell us what this drama is about."

"My play?" said Keats. "The title—"

"I know the title," said the magistrate. "My informants could not understand a word of it. They saw brawling, and immodest women, and a great red flag with Robespierre's wig in front. If you please, what is the message in that?"

"I suppose," said Keats, "the message is that man is not perfected."

The magistrate glowered under his cap. The clerk looked up, saw no direction and began hesitantly to write.

"It is a drama of weakness, and of failure," Keats said. "Yet in the confession of weakness is a sort of strength—"

"I am asking what is the code," said the magistrate.

"Code?"

The captain cleared his throat. "We mean," he said, with seeming effort at mildness, "that such a production—in a foreign language, with so much of the action incomprehensible—it is hard to conceive that it conceals no intelligence."

The trapdoor swung wide. "Intelligence of what?"

"The missing guns?" said the magistrate. "Someone knows where they are. You spent the summer in a place where powder is made."

"Was made," said Keats, "years ago."

"Your government does not love the Holy Alliance," said the captain. "More and more English arrive at Leghorn harbor. Ought we not to expect a ship of the line some morning, with cannons?"

"How many died last night?" asked Keats.

He had not intended to say it. The trapdoor was still open and he swung freely above, clinging with bound hands to the fact of their surprise—for he had at least surprised them.

"I saw young Leopoldo Vaccà struck down," Keats said, "who was the best lad in the city. How many more?"

The captain stroked his side-whiskers. The magistrate touched his shoulder and bent close in conference. The clerk stopped writing. He was fair-haired, hardly older than the students who had joined battle last night in the salon. The magistrate and captain glanced separately at Keats and back again, both of them gesturing; the magistrate's hand kept making axe-strokes to support some point of decision. The clerk bit his lip and seemed ready to break in, but at that moment the two older men nodded together.

"The questions are ended," said the magistrate, and lifted two fingers.

The guards came forward. Each took Keats under an arm, and as they pulled him from the stool he tried to move with them and preserve some shred of independence. But his limbs were stiff and could not anticipate their motions. They dragged him past a battery of writing desks to another side door, which was pulled open to a brighter space of oak paneling with high windows, before which descended a noose—no, that was the Grand Duchy's banner, seen side on. A bench was raised below it, and a large dock where three young men sat under an old Quixote of a guard, slumped and half drowsing against his tasseled pikestaff. As Keats was brought in, the young men began to whoop; the guard at fore raised a hand and they fell silent. It was Danton and Robespierre, both out of costume, and bright-eyed Leopoldo between them with a tight winding of gauze round his waist.

The dock's half door was opened just long enough to shove Keats within. The students too had their wrists in irons and sat hunched forward. As the guards marched from the room, Leopoldo leaned sideways to knock Keats's shoulder with his own. He smelled of sweat; his color was good.

"What have they done to you?" he asked in a half whisper. "Were you here all night?"

"Never mind," said Keats, and looked to one side; the old guard, who had briefly stirred to attention, was back in his dream. "I saw you struck!"

"I hardly felt it," said Leopoldo. "A coldness was all. And the blood, that startled."

"Of course it startled. You would never see an operation." That was Robespierre, who was a wag when not in character.

"But you should not be about!" said Keats. "Are you in pain?"

"With every breath," said Leopoldo, "now the swelling is up. But my father says I am whole enough." He touched the gauze and winced. "A rib deflected it from the lung."

"Luck, Leopoldo. You should never have needed it. Did you think the play was still going on?"

He shrugged, and Robespierre pointed out that both he and Danton had been held here overnight, with no fathers to watch over them. They wanted to know what questions Keats had been asked. The city governor had taken a new interest in the British Foreign Office; perhaps he had heard some story about English poets and his daughter. "And the other girl fascinates them, who came to the play in disguise. Do you know her? Is she a spy?"

"She is not a spy," said Keats.

"Does she wish to become one?" asked Robespierre. "I might have fallen in love when her hair spilled out."

"Stop that," said Danton, "and show him what you have in your pocket."

The old guard was thoroughly drowsing and did not stir as Robespierre lifted his hands to the lapel of his jacket, irons clanking. "See," he murmured, "they didn't trouble to search us."

He unfolded a slip of paper to show a newspaper frontispiece, sketched in pen and ink—the *Minerva Pisana*. As in the journal from Naples, the device was the goddess's head; here the city's tower slanted out from the crest of her helm.

"They thought to quash us," said Danton, "and will have us tenfold. There will be Carbonari in Pisa now."

"You have given us strength for it, Kitsa," said Leopoldo. "Look below."

Care had been taken to set down a lead article, or the opening of one, in tiny print. The title was "Il Morte di Danton," as written by John Keats and presented at the Casa Lanfranchi—a caution to tyrants! Keats read over the first lines and recognized himself strangely in them; it was his familiar work, but in a choppy image, as if glimpsing his own face on moving water.

"Who has translated it?" he asked.

"All of us," said Robespierre. "Vaccà understands best."

"You deserve so much," said Leopoldo.

But they could not owe him anything. He knew exactly what had gone out of him and into the play: weariness and laughter, no more. The fervor of these young men was something apart, and if they thought they had found it in his play, then it was his no longer. It half frightened him; it was like the dark glow that lit Giuditta's eyes when she passed outside his influence.

"Leopoldo, have you seen your sister?"

"She must have left with another," he said. "Signora Shelley, perhaps?"

"Perhaps," said Keats.

"You do not fear what she said last night?" Leopoldo leaned sideways, shoring up Keats's shoulder. "Come, Giuditta may talk, but I know you are not false."

"Leopoldo, you know not what you say. You are good." He looked up to the gray windows. "What is to happen here? A trial?"

"Not so soon," said Danton. "They will be setting their files in order. They must draw up the charges, the schedules."

"Do not worry for yourself," said Robespierre. "You are English."

"Is that a blessing?" Keats asked.

"Your fellow countrymen stood to defend you last night. If you had been an Italian before Italians, you should have been stoned. That is why yours is a great nation, and ours is—as it is."

"But not as it shall be," said Leopoldo.

The main doors of the room swung open, and the lone guard started to attention as more police entered in file, leading a shuffling crowd in damp coats. Some carried hats and had oilskins slung over their arms; others wiped rain from their eyes. There were students from the Ussero, older faces that Keats remembered from dinners at the Vaccà house; these frowned and lifted their chins to look over the prisoners in the dock. Were they here to cast stones? Professor Vaccà came haltingly with both hands grasping the great pendulum clock from his chambers, gift of the Grand Duke, a burden so large that the top cornice forced his head to one side. Signora Vaccà walked beside him and the white-haired footman came behind, looking as if he had already tried to take the burden and been refused. Giuditta was not with them.

At the sight of the clock the police descended severally on Vaccà; whimsical items were not to be introduced to the courtroom. His wife caught sight of Leopoldo in the dock and blanched, putting her hand to her breastbone. Leopoldo smiled and patted his gauze-wrapped middle. The clock was set against the back wall; Vaccà caught Leopoldo's eye, nodded and followed his wife to the seats. For Keats he had not a glance.

The side door opened, the magistrate stepped in with the captain and clerk and everyone stood. Hours before, when Keats had last faced a crowd, the stage and players were all around, the attendant spirits of his art. Now his companions were the same but the enchantments were unraveled; he was simply a man in a box, exposed.

A gavel banged and a bailiff gave leave to sit. The magistrate seemed annoyed that a crowd had shown up and informed them that this morning would have no spectacle to match last night's exhibition. Statements had been taken. The events in question—here he began to read from a sheet—had transpired at Palazzo Lanfranchi on the twenty-first day of August instant.

Keats would have liked to sink behind the front panel of the dock. He could have borne any denunciation from the bench, he thought, so long as he had from the Vaccàs a look of sympathy; but they sat propped against each other, with no children beside them and no strength to spare. The doctor, Keats's teacher, in whose knowledge and pride he had always trusted, looked tired and afraid, an ordinary man. His wife held his elbow. If Keats were out of the dock he would drop to his knees and beg their judgment on him; he would call them mother and father.

"On statement given before this body," read the magistrate, "Francesco Domenico Guerrazzi of Livorno, student at the Collegio Ferdinando, is found to have riotously, tumultuously, seditiously and unlawfully assembled with diverse others in open breach of the public peace, and is fined fifteen zecchini and discharged."

The bailiff gestured to Danton to raise his hands and produced a small key that snapped the manacles open. Murmurs of relief came from the crowd, but Danton himself dropped his arms with a perplexed look. Was that the whole of the affair?

"On statement further given, Giuseppe Mazzoni of Prato, student at the Collegio Ferdinando, is found to have riotously, tumultuously, seditiously and unlawfully assembled with diverse others in open breach of the public peace, and is fined fifteen zecchini and discharged."

Robespierre's hands were snapped loose. A brief cheer cut the room, silenced at once by some neighbor. Leopoldo crouched forward and sucked his lips.

"On statement further given, Leopoldo Vaccà of Pisa, student at the Collegio Medico, is alleged to have riotously, tumultuously, seditiously and unlawfully assembled with diverse others in open breach of the public peace, and having uttered oaths to the insult of his Royal Highness's subjects, to have assaulted officers of the law with a deadly weapon or instrument in ostensible form of a deadly weapon, on which report we charge the said Leopoldo Vaccà with aid and comfort to Carbonarism and set trial and sentencing for the third day of September instant, at half past nine in the forenoon, until which time the prisoner is discharged upon bail of one tabletop pendulum clock."

Whispers rose and died, the false start of a storm. Leopoldo's hands went up for the bailiff and Signora Vaccà dropped her head to her husband's shoulder. Two gendarmes hefted the clock from the back wall and hauled it across the courtroom, frowning as they went. It was not a thing meant to be carried about. Brightly gilded, listing to one side, it went orphaned through the door.

"On statement further given, John Keats of London, having no fixed residence or profession, is charged with no offense."

Keats's eyes shot up. The magistrate took a new sheet from the clerk.

"The said John Keats is found to be a foreign national who has neither requested nor received the necessary permissions to reside at the city of Pisa. By order of His Excellency the governor he is banished the city and the Grand Duchy. He is given four days to settle his affairs, following which he shall be escorted to the border of his choosing and given his freedom."

The gavel struck. The magistrate stood, the room followed, and the moment that Keats's hands were freed, he turned and stretched them toward the bench. Voices and footsteps had come up; the officials had already turned to go and Keats did not himself know what he wished to say to them. Was it not unjust to say he had no fixed profession? Suppose he could prove he was a working physician? The half door of the dock swung open and a crowd of students surrounded the freed prisoners, giving slaps on their shoulders. One by one they worked their way onto the open floor; Leopoldo's mother was there to embrace him, keeping wide of his bandages.

"Carbonarism!" she cried. "And all for a play—like Pellico."

"It was for his newspaper that Pellico was arrested," Vaccà said from behind.

"Who has not seen what Leopoldo reads in that café? They will hang him, Andrea."

Vaccà looked a little white. "The charge is aid and comfort only," he said. "That does not carry the death sentence."

"Where will they send him? Elba? The Spielberg?"

"What does it matter where they send me," asked Leopoldo, "when all Italy is in bondage?" His parents shrank back; nor did Leopoldo's voice seem quite so bold as his words. "Babbo," he asked, "how did you know to bring the clock?"

"It was arranged this morning," said Vaccà. "A reminder of services done His Royal Highness. It has won you a space of freedom, but we have much more now to arrange, if we can."

"But where is Giuditta?" Keats broke in.

They turned to him, terrible in sorrow. Mother. Father.

"Where is Giuditta?" asked Signora Vaccà, her voice shaking. "I shall answer to God, that I let you have my children."

At this moment a great shape intervened, beard and grin, and engulfed Keats's shoulders with such force that his feet nearly lifted from the ground. Hands were on him; Hunt was here, Severn too. Brown's laugh shook at his ribs, a free and generous note of triumph.

"My friend!" His voice was warm as a mother's; in another mood Keats might have dropped his head against the heavy shoulder. "Are you all right? Were you ill handled?"

"I am all right," Keats said, working himself loose.

The Vaccà family was gone. It was a wholly English party before the vacant dock—white faces, in watery light that might have been London in autumn. Severn looked freshly hurt, as if he had discovered his abandonment in Rome only five minutes before. Hunt's features were looser, but he had not lost the look of an aged boy, eyes dark and mirthful as ever. What a thing it had been to live among friends, all of them believers in his gifts.

"I knew they would give you no hard sentence," said Brown. "No one could have seen you in that dock without human feeling."

"Did you not understand?" said Keats. "I cannot stay."

"I think I understood well enough," said Brown. "I have spent one night in this city and seen quite enough of it. Say, where are we bound?"

An outer door had opened in the next room, letting in warm damp and a smell of wild sea. No, this was no English storm. He could not be the promising child among these men, not now.

"Is it back to England?" asked Brown.

"Brown," said Hunt, "what is it you propose?"

"I understand," said Brown, "you want him still for your journal. But can't he contribute from anywhere? He left England for his health, and that—my God, Keats, you are restored." He passed his large hand over Keats's shoulders, not quite touching. "I did not know that I should see you whole again."

"But why not Rome?" Severn asked. "They cannot banish you from there, surely—Keats, do you know I had to invite an Italian painter into your room, to make up the rent?"

"Joe, I am sorry."

"Everything is there still—the paintings, the pianoforte, all waiting for the work you were going to write. You have so much now!"

"I?"

"Your brother," said Severn, "your grandfather." He seemed near tears.

Brown took up the thread. He wanted Keats to understand what he had done. He had been the first to receive the letter from America, and he had gone personally to make inquiries in Chancery. Something in his tone recalled to Keats his dreams of the previous night, or the echoes of those dreams, for all he now remembered was that they had rhymed with the eternal sickbed in Rome, the blood in the mouth, the release never given. Brown was pulling a letter from his pocket—all those letters from England that Keats had left unopened, for fear they should tighten the mesh. He knew George's hand at once and looked the letter over as Brown explained, but its message was unfathomable. A matter of money? Was that all?

"Then you all shall have restitution," he said.

"Restitution?" said Brown.

"For what you provided in my need. You should not have had to wait so long for it."

"Man alive!" Brown said, "do you think this is a matter of restitution to us? It is about your having a proper season at last to yourself, to compose under the sky."

"No one deserves it more," said Hunt.

"You shall cut the gem," said Brown. "I know it."

Their loving eyes were fixed, it seemed to Keats, on a place where he no longer stood. His spirit had slipped from its costume and hung apart, perceived by none.

"Your pardon," he said, "I must find Mrs. Keats," and started for the door. Severn clutched his elbow.

"You cannot leave us again!"

"Leave you, Joe! I am only going—"

"To Mrs. Keats, you call her? A life in exile, where you will write strange letters, and stranger verses, and see no one? Keats—"

Brown pressed the letter into his hands. "I do not understand you," he said reproachfully. "I should have thought this was deliverance."

"Certainly, a year ago," Keats said hotly. "Then I wanted money—to marry on, Brown. You have not been here. I have debts not to be paid in that coin."

He thrust the letter aside and Severn snatched it up, letting go his arm. Brown stepped near, looming and gentle of face.

"You are yet young," he said. "I suppose you think this is the fifth act. You are hardly out of the first. Believe me that to turn down money is always the wrong thing."

"I have no time to dispute it."

"I understand you are in a stew," said Brown, still gentle. "I am saying that you have the means to get out of it. I wish you would come and drink a cup of coffee with me, and after that a glass of wine." His hand found its old place on Keats's shoulder. "No one will sneer at you for what happened here. Once you have left this foreign state, what claim could it exercise against you?"

"You imagine a dodge," said Keats.

"Well," said Brown.

"I swear to you, if you suggest I do to Giuditta as you did to your serving girl—"

Brown drew himself up. "Now, Keats."

"Severn's bastard in London? What of Shelley's first wife, that he left with the children and made a madwoman? I will not conduct myself so."

He had wounded them. They stared back in perplexity, just as they had stared at his play. A path had been cleared for him and he was not following it.

"We do not understand everything," Hunt began.

"The man who should have used that money, the man for whom it was intended, is one who died in Rome. All of you," Keats cried, "have come here after a man who died in Rome."

The murmur of the outer room had condensed to a single exchange, focused on some new object. Boots were rapping, quick and out of step. A figure in a gray cloak stepped into the court-room and halted between empty chairs. Small hands lifted from the wet sleeves and pushed back the hood to show Fanny's face.

Her hair was dark with damp and drawn clear of her familiar cheeks, chin, sea-blue eyes. Out of the strange costume, in plain daylight, there was no alteration from the figure that Keats had kept in memory—was that possible? Of course it was not pos-sible. Beneath her eyes were drawn new, thin arcs. She had gained knowledge somewhere.

"John," she said, "you must come out."

Outside the courtroom was a broad doorway open to rain and a stone atrium with benches where petitioners might sit. No one was sitting now. The crowd stood in a ring around the commissary of police, who was peering over a wet, dirty length of canvas stretched aloft between two officers. Mary stood at his elbow, hair still half pinned from the evening before and falling over her brow. She nodded tightly in answer to some question. The commissary gestured to the cloth's ragged edge and Mary drew his hand aside, pointing out the dark streaks just discernible under the surface grime. The largest of them, as long as a man's arm, was flourished in the shape of a "J." The "u" and "a" faintly followed, and no more; a tear in the cloth broke off the word.

The Tempest

OUT OF DOORS THE MORNING was dark as dusk. Keats pushed his way across streaming flagstones to a kerb where carriages stood in line, directed with a lantern by a gendarme in an oilskin. He climbed after the damp uniforms of policemen into the foremost car and found purchase on a seat corner just as the door swung shut. Reins were shaken, the floor rocked beneath him and dim slants of roofs began to slide past the windows. A broad back in a dark coat, pressing hard into his side, turned out to belong to Vaccà. The doctor held a scrap of sailcloth and rubbed his thumb along its edge as if palpating a wound. Finding Keats beside him, he stiffened a moment, then relented and held out the cloth.

"Do you see?" he asked. "This was cut loose deliberately."

Keats took it and felt the weave coming apart in his hand. "Why should they have done it?"

"A last resort," said Vaccà. "They could not lower the sails, and had no hope of holding a course."

Keats thought a moment. "But where was it found?"

"The mouth of the Serchio," said a gendarme opposite them.

"Then the sail alone," said Keats, "will have been driven farther than the rest of the boat. The wind—"

"Yes, northerly."

Their eyes met, and for a moment Keats felt the same unity of mind as when they had operated together.

"We must search the coastline to the south," said Vaccà, "between the Serchio and the Arno."

It took the gendarme a moment to understand; then he pushed open the windscreen to speak to the driver. They were out of the city already, entering a forest valley where boughs shook red and orange over choppy, charcoal-colored water.

"Poter di Bacco!" came a shout. "It is the girl spy."

Keats half turned on the cramped seat but could not make out who had spoken. From the crowded rear of the cab came an answer in rough-hewn Italian: "No such thing!"

That was Fanny. Again he twisted his neck, half afraid to meet her eye, but saw only uniforms. Her voice in the new language was louder than he remembered, pitched over the storm.

"As you like," said the first voice, "but you caused a fair row last night in the commissary's office. Didn't she, friends?"

The men laughed, and someone took up the thread. "They couldn't write a charge because they couldn't work out what to call you. Did you not arrive under your real name?"

"My passport—it is written for *un gentilhomme anglais.*" She was conceding no dignity; Keats knew that tone. They laughed and congratulated her. She had escaped a hearing. But she would not find it easy to get residence now.

"I did not come to stay."

"Then how shall you leave? If an English gentleman arrives at Leghorn, it cannot be an English lady who departs, or Florence will have questions."

"The Leghorn office will hate it!" said another. "Perhaps if you put the costume back *on* for them—"

The forest ceased and the valley opened, freeing the river's mouth to spread over a beach of pale rock edged by vine-wrapped cliffs. At the end of the road a short dock flanked a few low buildings; waves reared in crests, folded up as if biting themselves and crashed into spray. The farther waters were blotted in rain. Two police rode in the wet, their horses' heads lifted against the storm. The parade-ground hats and striped trousers that had once seemed farcical, and frightening because of that farce, were now emblems of hope. As the carriage drew near, both riders halted and called out, pointing north. The gendarme stuck his head out the window and shouted back, and the driver slowed and turned onto a muddy cattle track running the crest of the cliff.

"What do they say?" asked Vaccà.

"The wreck is found," said the gendarme, "over the next rise. They must have hardly made sea."

"The crew?"

He shook his head. "They say no one."

As they gained the hilltop a dark heap came into view, driven half ashore in an inlet between slopes of sand. Both sails were gone and the tilted foremast dangled shreds of rope. At its base the deck was buckled, the planks snapped. It was a litter, a moment's arrangement of the storm, and Keats's heart shrank to remember how it had run before the wind with Shelley's hands at the ropes. Two police walked the broken gunwale, picking up shards of wood.

The carriage halted, the gendarmes threw open the doors and leaped into the rain. Keats and Vaccà followed in their flapping coats. They scrambled down the cliff face, clutching vines and shelves of rock, and jogged to the shoreline across wet sand. The instant they reached it they felt the sting of an absurd trick, for here was nothing they wanted, only a wreck of wet boards and a sodden gray lump dangling from an officer's hands. That was Shelley's canvas jacket, soaked through. Keats took it, turned it inside out and felt cold water coursing between his fingers.

"Nothing else?"

The officer shook his head.

"If I may," said Vaccà, and turned the jacket about in study. At last he said, in a voice more icy than Keats had ever heard him use, "This was deliberate."

"Deliberate how?"

"See here!" He thrust the jacket out. "Nothing is missing, nothing torn. It was stripped to dive." He shook the garment; drops flew from it. "They drove for the storm, and cut the sail before they leapt to sea."

"It cannot be that," said Keats.

"Can it not?" he cried. "Your Mr. Shelley is not a man of sound mind. He asked me once for prussic acid."

"But you are not saying that Giuditta—"

"I say what I observe," said Vaccà, and flung the jacket to the broken boards.

White spume crashed up either side of the wreck, joined at the ruined prow and sank to a gray mirror that was sucked at once back to sea. Fanny stood behind Keats on the sand. Her gloves clutched the handle of an umbrella whose canopy flapped and ducked like a bird on a string. She lifted it for him, and he lowered his head to step into an old dream. How many times had he stood before her in imagination? But at arm's length she was a stranger. The lines about her ginger-lashed eyes were delicate, alien work; they would crush at his touch like a butterfly's wing.

"Where were they bound, John?" Again her voice startled, so much louder than in his thoughts.

"An isle of sweet airs," he said, "ringed by sea foam. It is not real."

The strangeness in her eyes eased. Was that compassion, for him?

"I am sorry," she said.

He nodded once, and shy of their closeness, turned his eyes back to the wreck and churning water.

"All the sorrier"—she choked a moment, but kept on—"if it is on my account."

"No, no." He shook his head. "It is a long tale. You must have seen that. I am very much to blame."

Was it some sign of absolution he wanted, from her of all people? Ashamed of his own need, he drew breath and looked her full in the face. "If you can," he said, "forgive the greeting I made you last night. I thought you were come as my judge."

She gazed at him a long time—struck, perhaps, to stand so near in daylight. "You set me puzzles, John. You are nothing but puzzlement. I came because no one knew where you were gone."

He joined hands and nodded, a formal gesture. "I set too little store by you."

She seemed about to smile in answer, but the spark did not catch. "I thought it was in my hands to save you. But I was another traveler, was I not, after something not real."

"Fanny—" On an impulse he wrapped her gloved hands in his own. Her face tightened but she made no answering move. It was spray and not tears that shone on her cheek; she held back her heartbreak.

"They will be found," she said.

"So they will," he said, "doubtless." There was a charm in saying so. But when he looked back to sea, something wrenched in him. "Yet—if not—"

"No," she said, suddenly afraid, "say not if!"

He had not known what he was saying. But he read the fear in Fanny's eyes, and understood that even on this wild coast, with the world tossing around them, they stood within the bounds of an order not theirs to overstep. He let go her gloves, and on the cliff above a second carriage halted and opened its doors.

"But on the ship," said Fanny, a new quaver in her voice, "I saw the sun on the waves each morning. I saw the rock of Gibraltar, John, with all its shadows. And of course I was with Brown, and tending his child, but I thought, here is the world, so much greater than I imagined. And last night I left a hired carriage behind, with my trunk still in it; I walked away with Mrs. Shelley, on my own feet, and no one came after—" She spoke quickly, eyes downcast. "I felt joy. I did, John, in a tumble with everything. And I thought, such a feeling is wrong, on this evil night."

A new party of blue and white uniforms was clambering down the cliff face. Mary came in back, clutching an officer's elbow as she stepped between the rocks.

"Quickly," said Fanny, and held out the umbrella to Keats. He took it, not understanding, and she drew the glove from her left hand to show a golden band on her finger. He knew it and had no words; but she had already tugged it loose, betraying a moment's wince of effort or pain, and dropped the mere weight into his palm.

Mary burst from the storm, unsteady in the wind with skirts and hair whipping behind her. She seized Shelley's jacket from the gunwale.

"It is," she cried, "oh, it is—" and clutched the sleeves as if to rip it apart.

Fanny dropped the umbrella and embraced her in the wet. To Keats's amazement Mary bent her knees and sank against the younger woman. He had never seen her yield so to anyone.

The commissary, portioning out search parties, waved his arm to bring Keats and his companions into the division. They were directed toward a northward rise, where the sand gave way to reddish stone ledges that hid the farther coast. Keats and Vaccà set out in silence, and behind them Fanny led Mary over the uneven ground, which she took with halting steps, as if in a dream.

Over the rise they met another beach of dark sand broken up with boulders. The landscape widened here and they might have gone singly, but none wished solitude now. The rain had found its way through their coats, and they shivered as the wind changed. They stepped over strewn shells, the pink joints of crabs' legs. Shapes resolved from the gray, fantastic twistings of bodies flung over shore; on nearer approach they became boulders and more boulders, trailing indentations in the sand. A vivid moss covered their seaward sides. Nothing else grew.

The sand snatched at Keats's boots step by step, and it came to him that this must be the wrong path. The police had set them this task to get them out of the way. He looked back at their tracks filling with rain, the rise behind which the wreck lay concealed. They had not searched it properly. Imagine Giuditta trapped under planks, the child heavy in her.

"Can this be right, to go north?" he called to Vaccà.

The doctor looked up, surprised at the address, and turned

his eyes to the sea. The water lashed back and forth, without boundary in the rain; it mocked any thought of telling its course. In the carriage, Keats thought, their minds had been clear.

"How should a swimmer go in these currents," he asked, "as against a boat?"

Vaccà shook his head. "I do not know. No more do you."

"But—"

"Do not ask!" cried Vaccà, and Keats saw he had misjudged. They could not use reason here.

Two police broke from the rain, riding hard. It seemed they were about to gallop past, but the rider at rear pulled up suddenly, throwing gouts of sand from his horse's hoofs. He shouted to his companion and gestured back at Vaccà; when Vaccà lifted his arm, Keats saw it was the doctor's bag that had caught their attention.

They scrambled up a break in the cliffs, catching handholds on wet stones. At top was a footpath through yellow grass. The rain was easing now, the inland sky perceptibly lighter and crossed by pale billows. Plumes rose from a cluster of wood-and-thatch huts. They skirted a stand of cypress, passed through a gate and found a crowd bunched at an open doorway. There were villagers wearing broad hats against the wet, and a few police who saw their comrades approaching and swept their arms to clear the way.

Inside was a close, windowless hut of the sort Keats had known in the marsh, its single room warmed and reddened by a fire in a brick ring. Two peasants, man and boy, stood to meet the strangers. Under a half-moon opening in the roof smoke tumbled without dispersing; bad for the lungs, Keats thought, and caught his breath as he rounded the fire to a pallet where two forms were laid. They rested face up, not touching, shoulders bare under a wrapping of blankets. Their damp hair was spread back from their faces. Breath moved in them. One after another their eyelids fluttered and showed the black of Giuditta's gaze, Shelley's blue.

Vaccà was already at Giuditta's side, pressing two fingers

to her neck and taking the auscultation tube from his bag. Her cheeks were flushed; a shiver touched her lips. She opened her eyes wider and looked between Keats and her father.

"Do you know me?" Keats asked, kneeling.

From the other side of the pallet, where Mary sat, came a high, weak whisper. "An error. I cannot pretend—"

"Hush," Mary whispered.

"Night heron," said Giuditta. "My mad love."

The room's quiet was strange after the storm. The fire whistled, the peasants moved softly at the door. Shelley murmured, "It was an exceedingly grievous error."

"You leapt into the sea!"

"There was no choice. I could not get at the aft sail. A grievous error, to have put two sails on the boat."

"You leapt," said Mary, "and you can't swim!"

"It was leap or be dashed on the rocks. And see, a Nereid took us in her arms. Unless"—his voice gave out a moment—"the sea change. All things through pearls."

"Hush!" She seized him around the shoulders. "You will hush! Half drowned and you talk so!"

Vaccà lifted his hands from Giuditta, not yet at ease. Her head rolled aside and exposed her mottled throat. "I wondered if you should come after me," she said.

Keats reached under the blankets and drew out her limp hand. He held up the ring she had cast away the previous night—so small a token, so quick to lose—and hesitated, as if asking leave, before beginning to work it onto her finger. She gripped his hand and made as if to fall against him; but as her eyes passed the doorway she tensed and lifted her head.

Fanny stood there, hair wild in the firelight and breathing hard with the effort of the climb. She met Giuditta's eyes a moment, then dropped her own in abashment. In the smoky warmth, with blankets all around, she might have intruded on a bedchamber.

"All is well," Keats called across the fire.

He felt reproached by his own voice, too loud in the stillness. He had wanted to reconcile. But Fanny seemed to take his words as a dismissal, and after a moment of silence turned and walked out of the hut. Giuditta's expression eased and Keats pressed her hands. His was the healer's office and he had nothing but gesture.

"It is finished," he murmured. She nodded, eyes shut, and did not ask what was finished—a mercy, for he had no sooner spoken than he felt nothing was finished at all. Never in his life had he been so forsaken by words.

Ai dolci amici addio

ONE DOES NOT RETURN ALL at once from the land of the dead. The climb is halting and slow, and if it leads through another realm, then the signs of that place will linger together with the hush of the tomb. Giuditta in bed seemed to have taken on qualities of sea. Her breath came in swells, leaving a sheen of brine on her lips; a pearly, wave-worn glow touched her fingers and face. When her eyes opened, Keats fancied he saw new green there, a Northern tint of cold spray. She was not the girl who had sailed into the storm; she had its knowledge now, and looking down at her, Keats could think he was looking into his own past sickbed. The quinine pills that she had refused in the country, she now suffered him to place between her lips.

Clear daylight transfixed the windows, vacant of heat. Summer's press was lifted and the air was golden and dry, without suspicion of past storms. New birds winged across the squares, blackcaps and swifts that might be weeks out from England. Keats and Giuditta watched them from bed. They had never before known how to be quiet together, but now each listened to the other's breath, curled on the bedclothes between the jumbled cabinets and desks of the top-floor room where Keats had once slept alone. The maid brought milk and toast; the infant Minerva, who could now chew her food, clambered over the blankets to snatch bread from their plates. Giuditta pressed Keats's hand to the firmness of her belly.

"Here," she said. "He is swimming."

Keats touched. "So do we all, unborn."

"No, you must feel; there are fins." But Keats could not feel them and she pushed his hand away. "You will see," she said, "he will be born a fish."

Minerva clung to his other side, eyes half shut and mouth working at a fringe of his coat. He dropped his face to her sun-colored hair and smelled milk and summer wind. The afternoon breeze was there, that had driven the marsh vapors from the hills. She clutched his forelock in one clever fist.

"Holly berries," he whispered to her. "Snowdrifts, where the buntings light."

England would soon be around them, clothed in winter. For the moment it was an idea, which they faced in stillness. Vaccà had seen to the buying of tickets, the stamping of papers, the neces-sary delay to Keats's banishment. Just now Keats had nothing to do in the world, and in this unaccustomed idleness a shape of light was taking form in his mind. It had been in the depths a while, it seemed, waiting for the surface waters to clear. It was a warmth with no name.

Giuditta's family stole at odd intervals into the room, usually to find her asleep. Her parents held back at the doorway rather than engage the welter of furniture. Vaccà seemed always to be carrying the world with him, or else to have left behind in the world some part of himself that was still at work, furrowing his face. Leopoldo too was abstracted, but sat at the bedside and held Giuditta's hand with a tenderness that Keats had never seen be-tween them. Each seemed to fear for the other.

If Giuditta was sleeping, Keats would rise and walk with Leo-poldo to the library, where they sat at the window and looked down the Lung'Arno. In the cool new weather the great houses were opening doors that had been shut all season, while their masters were at the mountains or the baths. Steps were being scrubbed and carpets beaten. Leopoldo told Keats the names of the families, distinguishing those friendly to his own house from those ill disposed, but halfway through an anecdote of his father's he broke off.

"It was always a joke to me," he said, "my father drawing up lists of friends and enemies. I should have done well to listen."

"Your father says you have not been going to lectures," said Keats.

"Why do it now?" asked Leopoldo. "Guerrazzi and Mazzoni came this morning to ask after me. Mother met them in the hall shouting thank you, you have done quite enough already, and drove them out to the pavement."

"I suppose she would like to drive me out as well."

"Not at all. She knows Giuditta goes with you."

That was little comfort. Keats ran his eyes up the shelves and thought of the family that this great house had been built to contain.

"Every day my father is at Palazzo Pretorio," said Leopoldo. "He says he is seeing to your travel papers, but I think he is really waiting on a miracle from his clock."

"What sort of miracle?"

"Indeed, what sort? They will keep it in a cabinet till trial. The governor has decided already."

"But what can he decide before trial?"

"Why, whatever he likes. At least two years on Elba, Father says, and not more than four. Of course we are supposed to hire lawyers, and everything else."

He spoke like a student resigned to failing an examination. Elba in Keats's mind was another stretch of rainy, rocky beach, unrelieved by any growing thing, against a gray wall of sea; haunted, perhaps, by the sorrowing ghost of Napoleon, reduced at last to the span of his footsteps. He would gladly have gone in Leopoldo's place. But his penance was otherwise, harder to picture.

"Do you think they will allow me pen and paper there?" asked Leopoldo.

"They cannot forbid you your eyes," said Keats, "nor your heart."

Hunt and Severn and Brown came to call. They were chastened, and when Mrs. Keats came down barefoot in a plain white dress for introductions, each outdid his neighbor in courtesies. Keats took them to the library, where they sat side by side on the sofa and seemed to pass some common secret among themselves, like the eye of the Graeae.

They had seen Shelley and found him well. They were glad there had been no greater loss in the shipwreck. As for Keats's journey—Brown took a bound packet from his coat and gruffly explained that it contained those documents he should need to present his claim at Chancery. Keats turned it about, surprised at its thinness, and gave thanks; for there seemed no point in trying to refuse the money, nor in remarking that surely none of his friends was actually going to turn about and follow him back to London. Brown had his son, Hunt his entire family; Severn was seeing his first success with portrait commissions. And all of them shared in the project of Hunt's journal, though Hunt seemed disinclined to speak of it.

"And Miss Brawne?" Keats asked.

They did not know. They had seen her at the Shelleys' but had not inquired. She must be on her own, at least until a letter came from her mother to call her home.

At that moment Keats saw Leopoldo in the entry and leaped to his feet. "Never mind me! I will need all of you to know Leopoldo Vaccà. You must be friends to him when I am gone."

Leopoldo demurred, but Keats pulled him within, and Hunt was first to recognize the fearless Camille from the stage.

"Why, you are a credit to your nation," he said.

"Hardly!" said Leopoldo. "Without Kitsa's words we are nothing."

"Words, but never deeds," said Keats. "Hunt, Severn, Brown, I charge you—as any of you ever saw promise in me, you must believe ten times more in young Vaccà."

No one seemed to believe him at all. But Leopoldo knew that Hunt had been in jail and could not help asking about it. Did such things happen even in England?

"Even in England," said Hunt, "if you happen to own a press, and your Prince Regent is a fat fop, and you print one truth too many concerning him."

"Do not let Hunt frighten you with his ordeal," said Brown. "He painted clouds on his ceiling, and had a rose trellis and pianoforte. When Bentham came to console him, he found him playing at battledore."

"Against the freedom of a man's spirit," Hunt said gravely, "battledore weighs only so much. Nor am I sure an Italian state will treat its inmates as Suffolk county did."

The introduction made, Keats would have been glad to drop out of the library. But Leopoldo would bring the matter back to his play, which he understood Hunt would have the courage to print.

"I most certainly hope to print it." Hunt's face stretched a little. "We have only to settle the question of funds—that is, to make up the balance of the contribution we should have expected from Lord Byron."

"Byron is withdrawn?" Keats looked between Severn and Brown and saw them wincing; that was the secret loosed. "He—Hunt, did *I* do this to you?"

"It was nothing you did," said Hunt, tightly smiling, "not entirely. I am certain we will print your drama very soon. And it will sell; there is publicity to be had around the circumstances of its première. But for the present you might count yourself fortunate that, through Brown's good offices, you have money from another source."

"I understand," said Keats.

"No doubt we shall print it very soon."

"I understand, Hunt."

They stood for farewells, but circumstance lay heavy on them and their pained smiles were worse than no smiles at all. They shook hands with lowered eyes.

"Next year in London, perhaps," said Keats.

"Next year in America," said Brown, "next year on the moon."

In a different tone it would have been the old jovial Brown, but this was the voice of disillusion. Keats's neck grew hot as he saw them to the door.

On the day before their departure, the Shelleys at last paid their visit. It was late afternoon when they called; the shadows of the palazzi were well advanced on the river, and Mary hung back in the yellowing light as her husband sprang into the foyer, folded his hands and bowed deeply and repeatedly to Professor and Signora Vaccà while the footman struggled to get his coat off.

"Forgive us that we have not called before now," he said. "I was ashamed to face you. My conduct has been unforgivable, but you must believe it was prompted only by the wish to relieve suffering." That wish, he said, led him so often into error. He had parted a young woman from her family against all enjoinment of law and custom, to say nothing of natural bonds, and in any case to put two sails on a boat, with no consideration of the prevailing conditions at sea—

"Mr. Shelley, my dear Mr. Shelley," Vaccà said several times, and at last, "For heaven's sake, will you stand up like a creature possessed of reason?"

"I told you they would hear no confessions," said Mary.

"Neither did you carry me off, wrapped like a parcel," said Giuditta, coming downstairs in slippers.

She moved more easily now, but a deliberation remained in her step, and she seemed to have been shut away longer than these few days of recovery. Shelley made her another bow. His apologies past, he too seemed altered by the sea, his breath and movement slowed a fraction. Imagine the change come upon them together as they stood on the storm-lashed deck, spray in their faces. But Keats could not really see it, not as it must have been.

They took coffee in the library. Shelley said this trial and banishment was the most ignoble thing the Tuscans had done since expelling Dante, and Mary nearly spat her coffee; but of course, she said, wiping her lips, it was a sore loss, not to be made up. The mercy was that they should have their own money. Hunt must continue to seek some path for Keats's play, but the prospects seemed few unless Byron were to tire of Greece.

"Greece!" said Keats.

They were startled. Did he not know?

"If Hunt is not giving that out," said Mary, "he must be pained indeed."

It was Prince Mavrokordatos—Keats would remember him?—who had recruited Byron to the campaign. Before that, he had been talking one day of sailing to America, the next of riding to Switzerland, though on the other hand Genoa or Lucca might be more congenial. God knew where he might have ended up, had the Greek cause not offered itself.

"And all from the outrage of a theatrical evening?" Keats asked.

Shelley laughed. "No! Well, I think not. Surely not in the main."

"He has been weary of the world a long time," said Mary, "and life in Pisa is not what he hoped. I suppose a war is the last thing he has not tried."

Keats tightened his lip, but Shelley wanted to talk of the play, the excellence of which he claimed to be slowly apprehending. "You go ahead of us all," he said. "Some turnings in the path are yet dark to me."

"It may be they do not lead anywhere," said Keats.

Shelley could not believe that. He was writing something new himself—if not quite on Keats's model, still drawing from a spring he should not have tapped otherwise. It was a *Triumph of Life*, in terza rima.

"Oh!" Keats said, and since some further response was waited for, "Have you a Virgil?"

Naturally, said Shelley, and seemed surprised that Keats could not guess. It was Jean-Jacques Rousseau, of course. What other guide was possible?

"I could not tell you," said Keats. "I think you are following your own star and not mine, and it ought to be so."

The Vaccà children sat in quiet conference. In the gathering dusk they seemed near identical, their faces answering each other like a pair of birds. Leopoldo was giving advice on travel. Giuditta must know not to gape at the streets of London, he said, or she would show herself a stranger.

"And when have you ever gone abroad?" she asked.

"You know I have been to Rome," he said, "and Genoa."

She broke out laughing. "That is not abroad!"

"Of course it is," he said, injured; "there were border crossings."

Their parents watched from across the room as if expecting some new storm. Vaccà went to Shelley's side and asked if he perceived no change in himself since his rescue. Was his sleep not disturbed? Did he suffer chill or fever at any hour?

"I am more whole than in years, Professor," Shelley said.

Keats found Mary beside him and felt the sudden small balm of friendship. They too were comrades; they had shared the trials of those who wait on shore rather than sailing into the storm. It was theirs to search and to tend. He realized he should miss her greatly.

"I wonder you have not asked after Miss Brawne," she said.

"Does she wish to be asked after?" said Keats. "She should have been welcome in your company."

"She was not sure that Mrs. Keats should say the same."

"Oh," he said, and could not quite strike the note of easy dismissal. "I do not think it is in Mrs. Keats to be ungenerous now."

"Miss Brawne has darned clothes for Percy Florence," Mary said, "and sat at Shelley's bedside. With me she reads French and Italian."

"She was always the quicker at tongues," said Keats, and felt a sudden choke. "Truly, I think it might have gone easier for her if

I had died."

"Perhaps," said Mary.

"It should have gone easier for all of them—Hunt, Brown, everyone. They should have a proper allegory then, and elegies to write. As it is, they came expecting they should extend my old life with ruler and compass, and find out the arc of the new."

"They came out of love."

"Of course it is love. I did not give them what they wished."

"If you are melancholy after your play," said Mary, "I will tell you that in the moment it seemed obnoxious work. But upon reflection I begin to think otherwise."

"The play is a failure," said Keats, "and I shall never again undertake the like. Do you remember this summer in the country, when Shelley said we were like cats in the Roman forum? It is just so. We live among broken monuments."

Mary considered. "Who then built them?"

"We must have done it ourselves. Every toppled door and arch has a motto inscribed above, speaking out the lives we thought to lead. Now we scarce remember how to read them."

She laughed aloud. "But Keats, have you never *seen* the Forum?"

He was perplexed. Then he understood; his conceit had crowded out his memory of the place, which was not of broken monuments at all. It was Severn who had looked up at the stones, named the emperors and read their boasts. Keats had watched the cat licking its shoulder in the grass, the poppies shaking their bright heads and the cypress behind. He had lost that picture a while, but it had endured by its own laws; and discovering it anew, he felt it linked to the shape of light rising in him, whose form he had not yet discerned.

"I am going to write something," he said to Mary.

"Are you so?" she asked in mock surprise.

"It will be small; not a pageant as was the play. Beauty runs always a step and a half before me. I shall never catch her. And yet!"

He gave a sudden laugh. The coming journey seemed to open before him as a discovery and not a loss; in one of those configurations of the mind that align for but a moment, he remembered his brother's letter to Brown, and realized that his brother too must return to London to exercise his claim. They should both be in London this winter: his sister also. Giuditta should meet them. And then—but the vision was fled. There had been snow and stars, hearth and kettle, a home as he had not known it since childhood.

He had forgotten his surroundings and became suddenly aware that he and Mary stood alone in the library. Shelley had been gone a while, it seemed, and the family was gathered in the foyer, except Signora Vaccà, who had lingered to draw Mary forward. Mary nodded and motioned Keats after in silence, just as the footman bent his back and threw open the great doors.

Shelley stood outside in the twilight. At his shoulder was Fanny, her eyes cast shyly at her boots, though she was dressed as if going to a ball in Hampstead, in blue lutestring and gloves. Her hair was parted and drawn up behind her bare throat, dark in the last light.

"Monsieur le Professeur Vaccà, Madame Vaccà," said Shelley, "permettez-moi de vous présenter à Mademoiselle Brawne."

"Enchanté," Vaccà said gravely.

They stepped inside. A greeting was ready on Keats's lips, but Fanny was not looking at him. She directed herself in soft French to the master and mistress of the house, thanking them for an invitation—when had she been invited? She was nervous, Keats saw, and using the foreign tongue to shore herself up.

"I do not wish to trouble you long," she said. "Mr. and Mrs. Shelley have made themselves my guardians in this city, and while they are here I would make bold to present a gift."

Was it the French that made her speech sound rehearsed, or was something here prearranged? Who had determined it? Not

Leopoldo and Giuditta, certainly; they stood together in hesitation under the painted lions, and Leopoldo started when Fanny faced him full on and drew from her reticule a folded sheet.

"This is yours, young Monsieur Vaccà," she said, "if you will have it."

Leopoldo's hand lifted automatically, but his face was blank. Fanny unfolded a page of official script: from abroad, it seemed, full of alien names.

"Please," she said, with strange urgency.

Something in the document's shape was instantly familiar to Keats, but he was could not name it till he made out the signature at bottom. Then he understood: it was the same that he had been required to pull out at every border crossing, presenting his own name and description with Lord Castlereagh's hand beneath. That despised minister, under whose seal he nonetheless traveled; the unloved government that yet wrapped its protecting shadow about him. Of course it was more than a government. It was England itself, the old green hills and fields, that had seemed somehow inscribed in the document, a last charm against destruction in strange lands. What would it mean to give that up?

"Fanny!" he cried. "You are giving up yourself."

"It is not me." She met his eyes, resolute as a painted saint, and again urged the sheet on Leopoldo. "May I present Francis Brawne. He is a young Englishman who arrived at Leghorn on the twenty-first of August, and has booked passage to depart tomorrow. He wants only someone to wear his name."

Leopoldo took it in his hands, not yet willing to believe, and looked to his father, his mother. The leap in his heart showed so plain that Keats was nearly drawn after. But he could not put Fanny aside.

"And what of you?" he asked.

"I am here."

"To live?"

"Just so," she said, and took a moment to settle her breath.

"You will recall we have an attic room," said Mary, coming half a pace forward to stand at her shoulder, and Keats remembered how she had sunk her weight against Fanny on the shore.

Leopoldo's parents made him solemn nods, one after another; they had already weighed and decided. Giuditta took his arm, marveling to see him in the new aspect of a traveling companion. For an instant their faces were a perfect mirror. Then she laughed and let him go.

"No staring with that gawp at Saint Paul's!" she said, "or they'll know you for a young monkey."

They were marked for departure, and Keats with them. The floor around his boots was already widening with the current of future time, and Fanny receding on the far shore.

"You too will have letters from Hampstead," he said, "calling you home."

"They may call," said Fanny.

She had found a new duty, she meant to say, for which she would give over the old. But her face betrayed that he had hit on the saddest thing. She was too young! She had not considered the half of it. The price was too high: see how the Vaccàs stood together, mother and father, veiling their hearts. How could they lose both their children at once? Would they not turn to statues in this house?

Giuditta leaped over the stretch of floor that Keats had imagined grown wide, caught Fanny around the shoulders and kissed both her cheeks.

"My sister!" she said.

Fanny smiled, abashed in her downward gaze. For the moment that Giuditta held her, she did not drift away. Oh, it was a tenuous thread. But Keats himself had come to Pisa on as little—perhaps less—and Mary was standing behind her now. All this unfolded from a night's lodging in an attic room.

"And are we to stand all night in the foyer," asked Signora Vaccà, arching her brows, "or will we dine?"

The smell of baked bread had stolen into the hall, roast and autumn herbs. They were hungry, and had forgotten that hunger could lay a claim on them; all at once it seemed to lift them from pitching seas back to firm ground. The Vaccàs passed under the painted lions, Giuditta and Leopoldo after, and Fanny still half in Giuditta's arms. Keats joined the Shelleys behind.

"You conceived it all!" he whispered. "Did you not?"

Mary waved him to silence. Of course he needed no answer. "But is it wise?" he asked.

"You will have to trust in us," she said softly, so that those walking before might not hear. "Who can speak for tomorrow?"

"Then I must look out for Italian postmarks."

"Of course you must," said Shelley. "From all of us."

"You must tell all," said Keats, "whether good or ill. She is young, Mary, she cannot know what it means." And when Mary began another silencing motion: "At least guard her well. She will not find it easy. I loved her, and did not give her her due."

Mary nodded. Keats saw Fanny walking in step with Giuditta, her fiery hair spilling back over her companion's arm, and felt it was an unearned grace. But that too was presumption. In this moment it had nothing to do with him.

"My tale here went awry," he said. "I should like to think hers might run smoother."

"Oh, Keats," said Shelley, laughing, "do not worry after your own tale. We ought not to *live* tales at all. It is enough that we write them." And more seriously, bending close, "Only write, Keats. Write all your days."

Keats nodded deliberately, to show he understood the charge. A cloud had dropped, veiling Fanny and Giuditta walking before, and he knew the world was once again getting ready its questions for him. He would meet it around the next corner. For himself, for everyone, there was labor to come.

"As for your journal," he began, "if there is yet no money for it—"

"Oh, not a word on money," said Shelley. "Not tonight."

They stepped into the dining room and saw autumn spread over the table. Lids were being pulled from silver dishes, steam roiling past the candles—but the greater part of the room's warmth seemed drawn from elsewhere, as if summer was still conserved within its walls, and the old ceremonies of chairs being chosen, plates brought forth and wine poured, the old gestures of hospitality between native and foreigner, visitor and host, had wrapped them so thoroughly in the warmth of this land that they should feel it around their hearts even long afterward, in colder climes.

"Tell me truly," said Shelley in Keats's ear. "What great or good thing should ever have been written, if the payment for it had to be settled in advance?"

ACKNOWLEDGMENTS

A WRITER IN ANY AGE is always stretching out imploring hands. For numerous assistances and indulgences I'm grateful to Ginny Carano, Juliet Clark, Ray Davis, Lyn Hejinian, Ed Kerschen, Dale Marlowe, Daniel Medin, Dan Pope, Molly Spencer, Doug Stillinger and Nik Zeltzer.

The spark for this book was struck during a study of Keats's *Hyperion* and nineteenth-century medical science with Kevis Goodman. None of my succeeding speculations can claim any academic sanction, but they were lucky to draw first inspiration from an atmosphere of generosity and inquiry that showed the academy at its best.

Peace to the ghosts of Georg Büchner, Henri Beyle and others from whom I borrowed without asking.

Jessie Ferguson is a reader of unerring taste whose word is good for a thousand pound. She and Rosalind Kerschen showed great forbearance over this book's slow making, and are daily confederates in wild surmise.